THE PRIVATE GARDEN

A NOVEL

OLY TL

THE PRIVATE GARDEN

Oly TL

WARM PUBLISHING
El Paso, Texas
www.warmpublishing.com

Original title: *Jardin secret*
published by Editsource
Paris, France

Interior design by Warm Publishing
Cover design by Angela Haddon
Art by Scarlett Lovell
Translated from French by Iris Clark
Edited by Emily

ISBN: 978-1-958447-03-1

TRIGGER WARNING

WARNING: Although *The Private Garden* is a romance please note that there are several themes within this book that may trigger those who have experienced similar trauma. If you are easily triggered by dark content like violence, sexual assault, drug, or grief, proceed with caution and at your own discretion.

PRONUNCIATION GUIDE

Océane = owSey-AEN
Anaïs = Ah-Nah-EESE
Gaëlle = Guy-Elle

PART I

LOCKED ACCESS...

Some things are worth taking our time for.

Like learning to understand someone or a given situation in depth…

Or letting a third party into a forbidden area, too private. We must not go too fast so as not to fail, not to regret.

After all, don't secrets often remain buried under a candid layer of routine and appearances for a good reason?

I prefer to seal off the entrances. No one gets in; no one needs to know…

PROLOGUE

TIGER

MISTS OF THE PAST…

"Stronger."

"We have already passed the critical threshold; I don't—"

"Stronger, I said!"

"Very well, Mr. Sexton," Lady Candice abdicates.

For the umpteenth time, I urge her to increase the intensity of the electric shocks. Recalcitrant, she contemplates the electrodes scattered over my abs, groin, and thighs. Then her gaze with smoky outlines probes mine. She frowns, more and more destabilized. I don't think she often loses her composure in this kind of context.

"It's not enough," I repeat to her.

Here's the deal. I'm half naked in bed; shirt open, no more suit jacket or tie, no more pants, shoes, or socks. Just my boxers, my erection, and those damn electrodes that send nothing but shit. My "lady" activates the control box. Is that all she's got?

"Again."

"No," she replies.

"I thought you were the toughest. Am I wrong?"

Her face puts on her usual sitting expression. Even if she loses it a little too often these days with me. Damn, this is the last one on the list of those recommended to me! At this point, she is proving to be as disappointing as the previous ones.

And yet, perched on her black stilettos, molded in her vinyl sheath, Candice stands up to me. She runs her tongue over her crimson lips and readjusts her fake glasses on her nose.

Does this accessory make her look like a stern and horny schoolteacher? Yes.

Is that enough for me? No. I want more, damn it!

As time passed, my patience wore thin, and my frustration was soaring.

"Have I misjudged your skills, Lady Candice?"

"No. But it's also my job to take responsibility when you put your life at risk during a session on purpose, Tiger," she says to me.

"*Tiger?* And are we on familiar terms now?"

"Look, I… I think we should stop, Mr. Sexton."

Right now, I'm one step away from panicking internally. My last resort is dropping the case too. It's been two years since I…

Damn it!

"Why?" I reply in a calm tone.

On the surface, I am. In the background, the turmoil is unleashed.

"You… You know that very well, Mr. Sexton."

"No, enlighten me, Candice. We have an agreement; you're not going to give up after a few pathetic sessions," I argue.

Our eyes lock, and I run my fingers through my messy hair.

"I knew that your requirements were more demanding… Even though I have been doing this job for a while, I am still a woman, and I know who you are, just like the rest of the country does."

"And who am I?"

"Tiger Sexton."

"Okay… Since when is that a problem?"

"It becomes a problem when 'the 19-year-old, head of one of the world's biggest fortunes' pushes me to fuck him up! This trend gets worse every night. You ask me to go too far, always too far."

I straighten up, tear off the electrodes and get out of bed. Grabbing the bottle of vodka that I had started, I take a sip. I wipe my mouth with the back of my hand and stare at the one who obviously forgets who is paying the other to satisfy him.

"No," I say calmly. "You're supposed to be a pro, and I'm the client. It's just a transaction. S & M fucking and boundaries. I know my limits; my name and money have nothing to do with it."

She turns in circles, then finally borrows my bottle for a drink.

"Exactly," Candice says gently, handing me back the bottle. "You're playing a dangerous game, Mr. Sexton. Even if you don't want to physically dominate your sexual partners, I wonder which of us is subject to the will of the other here."

With a smirk, I grab her by the waist and slam her against me.

"You love to hurt, and I'm paying you a fucking fortune to hurt me. It's a win-win situation, right?"

"Loving being bullied for a hard-on is one thing," she argues. "And, yes, I love how intense it is with you."

I like this version better… Our breaths come closer. My groin contracts.

"So, everything is cool."

"Not really… Not knowing where and when to stop is a real problem," insists Candice against all odds.

And despite her dilated pupils, all these warning signs normally announce a feverish body to body.

"Tiger…" she complains.

"Hmm?"

"Are you listening to me?"

"My cock is very attentive. How about, as you say, we make this night more intense instead of just talking? You choose how you want to correct me, and I'll take care of the cursor."

I nibble her on the neck. Candice sighs; she seems to hesitate, about to give in. Unfortunately, the next second she shakes her head and slowly pulls away.

"One of us is going to have to be more mature and responsible," she says. "Otherwise, this will end badly. You're young, too young, so it's me, with my few extra years… even if I don't look like it, who's going to have to control all this," Lady Candice concludes with a sexy pout.

My smile widens.

"We agree on one point: you don't look older, and anyway, age doesn't matter as long as we are all adults. Besides, my experience level more than makes up for it. No?"

"Yes, I realized that very quickly."

Her lips quirked into a smile, and desire could be seen in her eyes, but she controlled herself for good.

"I also noticed something else…" she adds.

No need to talk, I understand what she is implying, so I interrupt her and try to negotiate differently, "The deal stays the same, my lady; I said it, I set my own limits, and you have free rein on the… technical aspect. That was the deal."

"Right, only the more it goes, the more I realize we are on a slippery slope. I'm not going to electrocute you, Tiger! Even if all this unbearable pain for my most masochistic submissives makes you fuck like crazy afterward, I'm starting to get scared. And that makes me trip less."

Cornered, I try not to panic.

"Don't fucking do this!"

"I have to. Damn, look at your body. Your fists are constantly banged up. You're covered in bruises, but you want more. It's getting toxic, dangerous. For you. And for me."

"I have it under control."

"Of course… But I don't know where we're going, and it's impossible for me to control you. Obviously, no Domina can do that… Better… better to put the brakes on. Believe me, I would have preferred to continue, but under these conditions, the risk of things going wrong rises every time."

"What the hell? Risks? It's just sex; you're used to hardcore stuff, right?"

"I'm done, Tiger."

Okay, take a breath…

I control my nerves for a long time, in the silence that falls again. Then my bottle flies and crashes against the door after Candice crosses the threshold. The alcohol spreads over the surroundings with its heady scent. I walk through the debris and leave the room myself. No need to run after her; not my style.

I barely take a few steps when I run into Peter, our butler. He's always around at the wrong time; this place is too cramped. I need more space. I feel like I'm suffocating as Peter inspects my "condition."

Shit, I didn't get dressed!

His attention crystallizes first on the ring that shines on my ring finger. Then, thoughtfully details my bruises and other traces of game… Despite his best efforts, Peter tries to erase the disapproving look that he displays quite regularly. And, straight in his shoes, he finally clears his throat and locks his eyes on mine. At the same time, the front door slams, signaling the departure of Lady Candice.

"We need to talk, sir," Peter says.

"Later."

"With all due respect, sir, you need to hear what we have to say. Now."

I raise an eyebrow, taken aback.

"Who is 'we?'"

"I took the liberty of contacting Anatjari, sir. Since I had a hard time channeling your… Anyway, I felt his opinion might give more weight to my words. We only want what is best for you, sir."

Anatjari then shows up. I breathe in, then out, raking my hair.

Is it just me, or does this look like a fucking ambush?

The two wise old men who have known me since I was born suddenly come together to… what did he say already? Channel me. Is this a joke? I gasp again before declaring, "What is best for me? Peter, believe me, you have no idea what makes me feel good or not. And I will certainly not discuss this with you."

"Please, Mr. Sexton. We have just one request for you."

I tense up but ask, "What is it?"

"Allow me to reconnect with the doctor who followed you during your childhood, sir. In order to…"

He leaves his sentence hanging. Peter and Anatjari, after going over my torso through the flaps of my shirt that I button up clumsily, explore the marks, my thighs… Then they seem to be a little too interested in my bare feet afterward. Anticipating their silly sermons, I shake my head to stop them.

"No, it's useless."

"Did you step on broken glass, big boy?" Anatjari worries in his native language as if he doesn't want to hear my refusal.

I look down at my feet and notice the blood prints in my wake. Okay, in anger, in frustration, I didn't pay attention. However, this solicitude has the gift of annoying me; I'm an adult now, damn it!

"It's nothing," I reply. "And you shouldn't have come all this way for so little, Anat."

Determined to get away from them, I don't expect them to stand in my way. Technically, I could force my way through, but I don't want to hurt either of them. They may still see me as the little

Tiger who used to run around with his dog, Sausage. They are so far off now…

"Yes, I had to, my boy."

"It's important for us to look out for you, Mr. Sexton," Peter insists. "For once."

"Give us your word for the doctor," adds Anat. "Commit to resuming check-ins, and I'll be back on the road to Canberra."

"We want to, sir."

Sterile fight, dialogue of the deaf. They won't change their minds, and I don't have the energy for this bullshit. I want to go for a run and evacuate the tensions that are crushing my brain. Blasé, I capitulate.

"Okay. I'll do it."

This is the first promise that has been extracted from me since Sophia. It will be the last. I'm going to lock everything down and keep a damn control over everything from now on.

1

TIGER

NOWADAYS, NEW YORK

That's enough!

I stop watching the umpteenth video—already seen, reviewed, re-reviewed—and straighten up. As determined as I am, I get tired some days. I grab my cell phone and go out onto the terrace of my suite, next to Sophia's. The latter is busy hiring a vegan chef from New York to run her new restaurant on the corner.

Works for me; that way, I don't have her around.

The phone call from Anaïs, my main assistant, cuts short my frantic thoughts. I go back to business as usual, dropping in a firm voice as soon as I pick up, "Sexton."

"Hello, Mr. Sexton," greets my employee on the phone. "I wanted to remind you that your wedding anniversary is coming up in three days. I've confirmed with the florist that we'll send the usual bouquet of one hundred roses to your hotel in Washington, D.C. since your schedule indicates that you and your wife will be there on that date. Does it suit you?"

Lost for a brief moment, I pull myself together. The anniversary, damn it! Sophia obviously expects special attention… It's more convenient to repeat a familiar pattern. The idea of the hundred red roses is the classic ritual borrowed from my parents…

I look at the time before answering, "Perfect, Anaïs. Indeed, I still have a few meetings in the United States that will end in Washington… Contact the Cartier house. Tell them to send me someone with the necessary items to the airport on the day, let's say, an hour before takeoff. They know Sophia's tastes."

"I'll do it right away. I wish you a good day, Mr. Sexton."

Let's move on to the next thing: the lunch scheduled with business partners and their spouses this noon, which I will show up to with my wife.

As a straightforward man.

OCÉANE

Bondi Beach, Sydney, Australia

The heat is suffocating. I'm in sync with the weather. It's as heavy as this leaden screed in my chest; even the coolness of the ocean doesn't change that.

But I'm a better person today. I'm a better person, aren't I?

I immerse myself as much as I can in this thought as I emerge from the bluish and sun-drenched waves.

Dear Océane,

I can't get over the nerve you had for daring to write to Lucas.

I had to answer you to tell you two things:

One, we're going to change our address, so you can never reach him again…

Stop! Alas, my brain is replaying the words contained in this letter. I take some salt water in my palms and splash it on my face. I adjust my bikini top, trying to swallow it all…

I respond as best I can to the blissful smile of Louane, my new girlfriend in Sydney. I only have to think of the people who are freezing at my house in France at the moment to measure my luck and learn to savor the moment. Even if one of the relics of my past must be scouring Paris to find me… I may be far away physically, but my mind seems to have remained stuck there.

"That deserves a first swim selfie in Australia!" says Louane to me.

This Canadian language student, as comfortable with French as she is with English, instantly become my favorite friend. The language barrier doesn't exist when I'm with her. And then, she has the gift of pulling me out of the gloom that has sometimes plagued my thoughts since my first days here. Hanging out with her makes me feel…almost good.

"Cheeeeeese! "I say in unison with Louane.

"I post it on my Insta and my Snap?" she asks me.

Oh no!

"No, I… I don't really like exposing myself on social media," I say. "Can you just keep it to yourself and send it to me, please?"

"No problem, sweetheart," concedes Louane.

We settle down on our beach towels. I slather on sunscreen and put my straw hat and sunglasses back on. Louane's hand comes out of the picnic basket with Vegemite toast. I haven't gotten used to it yet; the taste is quite particular. I pick on it, letting my gaze wander to distract my brain. My girlfriend, believing I am interested in the male sex, starts watching and commenting. Technically, she's in a relationship, and they seem very much in love, Trevor and her. But "looking is not cheating," she philosophizes, laughing.

"It's a passive market watch for high-potential males, you know?" she justifies herself. "On the other hand, I advise *you* to go for it. Nothing better than a good dose of fun to erase this sad face."

I smile at her.

"What's your type of guy?" Louane asks me.

"Very good question… I'm still thinking about it," I evade, laughing.

The only relationship I had when I was sixteen has also become the mistake of my life with a monumental "M." I don't want any more illusions, and I willingly gave up on love. I already have to convince myself daily that there may still be a little crumb of happiness left for me. Somewhere. If I deserve it. And that I will learn to have fun again with no worries if the opportunity arises. Well, we'll see…

"Thin? Chubby? Beefy? Brown-hair? Redhead? Blond? Bald?" insists Louane, relaxed. "Well mounted or small dick?"

"Hey!"

"What? It takes a bit of everything to make a world, right?" she laughs.

In the process, she leads me into a game that consists of trying to guess the "equipment" of the surfers and swimmers around us. I appreciate this lightness, but I hope that no one around us understands French. Myriam's advice at the airport teases my memory, *"People's opinions are too important to you, my little Océane. Especially the negative ones. You have to get rid of that. Free yourself, let go! Go live your life!"*

I want to… Much more often since I've been in Australia. I just can't do it yet, not like before, not totally, intensely, freely. I know I can be wild; I used to be. Only the blockage is there, less strong, but still present.

"Oh, the poor dear, he has a tiny one!" laughs Louane, who focuses on the tight suit of a surfer at the crotch.

I'm suddenly stressed, "He more or less understood, didn't he?"

Yes, this kind of self-censorship easily reappears in my head despite myself.

"So what?" Louane answers me, licking the salty spread on her index finger. "Guys do the same about girls' tits. Equal rights, honey! Didn't you remember anything from *Sex and the City* or what?"

"You're right; let's drink to Carrie, Samantha, and all these women who are happy with themself!" I agree, uncapping my soda.

I hope that one day I can feel the same confidence and enjoy my stay.

I'm a better person today. Well, I guess.

2

TIGER

The gym is empty, my staff made sure of that ahead of time. I start my session alone, an hour early. Time passes, and it's getting dark outside. He will soon show up at the agreed time. Indeed, I notice the arrival of my appointment while continuing to whip the ground with the heavy and thick battle cords. Faster and faster, knees bent, legs apart, I push each of my muscles to endurance by lifting and waving the ropes in front of me continuously.

At the end of my series of exercises, my T-shirt drenched in sweat, I join the tall, silent black man. At first glance, we look like two guys who come across each other in a gym to work out. He blends into the background by getting on the pull-up bars. I do the same. My fingers wrap around it; I start to pull myself up and down.

"What was the emergency, Terrence?"

"I need a guy. He's expensive."

"Whatever, hire him if I can get something out of him."

"Roger that."

Terrence's succinct answer says more than a useless speech. His background as an MI6 agent makes him organized, efficient, and surgically precise. He doesn't blather for anything, and I appreciate that. I continue my pull-ups, focused on the follow-up during the sustained physical effort. Our face-to-face meetings are extremely rare. For the discretion and the success of the operation.

"It's been ten years, Terrence, ten fucking years."

"Affirmative, sir. We're close. I'll send you the pedigree of the new guy. He'll be very useful to us in Europe."

"Okay, you'll receive the necessary funds in the offshore account."

"Yes, sir."

"I'm going back to my hotel; my wife is waiting for me."

"Yes. Enjoy the rest of the evening."

"I need results."

On this last push, I leave Terrence. I put on my sweatshirt, pull the hood over my head, and take short strides. I run for a long time without wanting to return to my suite. Things are flowing into my head…

I'm what, nine years old? I stole a lighter from the kitchen. And now my palm is open over a lit candle. It goes down and gets licked by the heat of the flame. I count… Twenty-five, twenty-six, twenty-seven—

"Tiger! What are you doing?"

My mother screams and rushes towards me. An indescribable smell floats around us. I could have lasted longer. I could have, I know. My mother grabs my wrist and looks at the palm of my hand. Why does she have that panicked look? It's just a little burn.

"Oh my God," Mom whispers. "You… you… don't ever do that again, and don't tell anyone. Can you hear me, Tiger?"

"It's just a game, Mom."

"No! Never again, do you understand?!"

I arrive at my hotel and begin to stretch, breathing steadily. I anchor myself in the present. I have files to manage, I have Sophia, and I have a hunt in progress…

As planned with Anaïs, Sophia's favorite luxury jeweler is waiting for us in a private lounge at Washington airport. I put an Amex card on the table and left Sophia in personalized shopping to isolate myself in a corner. While my wife is trying on Cartier rings and necklaces, I quietly begin a brief online meeting with Terrence. He gives me his daily report.

"I can confirm, sir, that our investigations have made a considerable leap forward," he tells me.

"Do you have a distinct target?"

"Affirmative. I will send you the latest information collected by a secure channel. We still have to dig, but the lead is serious."

"I want all the details."

I hang up and pinch the bridge of my nose. What's bothering me? The stress? Fear of failing and being frustrated and disappointed again? Or something else?

My eyes meet Sophia's. She obviously fell for a jewel or two because my card goes from her hand to the jeweler's. Satisfying her materially and financially is the easiest thing in the world.

Focus, Tiger.

I nod a sign to the pilot of my jet, who is waiting in the corner of the lounge.

"Are you ready to take off, Mr. Sexton?" he asks me.

Turning my attention to my wife, I refer the question to her, "Sophia?"

"Yes, I'm done, Ty."

She puts her things in her bag and gets up elegantly to come and give me a kiss and give me back the credit card. But I leave it to her.

"You can keep it; I have more," I grumble as my mouth avoids hers.

Her lips crash into my jaws.

"Happy anniversary, Ty," she simpers. "I love my gift and the Amex, too, of course. Hope you like mine too."

I doubt it. What can you offer me that I really want, that I don't already have or can't get on my own?

"Perfect. Let's go," I decree.

Closed to her banter and any dialogue, I cross the tarmac with my wife, looking at my phone.

In the jet, I stare outside without really seeing it. The projection of images in my head is more tenacious than the present moment. Collateral damage.

Hair bristling… Arousal rising… Hands… More words… Immaculate fabrics… Brushing… Moans… Crushed flowers… My cock, tongues… Moist heat… Green light… No, red… Yellow… Indigo? Hugs… Breasts… Bare curves… Desire… Fluids… Lust… Glitter of sweat on the skin… Pleasures the lips…

"Ty?"

Sophia's voice pulls me out of my silent drift. Shit, it went too far this time! I stop staring at nothingness, pack up these snatches of unspeakable images and turn my head toward my "tender wife." What a brilliant idea to take this trip together!

"The Sexton couple were spotted in Washington-Dulles today." "It is whispered that they are celebrating their eleventh wedding anniversary…"

Just to feed these kinds of predictable headlines into the papers and maintain a smooth surface, I bend to a few such compromises like this. Like any other couple in our sphere. Rich, unattainable, happy…

"Ty?"

"Hm?"

I can't help but notice the empty seats in my flying cab. And notice that despite that and the onboard WiFi that should keep us engrossed in our PCs until landing, Sophia has invaded the seat next to me. I don't know why; she could have taken a nap in the bedroom. Instead of inviting herself into my living space when my head is overheated and in a fucking mess.

"So?" Sophia insists.

I haven't heard a word.

"About?" I ask, shoving my fingers into my hair.

I blame it on successive jet lags and lack of sleep. I hope Sophia doesn't pull out her "what if you calm things down a bit? Take at least a day off…" Or "let me take care of you."

My wife sighs and turns her computer in my direction. I resolve to read a piece to discover her virtual exchange with a rare "girlfriend." Correction, the wife of a man I get along with pretty well because his network opened up prospects for me a few years ago… I raise my interrogative look at Sophia to ask her, "Why are you showing me this discussion?"

"Ty! So, I've been talking in a vacuum for several seconds," she punctuates with an affected look.

With her thumb, she twists her wedding ring. My features become expressionless, and the pad of my thumb presses hard on my own ring. I feel like it's been an eternity.

"Get to the point, will you?"

Her pupils are moved; mine remain emotionless. Sophia swallows and continues, "I was telling you about my present for you… and also asking you a small favor for my friend."

Her friend, that sounds biased. But Murphy approves of such initiatives…

"What kind?" I ask her.

"The Lilas Hood Charitable Foundation is setting up a contemporary art exhibition for its donors. Her husband, Steen, told her about your Basquiats. The ones he admired in our house in Melbourne."

I groan.

Talking about paintings brings me back to the missing heritage also on my list: the Frida Kahlo evaporated with other works of art… I look at Sophia.

"Lilas would love them to be among the works she is gathering for the occasion," she tells me pleadingly.

"I don't play the philanthropist for show or for interesting tax reductions behind a 'good deed,' unlike some of my peers."

"I know, Ty."

"Then stop asking me to do stuff to look good because those kinds of considerations will never be part of my motivations. And my paintings never leave our properties."

"I know. But could you make a small exception? For me. Lilas has largely contributed to attracting the best of Paris and Hollywood to my restaurants. And Steen will be indebted to you for having fulfilled his wife, as he can't refuse her anything…"

A little exasperated by the comparison I feel coming, I counter her curtly, "Am I not doing enough, Sophia?"

"Yes… I just wanted to point out that Steen Hood will return the favor to you one of these days. But you know that."

Okay, I get her point: this reasoning pretty much defines my way of seeing the world and the way I do business. It's mutually beneficial. Sophia's fingers touch my hand. I tense up, holding her gaze until I feel her become troubled.

"I'll thank you any way you want…" she begins. "And going back to your gift, I thought back to Murphy's suggestion…"

Sophia caresses me; I stiffen more and sneer. If I didn't know her so well, I wouldn't tense up.

But I know her.

"I listen to you."

"I'll follow his advice," she replies, evasive. "At least, I think about it a lot."

I recover my hand under hers; the contact has lasted long enough. Exhausted, I rub my face.

"I'm old enough, Sophia. For that… I don't need your intervention. In any way."

Her features twist and a veil of sadness obscures her eyes. I open my computer again to signal the end of this discussion that is getting out of hand. We stagger towards the sempiternal negotiation, which I always cut short.

"I know, but since Kelly, I… I really try… Please, Ty," she stammers.

I sink into a pensive silence. Kelly was useful for a while before almost screwing up by contacting a tabloid… I decide to end this debate, "Ask Lilas Hood where to ship my Basquiats and for how long. You will take care of the insurers and the transfer?"

Me, I have to maintain my focus to the maximum, away from these trivialities.

"Oh, thank you, Ty!" rejoices Sophia. "I promise you a sublime gift."

Her promise leaves me marvelously indifferent. I just nod my head before going back to my emails. Sophia returns to her online conversation in her chair on the other side of the plane.

As for me… things are reeling in my thoughts. Between the idea that Murphy stuffed into Sophia's head and the way Terrence and his guys' research may turn out… My body, my head, and my locked fantasies threaten to give way under the pressure.

And yet, it is better to reinforce my locks, to keep control.
Whatever it takes.

3

OCÉANE

Days later, Sydney

Hello Miriam,

Here, everything is fine. For you, too, I hope. Here is my new number. I will send you photos by WhatsApp. To keep to yourself, of course…

Anyways, everything is so beautiful in Sydney. The opera is even more gorgeous in person! And you know what? There are as many colorful parrots in the trees as there are pigeons in Paris. I also came across koalas without even having been to a zoo. It's crazy!

I just have to find a job to enjoy it better.

Big kisses. Kiss the others for me. I miss you.

I send my email. Then I motivate myself to take some pictures with my Instax hanging around my neck, a departure gift offered by the educators of the children's home who have chipped in for me. A rare sign of affection that still warms my heart today.

Playing the ecstatic tourist isn't so difficult after all; the scenery is up to my expectations. Yes, I feel better in this country. I'm now wandering around The Rocks, shaking and blowing at my slides as the images appear.

Everything is on track, moving forward.

I repeat it to myself once, twice, three times… until my brain and heart buy into it and feel positive too. I put my photos and camera in my bag and grab my cell phone to check the time. I still have time, but I have to look for The Sexton's restaurant by memory. I've been there once before. I can't believe that the owner of this fancy establishment called me back.

Would my luck be changing favorably with this new start? For once, Mom would have been proud of her daughter. After my mediocre career in some aspects, giving up on of my law studies when I worked hard to get my high-school diploma with this only objective: to become a lawyer and defend minors in need…

This dream is dead and buried. Another, more vivid, turned into an almost vital necessity afterward: to go far away.

Unfortunately, it also costs money when you finally find the motivation to make your dreams come true. As far as money is concerned, I only have the bare minimum required to get the Working Holiday Visa. My meager savings are disappearing, and I won't benefit indefinitely from the hospitality of the students who welcomed me as their roommate. The relocation agency offered me this temporary accommodation—right in my budget—until the boy, a Peruvian whose room I occupy, comes back from vacation. Which is very soon.

Anyway, I need a job. This job! And to finally have my own place.

I look up at Harbor Bridge which overlooks the place. It's so majestic.

My friendly network is currently limited to the young people who are my roommates. Especially Louane, with whom I get along with. If my interview today is successful, I will have plenty of time to follow Myriam's advice: learn how to have fun again, to finally free myself from other people's opinions.

Every time I go job hunting, I still find that my stammering English is a bit of a problem, but I persevere. If I want this to work, I must be the first to believe in it and myself. The cheerful stalls of bohemian products in the market, the tourists strolling around, and the residents going about their business, all this makes me want to enjoy my stay. And to be this new version of myself that I aspire to…

So, this restaurant? The Sexton's! Here it is!

I look at the time on my phone before stopping in front of the fancy sign. It's the kind of place where a lettuce wedge costs you an arm and a leg. Kind of the equivalent of Fouquet's in Paris or other overpriced starred culinary wonders. The colonial building stands before me with its breathtaking view of the port. On the terrace, a wealthy clientele is sipping fine wines. Just like the first day when I timidly submitted my application, I hesitate to set foot there again, dazzled by the high standing of this place. My attempt at being five minutes early suddenly seems difficult to manage. I was freaking out about getting lost or being late, and now I'm stressing about messing things up.

Am I presenting myself well enough? I shouldn't have put on that skater dress!

An ounce of doubt belatedly manifests itself in me. But I have no more time to procrastinate. I take a deep breath, pat my loose bun from which wild locks are escaping and arm myself with nerve.

Remember: no Frenglish, Océane. You can do it!

I breathe out, my flat gold sandals treading the floor of the restaurant, a polite smile plastering on my face. A delicious smell of gourmet food floats in the air; the very light background music punctuates the forks and discussions at the tables. I look around, definitely impressed by the refined decoration.

"Hello, miss."

I recognize the guy I gave my resume to last time. Looks neat, straight as if he had a stick stuck in the… Don't be silly, Océane, he might be your future boss! I stop myself from giggling nervously and opt for self-motivation.

No more Bryan is in ze kitchen. *Get me that job, baby!*

"Good morning. I'm glad you called me back," I say as we shake hands.

I managed to say it in one breath in English! A micro pride germinates in my little edgy body. Having dropped out of college a year after my high school diploma may not have affected my English skills too much after all.

"Good to see you again. You submitted your application in the middle of a rush the other day, so we have some time to talk more quietly today," explains the gentleman.

"With pleasure."

"Thank you for agreeing to make the short video presentation with such short notice. The owner has viewed it, and she is ready to receive you. Please follow me."

The owner? Okay, she's a woman.

And the video was new to me. So, I didn't do so bad? I trot along behind the guy, blocking out my stressed brain's attempts at derision at his stilted demeanor. We leave the room. Nervousness doesn't help me channel my thoughts which go all over the place; I might as well speak, "Excuse me, and you are?"

"I'm Mike Woods, the manager of this restaurant. Mrs. Sexton owns others across the country, as well as overseas."

"Oh, I see."

Mrs. Sexton, got it.

He pauses at the kitchen doorway and turns to look at me.

"Really? You see?" he repeats in a funny way.

The stress is probably screwing with my perception. Unless he noticed that I still had no idea who runs this place; or felt my involuntary urge to giggle. Or maybe he knows… No. I have to pull myself together; they don't know anything about me except what's on my resume and the short video on the manager's smartphone. However, I should have asked the internet about The Sextons before showing up. It seems like a girl who's not prepared at all. My positive attitude is fading.

What if I didn't fit in and was kicked out in three seconds?

The owner surely has no time to waste with a young expat who can hardly put together a correct sentence in English without searching for words. A girl who ignores the essentials of her potential future employer.

The defeat!

"I imagine she's very busy," I catch myself, a bit depressed.

"Indeed. But after the pre-selection, she wanted to meet you… Go straight ahead; Mrs. Sexton is waiting for you at the back in the chief's office."

Mike Woods turns back; I take another breath and follow his instruction. Nobody pays attention to me. I'm the transparent chick slaloming between the members of the brigade circulating under the orders of a man in a chef's outfit. He barely glances at me before getting annoyed at a clerk. I tuck my shoulders in and pick up the pace.

I knock on the door and turn the handle with a lump of apprehension in my belly when I hear a "come in!"

"… My babies are doing great; they've grown up a lot since the last time you saw the little one," finishes a soft voice. "They make me proud."

Inside, I discover a beautiful mixed-race woman sitting on the edge of the desk in a tight skirt, her legs crossed. A specimen straight out of a Dior show. Nothing is out of place, from her brown hair to the tip of her sandals with vertiginous heels. I swallow, feeling even more intimidated. Her phone glued to her ear, she stands up. The stone in the hollow of the neckline of her blouse must alone be worth the price of a house in the Parisian suburbs.

Why the hell does my mind get stuck on a detail like that? I'm getting consumed by stage fright.

"Excuse me, can I call you back?" interrupts the woman. "The person I was waiting for has just arrived."

She addresses me with a sign while listening to her interlocutor.

"… I will not miss it. See you soon," she finishes.

She hangs up and holds out her hand to me.

"You're punctual; you're even a minute early. We appreciate that. Sophia Sexton, delighted to meet you, Miss Rousseau."

We?

"Me too, Mrs. Sexton."

Her hazel eyes scrutinize me. It's hard to know if that's a good or bad sign.

My outfit? My body? My makeup? My hairstyle? Oh dear, is something wrong?

It seems that the first impression is often decisive; I put on a good face by remotivating myself internally. I finally have this unique opportunity to give a better image of myself, very far from France. True, appearances counts when serving in a place of this caliber, but this gorgeous boss surely doesn't take the time to interview every applicant, given the volume of her business. Besides, I was a waitress for a large part of my working life… Okay, those were student jobs in low-key bistros and a crew job at a McDonald's. Nothing to do with this. I must do well in front of Miss Australia.

I take a deep breath. She shifts and points me to a chair.

"You're as cute as on the presentation video," she surprises me.

Cute? Okay. Let's say my appearance is validated. And I'm not going to get on an anti-sexist high horse and on the #MeToo, considering who's giving me this confusing compliment.

"Uh…thank you, Mrs. Sexton."

"Sincere observation. Take a seat, please," she says to me.

She puts aside the chair opposite to settle down again on the table's edge. No need for obstacles to impose, and this woman obviously knows it. She grabs a file and opens it, and I see my resume and photo.

"Good. You are Océane Lilia Rousseau, 20 years old, French, with a Working Holiday Visa allowing you to work in Australia. Is that right?" she continues in my language, to my great surprise.

Phew! I will stammer less.

"That's right. I arrived a few days ago with my one-year visa, and I am relentlessly looking for a job."

"In order to earn some pocket money to better enjoy it?" she deduces in impeccable French with a hint of an English accent.

"Exactly. I wanted adventure and to discover your country."

And incidentally, to relearn how to flirt. To drool over surfers with Louane, or even more if you have an affinity to forget… Stay focused!

"Work, adventures, and tourism let's say," I rephrase.

A slight smile appears on her features. Damn, she's even hotter, it would almost make me cringe to admit it. It's like a Photoshop design of a life-size feminine perfection, but for real. People certainly look at her as soon as she walks in somewhere. I push back my little complexes and smooth my modest Pull&Bear dress over my thighs, trying to look like a confident girl under her scrutiny.

"So far, are you charmed by Australia, *Mademoiselle* Rousseau?"

"Oh yes! But I… I need to find a job… and a more permanent place to live."

Shit, now you sound a little desperate, girl.

Mrs. Sexton nods. The silence lasts a few seconds, the feeling of not fitting in start to show up in her eyes and increases my stress level. Her manicured nails endlessly tease a ring on her ring finger, and then she brushes the folder of documents as she watches me.

"Let's see if I can do something about that, Miss Rousseau. Tell me a little more; why should I choose you among others?"

"Because I would be honored to better my experiences and professional skills within a prestigious establishment like The Sexton's."

I can see in her eyes that she's used to kissing up to her without feeling any effect whatsoever. I clear my throat and think about finding something better.

"I'm reliable, hard-working, and determined, madam. I saved for this trip and left my comfort zone and my little habits to seize an opportunity such as this in the country of my dreams. I will do my best to be worthy of it."

She doesn't need to know that the opinions of new people I meet help me rebuild the tainted image I've accumulated at home. However, I hope she's convinced of my sincerity and motivation. In any case, she reopens the file in her hands.

"Any ties here or in France?" she catches me off guard.

"Not really... I'm free as a bird and finding my feet in Sydney."

"Hmm... In that case, you could potentially be a good fit."

Don't gloat too quickly, Océane. Calm your little heart.

She lifts my resume. Underneath, I can see other papers instead of the pile of various pre-selected applications I expected. If this file is only mine, what is all this paperwork?

"However..." started Mrs. Sexton, "I need us to agree on the formalities of your possible hiring."

She said possible hiring?!

I try to keep my restraint. She hands me the paperwork, and I read the header. My eyes widen as they move toward her. This is not the classic work contract I was expecting...

"But this... is this a non-disclosure agreement?" I say.

"That's right; we commonly call this an NDA for Non-Disclosure Agreement. Our lawyers have taken care to write it in French and English so that you know exactly what you're signing."

Breathe, Océane. Stop your crazy imagination.

4

OCÉANE

I stare at the restaurant owner, my heart pounding, and I repeat, "A NDA?"

"Yes, in both languages, because Mike briefed me on your difficulties with our language," she says.

Ouch, busted for English!

Nevertheless, Mrs. Sexton shows either a delicate attention or a formidable reactivity of a businesswoman with this translation planned just after a small report from her manager. Efficiency and zero waste of time. Or just a routine; other expatriates have probably passed through his restaurants in their job search…

I still try to minimize my weak point. I'm too close to the goal.

"Thank you for this effort, madam. I plan to improve my English during my stay, and of course, my goal also is to practice English every day."

"I have no doubt about it. You will have the opportunity to do so… However, if I decide to let you in, I want to ensure that nothing will leak out. You see, the slightest trifle about us is sold to the vultures; we take precautions to keep them at bay."

We? Who is this "we" that's come back? Her? Celebrities who probably come here to eat?

"I understand about the press. It's not my style to peddle, and besides, there's no way that by serving at Sexton's, I'm going to be involved in the lives of the customers and—"

"Working here, maybe. But you're not selected for the position for which you applied. You don't have the profile."

What?

What am I doing within these walls, then? My professional experiences relate only to room service. I hardly hide my disappointment, a bit offended at not fitting in with what she was looking for. Am I not pretty and classy enough to deserve to serve in her restaurant? Or is it because of my poor English? Or worse, both? That's it; I'm losing my confidence.

"I don't get it, Mrs. Sexton. Why this appointment and this non-disclosure agreement if my application is rejected?"

"I offer something else to you, *Mademoiselle* Rousseau."

"Oh."

"You have the choice: sign the NDA, and we discuss it. Or we'll stop here if you prefer," she says calmly.

I try to think, confused. I want a job, right? Apparently, I have the skills for this special offer, so I might as well browse the pages of this thing and see what happens. My heart is still filled with hope, and my optimism rises again. I start to read the content again:

"This confidentiality agreement covers all exchanges and interactions between the parties… Bla-bla-bla… During her time with the Sexton family, Miss Océane, Lilia Rousseau, hereinafter referred to as Employee, agrees not to disclose any information of any kind to any third party regarding Mr. and Mrs. Tiger Sexton hereinafter referred to as Employers… The Employee will be…"

My brain cells freeze. I look up with bewildered eyes at the sophisticated woman who is patiently scrutinizing me…

"I… This Tiger Sexton is your husband?"

"That's right."

My interlocutor does her thing again; she fiddles with her ring. Her wedding ring, actually…

"So, I'll have two employers because the restaurants belong to you both, I guess?"

"As I explained to you, it's not about my restaurants. Tiger is no longer involved in my management nor in the staff I hire. He has his own business in shipbuilding and related business… However, confidentiality covers both of us, of course."

Okay… What I can see at the moment is that they are rich and overwhelmed. In their position, of course, they control their image. It doesn't tell me what job I'm interviewing for.

You prepare to serve food at Sexton's and find yourself signing a deal to shut up. What's the story?

My curiosity is piqued. Not to mention the rush to replenish my new Australian bank account. So go for confidentiality if it makes them feel better. I hesitate, then sign the sheet in triplicate. Sophia Sexton lets out a discreet sigh. At least, I guess so.

"It's done. I'm all ears; what is your proposal?"

"Very well. Here's the job offer," she decides, grabbing the papers and handing some more to me.

My slightly sweaty fingers receive them. My irises come alive on the written lines. Mrs. Sexton collects the signed sheets and leaves some for me. In the meantime, her cell phone rings; she picks up and whispers to me, "take your time."

I'm focusing. It doesn't take long for my mind to process this information. My questions find their answers. Two other first names—Byrne and Annie—appear. I guess they are the Sexton children.

An au pair! *They are looking for an* au pair!

Hence the precautions; this job involves living in their house(s), sharing their daily lives. I didn't expect that, but I think I can handle it with their children. Kids love me, so that should do it. Six-month contract, housed, fed, the jackpot in my current situation. Cool, right? I'm in the middle of my reading, my mind overexcited, when Miss Australia ends her conversation and gives me an uncertain smile.

"So?" she asks me. "Do you need time to think? I'm sorry, I have to cut this short; I have an emergency."

"Uh… first, I'm very honored. And I want to assure you that I'm great with kids; you can trust me. I'm tempted. I'll finish quickly and give you an immediate answer if you like."

A fleeting expression appears on her face. Did I screw up? She looks at her watch. Damn, but yes, that's it! For people in her sphere, time is money, and I'm wasting it. I fear that this will work against me and see this opportunity slipping away from me, so I hurry to skim over the terms. I have never absorbed so much legal jargon in such a short time. The Sexton family opens their doors to me for six months… Travel opportunities at their expense… Boy, that sounds great. No more stress of having to find a job for an entire semester! Overexcited, I turn the pages and get to the end. Sophia Sexton paces around the office, kicking her heels around the room. She doesn't stop turning in circles.

"It's good for me," I say. "There is just one thing…"

I hardly dare to make my request, but not everyone is Croesus.

"I… I'm a little embarrassed to ask you since you've already offered me food and a place to stay for 6 months… Is that why there's no salary mentioned?"

She stops and locks her hazel gaze on mine. I fidget and nibble the inside of my cheek.

Skip the poor beggar effect you feel and smile politely.

"Oh, don't worry about that! There's no way you're not getting paid; let's see. This field is left empty on purpose; it is up to you to indicate a number in the space. Your price will be ours."

What? That's it, I'm dreaming. A glittery unicorn riding by a hot rider will appear, and I will wake up disappointed.

My face must be super comical at this moment because it extracts a completely unexpected crystalline laugh from Sophia Sexton. My lips close and only then do I realize my mouth has fallen open in disbelief. In my defense, this is too crazy to be real, right? Or maybe their kids are terrors, spoiled, insufferable airheads who have exhausted the country's supply of nannies. I can't think of any other logical explanation.

"Really? I set my own salary?"

"Absolutely, Miss Rousseau, you have free rein within… reason. Don't ask us to pay for a jet and a yacht," she comments, grabbing her designer bag.

Her amused look would almost makes her approachable and friendly. Money is clearly not a concern in her world. In mine, I'm too stunned and used to "normal life" to take it lightly. I finally respond to her smile by shaking my head. Despite the shock, my cheerfulness takes over. Sophia Sexton seems so casual now that I dare make a joke, "You're right, maybe not both at the same time. Why not get me a private jet first? That would be quite a start."

This accentuates her laughter. She runs her fingers through her mane and seems much more… cool to me? Yes, I think.

"If you like traveling by private plane, I think we will get along well…" she answers me. "I'll let you decide. In case you agree, fill out your initial and put this in an envelope. Mike will take care of sending me the contract. Take your time, so our lawyers will do what is necessary to send you the final document with the salary of your choice."

It's insane! No matter how much I pinch myself, this interview exceeded my expectations.

"Of course, we will take care of your move. Do you have a lot of stuff?"

"Uh… I don't have a lot of stuff."

She checks her watch again.

"Someone will contact you when it's finalized to organize all this. I really have to go now. Bye, Océane."

With that, she presses my shoulder and looks at me for a moment. Then the luxurious creature turns on her heels and leaves me stunned. God, is she hiring me? With four zeros for my weekly pay?

No matter how big the task is with this woman's offspring, her children may be dirty little monsters, baby tigers as their father's name would suggest, I'll hang on! No way I'm letting go of this! Leaving the restaurant after the signature and the final formalities agreed with Mike, the manager, I felt like I was floating on a gigantic cloud. I have better than a job. I can't wait!

I branch off to the beach, lay down on the sand, and grab my cell phone, freshly bought on my arrival.

A crazy contract to become an au pair. Too cool, right?

The only thing I have to deal with is that I still don't know much about the people who hired me. The Sextons may be well known here, but I've never been interested in big fortunes. Whether in France or elsewhere. Nor what they do with their lives. But now, since I'm going to spend six months in the wake of these people, I need to know more.

Google, to the rescue! Almost immediately, a row of photos appears in the results. One of them catches my eye. I click, and confusion invades my neurons. A certain shock too.

Mrs. Sexton's guy. He's… Damn, he's living up to his name.

He's not what I had imagined. An old billionaire with the face of Donald Trump or something like that? Anything but this tall, dark-haired guy. Young. Raw charisma. His manly jaws, his piercing blue eyes, his stubble, every detail catches me off guard. Including that harsh, closed expression.

A little on edge, I continue to snoop around. Images of the couple follow one another; not a single one shows the husband smiling, even when his wife presses against him, all radiant. He keeps the same intimidating presence and this kind of coldness. Designer suit, Rolex, sometimes hands in his pockets when he stands alone or an arm around the waist of his sublime wife when Miss Australia shares a pose with him. The guy, self-assured, inaccessible, and magnetic in front of the lens, seems to be staring at me.

Breathe, Océane, and say hello to your future boss.

My mouth goes dry. I close the images, suddenly disturbed. Am I going to share these two's daily life? Well, I mean him too? I was already impressed by Mrs. Sexton alone. Him, it will be a million times worse. Just through the screen of my phone, he gives off something. So, in person…

Stop! Don't chicken out on pictures. You've got a crazy job; you've got to do it!

My self-persuasion is half working. Or not really. My mind is confused. I decided to poke around in the rest of the Google results. A logo with an intertwined T and S appears in the results. The Sexton's initials. The extent of his company and his fleet of ships… A stern-faced uncle; who cares… The Sexton clan… The list of The Sexton's restaurants, the inaugurations… Their appearances at prestigious events… Articles from specialized magazines and newspapers… Charity evenings…

Damn, a more than full, stunning life! No wonder they have less time for their kids. How many names were in the contract again? Two! But what ages? What an idiot; I didn't even ask! Their parents must fiercely protect them from the press, there is nothing for the moment. Wikipedia might tell me more. With their faces even, who knows. I type the name of Madame plus the word children.

"Sophia Sexton, wife of Australian businessman and ship owner Tiger Sexton, opened her first restaurant six years ago. At the time, she considered this restaurant her baby and aspired to enlarge the family, or rather the naval and financial empire built by her husband. This goal has been achieved, as this formidable duo's fortune and number of acquisitions continues to grow. This childless couple is expanding their wealth indefinitely…"

Wait… what?! I stopped browsing the internet and froze, shocked by my discovery.

No?

I nervously reach into my bag, and pull out my copy of the contract to check. Damn, I hadn't paid attention to the asterisk next to the first names! Who are Byrne and Annie? The little star next to it refers me to… the ambiguous mention:

"May be subject to additional clauses to be determined by The Employers."

Oh no! I realized that when I arrived, the half of the telephone conversation where Sophia Sexton mentioned her "babies" and my hasty conclusions skewed my reading. I signed in a hurry. There is no specific mention of kids anywhere. Now that I think about it, Ms. Sexton deftly let it slip when I brought it up. She didn't correct me or confirm their existence.

Because they don't have children? Who were those two? And if they don't have kids, you committed to shut up and do what with them?

5

TIGER

Sydney

While swimming under the warm, turquoise water of the pool, the more I run out of air, the more a memory materializes under my eyelids:

The bag is held on my head, and the plastic sticks to my lips, seeking a breath of oxygen. I suffocate, and my fists clench. The hot wax gets closer to my chest as I gasp loudly. Very close, too close. I feel it running, dripping, freezing, piling up on my bare skin. My whole chest is covered in it. Now the flame of a lighter flickers through the transparency of the plastic bag… because the candle is no longer enough… I struggle to breathe, and I fidget, trying to move.

I want air! Air. Air. Air…

I inhale with all my might, pulling my head out of the water. This crap evaporates. Like the other lurking in there, they dissipate to come back better. Tirelessly…

I pull myself together and leave the pool, moving towards a deckchair. My wet hand grabs my phone, and a drop falls on the screen as I read the name of the person who dares to reach me at this hour. It's Shanna, my "trustworthy man" in business. Technically, Shanna has a pair of ovaries, but she's got more in her pants than a lot of guys in my circle, which earned her the privilege of holding this number for private use. Since she never abuses it, this late call is surely justified. I pick up.

"Sexton."

"Good evening, Tiger, sorry to bother you—"

"I guess that the informal tip I gave you is true?"

"You're right; your flair did not deceive you. My contact confirms Harry Carter is indeed entering the fray. He wants to acquire the company you are targeting."

Okay.

I may be busy with other fights, but with my legacy, I keep proving that I have taken up the torch perfectly. Prove it to others, prove it to myself. So there's no way I'll let that buffoon Carter jeopardize my plans to expand and diversify.

"How are we gonna play this?" Shanna continues.

With my other hand, I grab a towel from the back of the lounger and rub my hair, thinking about the plan of attack I finalized an hour ago. I return the question to her, "What do you suggest?"

"Play it fierce, like when you struck last summer? We pull the rug out from under them and launch a hostile takeover bid before Carter gets an amicable agreement to trigger his own. He'll be caught off guard."

This aggressive response had indeed been effective. This made it possible to clear the passage between the horizon and the TS Naval. Incidentally, she spilled ink about me in the financial press.

And not about my private life…

Shanna has seen me crush the world to anticipate this tactic. She manages with an iron fist the battery of experienced traders and the investment fund that grows part of my personal assets and those of TS Naval. A certain professional collaboration has developed between us as we have won. In fact, she is not wrong, and I could slap his head immediately.

But the Carter heir will naturally consider the same thing from me. From the beginning, there is too much of a tendency to compare us. But I have nothing to do with this jerk. Each of us may have been born with a silver spoon in our mouths and find ourselves managing the family fortune, but the similarities end there. We don't have the same things in our guts, and it's time to bring it into line to master my whole environment. Not to be caught short, to stay on top, and to live up to the expectations of the great Nick Sexton. Damn it!

I drop the towel to light a cigarette. I want a surprise effect. And pain. Harry Carter must suffer in his pride to stop stepping on my toes.

"Tiger? Are we planning the takeover bid?" Shanna asks me again.

"No. Let this daddy's boy gloat and believe he's kicking my ass. While he's busy convincing the board of directors of the company he's after, let's put our guys on to something else."

"Which one?"

"I want control of the sales of all the suppliers essential to the operation of the company that he will take over. Gather strategic shares on the sly. Make a raid, a silent carnage, and let's see what happens next."

Shanna assimilates without flinching, then suddenly she laughs, "Damn, it's always more twisted with you. I'm in!"

My lips form the shadow of a smile.

"You can't afford to miss the timing, Shanna. I don't tolerate failure."

"You can count on me. We act like a submarine and let Carter go into debt and invest everything he's got to acquire a company whose supplies you'll be blocking behind the scenes. His supply costs will soar and weigh down his production. We're helping him dig his own financial hole.

"More fun, right?" I retort.

"You bet! Once cornered, his only choice will be to beg you to make a deal," Shanna analyzes. "Can't get around you."

"That's right. Whatever he does, he'll be blocked. Then I'll be able to kick his ass a lot deeper when I show him the three remaining perspectives: either I'll be his only supplier around and suffocate him. Either his pride prevails, or he resists and files for bankruptcy. Or… final option, he'll dump the company in my lap."

The company that he should have let me buy without getting in my way.

"Back to square one, and you get your target back. Damn, this will be humiliating for him," Shanna enthuses.

"I want him to learn his lesson once and for all."

"That you don't covet what Sexton covets? And you always get what you want? I think it's crystal clear everywhere," she adds, deadpan.

"Obviously not enough. This isn't the first little clown on my path, so I might as well set the record straight."

Shanna laughs; I take a puff of nicotine, staring at the water in the infinity pool.

"Great. It will boost the troop," she concludes.

I sit in the deckchair without superfluous comment.

"Good. Anything else, Shanna?"

"No, I'll leave you. I have shares to steal on the sly," she adds.

"Keep me posted, and put my CFO in the loop. He had twenty-four hours to mourn his father, that one. He's got to get back in the ring. And remember to reward your mole at Harry Carter's."

"I'll get right on that. Have a good evening, my regards to Sophia."

I hang up and crush my cigarette butt. Speaking of my sweet wife, it looks like she passed by when I was swimming. I believe the file was placed under my ashtray. With a scribbled word:

Ty, I'm in the sauna if you're looking for me.
Remember what we talked about on the flight two weeks ago?
Take a look.
Kisses.

I open the documents folder and convince myself to close it in two seconds.

Or not…

My gaze lingers on the photo that accompanies a resume. Océane Rousseau. Blonde, doe eyes with green tints… Fresh and rather cute… A flower. I take a deep breath, staring at her. How do I maintain a stable border between my quest, the videos, the things that still obsess me, and my daily life? This glossy face is likely to be a problem, depending on what Sophia might have in mind…

Damn! I have to keep my filter in place and keep the situation under control.

6

OCÉANE

My roommates are laughing in the living room. The rather nice appetizer dinner with a few other students is coming to an end. They are getting ready to go down to the city.

And me, I remain a spectator of this ambient lightness. There was a time when I could be like them: carefree and joyful despite the little worries of everyday life. But tonight, I'm less inclined to do Sydney by night. My interview this afternoon is running on a loop in my head. My tendency to get excited hasn't always led me to the best choices, but I don't want to miss out on something great out of an abundance of caution, either. So, I can't help but hesitate. Should I back out or take advantage of the opportunity? Damn, a roof, a job, and more money than expected! It's an opportunity I'll never have again.

Yes, but…

"Océane, are you coming?" Louane asks.

"Nah, not very excited tonight," I say, thoughtful.

I go out on the terrace and sit cross-legged on the floor, my half-opened glass of apple vodka in my hands. Louane joins me, and I steal her cigarette. She pouts as she watches me take a drag.

"Hey, say! We didn't have a chance to discuss it when you got back. How was this interview?"

"How can I tell you?" I reply, handing her the cigarette, which she drags in her turn.

"Don't worry; odd jobs are easy to find here. You'll see," she comforts me.

She hands me the cigarette; I give her a wink and grumble, "Yeah…"

"Come on! You're all calm tonight; where's the funniest Frenchie hiding in there?"

Not so far… I hope.

"Too bad if you have nothing to celebrate today, have fun and try somewhere else tomorrow," she encourages me.

"Actually, I… got the job."

Louane's eyes widen, then she applauds, delighted.

"But that's great! Why are you making that face, then?"

Because they are rich, famous, and I don't know why I was offered this job.

Confidentiality agreement, Océane!

"You don't like the job? Ungrateful tasks?"

"No, it could even be the opposite… Well, I don't know."

Damn it, shut up!

I take a puff and quickly add, "I'm hesitant. Weighing the pros and cons."

Not sure if she understands more than that. What can I say without betraying my contractual commitment? I'm a little confused; my excitement at hitting the jackpot is dulled over the hours. Questions swirl around in my head.

"Loulou? Here we go, babe!" shouts my friend's boyfriend.

An Australian student gestured from afar, ready for the party.

"Go, your boyfriend is waiting for you," I say without moving.

"Wait, Trevor!" exclaims Louane before starting again slowly for me. "If it's great, go for it! You are thinking too much, live, darling! And if this offer is not great, tell yourself that there will be others, much better."

I don't think so, no. An opportunity like this doesn't come along very often. And, yes, I want to live, to fully feel all the good vibes, but…

Boy, it's the first day, and I'm already tempted to break the agreement. I just wanted to get an outside opinion so that I don't regret later on having refused… or accepted Sophia Sexton's offer. What would someone else do in my place?

Okay, I used to be pretty confident, even too confident. Only, my mishaps are supposed to teach me to show a little more common sense now.

Like, if it's too good, is there a wolf?

I don't know, that wouldn't be new… Something bothers me with this absence of children and the vagueness around the two names on the contract. And then these people probably have an army of servants serving them in their house. What do they want from me?

The question burns my lips, and my eyes lock on Louane's.

"Thanks for the advice, sweetheart. Go, your guy is getting impatient! Go dance," I answer, smiling at him.

"You really don't want to go out with us?"

"No, not tonight. Maybe next time."

"I hope so!" she promises me before getting up. "I know that as the return of our roommate Ben approaches, you occupy his room and that stresses you in your research. But we can help you out if you need… Don't worry too much, okay?"

"You're adorable, thank you."

"It's no problem. So, you still don't want to come?"

"I'm going to watch the series Garrett has been talking about and eat all the ice cream."

"That guy's awesome! He convinced you, too."

"Yep!"

Garrett is a business school student who also shares this apartment with the gang. As far as I know, he would sell anything to anyone. I'm going to make up my own mind, especially about the job I've been offered…

"No matter what Garrett said to you, you'll have a better time with us," my new girlfriend baits me again.

In reality, the Netflix argument is a trick to be able to think in calm. I hold to it, and my friend finally gives in.

"If you change your mind, will you call me? I'll tell you where to meet us."

"Sure."

We say to each other a goodbye. She starts to move away, but suddenly I can't hold myself back and says as innocently as possible, "By the way, Louane, you have been living in Sydney for a long time. Do you know anything about the Sexton couple?"

My question confuses her. She turns around.

"Erm… no more than most people. He's as hot outside as he is evil inside, according to the gossip."

Thank you, I'm so much better now.

"Nevertheless, he is feared and respected, good at business. And her, apart from brilliantly managing her restaurants, being brilliant and beautiful to make us jealous, what else could I add? Oh yes! The tabloids got excited about something for a while; I don't really remember…"

Shit, what was that? She can't leave me hanging like that.

"About the couple or one of them?" I insist, totally interested.

"I don't remember. I vaguely remember that there were public denials and public apologies from the media, probably attacked by the Sextons' lawyers for defamation, I guess… Then nothing. I'll ask Trevor. In any case, the urban legend says never upset Tiger Sexton… In the end, not much filters through from their lives."

Great! It helps me a lot.

"I see."

"Why are you asking me that, anyway?" Louane asks me.

"Oh, just to get to know the Australian aristocracy and jet-set better, for my general knowledge."

Her face tells me she's a bit ticked off. She's the French-speaking person in the gang, so she is the one I've chatted with the most easily since the beginning. This morning, I told her to have an interview in a restaurant at The Rocks. Fortunately, I don't think I mentioned the name. I don't know if she would have made any connection… She's about to question me again when her boyfriend comes up behind her, hugs her, and makes out with her.

Phew, saved by the bell! Or rather by Trevor's hungry tongue. My lie may not have been very convincing.

"Have fun!" I say before sipping my apple vodka.

When the house empties of its occupants, my hesitations reappear in the dead calm that sets in. I grab my smartphone and start making a list of pros and cons.

Arf, my mind is scattering! "Au pair," this title seems foggy to me in the end.

I don't have a phone number to contact Sophia Sexton again, just the contact information for the restaurant at The Rocks. Tomorrow, I'll call the manager, this Mike Woods. His boss owes me two or three explanations.

On this resolution, I squat the sofa to chain the episodes. But my attention goes elsewhere. Images of Miss Australia with her dark and intimidating husband run through my head. I end up turning off my screen to go to bed. My thoughts are racing in all directions; I would have done better to go out with my friends.

TIGER

I want to get high! Soak it all up.

Strobe lights, background music. But it's the breaths, sighs, and jerky breaths that invade my ears. At the same time as the mouths, the hands, the curves of a pair of breasts glide over my skin.

"I want you," Eve meows.

My fingers sink into blonde hair. I feel the caress of the ball on her tongue along my cock. I groan, pressing harder on her head. Eve's mouth comes to beg mine. Our kiss is as wild as the primitive growl in my insides. Greedy, hungry, unquenchable, endless. Someone grabs my ass, bites me, licks me, kisses me. One, plus another, plus another. Fingers, almost all over my skin. And that fucking blowjob. Is her name Chastity? Or Amber, or maybe Jemma? Who cares about their pro nickname?

No first name, no last name. Nobody matters. Ages don't matter, either. I am 17 years old, I have money, and want to fuck. Let them all fuck me! And fuck that asshole Uncle James!

My cock gets into the throat of… Who cares who it is. Just don't stop, don't think, don't touch the ground.

Arousal… Mixing of bodies… All together, their hollows, their curves… Intimate perfumes… A warm and wet cocoon… My erection… Lights… Closed eyelids… Primary desires… That feeling…

She abandons herself and sucks my neck. With all of her strength. Her fingernails and those of others scratch me, furrow me. How many of them are there? I don't know anymore… Who cares…

I get lost in an incalculable number of frantic coitus. No longer knowing in which orifices of submissive nudity, offered, wet but so thirsty, I stuff myself. I no longer differentiate their bodies. They are interchangeable…

They make me hard again, each one in their own way… How long does it take me to recover before going for another orgasm deep inside one of them? I don't really know anymore… I feel like I'm going downhill too fast, like I'm not on enough endorphins anymore, of…

FUCK NO!

I grab a neck, and lips come to stick to mine. Here we go again!

It goes on and on. I lose track in the smell of sex, of fluids. Blackout of sensations… Time stops or flies, I don't want to know… In sweat, I realize I'm embedded in a chick pressed against a wall, her leg held firmly in my hand.

"I'm yours," she gasps. "Tell me what you want."

What do I want? My eyes search in her… Drifting landmarks… Violent need, omnipresent…

"I want you to scratch me! Scratch me, everyone, everywhere!"

I order this by thrusting myself with ardor into her. She executes. Others, also, behind me, while my abrupt comings and goings tear cries, "oh, yes!" to the one I take without respite, each thrust becoming more invasive. She moans, her teeth close on my ear, then she whispers it to me with a sigh…

Then I lost it… It swirls, tilts. Her eyelids flutter.

"Oh fuck!" she cries.

I maintain the rhythm, the vigor. She starts to cum loudly in my arms. I refuse to stop; I continue to thrust her. To eat her sighs. A taste of blood spreads over my palate, my lip bitten during her orgasm…

I know I'm going to collapse from fatigue afterward in the middle of used condoms. That I'll want more when I wake up. I can't manage to frame it, to control this dazzling instinct. To fuck until I collapse. And start again as soon as possible…

"Ty?" I hear a voice that comes from elsewhere.

A kind of echo. Someone touches my shoulder, and I suddenly open my eyes, on alert. Sophia jumps slightly at my reaction. Shit, I fell asleep outside by the pool! I regulate my breathing to release my nerves which are on edge. Sophia smiles at me.

"You fell asleep, it seems," she says. "I woke up to drink and saw you in the deckchair. You look exhausted."

And I'm sure you noticed my erection too.

I press my fingers to my eyelids, and I grab my phone to look at the time: three in the morning.

"I'm fine," I say, already deciding to go back to work upstairs.

I have front pages of the press—foreign and Australian—

to dissect, looking for the smallest useful detail. Sleeping more than necessary would be a monumental waste of time.

"Are you going to bed?" Sophia suggests to me, whose gaze envelops my body in swim boxers.

My member is not hard anymore, but she still looks at it. My other muscles tense up.

"No."

"Okay," she concedes with this eternal sad face, made to stir up my discomfort…

What she has just interrupted would be enough to ripen the guilt and feelings buried in my guts… But I don't talk about this kind of thing with her. I don't do it with anyone. Hermetic, I ruffle my hair, straighten up and let go, "I've rested enough; I have to go upstairs and work. You can go back to sleep.

Sophia fiddles with her wedding ring, hesitates, and glances at the papers she left me earlier in the evening.

"Of course," she whispers. "And you… did you take a look at the file?"

About the little French tourist? Shit, is there a link between the photo of this blonde, what I could imagine at the moment, and this damn dream that stirred up old memories?

Fuck, no, the filter! I remain impassive and simply nod my head.

"What do you think?" asks Sophia.

We stare at each other for a long time.

"Give up this idea," I end up saying.

I pick up my cell phone and the paperwork and walk away without dwelling on the subject. It's better never to open that trap door.

It's a dead end, like all the others…

OCÉANE

The next day, the whole house was asleep when I woke up. Normal for a Saturday morning after a night of drinking. No one will emerge before three o'clock. The positive point is to be able to take a long shower and dress myself up without having to free up the bathroom for others. I head to the kitchen to find some coffee in my small stock of groceries.

"Oh, hi, Garrett!" I say. He is in a T-shirt and boxers, and his hair is a mess.

He drinks from the bottle of orange juice, obviously the only one who has fallen out of bed to quench his thirst.

"Hi, Frenchie. We didn't see you last night."

"I wasn't feeling well. I preferred to watch that show you're into right now. Pretty good."

"I told you so! Still, you missed out on something with us."

"I can imagine, just by looking at your tired smile."

He stifles a yawn and laughs.

"What would be the point of weekends without parties?" he says to me with a wink. "Tonight, you go with the flow, or we'll drag you to the club, got it?" Garrett teases me.

"You won't have to force me."

While he's laughing and drinking again, I think back to my job offer. What if Garrett could help me get a second opinion?

"Say, my friend, did you or anyone from your business school do an internship or work in a company owned by the Sextons?"

I spoke my sentence in one go without hitting a word! I guess my English is getting a little better as I've been snooping around about potential future employers.

"The Sexton clan or the other?" Garrett asks me.

"Why? Is there a distinction?"

"Yup. The clan is the Sexton family in the broad sense, a long line of Australian high circles, or at least what remains of it after the death of Nick Sexton. The other just includes Tiger, the alpha male who took over the reins, and Sophia Sexton, his hottie. Their power and level of influence outweigh the rest of the clan."

Okay, in the broad sense, there's the uncle I saw on Google… But that's not what interests me right now. I try to stay natural by saying, "The couple, then. Do you have any tips?"

"Why? Do you want to apply to one of their companies?"

"Uh… maybe, I'm just asking around."

"Cool. Yeah, a buddy worked at a TS Naval branch one summer," Garrett tells me as he casually puts the juice bottle back in the fridge.

Except that—by the way—the name written on it is another roommates. Seven of us live in this house, with rules and all the crap. Garrett doesn't seem to care about that, helping himself to the groceries. When he notices that I have busted him, he smiles at me and signs to keep it under my hat. I laugh, shaking my head.

"So?" I resume.

"So what?"

He has already forgotten. If I go on, he might find my curiosity a bit suspicious.

"How did it go for your friend who worked with Tiger Sexton?"

"Oh, no, not directly with Sexton himself. Are you kidding, or what? But basically, he didn't last. He was quickly ejected with no concessions and lots of demands at all levels. The big boss has a reputation as a war machine. You have to earn an internship or a job in his matrix, and he only goes for excellence."

"Okay, I get it…"

"Me, I'll get in one day. I will join his teams of killers on the financial markets. And who knows, I'll even work with him live. Can you imagine it?" Garrett continues.

Right now, with his improbably colored boxers and his face ravaged by the excesses of the day before?

I just have to mentally compare it with the pictures I saw of Tiger Sexton online to shake my head and giggle. No, totally the opposite! Miss Australia's husband is so much more serious and so…

Océane, you are losing it!

I push my scattered thoughts back into place, unsettled by the turn they were taking. Luckily, Garrett still marvels on his own. He is inexhaustible when he's into something.

"Yep, I'll be a fucking tiger like him."

"Right now, big guy, you don't inspire the fear or respect you feel when faced with a fearsome feline. You should go back to bed," I tease him.

"Keep laughing. This guy is a missile. His methods are dissected in my business school… An example for the future leaders of the country."

My amusement is half-hearted when Garrett reaches the door. He pauses to mention the sexiness of his idol's wife in passing—

as another example of excellence in this Tiger Sexton's perfect existence—and winks at me again.

"Océane? Hush for the orange juice. I'm working on my Tiger 2.0 tactics: take what I want when I want it. And soon, I'll be grabbing business, millions, and a Sophia Sexton-style fighter plane in the same way."

"So, you plunder your comrades' supplies for training? Would your demi-god approve of this sort of thing?"

"How do you think he is the most powerful at the top? Feelings and moods are not his things."

He laughs, happy with himself, and goes back to his room. I remain pensive. How does it feel to get so close to this couple? What about a man with such a reputation? You should already know what I'm going to do under their roof. Dust the furniture? Take care of invisible beings whose first names appear in my contract?

Ah, well, maybe they are pets?

I make sure no one else comes into the kitchen before I fall back on my phone. Determined to find out for sure, I decide to call the restaurant immediately. They pick up after two rings.

"The Sexton's, Mike Woods speaking."

"Hello, Mr. Woods, it's Océane… You know, the one who had the interview yesterday."

"Yes. Good morning miss. I forwarded the signed contract to Ms. Sexton. The salary you have chosen has been validated; an amendment will be sent to you during the day. Your contract will be effective today."

Oh shit! It's going too fast! I lose my words and start babbling in English, "Uh… yes, precisely… I want to discuss the terms."

"I'm not qualified to discuss this with you, miss."

"With Mrs. Sexton then. Ho… how can I reach her?"

Mike remains silent on the phone.

"I don't give out Mrs. Sexton's contact information. But I can inform her of your desire to speak to her," he finally eluded.

"Okay. Let's do that. If you could tell her it's urgent… Thank you."

I cut the call. With my coffee and my computer, I go out to sit on the step in front of the house.

Why did Sophia Sexton pre-select me? How can "my profile" which was not suitable for her restaurants, be interesting to live at her house?

7

OCÉANE

A look on social media—time to spy on the actions of some ghosts from the past—and two coffees later, I look at the time. Thirty minutes gone. Thirty long minutes, the phone near my buttocks waiting for a call, a sign from Sophia Sexton.

I almost don't believe it anymore when a black Bentley pulls up in front of the house. Luxurious, tinted windows. But everyone is sleeping. Is someone expecting a visit? Quickly, a driver in a suit comes out, bends down to…

It looks like someone inside is telling him what to do.

I straighten up. Would an ambitious guy like Garrett would be thrilled if he knew that a car worthy of his dreams of greatness was parked in front of his roommate, I wonder? Meanwhile, the driver nods, closes his door and heads in my direction.

Maybe he's there for me? There was the address on my resume, and I… No, don't panic!

I check my cell phone screen again in my palm, which is getting sweaty. The manager didn't forward my message? The driver is already close by; he calmly gives me his identity before spilling the rest. Stunned, I blink.

What the hell is this?

"Miss Rousseau?" he repeats. "Please show me where to get your luggage."

"I… Excuse me?"

I was hoping for a phone call, not a giant wardrobe determined to obey orders and take me I don't know where. And then, who's in there?

"Your personal belongings, miss."

"But I… No."

"You're an employee of the Sextons," he tells me. "You're starting your job today. I'm in charge of helping you with your move."

His eyes locked on me, and the guy in the suit waited. I clear my throat and collect all my English vocabulary in my messed up noggin to try to express myself as comprehensively as possible.

"Look, you may not know this, but I left a message for Mrs. Sexton… about this. She must not have gotten it. For now, there is no question of … moving until I talk to her."

The giant finally blinks, and his expression changes imperceptibly. He moves away from the porch and shows me the vehicle from which he got out.

"Follow me."

"Huh?"

"You want to talk before telling me where your luggage is, is that it?"

"Yes… yes, but—"

"Come," he insists.

I take my courage in both hands and resolve to move forward.

"Who's in the car?"

Mr. Muscles becomes mute. Is he on a word ration or what? I give him an annoyed grimace. He continues to walk to the Bentley. He knocks on the window, and I can't think straight when he opens the door and steps aside to make room for me. I don't want to admit it, but my heart is beating faster, and my legs wobble a little as I lean in.

"Hello, Océane."

I inhale sharply. It's her. Just her. Damn, what was I thinking? I relax more or less to reply, "Hello, Mrs. Sexton."

"Sophia. Get in; we're not going to drive."

"Okay, but I… was expecting a phone call, not a young version of Jean-Claude Van Damme in my house."

The nickname is easy to find because this guy is muscular everywhere but in the brain. The only notable difference is that he is taciturn.

Sophia starts laughing, and my nerves relax. Not completely, because the not-talkative Van Damme slams the door on us and stands outside. We are locked in the car, and the heady fragrance of Sophia infiltrates my nostrils. My attention crystallizes on her, who tries to regain her seriousness after my joke. Her eyes still sparkle with amusement when she says, "You change me so much from social or business discussions, Océane. This freshness… I hope my driver didn't scare you. I preferred to come in person."

Well, you're a nice change from my temporary roommates, too, believe me.

"To be honest, he doesn't look very friendly. Anyway, it's probably better to be able to discuss face-to-face."

"Indeed. So, what's the problem?"

I moisten my lips and say, "Who are Annie and Byrne mentioned in the contract?"

Sophia's face freezes; she bats her eyelashes and chases a *je-ne-sais-quoi* from her pupils.

"As the asterisk indicates, we will eventually see if your contract extends to this subject or not… At the moment, this is not up to date. So, no problem there."

So my second guess also falls apart. They are not Chihuahuas. Nor real baby tigers, koalas, kangaroos, or other exotic animals that I imagined when I discovered the absence of kids to keep.

Confused, I bounce back, "Conclusion: something not to bring up at this time?"

"Let's just say that this subject could be a bit touchy. Especially in the presence of Tiger… thought it was important to mention them in case it would come up in time… Just know that in the current state, you have no commitment contractual vis-à-vis Byrne and Annie."

"Alright… let's move on to the next one. So, you don't have kids, right?"

"Right," she replies under her breath.

"Then why did you let me believe otherwise? What exactly will my role be? I thought I was taking care of your children, helping them with their homework, keeping them company when you're busy. I mean, you know what I'm talking about?"

She closes her eyelids, then whispers, "That's a lot of questions in one go, Océane."

"Lots of gray areas too. I'm sorry, but you cut the interview short, and in the end, I didn't know what was important. I was convinced that your babies were real ones."

"Indeed, we have no children. I didn't clear up this misunderstanding during our interview. I'm sorry."

No kidding! That's all?

"Well, I could also be sorry to give up on your proposal… a little too opaque now."

I'm about to go out, but Sophia Sexton holds me by the arm.

"No, wait for Océane. Apart from this mistake on my part, our interview went well, right? You were excited… motivated, and this would solve both your housing and work problem. Am I wrong?"

"It's true. However, I am no longer sure I understand why you are offering me this position and what you actually want from an au pair."

"Okay, let me clarify that. How about seeing it from a different angle? Consider yourself as 'my guest,' of course, with a salary to match."

I stare into her hazel eyes, wondering why she would pay someone to pretend to be a guest at her house. What is this, a kind of charity or fad, a distraction from the bored rich?

"Sophia, I still don't get it."

"Instead of a child to keep company, you will keep me company. Sometimes I… Let's just say the loneliness can be a little heavy some nights when I come home."

"Oh…"

Is that the thing? Does she feel isolated in her extraordinary life?

"I'm used to hiring personal assistants, but it's not the same. Tiger is often absent, and it would be nice to be able to share small moments of everyday life with someone real, sincere. And that's what I perceived from you during our discussion yesterday; you stayed natural, you didn't even seem to know who we were."

Busted! I hadn't prepared for my interview.

"Theaters, trips, etc. Together… A person with whom to open a bottle of wine in front of a movie at home. Does that make it clearer to you?"

Some sort of female companion? In other words, she pays for a friend on fixed-term contracts, at least a banal presence at her side?

Damn! Suddenly, she seems embarrassed to show herself in this light. A beloved personality who seems to have it all, yet plagued by loneliness at the top. It's crazy. Moved, I moisten my lips and find myself nodding slowly.

"Yes, it's clearer. But can I ask you a question?"

"Of course, Océane," she replies, a soft smile on her red lips.

"Why don't you just invite friends?"

"Friendships are rarely disinterested in my surroundings. I maintain a few, but it remains superficial. And then, Ty… Tiger has his way of working; I have mine…"

Where is the connection? Does he have a say in his wife's friends?

"Anyway. The only one I like to spend time with lives in South Africa. She travels a lot, too; we see each other from time to time," continues Sophia. "I no longer have personal assistants; an au pair seemed like a nicer opportunity to have someone more at home. However, if you want to back down, I won't insist, Océane. But the confidentiality still applies."

We mustn't let it be known that the wife of the great Sexton is so bored that she has to hire an extra on her property, right? I don't intend to tell anyone about it anyway. I feel rather sorry for her.

"And your husband, in this deal? I mean, about me barging into your house and all?"

"Tiger appreciates things that are well framed. That's why I formalized all this. Don't worry about that. Moreover, he is not often with us."

Basically, a control freak, absent most of the time? No, let's not jump to hasty conclusions.

To think that many women in this country must envy the one who has put the ring on the finger of one of the best parties in Australia without suspecting the kind of existence she actually leads. It sounds complicated… My emotional side will lose me as I sympathize, although I know little about the couple and their life. I breathe in and smile at Sophia.

"Say yes, Océane. It worked out pretty well between us, didn't it?"

"I… Okay, I'll scribble a goodbye note to my roommates and get my things. I'll give it a try," I answer on impulse. "Me too; I need to change my mind."

This one won't hurt, as we say. For the first time in a long time, I would like to follow my feeling and take things as they come. A fresh start with a bit of daring!

"Marvellous! Thank you very much, Océane. I'll be waiting for you here."

In the meantime, the courier arrives with my contract change. Barely twenty minutes later, the Bentley is driving with the two of us seated in the back. I fiddle with my Instax around my neck.

I can no longer compartmentalize Sophia Sexton in the "refined woman on a pedestal of beauty and success" box. Of course, she reflects all of this in a general way. On the other hand, at this precise moment, I see a more human facet…

Obviously, my friendship isn't for sale, but now that I understand why, I'm willing to stay with her and enjoy the moment. Even if my nervousness about meeting her husband intensifies.

We'll see. Maybe he's not so intimidating in real life?

"Shopping?" suggests Mrs. Sexton, pulling me out of my thoughts.

"Admit right away that I don't look good," I say playfully to lighten the mood.

Her features light up.

"No, I really like your style, but a woman never has too many clothes," she laughs. "It's Saturday, and I don't have any appointments today; let's make the most of it."

"Uh… if you like, but I can't afford a piece of fabric in the kind of stores you must go."

"Admit right away that I'm a snob," she replies.

Her eyes sparkle as if she were rediscovering the simple pleasure of chatting, of being teased. I take a falsely serious air to reply, "Oh, no, Mrs. Sexton. I would never dare to call you a snob; I don't want to get fired on the first day."

She starts to laugh, and it becomes communicative.

"You see, that's what I liked when I met you. You're natural and frank. Can we move on to familiarity now? Please call me Sophia."

"Okay… Sophia."

We end up in a private CBD lounge in an increasingly good-natured atmosphere. The Central Business District of Sydney is the center of the city for the big fortunes. I have often heard about it. We enter a showroom with velvet boudoirs, cups of *je-ne-sais-quoi*, macaroons, and saleswomen entirely devoted to us. Well, only to Sophia.

"Mrs. Sexton! What a pleasure to see you again. You are looking as gorgeous as ever. How are you?" welcomes us a lady of a certain age with a bohemian chic look.

I look transparent by comparison.

"I'm very well, Solange, thank you. I present to you Océane. Océane, Solange is my personal shopper. She has an eye for finding strong, unique pieces wherever they are," Sophia explains.

I don't doubt it, especially if there are no price restrictions. The professional lick's boot is now interested in me. Too bad for her, as my casual look indicates, I have neither the habit nor the means.

"Nice to meet you, Miss. Tell me what styles and designers you like, and we'll take care of the rest," promises the personal shopper.

All eyes turn to me. Uncomfortable, I waddle and opt for derision.

"I'm a big fan of Mister Sales and Miss Promo," I say. "Don't worry about me; I think it's Sophia who would like to see some clothes."

This one is laughing. The lady, confused, ends up smiling in turn.

"We will choose together, Solange. It would be necessary to have evening clothes, accessories, swimsuits, and why not two, three day outfits in phase with the trendy style of Océane," says Sophia.

The saleswoman bows again and happily obeys. She disappears very quickly to go in search of the items requested by her wealthy client. I turn to Sophia.

"You don't have to buy me clothes. With my salary, I will be able to—"

"Don't tell me no already, Océane. You've been very reasonable—too reasonable—about the amount of your pay. Given the little luggage you have brought, you'll need a bigger and better wardrobe for future occasions."

"Yes, but—"

"Tut-tut-tut! These are benefits in kind included in your job," she whispers in my ear. "And that makes me really happy," she decides, grabbing two cups from a tray to offer me one.

"Okay, presented like this… I just have to toast with this orange juice served in a glass of champagne to make it more classy," I tease, capitulating.

"Actually, it's a mimosa. I thought you would know, this cocktail was invented in France. Go ahead, taste it!"

"Oops, I look a little uneducated now?" I laugh at myself before soaking my lips in it.

"Not at all. I'm sure you have a lot to teach me, too," says Sophia.

"Maybe…"

It might be fun to take her out of her posh environment for a bit. Making her laugh also erases the gloom that often plagues my thoughts. Each one distracts the other. This idea draws a knowing smile from me. Then I take a sip of the mixture. The flavor of freshly squeezed oranges is indeed enhanced by that of sparkling alcoholic bubbles.

"So?" Sophia asks me.

"Hmm… not bad. But it's not too early to drink?"

"Too early for champagne? Never! Might as well celebrate your hiring with dignity, right?"

"Of course! It feels weird; I feel like a Pretty Woman 2.0."

This feeling is reinforced when the saleswomen bring racks loaded with masterpieces of clothing into the private room.

"So, enjoy, my pretty! We're going to burn the Amex!" declares Sophia, who is already falling for a superb red dress that is being carried for her behind a large paravent at the corner of the lounge.

This is crazy! There is not even a price displayed on the labels, as if no one cares how much it costs. I resolve to follow her example when I am offered clothes to try on behind the second paravent. I'm definitely going into Julia Roberts mode for the day. The most euphoric thing is that there is no Richard Gere or any male waiting to be rewarded for blowing his money on me. So, I don't ask myself any more questions. My head spins a little at the end of the third cup of mimosa. My eyes are shining, and my cheeks are all rosy. I stare at my figure in an emerald-colored dress with a very low cut in the back and vertiginous nude sandals in front of the mirror.

"A hottie! It flatters your morphology, your complexion, your hair. Just perfect," comments the saleswoman.

"I agree," approves Sophia, who is staring at me now. "I know exactly when you will be able to wear this wonder…"

"Really?"

"Oh yes! We take it all on."

I'm not sure I feel comfortable in something so sexy once out of this frame. We'll see… Enjoy, as Sophia says!

She gives me a wink. Tipsy, I let go and take pictures. The slides follow one another, and I begin to hum the famous song from the movie with Julia Roberts while parading in my turn, ""*Tan tan tan tan, tan tan… Pretty woman, walking down the street. Pretty woman…*""

Soon, Sophia gets into it, too; I pose for her. We laugh like drunken teenagers shopping with an unlimited credit card.

So, this is his world?

8

TIGER

"Friction" by Imagine Dragons resonates loudly. In my jogging bottoms, barefoot, I remove my soaked T-shirt to finish my stretching. The traces, the few not buried under some of my tattoos, appear, barely discreet. Those who work for me never have the guts to ask questions about it. My two sports and close combat coaches are no exception to the rule. I dismiss them by mopping my forehead, which is beading with sweat after hours of intensive physical effort.

"Have a good weekend, Mr. Sexton. See you next time," one of them greets me on the doorstep of my room.

I turn off the music and say, "See you guys later!"

Grabbing a bottle of water, I walk out of the room, the towel around my neck. I have to check my emails first to make sure nothing will disrupt the rest of my day. I spent most of last night dealing with an emergency at one of my branches. Didn't have time to talk to Sophia about the resume… Knowing her, she might insist. We'll have to make things clear if she intends to persist despite my refusal and show off this little French girl under my nose for six months.

The young lady won't last that long… Sophia either…

Usually, on Saturdays, my wife spends the morning in one of her restaurants, shopping, or having brunch with some upper-class chick. I'll wait for her to return and leave our talk on hold for now. I leave my private wing to go downstairs in search of the newspaper I left lying around after my morning coffee. As I pass him at the bottom of the stairs, I ask the butler for another coffee.

"Shall I bring this to you on the north or south terrace, sir?" ask this one.

Through the open windows, laughter punctuates this question. I check the time on my wrist and squint; my head turns to the butler.

"Is Sophia there?"

"Yes, sir. Madame is back. With… a new friend. A young blonde woman, sir."

I rub my growing beard. Peter continues, "They are on the south terrace."

So, Sophia went all the way and really hired her? I'm still puzzled by this phase that Murphy set up. But that would have been too simple if my *dearest* had stuck to my "no" last night. But nothing is ever that simple here…

And a young lady will now be living under my roof unless I kick her out myself right away and put the brakes on. This deserves an efficient and quick analysis. With an impassive face, I glance at the head servant and mechanically correct, "Our *au pair*, Peter. If she stays… She's not a friend."

Framed, clear, net.

For the moment.

"Very good, sir. And for your espresso?"

"In the library," I decide. "Thanks."

So, I move to the room downstairs, whose bay window looks directly onto the outside, which my wife has taken over with "her guest." Phone in hand, I go there.

11:10 a.m. Let's observe first before determining what's next…

OCÉANE

The exterior of this gigantic property alone impresses me. Everything is so perfect. The vast expanses of greenery maintained to the millimeter, the dimensions, the chic, and the beauty of the place. The whole is bathed in sunlight. I turn on myself, exclaiming, "Holy cow!"

The only problem is that it's the middle of the day, and the mimosas we put on in the showroom are getting to my head. It radiates too much; I should have put on glasses. I think we bought some, right? I don't know… We couldn't stop laughing. And cup after cup, hearing Sophia keep saying to the sales assistants, "we'll take that too," seemed almost unreal to me. I have never been offered so much stuff in so few hours.

I feel like I'm stuck on a merry-go-round. In a bubble. With my arms spread out, I keep spinning, laughing: "That's crazy! Maybe I'll wake up."

Dazed, I fell on the grass and burst out laughing. I think I'm tipsy. Sophia too. She sways, all seriousness gone, all pressure released. She's put "The Fade Out Line" by Phoebe Killdeer on her cell phone, turned the volume up to the max, and is shaking with yet another drink in her hand. A discreet woman in uniform brings bottles and steps aside. Mrs. Sexton obviously hasn't finished letting off steam, and I have to admit it feels great! Stop thinking; stop worrying about anything.

"Come on, Océane!" she invites me to join her.

I'm a little too drunk by everything going on since this morning. The shopping, the astronomical quantity of shopping bags that the servants have put up in "the lady's dressing room," this radical and destabilizing change of life makes me dizzy. Or maybe it's all the alcohol I've drunk in the last few hours? I get up, giggle uncontrollably, and start to wriggle in rhythm too.

Everything seems so easy in her world.

"Wow! You move well, Océane. Could you teach me?" Sophia compliments me.

She comes closer and sets her dance steps on mine. She hugs me, or it's me. I don't know anymore. I guide her.

"Just let your body… soak up the music. Like that…"

She hands me the opened bottle of wine to better imitate me. No more glass. Miss Australia, so classy, has passed the bottleneck. She is funny. So much alcohol, it's about to make me lose control. Uninhibited me. Don't do anything stupid like with regular buddies; we hardly know each other. And she's my boss.

No, my… boss-girlfriend?

I laugh stupidly, my brain doesn't work anymore. Damn, I think my reason is drowning in the mists, my hips are swaying, and the bottleneck is getting closer to my lips. I tilt my head back, close my eyes and savor while undulating my hips.

Musical notes… Not the kind I usually listen to, but I like it… The warm air in my mane released on my shoulders… The cool bottle on my thigh… The wine goes down my throat… Lyrics in English… I sing in fake English. Sophia waves her beautiful brown hair, and I do the same… Rocking… I didn't think I'd have fun like this in my work so quickly, so naturally, so well…

"I'd have to… show you around the house… Your room," she says.

"It's… huge here."

"You think? We have bigger ones, you'll see… Damn, I'm hot, aren't you? Shall we… take a dip first?"

I watch the gorgeous infinity pool next to us and shake my head, giggling like an idiot.

"We're going to sink."

"You don't know how to swim?"

"Yes… but too drunk."

We burst out laughing like it was the funniest thing in the world.

"No, we're all light; we're going to float," insists Sophia.

Damn, she begins to unbutton her blouse and throws her overpriced shoes. They disappear into the hedgerow.

"Come on, Océane! I haven't felt this happy in… so long."

"Me too."

"So come!"

She staggers while trying to get rid of her pants. Her contortions amuse me. I follow the movement and eject my T-shirt. In my bra, I fight with the fly of my denim shorts. I've definitely crossed the threshold of one drink too many; I'm getting hilarious for nothing. I can't control my movements anymore.

"Yes! You are going to swim with me!" Sophia enthuses… "The water is good, you'll see."

The beautiful, distinguished woman is as drunk as me now. She doesn't give a damn about anything. She laughs and struggles to take off her suit pants.

"Watch out… You're going to make a splash, too… Like your Louboutins."

She laughs at my remark. Then she tries to take off one leg. Oops, she loses her balance… A guy appears from nowhere. Where does he come from? He catches her before she falls into the turquoise water and yells at us.

"What the hell are you doing?" grunts this bare-chested hottie in jogging pants.

My irises lock on him while my brain freezes on the image: large aboriginal designs cross his side in an assemblage of complex patterns and disappear on his back, which must be tattooed too. I don't know which is hotter: his abs, his tanned skin, or the raw graphics of his tattoos? I try to come back to his face.

Uh, I know him, right? Brown hair, sexy, and… Oops, it's the boyfriend from Google! I mean… Sophia.

His blue eyes focus on me draining all the oxygen from my lungs. My cheeks are on fire. My brain melts away for good. Fuck, they should put shirtless pictures of him on the internet. In jogging bottoms and his hair disheveled like now. A fucking detonator with his gaze fixed on me.

TIGER

Sophia landed in my arms, at the very last moment. She is not even in a state to answer me. I detail the number of empty bottles of Côte de Nuits on a table and finish by stopping at the one Blondie is holding in her hand, leaning on her pale thigh.

Fuck, the trouble is already starting!

The doe eyes of the little French girl stare at me. Her cheekbones were as pink as her moist parted lips. I clench my jaw, and my irises run down her curves, going up to lock themselves in hers. She swallows, me too.

"Ty, my love… are you joining us?" whines my wife against me.

I inhale sharply and tense up.

"It's not even noon, Sophia; how many glasses have you had?"

Both laugh, completely drunk. My wife tries to sit up.

"How much did we drink, Océane?" Sophia hesitates.

A pout appears on the girl's face, the kind of half-innocent, half-candid expression that inspires an X-rated reaction.

And I… No. Stop, Tiger!

She is not aware of it; she is obviously trying to count in her head. She unfolds her fingers to list, then gives up after three seconds.

"Uh? A lot?" she replies, then she writhes with laughter.

"You got it! A lot of glasses, Ty," Sophia confirms. "And now… we're going to play mermaids. You know when we used to swim in the lake, you and me… It was so good. Come on, my love."

"Certainly not! You'll go upstairs and sober up."

The evocation of this memory disturbs me, and the inexplicable laughter of the two, ditto. Sophia suspected I could see them through the window, but damn it, she's really drunk and starting to lose her filter.

"Or maybe you'll ride me and intoxicate my senses like you know how to do, my stallion."

"That's enough, Sophia!"

"Wow, does he ever relax?" intervenes the blonde in a bra that I try to avoid watching again.

"Nah… Let me introduce you… Mr. Killjoy Sexton, my husband," giggles Sophia, totally unsteady on her two feet.

"Hi, Mr. Sex… I mean…"

The *au pair* implodes once again, clutching her stomach. The more my features harden, the more her hilarity seems uncontrollable. At the same time, my wife softens against me, in off-duty mode.

"Sorry… You're so serious… It's disturbing with the… face you have and those… those crazy abs, your tattoos, and… your warlord wounds… Can I touch?"

Unaware of overstepping the bounds, she points her fingers toward me. I give her an immediate slap on the back of her hand, which makes her jump.

"Ouuuuh! Mister Sex gives slaps, Sophia?!" she comments in a mocking tone.

My *dearest* does not speak another word, and this one collapses almost at the same time. My lips are sealed, and my eyes glare at Blondie. I hoist my wife on my shoulder while piercing the gaze of the alcoholic lady who vacillates.

"The big boss is not happy, she jokes… You want to pose for me? It will relax you! Where is my Instax, by the way?"

I signal Mary, an employee, to confiscate the flashy turquoise camera lying in the grass before this walking disaster finds and uses it.

"Arg, I may have lost it at the showroom… Too bad, beautiful scarred tiger… Uh… You speak French, by the way?"

I walk slowly towards her, my load on my shoulder. She blushes but can't help but giggle again.

"I'll take care of Sophia," I reply in my language, which I've been using since the beginning of this disastrous conversation.

"Oh, he only speaks English," she concludes in hers. "Good… You won't know what I'm talking about… You should put something on this chest… Mr. Not Funny. Because, right now, if I had your number, I would have sent you a good big eggplant," she says before bursting out laughing. "You don't know, do you? I'm sure Louane would have validated what I see through your joggers too. Little lucky Sophia!" she congratulates my wife.

Damn, that was all I needed! I move closer, lean into her ear, and whisper, "I forbid you to swim in this state. Someone will show you your room, and you will stay there long enough to sober up."

"You… you are not my… boss, first of all."

"Obviously, my wife hired you. Unless you issue my veto, you will live under my roof. So go ahead and do it! I want you to have clear ideas when we talk again about your behavior, who this Louane is, about everything *you won't tell her*, and sexual emojis."

She shudders as I step back. Her green eyes widen as I tell her all this in her language.

"Shit, you…? French?"

She is drunk, and her pink lips open dangerously. I prefer to take a deep breath and turn on my heels without comment.

"Hmmm, your backside is even more…" she chops behind my back. "These twisted designs make you want to touch them too much… How far do they go?"

I walk away carrying Sophia and order the butler to make sure she obeys. Damn, she's still raving about my butt as I walk away!

"Oh, yes, yum! Worth a fucking eggplant."

9

TIGER

Fourth coffee, my mind in turmoil. I smoke the last cigarette in my pack and open a second one, dissecting the financial press. This mental diversion works for a while. I focus on markets, numbers, and strategies to erase from my head everything I have witnessed in the past few hours.

Sophia, blouse open. The lace on her breasts… Blondie, loose mane… Micro shorts, a kid's bra… Damn, that pearly skin under the cotton fabric… Both of them were drunk… Their undulations… This languorous cadence… The little one unconsciously making advances to me… Her button undone on her lower abdomen… A damn button and a torrent of debauchery promises are trying to get into my skull.

My mechanism must not jam. Not now, not ever.

The ringing of my phone puts my thoughts back in place. Irascibly, I pick up, growling, "Sexton."

"Hello, Mr. Sexton, this is John."

I blow out my nicotine puff and run my fingers through my hair, listening to my CFO. Shanna had to give him my message to get back to work. Mourning is fine for a while, but whining about the corpse of your dad for more than twenty-four hours doesn't sit well with me. I didn't need to when I lost mine, even as a kid…

I'm going straight to the point, "Shanna briefed you?"

"She briefed me, yes… I'm also calling you to thank you for your gesture. My mother was very touched."

I would have to ask my assistant, "what did I do" to express my condolences to the family of my employee. She's the one who takes care of these kinds of details and who determines who deserves how much attention.

"Glad she liked it," I say.

"And, I was thinking of staying in London a little longer to help my mother, if possible. She can't handle it. I will be working remotely and will be in Melbourne for the annual Sexton reception… for sure."

Basically, he doesn't want to return to the front before next weekend? To see Sexton Sr. parading around, scorning my methods, and being condescending to me to my face despite the dividends he gets from me? I stump out my cigarette and inhale calmly.

"Tell me, John, when did you say to yourself that it was more important for me to have you as a guest of that old fart James Sexton instead of fully assuming your responsibilities as administrative and financial director of my company?"

I feel his breathing suddenly become uneven on the phone.

"Sorry, Mr. Sexton, I thought that—"

"Yes, what did you think? Why did I ask Shanna to tell you what we were up to, John?"

I hear him inhale; I can almost make out the look of disappointment on his face. Does he finally understand?

"Because on the list of targeted suppliers is my ex-girlfriend's family business. I will be more effective than Shanna in convincing her to give us the majority shares in time to counter Carter," he summarizes.

"You do what you want. That being said, you are free, John. You can hang around as long as you think necessary in London. You will bear the consequences. Make the choice that suits you."

I hang up without giving him time to argue. It's a waste of time. I dig into my hair again and let out a moan. It's three o'clock, my wife and "her guest" are still sleeping their hangovers off, and I feel like I'm going around in circles in a barbed wire cage.

I abruptly get up from my chair and leave the office to head for the wing opposite mine. I left enough time for Sophia; we need an immediate tune-up! I knock on her door, turn the handle and find her in the same state as when I put her to bed.

"…"

When I try to extricate her from her alcoholic mists, she mumbles something almost unintelligible to me. Words I can't stand to hear come out of her mouth in a mushy litany. In response, I raise my voice, "SOPHIA!"

"I… need… to sleep," she grumbles.

"No kidding? Out of the question. Open your eyes and stand up straight. You did what you wanted to do. You wanted my attention? It's your turn to listen to me carefully."

In the darkness of her drawn curtains, I turn on the light and pull out the comforter. This makes her react in a fraction of a second. She holds her head and stifles a grumble as she sits down.

"Ty, can't it wait? My head hurts too—"

"Whose fault is that? I won't be long. Just listen. You brought "that guest" despite my warning. I don't care what Murphy thinks; I'll set the rules for the rest of this since my space just got smaller…"

"Can we… can we talk about it later? Please, Ty," Sophia begs me, completely off.

Obviously distraught too.

"No, now! What I have to tell you is take it or leave it, so you're going to listen to me carefully…"

When I finish stating the terms of the new "arrangement," Sophia feels the effect. I'm not convinced that, in her condition, she has assimilated everything. However, I don't have time to wait for her to sober up, and my nerves won't last a second longer, so I add, "Last point, Sophia: I have brought forward my trip to Qatar. My jet leaves tonight."

"But when are you coming back? Are you going to avoid us? Punish me?"

I'm just taking a step back before the James Sexton reception. And I refuse to be destabilized, to let this breach in my filter get bigger. It took me a long time to set it up, damn it! Maybe it's not just Sophia who's been pushed around this time, Murphy suspects it, and I don't like it…

"Ty, please… These new rules… You can't mess everything up like that; that's not what we agreed on."

"What are you afraid of now, Sophia? That I end up having a hard-on for another woman under our roof, a woman you've chosen? Because that's what it's all about, isn't it?"

"I just want you to reconsider our—"

"The debate is over. You know my position. But did you warn her? Did you think about it yourself before going for it like this?"

"I—"

"Make an appointment with Murphy."

Despite her pallor and the consequences of too much drink, a familiar glow burns deep in her eyes. The one I have seen shine hundreds of times amid her sighs. Our fluids mixed, our sweaty bodies… Damn, this is getting out of hand. I really need to get away!"

"If I convince Océane, you could have her and me," she insists.

"Do you hear yourself haggling? Hey, come down, for God's sake! Do you think you can convince an innocent young lady to enter the intimacy of our couple?"

"Who knows? I might… I miss it, Ty. I miss you."

Everything is going wrong, damn it! My jaw clenches again, my fingers digging into my hair.

"Get your strength back and call Murphy," I tell her again. "I'll be back for that damn gala. Whether the blondie comes with us or not will be your decision. You can still kick her out…"

OCÉANE

Argh, damn, my head!

I tap my tousled hair, and it feels like a vice is crushing my temples as soon as I open my eyelids. What time is it? What did I do? Partying too much with my roommates? I close my eyes, the pain pulsing in my skull. I reopen them, moaning.

A refined room with impeccable, bourgeois decor. What's the big deal?

Where am I?

Shit, shit, shit! I don't recognize the place at all! I panic and dart up off of the bed. A moan of pain escapes my pasty mouth. I hold my forehead and close my eyes again. I try to connect to something, to find a valid explanation, fragments of memory…

The contract. Yes, I signed a contract! And a confidentiality agreement too.

The Van Damme look-alike! The famous driver in front of the roommate. No, more like my old home. Damn, yes! I accepted Sophia Sexton's proposal. We went shopping, we did… blank… We did what? And this is her place?

I use my wobbly reserves of energy to get up. My denim shorts are open, and I'm not wearing a top, just a bra. How did I… Blank… Misery! I inspect around me. A basin and a glass of water sit on the bedside table. As well as a box of migraine tablets and a washcloth. Who gave them to me? Sophia? She was as soaked as I was in my loose memory. Note to self: never again abuse this thing that we have not stopped drinking in the showroom. It's the first day of my *au pair* stay, and I already feel like a wreck.

My T-shirt, where's my T-shirt? And my phone? My God, what if I had done something stupid? Sent messages in France or online?

I wince as I move. Let's not panic; let's get the facts straight first.

And what the hell, it smells like… I don't know what's worse. The gaps in my memory to fill in or the fact that I let myself go so much, with an almost stranger and so far from home? I stare at the room, my eyelids wrinkled. Roses, lilies, and white tulips, that's where the delicate smell comes from that would almost dissipate the alcohol I'm soaked in. A large, refined crystal vase is filled with these fresh flowers on a chic vintage chic dresser. My Instax and my phone are next to it. Yes! At least two things found!

I grab the phone. No compromising photos or videos. Phew!

Text? No, too much right now; my belly is turning over. And I have to locate myself first. Nothing else belongs to me here. No clothes. But I'm not going to walk around in a bra, am I?

Maybe I already did? Total blur…

I continue my quest and find the adjoining bathroom. Easy, there is only a glass front between it and the bedroom. A gagging heart pushes me to rush in. I fall to my knees facing the toilet, and throw up an excess of liquid. Misery!

I flush the toilet. Above the vanity top, a sophisticated mirror displays the date, time, and weather in one corner. Saturday, seven twenty-six. Still sunny, eighty degrees outside. Have I been sleeping for *that* long?

Great, Océane. You are off to a good start! Masterful crash!

I discover my tidy toiletries... That's already a beginning. Might as well brush my teeth and agonize under the shower until I feel less lame. Under the warm jets on my body, my mind looks like a smokescreen. From 11 a.m. to 7:26 p.m., what the fuck did I do? Where did this bruise on my knee come from? No explanation comes to me...

You created a remake of The Hangover, and you screwed everything up?

This possibility is just scary because it is too likely. I put on a bathrobe and go to swallow a tablet of paracetamol. I lay back in bed again, eyes closed... Music. Was there music? Maybe my phone will fill in my memory gaps if I used playlists or something? I go back to grab it near the vase, and suddenly I see something I had missed... A card is slipped in the middle of the floral composition.

Uncertain, I extract it to read the words scribbled on it:

Well done, pretty Lily?

If you can swallow solids, I have asked the kitchen to conform to your tastes.

Eggplant and any other vegetable of similar shape that you want to eat...

You won't say anything to this Louane, of course. We will have a discussion when I return.

TS

My eyes widen. TS like Tiger Sexton? Vegetables? Eggplant? Did he take me for a vegetarian or something? Why does he call me pretty Lily in the first place? And what does he want to discuss with me? Why Louane? What would I want to confide in her?

Oh my, I'm losing my footing!

My mind is not working; I can't find any answers to my questions. Let's pick up the phone... No call. I didn't send anything to anyone or ruin my social life on any social networks, and obviously didn't call anyone. Confused, I stuff the TS-signed card into my bathrobe pocket and stare at the white petals. I'm trying to see it more clearly.

Sophia! Yes, she, she might help me remember. I venture out of the room, a ball of apprehension in my stomach. I don't know how to interpret all of this. What if, being drunk, I've screwed up? Why did my boss's husband leave me this fucking message? I haven't even met him yet. At least, I think so...

Great, did I meet him? Did I talk to him?

I walk along the hallway, trying to probe my exhausted neurons. Doors follow one another. My stomach growls, and my head hurts. I advance to the staircase that serves two different wings of the house. Is the side I come from reserved for servants, for guests? And the other opposite probably houses the private quarters of Mrs. and Mr. Sex… Lightning flash.

Damn, that name! Manly abs, Australian Aboriginal tattoos… It was on him. He was there, and I called him Mr. Sex!

In shock, I squeeze my eyelids and grip the railing at the top of the stairs. I'm not sure I want to come down anymore. He was angry, I think… It's blurry, but my mind brings up this image: him glaring at me.

Oh no, what the hell did you do, Océane?

10

TIGER

"Are you ready, Mr. Sexton? The pilot informs you that we can take off."

I take one last look at the runway, buckle my seatbelt and confirm, "Let's go."

"Yes, sir," the flight attendant obeys with a polite smile.

I put on my sunglasses and dive back into my thoughts. Not the ones including the girl's bra on the blondie's curves; I must repress that. Unfortunately, I'm afraid that I'm less successful at locking up old habits. Especially with this as a bonus: the slides Peter retrieved. "The au pair" dropped them by the pool. My butler saw fit to confiscate them. Good old Peter was certainly annoyed at having to give them to me—he has his reasons…—but they better not fall into the wrong hands either. Only, I don't know what to do with them now that I have them. Destroy them? I should probably. And certainly not to look at them like this. This pile of photos is like a detonator between my fingers. Yet, I can't stop staring at them.

On one, Sophia and Océane are playing pin-ups in what looks like a showroom. A saleswoman probably captured the moment at their request. Then little by little, the photos become more enticing… Maybe unintentionally… Because my wife and her new girlfriend look progressively tipsier. In some poses, there is only Sophia. I guess it was Océane who must have taken the photos. She changes outfits, has fun, and plays with the lens.

On others, there is the Frenchie. Alone. In dresses to make you crazy. A woman child metamorphosing into a femme fatale, image after image. Sophia's work. And this gleam in Océane's eyes reveals itself… The resemblance is subtle, but sometimes she looks a little like…

Fuck no! Don't compare! Holy shit, what have you started, Sophia? How do I handle this?

A voice evaporates the tumult in my head, bringing me back to the present, "This your pilot. We're ready for takeoff, Mr. Sexton. I wish you a pleasant flight."

I put everything in the kraft envelope and put it in the bag. Then I look at the time and open my computer. At least the old fart's damn reception will be less of a headache with this intrusion into my home. But the Frenchie is not a sex worker that I could possibly pay for… And then, I turned the page on the Dominas. But there's a big problem: I've also watched too many indecent videos in the last few years, and I've stayed clean a little too long.

Much too long.

So how can I try to tame these things that trouble me in spite of myself with a brand-new temptation under my nose?

Océane

I hope I run into Sophia first before I confront her husband. I reach the first floor. An elderly gentleman in uniform and with a strict appearance greets me with deference. His face vaguely reminds me of something. Another person I must have seen without remembering clearly.

"Good evening, Miss Rousseau," he says to me.

"Good evening, sir…"

He knows my last name. Did he introduce himself beforehand? I think he took care of our shopping bags when we arrived. But that's all I can think of. Empty space. Defeat!

"I'm Peter, Miss. Just Peter. Mr. and Mrs. Sexton's butler."

"Oh, right. Nice to meet you, Peter…"

"Likewise. Are you hungry, Miss? Mr. Sexton gave directions to the kitchen."

Let me guess: eggplant moussaka? Zucchini casserole? Cucumbers with vinaigrette?

"Uh… no," I answer, feeling the embarrassment and nausea rising together in my depths. "Not right now, thank you."

I still don't know how the master of this house came to this deduction about my taste in food… He doesn't know anything about me.

"Very well," says Peter, always very respectful. "Otherwise, what can I do for you, Miss?"

"Actually… I'm not sure where to go. Could you help me locate Sophia?"

"Mrs. Sexton is in the library. Shall I take you there, Miss Rousseau?"

"I'd like that. But please stop giving me "Miss" in every sentence."

"I'm sorry, Miss, Mr. Sexton insists on it. Everyone has their place."

What a psychorigid this "Mr. Sexton" is! After deciding what I eat and what I say or not to my friend, he also decided what to call me?

I waddle over and pull the sides of my robe tighter. Being naked underneath doesn't help me regain a minimum amount of confidence, and the fog in my head still isn't clearing.

"I see… And… Is Mr. Sexton around? In the same room as Sophia? I'd prefer not to disturb them."

Océane, the chickened-out amnesiac alcoholic, would she be afraid to see the tiger again?

"Mr. Sexton left a few hours ago, Miss. He's out of town," Peter replies without losing patience.

"Phew! Well, I meant… shit! Never mind," I mumble, noticing the model employee's raised eyebrow.

He doesn't comment and brushes off the expression that briefly crossed his face. I feel sorry for myself but find it hard to hide my relief. "TS" signed the card and vanished? That's one less immediate worry for me…

I try to pull myself together. Unfortunately, shame and doubt are starting to grow in me again. I hope I didn't make a fool of myself at some point. Worse, I didn't blow my chances of keeping my job in the first few hours.

"I would like you to direct me to the library, please, Peter."

"Of course, Miss. If you would like to follow me?"

I follow the butler's lead to a stately room. Graphic ebony shelves line the walls elegantly. They run along almost every side and are abound with books. Lush plants in large pots adorn the corners. And a huge bay window overlooks… the pool…

Second flash!

I recognize it. I see myself drinking with Sophia at the edge of this overflowing splendor… Then black out… My eyes freeze on the breathtaking view from here, and my belly twists. It kills me not to know how things turned out. For example, could Tiger Sexton have seen us from this spot?

We don't panic; we don't panic.

There's no indication he was around, and maybe I wasn't messing around that much.

I wouldn't have, right?

Otherwise, what kind of a messed up first impression is that!

I swallow, trying to control my breathing. Peter stays back; I move forward and discover Sophia in one of the meridians.

"Well, you're awake," she says immediately when she sees me.

Her smile is faded. I notice her puffy, red eyes. Just due to the hangover?

"Have you been crying, Sophia?"

"No, no… don't worry. I've had a bit too much wine and champagne; I can't hold alcohol so well anymore," she justifies herself, clumsily putting on her usual assurance.

I'm not fooled. I come closer and sit next to her, thinking about what I could say or do.

"You look sad, Sophia. And I have to admit, I don't remember much. I'm freaking out that I embarrassed you or hurt you or—"

"Not at all, sweetheart… It's nothing. You haven't done anything wrong. I'm just… a little emotional at times, and drunkenness makes it worse for me," she persists, fiddling with her wedding ring.

She stands up and leaves to stand in front of the window, graceful despite everything. Lost, I stare at her back. Is it time to prove myself? A true friend would have known how to act. A simple friend would have tried to minimize this by distracting her.

An au pair paid to keep her company, how are they supposed to act in this scenario?

What if I just listened to my heart? But I'm still an employee, and as the butler just told me, everyone has to stay in their assigned place in this house, if I understood correctly…

Argh, my hair hurts too much. Sophia runs her fingers through hers and turns toward me, a little more cheerful.

"Let's stop talking about it. We both drank too much; it's all my fault."

"Tut-tut, you didn't force me. And overall, we had a good time… As far as I can remember," I plead derisively.

"It's true…"

A moment of silence follows. She sits back down and holds my hands.

"Neither of us remembers the whole morning, so I don't know if I welcomed you. So I want you to know that I am delighted to have you here, Océane".

"Thank you."

"I hope you haven't changed your mind. You're gonna stay, right? I want you to stay with me."

"Yes, I'm not letting you go."

Why is she so worried about it?

She presses my fingers, and her face becomes warmer. I find a little bit of this beginning of complicity that we shared. Our fingers intertwine, and I smile back at her.

"By the way, can I ask you a little question, Sophia?

"Sure."

"Have I met your husband? Did we… talk?"

An almost amused astonishment emerges on her features.

"I don't know. Well… not clearly. I think we'll have to make more formal introductions when he comes back."

"Tell me he's not coming back for six months," I beg, half-serious, half-desperate.

Against all odds, her lips stretch, then she bites her lip, massaging her temple.

"Ty is coming back at the end of the week. Don't be so intimidated."

"I'm not intimidated," I lie. "I was just worried that he saw me drunk… Is that the case? Was he angry? Did he say anything to you?"

"I don't think so… It's okay, sweetheart. Don't worry about it… And you know what, you're welcome to come with us to his uncle's party next Saturday."

Like, the three of you at a social event? Hell, no.

Before I can get away, the ringing of her phone—although not so loud—twists my brain and interrupts us. Sophia picks it up hastily. An unknown number and a kind of incomprehensible uneasiness make her a bit feverish. Well, I think. I have to admit that I'm not in top form.

"Sorry, Océane, would you mind leaving me alone, please? I have a phone appointment," she says. "Can we meet later?"

"Yes, of course."

I get up. She whispers something in a language that I don't identify, picks up the phone, then takes the phone away from her mouth to add, looking at me, "Peter will show you around meanwhile. Your things have been put away in the dressing room in your bedroom. Unless you prefer to walk around half-naked?"

"Oh, no, I'll be happy to put on real clothes. See you later!"

"See you later, sweetheart. We'll talk about that night in Melbourne later."

I leave the library after a wink from Sophia. Confused, I lean against the wall, tighten my belt and stuff my hands in my bathrobe pockets. I almost forgot the card; I sigh as I brush it off on one side and my cell phone on the other. I pull them out and stare at them. In my left hand, my foggy new life and enigmatic words. And in my right hand, text messages from Louane belatedly invade my screen.

Louane: Seriously, you're leaving like that, sweetie?
Where do you live now? And the job
we talked about… Give me a sign.

Louane: It's me again, honey. Are you okay?
Call me back, or I'll pout at you
like, for a hundred years.
Kisses.

My confidential job might be in jeopardy if Louane digs too deep. I'm not sure what to tell her yet. Apparently, Tiger Sexton wants to control that aspect of my social life. I should go back under the duvet, in this room that smells of flowers and…

And what? Wait to see clearly?

"Is everything all right, Miss?" asks the butler, wisely posted near the steps.

I moisten my lips and nod.

"Would you like to visit now or later?"

"Not right now, Peter. This property is huge, and I have a really bad headache. I'll walk around to discover the places on my own when I'm in better shape. If you don't mind."

"No problem, Miss. But in this case, I must specify your accesses."

"My access?"

"Yes, Miss. The entire first floor, the exteriors, and the left wing upstairs is wide open to you."

"I see… And the right wing?"

"Those are Mr. Sexton's quarters. Strictly private. Your room is in Mrs. Sexton's area, on the left, as you may have noticed."

Shit, they're in separate rooms?

So even when Tiger Sexton is not on a business trip, he remains distant and doesn't share his wife's room. I try to hide my stupor and whisper, "Very well, got it. Thank you, Peter."

"You're welcome, Miss Rousseau. If you need anything, the whole staff and I are at your disposal," he says before slipping away.

Too much info to take in; my migraine seems to be getting worse. I press my temples and sigh again.

Well, welcome to the Sexton's, baby. But obviously not in the right wing… Argh, prohibitions have a way of exciting the imagination.

Mine gets carried away in spite of myself: Mr. Sex, so hot, so unreachable, so intimidating, what is he doing there alone?

11

SIX DAYS LATER, KINGSFORD-SMITH AIRPORT, SYDNEY

"I hope you had a good trip, sir. Where should I take you?" asks the driver, opening the door for me.

"Home?" Except for the stud farm, this notion is futile and non-existent when one has several homes scattered in different places while feeling no attachment to any of them. They are just stones, walls, and spaces that belong to me. And various content, works of art, staff, and my spouse. In short. Not necessarily in that order, but the result is still the same. I don't feel at home anywhere. Wearily, I mechanically order, "Sydney's property."

"Yes, sir."

It's Friday; it's six o'clock. Sophia and her "guest" have had the week to recover from their emotions, to get used to each other… I know that Océane is still with us. I guess Sophia made a choice, with or without Murphy's opinion. What will happen when "her new girlfriend" understands that all the expectations of her stay at our property are not written in black and white in her contract? We have never had to deal with this scenario. I didn't plan on banging a little novice in the marital home. Hell, I shouldn't even begin to consider it! In the beginning, with pros like lady Candice, then a slew of call girls, each of us always knew what to expect. And everyone enjoyed this situation until some things got out of hand…

Sophia lost her mind; I lost control of the situation.

She tends to get too emotionally involved. This rarely turns out to be beneficial for all parties involved. In conclusion, if I don't regain absolute control, someone will get screwed, and not in the orgasmic sense of the word.

After Kelly, Sophia ended up in a very poor state, and I had to take care of her. The press almost went too far into the breach… This was a lesson for us.

Knowing my wife, I assume that when I get back, it will depend on what she really wants… No, I know what she really wants, and it's inextricable, damn it!

I think as I watch the city pass through the window. Then I go back on my phone to think about something else.

Peter: Nothing to report, sir. Today, beauticians are at the house. They are in Mrs. Sexton's wing.

Tiger: Thank you, Peter. I'm on my way. Let my wife know about it in thirty minutes.

Peter: Yes, sir.

The irreplaceable Peter. Always faithful, he sent me a daily report of each day in my absence. The schedule of each of them.

Sophia hasn't seen Murphy, which bothers me… Even if she seems to have spoken to him on the phone… I also heard about Océane's little coffee date with a friend named Louane. My security service has, in fact, collected the necessary information on this friend. You never know. It's always best to prepare all the parameters of a transaction in advance, hoping that Miss Rousseau is smart enough to have respected our confidentiality agreement.

The ride takes place in silence. I think about the progress of the quest in the field. My guys managed to get their hands on a copy of the French police files… An ouroboros and other details stand out.

Some similarities are too striking…

I clench my fists; my stomach contracted with contained rage.

After the stops in traffic jams, we finally arrive. Sophia is the first to appear at the entrance to greet me; her figure is draped in a long silky kimono.

"Welcome home, Ty. I wasn't expecting you until tomorrow morning."

I guess the desire to go back was a little bit more than I wanted.

In any case, all this shakes me up inside. The uncertainty and the impression that a vice is holding me back are coming back at full gallop. So, when she hugs me, I let her do it.

"I see that, Sophia… How are you? Rested?" I answer her. "Am I interrupting something?"

"Oh, just my beauticians; we're getting ready for tomorrow night. And I'm doing great."

This "we" makes me smile. Blondie gets dolled up too. Translation: she intends to keep her. I hug her back and kiss her hair.

"Good."

"You, on the other hand, look tired, Ty."

"Long flight time and a lot of details to take care of in Doha. A shower and a whiskey will fix everything."

"If you ever want a little massage—"

"There's no need, Sophia," I cut her off more curtly than I should.

At least, according to Murphy, who is adept at tactful language. Bullshit! Sophia bats her eyelashes.

"Okay…" she gives in. "I'm going back; the girls will take care of Océane, then we'll get ready for dinner. You're not going out again, are you?"

"Not if I have a reason to stay. I'm waiting for you to introduce me to her now that you are sober, and she is obviously staying."

She hesitates for a few seconds, then nods.

"Okay. I'll see you later, Ty."

I continue on my way and greet Peter before going upstairs. I could have branched off to one of my "bachelor pads" in town, brought someone in with specific skills, and unleashed whatever I've been locking down for a few years. No longer needing to filter anything, just fucking in the only way that really gets me high. But no, I went "home."

I undress, turn on the music and let the warm jets run over my skin. "Running Up That Hill" by Placebo at full blast, my eyelids shut under water. I've been exhausted and sexually frustrated for a little too long. And abstinence has never been my thing. That's probably what generates those pesky, stubborn fantasies that seep into my pores with the fog.

Hot water. The lapping… Fresh petals… Moaning pink lips… The wet white silk plastered on the areolas… Delicious erect nipples… Immersed bodies… My fingers in the hollow of this moistness… This undulating pelvis… Fevered doe eyes, blond hair floating around, and…

Shit! The new one's face and body are encrusted in the middle of the images. Masterful mess up filter… Cold shower, damn!

OCÉANE

The girls are packing up their gear. I'm still a little puzzled by the result. Looking at the whole thing, I feel like I'm discovering another version of myself. But Sophia was so excited and happy to share her little beauty secrets that I don't really regret it. We had fun. And I tried out some different skincare products than I'm used to.

Sophia comes back into the room, all dolled up.

"Are you done, girls?"

"Yes, we are."

"Perfect! Océane? Tiger is back; we'll have dinner together," she says.

Damn it!

I nervously tighten the flaps of the silk kimono around my body. She is delighted with the return of her husband: normal. But personally, I would have preferred not to meet him anytime soon. Okay, that's downright selfish of me. I should be happy for her and smile. The absence of "sir" only suited me well because I couldn't fill in the countless blanks of my first morning here, of my probable exchanges with him. It disturbs me.

"Happy for you, beautiful. But you know what? I'm going to slip away and spend the evening with Louane; let you get back together," I say, trying to escape.

Sophia stares at me with a little pout.

"Don't even think about it! Come on, let's meet for an aperitif on the south terrace in half an hour," she decrees before crossing the threshold again and disappearing.

Did I already say, "damn?"

I watch the beauticians leave, trying to still look as zen as five minutes ago.

But he's back! How am I supposed to behave?

The question goes round and round in my head for the next twenty-seven minutes. No clothes seem adequate enough to make me blend in, to make me look tiny. A special outfit for "let's forget the first rotten meeting and start from scratch." Unfortunately, I can't find that one. Twenty-nine minutes. Damn, I'm going to be late too! This guy is surely the super-punctual type.

Be natural.

But precisely… The part of me that hadn't come to light for four years should be completely on the back burner this time around. I'll learn to be myself again later, far from the big boss. Here, I'm just going to do my job, keep Sophia company, and be a great *au pair*.

So, what am I going to wear to keep a low profile?

Tried and removed clothes litter the bed, and I was still in my underwear. Thirty-two minutes gone, shit! Caught up in time, I end up putting on a little flowery dress. Simple, ordinary. Then, I arm myself with the courage to leave the room.

The second one will be the right one. It's gonna be okay, whatever you did that day.

He may have forgotten all about it, and his head is filled with numbers and financial strategies.

I motivate myself as I walk outside. Yes. He is a robot dedicated to business and the omnipotence of TS Naval. Me, I'm just another insignificant domestic employee. So, I'm nobody, and Mr. Sexton has better to—

Damn, I wasn't ready!

His gaze freezes on me as soon as I appear in his field of vision. What was I saying again? That I did not screw up and that, at worst, he will have forgotten everything? I swallow and move forward, believing in it less and less.

I don't detect any expression on his closed face. Just an impassive hottie in jeans and a white T-shirt, hair styled in an obvious post-shower style. His facial hair, sealed lips, and mysterious blue eyes give him an intimidating air despite his casual attire. The pathetic thing is that, unlike the rest, I remember his fucking eyes a little too well. They're more striking than in the photos.

Damn, I can't think straight. He looks briefly at his watch and manages to notify me of my delay without saying a word. I swallow my saliva and keep walking.

"Ah, finally! Ty, this is our guest. Come here, Océane," Sophia tells me in English as she gets up with panache from the rattan sofa.

At least one person here is warm. In her powder pink dress that hugs her figure to perfection and with a beautiful smile, Sophia is welcoming. Quite the opposite of the other one. Stage fright swells in my stomach as I walk towards her, relaxing as much as possible. The husband lowers his glass and puts it down without deviating for a moment. His irises lock on me.

Breathe, big girl. The tiger won't tear you apart.

"Océane, let me introduce you to Tiger," continues Sophia.

I awkwardly hold out my hand, my mouth dry, and spout in their language:

"Good evening, Mr. Sexton. I… I'm delighted to meet you."

A slight raise of his eyebrow; his blue eyes fork over my outstretched hand, then slowly move up to root in mine. Is he going to ignore me? He finally shakes my hand, and his grip envelops me. Firm, big, soft, manly, and…fuck, he squeezes my fingers a little too hard.

"Océane, Lilia Rousseau, originally from Paris, right?" he asks without releasing me.

"Yes."

"Welcome."

"Thank you, sir."

He scrutinizes me for a long time, and I feel awkward.

"Amazingly polite today…" he notes, finally letting go of me.

I have the insane feeling that my palm is burning from this harmless contact. Pathetic! Sophia gently rubs my back.

"She's adorable," she comments, no doubt to calm me down. "I'm glad you can finally talk."

Her boyfriend makes no comment. He picks up his glass which has been miraculously filled with an amber liquid, and takes a sip. I may have lost my tongue. That sucks.

"With Ty, we were talking about Doha. I haven't been back there in a while," Sophia tells me.

"Me neither… I mean, I've never been there," I try to pull myself together.

"Really? Well, who knows? Tiger will be going to Qatar again in the next few weeks. If our schedules allow it, we could go there," she projects most naturally.

May she not start including me on a trip with him. I'm willing to be a stopgap and help her have fun when "her Ty" isn't around, but what's the point when they can be together? And above all, me, very far from him.

"We'll see," cuts Mr. Sexton, still standing, distant and unreadable.

"That would be wonderful; thank you for thinking about it, Ty… Anyway, what would you like to drink, my little Océane?" asks Sophia.

"Uh… whatever, as long as it's not alcoholic."

No sooner have I said those words than Tiger Sexton's azure beads lock on me again. The shadow of a half-smile passes furtively over his features. Shit, is it me, or is the episode of an inebriated Océane anchored in his head and ruining all my attempts? Uncertain, I lick my lips. Sophia speaks to a maid. As soon as she turns on her heels to get back to the garden sofa, Tiger closes the space between us, leaning in ostensibly. His smell and his body heat invade my security perimeter. Unwittingly, he reminds me of an infinity of imaginable prohibitions and makes every down on my skin bristle when his breath touches my ear.

"So, you're going to play the scared well-behaved virgin now?" he whispers to me in French. "Too late. I want to have this little chat in private…"

My brain, my breathing, and my heart suddenly stop working. My eyes widen. He has already restored the distance between us. He goes to sit next to his wife—well, not so close—and lights a cigarette.

God, what does that mean?

Satisfied, he takes a drag and blows his smoke with a false nonchalance, still staring at me.

No more doubt, you must have slipped badly, and this guy has memorized every detail.

To do what with it? In this embarrassing situation, I start to blush horribly, shamefully, inevitably, and stupidly. I know he senses my discomfort, but his observation becomes more intense and disconcerting. Damn, why didn't I bring up the subject of the bouquet of flowers and the card with his wife? She was so sad in the library, and I was so woozy that I forgot. What if this was a test from Tiger Sexton to evaluate me? Or maybe I'm just rambling.

"Come on, Océane. We'll bring you your drink," Sophia invites me.

She may not be paying attention to the suffocating tension.

"Yes, come sit down, young lady. And remember to breathe," Mr. Sexton commands me.

Am I hallucinating, he's savoring?

My mind gets confused with assumptions; being sober doesn't change that. It looks bad.

12

Tiger

Pupils on alert, Miss Océane, Lilia Rousseau seems destabilized just as much as me. At least, it is new for all of us… Her cheekbones and the base of her neck are coloring, and it makes my nicotine puff suddenly more exquisite.

Guilt or awareness, pretty little bud? What I've read about you has given me some guidance in my decision-making… This purity on your face is only a facade, isn't it?

The warm air of this early evening stirs her small dress. Interesting choice, as if with this, I wouldn't guess the contours of her body, wouldn't remember what's underneath. It's so easy to undress her mentally. Does she know it? Maybe she chose it on purpose. To urge me to venture on this pearly skin that blushes visibly under my insistence.

In any case, in addition to the physical criteria, I note what must have seduced Sophia: one has the false impression of reading this young lady like an open book. As if she were unable to hide the slightest emotion… And yet, everything lets me suppose that she could have her place in the dead end where we are…

I exhale and take a sip of whiskey. Once the mists of alcohol were gone, did this young lady think about how to manage "our official presentation?"

My wife chats with her, and gradually the tongue of our guest loosens up. The discussion revolves around banalities, Océane's opinion of our country, what she would like to discover or has already visited, and other trivialities. I continue to probe her and participate mechanically from time to time. Sophia promises to show her the must-see places in Australia.

For now, Blondie is sipping her virgin cranberry cocktail, carefully avoiding eye contact with me. She knows I can't take my eyes off her. Sophia realizes this too, hence her attention on me…

"Would you like it, Ty?" she asks me after a while.

"What?" I ask.

I sigh, then her smile returns.

"I was telling Océane how fabulous it is to watch herds of brumbies galloping in nature from a helicopter," she explains.

"Oh. A beautiful natural spectacle, indeed. Do you like horses, Océane?"

She was obviously not expecting my question. She swallows hard and coughs, forced to hold my gaze.

"Yes… I love animals in general. But I've never had… the opportunity to see so many horses… in the wild. Nor to get into a helicopter. That… that must be worth the detour," she stutters in English.

"In that case, organize an excursion for you two, Sophia," I say, screwed again to the green marbles of our guest. "Check it out with Anaïs for the helicopter and the pilot."

"You could come with us, Ty. Choose a date that suits you, and we'll settle on it."

"No way."

Sophia frowns at my refusal. Why is she suddenly so invested? Or rather, *despite everything*?

On the other hand, Blondie's expression changes. That's it; she judges me in "so compassionate" mode towards my wife. Are they in cahoots in some way? Does Sophia know about the note left in Océane's room? Is the Frenchwoman already instinctively trying to protect her? Or is she able to bond with the one who hired her while hiding things from her?

Any of these options would be vicious. And I'd prefer to go for the latter…

There was this hip wiggle, this start of stripping with my wife by the pool. Not to mention the words of Océane as a little drunken provocateur. So, no. Impossible to let this embarrassed and flushed face make me more innocent today.

Given the chaos in my thoughts in the shower earlier, the question is no longer whether I want to fuck her. But for how long before we get rid of her and return to our unbreakable fucking routine? As with Kelly and others, patches come and go. In the end, it's always Sophia and me.

I intervene calmly.

"Here's what I suggest: you both go for a helicopter ride, and if our… guest still likes horses, I'll bring her closer another day. That way, I can spend some time alone with her."

My wife, baffled, understands the turn of phrase. Océane, not at all.

"Uh… what do you mean?" asks Océane, dissimulating badly her beginning of panic.

"At the stud farm?" completes Sophia in front of my voluntary silence.

"Yes," I answer.

"I… I didn't expect that, Ty," my wife says in surprise.

"I don't think it would be necessary," tries to fight back Océane.

At the same time, Peter walks towards us, my office phone in his hand. I cut our *au pair* off by straightening up.

"Yes, it is. You live in my house; my wife seems to like you. It's important to get to know each other better in order to make this cohabitation possible. Isn't it, Sophia?"

"Well… I… okay, let's do it that way," she says.

"No. I mean, I don't understand. The three of us will go?" asks the girl in a troubled voice.

"Excuse me. Mr. Sexton? Dinner is ready to be served, but your CFO, John Parker, is trying to reach you," Peter explains.

Anyway, I had no intention of answering Océane's question. It's more fun to feel her getting alarmed at the idea of being alone with me. And to let Sophia deal with the decision I just made without consulting her.

"I'll take the call. Thank you, Peter. I'll join you ladies at the table in ten minutes."

I walk away to call my CFO back. About this girl, I have set my own rules. No one defines my limits for me. I hope that after sleeping it off, Sophia got the gist of it…

OCÉANE

I try not to stare at his ass and his long legs in his jeans as he walks away, his phone pressed to his ear.

Mister wants to be alone with me for an inevitable "discussion?" No, but what kind of one-sided way is this to decide for everyone?

I turn to his wife. She seemed as surprised and annoyed as I am by the famous excursion that her man wants to set up. And how she feels about it is what I care about first.

"Sophia," I say softly. "You'll come with us to this stud farm, won't you?"

"He invites you, Océane. Alone. Ty rarely trusts… I think he thinks he can judge you better without me around. This place is special to him. It will be a kind of trial period of just a few hours," Sophia says.

"But I… No. I'm here for you. I'll only go if you go too. Period!"

She opens her mouth, then falls silent and runs her fingers through her hair. I don't know if she's torn or upset, but her thing with her wedding ring starts again. Like a gesture forged by habit without even realizing it. Sophia looks much less playful as she fiddles with her ring.

"Nobody forces you to do anything, okay?" she says.

"Okay."

"Let's focus on tomorrow's gala. I'm glad you're coming… Tiger gets darker with each annual visit to old James Sexton's lair," she deflects the conversation. "He's already on edge, so let's just let it go for now."

I don't give a damn about her man's mood! Unfortunately, there is every reason to believe that his mood affects hers. Does she often go from smiling to sad, from happy to frustrated at a word or an action of her husband? Sophia is still fiddling with her ring as she watches Tiger walk across the garden in the middle of a phone conversation.

"I'll be with you, don't worry. We'll find a way to make it less burdensome and have fun together," I told her impulsively.

She smiles at me, nods, and looks at her husband again.

It is with him that she wants to have fun. She's crazy about him; it's obvious. But the opposite is difficult to detect…

Sophia just set up a nice dating program together, and he kicked it out. Why is he doing this?

Sophia tries to play it cool. She pretends she has to go to the bathroom. As soon as she leaves, I get up too. I am not very sure of what I am doing. I walk, bypass the infinity pool, and start walking in the direction of the big boss.

Do you want to get fired or what? Turn back right now! shakes my conscience.

"… Winning is the only option. Always. Knock down his reluctance; I don't care how you do it as long as it produces the desired result…"

Don't come any closer, Océane; turn around. He's on the phone and—

Damn, he turns around. He stops in the middle of his sentence when he discovers me.

"I'll call you back, John."

Tiger cuts off the call and frowns. Part of me is trying to shrivel up; he must have this effect on people all the time… on men, on women. This super-confident male side at the top of the food chain is just terrible and is already threatening to undermine my self-confidence.

"Look who's here. What do you want, Lily?"

"My name is not Lily. Let's stick to Océane."

My unexpected nerve surprises me. Not that I am incapable of asserting myself, but because now, in front of this man, it looks like a real achievement.

No, but *Lily*? Seriously? His nickname probably comes from my middle name, Lilia. If he doesn't like the first one, it's his problem, but he will call me Océane, like everyone else!

During a fraction of a second, the tiger shows an ounce of astonishment quickly replaced by a half-smile. Uncomfortable, I continue to brave him anyway.

"Should I add it to my notes? 'She loves eggplant emojis and hates nicknames,'" he spouts halfway between sarcasm and disarming seriousness.

Emojis? Chaos in my skull and a hot feeling on my cheeks. My God, was that it? I don't know where to put myself, yet I proudly hold my head up.

"What are you talking about?"

"I'm talking about you making advances to me almost naked in front of my pool. And you magically forgot all about it," he quips. "Alright, I'll cut it short. Did Sophia send you, or are you a big girl who decides by herself?"

"Shit, I have? I…"

He comes closer, and I swallow. He reduces the distance again; I take it upon myself to stand up to him and not retreat. However, my heart is beating wildly, and my two still active neurons advise me to get out of there.

"You what?" he says too close.

His smell, tinged with a hint of Scotch, invades my nostrils. The proximity of his body disrupts mine. His irises turn on my dry mouth, which he targets for a long time before coming back up to lock on mine.

"I'm listening, my Lily."

Damn, he's really pushing it!

I am less and less able to censor myself.

"My name is not Lily! What do you have against my first name?"

"Nothing."

"Then say it!"

"I don't want to."

"Damn it! I want… Note that I'm here for Sophia."

"I know you are."

"Not to… receive bouquets from her husband, to go horseback riding with him. Or for him to give me nicknames," I manage to say. "And if I said inappropriate things when I was a little drunk, it wasn't really my opinion…"

"I see."

He doesn't elaborate on the last point. He stares at me without blinking.

"You're done?" he asks me, inflexible.

I stare at him without answering, inwardly too troubled and outwardly too stubborn to admit it. This paradox becomes more pronounced as the silence continues. Then Tiger starts to unfold his index finger in front of my eyes.

"Let's get this straight, miss. I won't repeat myself, so record what I'm about to tell you: what you did or said on the first day; I'm old enough to draw the conclusions I want."

Crap!

"I don't take orders from anyone, not even about what to call you. Besides, from now on, you will be Lily to me. Because I said so."

No, but is it natural for him to be so stupid, arrogant, and stubborn, or did he get a Ph.D. for it?

He keeps on. His middle finger joins the other finger in front of me.

"Secondly, you never interrupt me again for such trivialities!"

I blink while his ring finger sticks up under my nose, forming three. My breathing hitches and my blood heats up. He's got the wrong girl, employee or not!

"And just so you know, Sophia has hired many personal assistants over the years. Young men, mostly. I've always made a point of spending a day with each of them at stud. You should thank me for my hospitality; I usually only bring males. Even my wife doesn't go with me."

Personal assistants? Men? So, first of all, they never had women in their service? And secondly, mister is "summoning" me to his lair because he has done it with all those who have worked for his wife?

My brain gets foggy and stumbles on this while Tiger tells me the rest by unfolding his fourth finger.

"Finally, I need to know those who come close to us, to Sophia. Watching over my wife, protecting her if necessary, is a duty I take very seriously. Since she has chosen you to live here for some time, you will not deviate from this rule. Therefore, getting to know you better is imperative as long as a contract binds you. Is that clear?

Clear. As clear as he is a control freak in all his glory!

"If you thought you got some kind of date, if you thought you were special, pull yourself together right now," he says. "You're a contract, and I will treat you like one, Lily."

The slap! Yes, verbal, but it's a slap in the face. I blink. He steps back, his eyes darkened. Stung in my self-esteem, my side that I held on a leash, well muzzled, awakes without warning. The desire devours me to slap this rich bastard!

Unfortunately, my ardor would immediately cost me my job. This guy just infantilized me in a few sentences to the point of feeling ridiculous and hurt. He doesn't hurt me like Christine and her relentlessness; it's different. Because against my past, I didn't have, I don't have, and I don't deserve a weapon. But against this arrogance, his need to rebel is stronger than anything!

My pulse is racing; I try to take a deep breath. This is not the time to break the shackles I've put on myself, to fit into the mold, to make amends… Here, it's the present, facing a billionaire who annoys me and thinks he can do anything! Tiger Sexton may be powerful, wealthy, feared, respected, married to my boss, and intimidating as hell, but right now, my little pride, too often abused, doesn't give a damn!

I breathe in, breathe out. The naturalness suddenly reappears in me at full gallop. The free and cheeky 15-year-old that I used to be shows up and the words cross my lips, "Tomorrow night, okay. For Sophia, not for you. For the side trip to your stud farm… Okay, if that's a mandatory step to take… But stick this in your head: you don't have anything special either! A miserable day alone with you will have no impact on me; it just eats up time I would rather spend with your wife! I really like *her*. And while we're at it, keep your cards and your flowers in the future, or give them to Sophia! Fuck you, Mr. Sexton!"

With that, I turn on my heels and take off before his answer. I feel his pupils following me. Wasn't he expecting a scathing retort? Maybe… And he has the power to get me fired. I know I've gone too far and will regret it in a few seconds. But right now, a warmth radiates from my body, and a smile of girl power pride blooms on my lips.

Now he knows I bite, even in front of a tiger that could crush me.

Fuck, this is it! I have my click, and I don't want to be this girl in quarantine on the edge of her own life anymore. The one who refused to live, who didn't return the blows anymore, thinking that she only had to take them. I have just recovered my pride and my fighting spirit lost in France. After four years, on the other side of the world. I finally stop bowing my head and hug the walls. Especially with a guy like that. And it's exhilarating as hell!

Yeah, fuck you, Mr. Sexton!

13

OCÉANE

Victor takes a big puff and smiles like a guy who is happy to be high.

"This weed… it's too good," he raves.

"Come on, don't be an asshole; share it," one of his friends teases him.

This one catches the bong; after a long aspiration, he feigns the tended hand of another and looks at me.

"Your turn, Océane," he incites me.

I hesitate, then shake my head.

"No, I'm good."

"Come on, princess, you're not that uptight. Take a drag," Victor insists. "Yeah, you're gonna love it."

The five boys stare at me. I'm the only girl in the group. A privilege that I adore; I feel integrated and surrounded. Originally, I spent time with Victor, we live in the same place, and he's pretty cool with me. These guys are "like a real family, you know? We are the same, them, me, you…" That's what he told me when he introduced me to them when I first came to this shelter. The other girl in our age group left. I heard she ran away with her boyfriend when she found out she was knocked up. That may have had something to do with the fact that they gave me a small place among them.

Victor sits on the rug beside me and brings the bong to my lips.

"One puff," he whispers to me. "Make me happy."

I stare into his dark eyes for a long time. Somehow, I think it's also flattering that he looks at me like that. As if he took me for a girl of his age. He'll be 18 soon, and he'll leave the shelter. I'm just 15. One of them is of age, and he got social housing. It's at his place that we meet.

I feel like I'm bigger, more important. And Victor looks at my mouth by sticking the mouthpiece there.

"I know you want it," he says, half-charming, half-confident.

Damn, yes, I want to. I finally give in.

"I… okay, I'll try."

I take a drag and hear him whisper to me, "Again… again, princess. Longer, stronger."

The steam shoots me up, and my limbs get heavier. Victor's smile comes closer.

"So? Do you like it?" he asks me.

Wait, what's going on here? Is he going to kiss me? His tongue is becoming scoundrel, and I see the tip ready to lick the corners of my mouth. I'm high, I think. Lucas, Victor, the faces get tangled up.

"Not even in your dreams, you little prick. Back off!" a more virile voice summons him.

Suddenly, I'm disoriented. My eyelids are struggling to stay open.

Where did he come from? How did he get there?

"Who's this son of a bitch?" Victor gets angry. "Dude, that girl is ours, mine."

"I don't think so," protests Mr. Sex.

Wait, is that really Tiger Sexton?

His hands grab me and lift me up. I crash into his rock-hard body. Before I can figure out what's going on, he's holding the back of my neck and…

And it's finally him who kisses me. A devastating kiss. I go numb…

… And I wake up with a start. Holy shit, what was that?!

A dream? No, a nightmare that was going completely out of control. Disoriented, I sit up. I guess last night's altercation with Mr. Sexton has left its mark on my mind. After my outburst in front of Tiger, I was prepared for an immediate explosion from him.

But nothing.

He ignored me and resumed the call I had interrupted. When he joined us at the table, he remained cold and calm and kept himself to himself. Sophia has worked to make the meal times less painful. However, her man's attitude gave me a strange feeling. And his eyes often came back to me during dinner. As if he was analyzing me…

Damn it; I lost my nerve even in my troubled sleep.

A grenade is now unpinned between him and me. Through my window, I see him leaving for his morning jog. The hectares of greenery and leafy trees engulf his stride.

I take this opportunity to get ready quickly and leave the room. It will be impossible to avoid him systematically today. I venture towards the kitchen.

"Oh, hello, Miss Rousseau," the cook greets me.

"Hello, Mary."

"Slept well?"

How can I put it? Your boss got into my dreams, and it was quite… weird.

"Yes, very well, thank you," I lie. "Could I have a coffee, please?"

"Of course, Miss. Want something else for your breakfast?"

"No, just black coffee."

"All right, then. Shall I bring it to you on the terrace or somewhere else?"

No, definitely not. The risk of running into Tiger would be maximized. It's too early, and I don't have a battle plan set yet. Besides, where is Sophia? Still in bed?

"I do not know. Is Sophia awake?"

"No. Mrs. Sexton is still asleep," the employee replies.

"Okay… In that case, do you mind if I stay here with you?"

"Oh… not at all," the lady hastens to answer, pulling out a chair for me. "Please have a seat, Miss."

We exchange a smile, and I offer to help her. She declines my offer but seems to relax and starts chatting, talking about everything and anything.

I check the time. What is the probability that the big boss will come at any moment to the kitchen? Almost zero, I guess.

Sophia doesn't need me to get into a fight with her boyfriend. And I'm here for Sophia.

If she is still hanging out in bed, it is because her reunion with her globetrotter has undoubtedly lived up to her expectations. Good for her. Me, I'm still in shock from the revisited version of my past intertwined with the Tiger effect in my sleep. Nonsense! Talking to Mary doesn't tell me anything, no info leaks about her employers…

A long time later, Tiger reappears. Two strong guys came out at the same time as if synchronized to his running time. I was about to go back upstairs, but I immediately turn back towards the kitchen, under Mary's amused eye.

Let her draw the conclusions she wants; I'm not sure yet what kind of retaliation is likely to fall and how to deal with it effectively.

"They're Mr. Sexton's sports coaches," Mary explains to me. "Don't worry; sir will lock himself up with them in his room located in the right wing. Their session lasts at least two hours."

A little embarrassed, I deny it.

"I'm worried about it. Thanks for the coffee and our little chat, Mary. I… I'm going this time."

Back in my room, the day seems to stretch out, left to myself in this vast property. Playing hide and seek with the feline of the place. I fall back on a show on my computer…

In the middle of the afternoon, I finally have the pleasure of meeting Sophia, fresh from her sleep in. Her personal hairdresser and makeup artist show up. The preparations for the gala begin with excitement in the heart of the left wing. We snack, chat, laugh, and drink glasses while being dolled up. I avoid any trace of alcohol; I want to have clear ideas to fight if necessary. Around six thirty, we become femmes fatales. I measure the quality of my physical transformation in front of the mirror in my dressing room. Smoky eyes, mouth with a bitten effect, fresh complexion, hair artistically tamed in a loose bun…

Gosh, I've never been so sophisticated.

I barely recognize myself when Sophia's head reappears in the crack of the door.

"Océane, have you chosen what you are going to wear?" she asks me as she walks forward.

She wears a sublime black evening dress.

"You are beautiful," I tell her, doubting to match such a level.

She is always sumptuous.

"Thank you very much; it's your turn now! You're not planning to go in a bathrobe, are you?" she teases me.

"I can't choose among all these designer wonders. It feels funny."

I'm a little nervous too. Your husband is going to see me in one of these expensive splendors, and it's impossible to predict his reaction to my temerity yesterday…

And now that I think about it, is it his money that paid for all this? It bothers me even more.

"Sophia, I'm going to insist on one more thing," I say, looking her straight in the eye.

"What is it?"

"For all these things, it's just a… 'loan,' 'work clothes.' I will return them at the end of the contract."

She hesitates, even look upset, then nods.

"If you want…"

"I want to."

"Okay. Well, can I still offer you my help to get dressed?"

"With pleasure, you're more familiar with the dress code for this kind of occasion."

"Yes, and I know exactly what you need tonight…"

"Really?"

Sophia smiles at me, so I relax, imagining myself brightening up her evening, having fun with her, and not worrying about anything.

And to royally ignore her husband…

TIGER

——

Sir,

We have names. Some are probably aliases or false identities. Our guys are doing everything to make a formal identification and a careful comparison with our screenshots of the faces that you sent to me.

According to our data, these individuals regularly meet in a castle on the edge of the city of Paris. For each of the following names, we establish a file and try to obtain recent and clear visuals. Here are the names:

Sir Alistair Sinclair

Morgan Sinclair (possible blood relationship, to be determined…)

Aaron Dennis

Cecilia Fournier

The aliases: the Shadow, the Dark Goddess, Snail, Air, Typhon, Echidna, and finally, one that will certainly interest you given the choice of his pseudonym, the One-Eyed Man.

———

Damn, this might be the one I'm looking for…

I close my box, nervous and pensive. It's finally coming together. Who are the people behind this new data? Is there any chance that it will work this time? The possibility of it being a false lead like we've had in the past gets me on edge. We've been through too many dead ends and failures in this hunt. It's mentally exhausting, even if I won't give up until the end.

I smoke my umpteenth cigarette to tame my nerves.

In less than two hours, I'll have to look good. To put the investigation work of my mercenaries in brackets and to face what is happening here and now. To control everything, to master everything in Paris and in Melbourne. Especially when we will be in my uncle's fiefdom for his social parade. It's never a pleasure to endure this kind of high society masquerade, and spending it supporting that bastard James Sexton doesn't help.

In these tense conditions, Miss Lily could become a more interesting distraction since her mini blood stroke. The need to take my mind off things, to let off steam for a moment, is getting stronger by the hour to better lead my various fights.

A decompression period between two fights… Moreover, the challenges excite me, and the one that the little Frenchwoman now represents will perhaps prove to be more fun than I expected.

So much the better if she hasn't caught anything yet…

It's time to leave my terrace and my wing of the property. I look at my watch again; almost seven o'clock. The jet will take off for Melbourne—where the oldest Sexton family residence occupied by Uncle James is located—in an hour. I don't compromise on punctuality, old James, either.

The more I go around in circles outside, the more my patience crumbles. A kind of negative wave is slowly eating me, the one that precedes the appointments with my father's brother. Too much unfinished business… My butler's throat clearing stops me in my tracks.

This good man saw me being born; he almost raised me at one time. Him and the employees of the stud farm. He knows everything about the Sexton line, and it is to me that he decided to give his loyalty when I took the reins… When, at the time, between 17 and 19 years old, I became "uncontrollable" in his eyes, he did not hesitate to put his job in danger by calling Anatjari and the doctor of my childhood to push me to better manage the situation.

I have all the more respect for him today. There is no one more loyal and dedicated to the late Nick Sexton.

"Yes, Peter?"

"May I offer some advice, sir?"

I look at him, surprised, before saying, "I'm listening to you."

"I know that Mr. James Sexton has a bitter grudge and that he won't stop trying to make you pay for his dismissal…"

"Among others."

The list of things that the oldest living Sexton blames me for is actually quite long. Peter knows this; he just has the decency not to refer to it…

"Yes, sir," he continues. "So, I think… with all due respect, it would not be wise to bring… our guest to this party," the butler says.

I stare at him, aware of what he's implying. I had just made it clear after giving in to his ultimatum when I was younger, more impulsive: he was never to lecture me again, nor to dictate my conduct. That's not his role anymore. I am an adult, vaccinated, and the only one in charge. Nevertheless, think twice not to hit him with a scathing reply. Out of respect for his person, his age, and all his years of service to my parents, then to mine. I think he sees it in my eyes and realizes he has crossed the line.

"I apologize, sir. I didn't mean to interfere," he continues.

"Indeed, it is not your concern. But I appreciate your sincerity, Peter, and your advice will always be valuable."

He nods; I press his shoulder without dwelling on the subject. I notice movement inside, which cuts off the discussion and my time waiting.

It's about time!

I glance at the dial. Nine minutes late, great! The sound of heels echoed on the marble, then on the stairs. I enter and stand at the foot of the stairs. A vertiginous slit opens on Sophia's tanned thigh as she arrives, all in black. After all, she was raised with a sense of showmanship, so making a big appearance and seeing me in the front row can only delight her. She parades like a prom queen. It's ridiculous! Nevertheless, I let her enjoy her moment, and then she is closely followed by...

Unanticipated heat wave.

This time, it is not calculated. Everything is different. I take a deep breath. Despite appearances, my hands in the pockets of my tuxedo, and the confidence I display, I tense imperceptibly as I discover *our young au pair*. This emerald dress on this body has everything to set the world on fire. Especially tonight. It's more sumptuous in real life than on one of the slides stashed in a drawer of my desk. This outfit is made for Océane. Our eyes catch each other as she descends. The black around her doe eyes gives a much too sexy depth to her irises... And the whole is...

... breathtaking, terribly dangerous for my self-control for the next few hours.

I make an effort to turn my attention back to Sophia and whisper to her, "You're splendid."

"Thank you, Ty. You're not bad either," she replies, delighted. "And what do you think of Océane?" she continues, brushing against my bow tie.

Looking neutral, I pivot towards the Frenchie. I feel her stage fright, her uncertainties, and above all, her irises locked on me. Her little bravado of the day before is long gone now. But with the weapons she's pointing at me and everything she's giving off, it's hard to continue feigning intimidating indifference in front of her.

"She's late," I reply without looking up. "You're ready?"

"Yes," says my wife after a brief moment of silence in the face of my lack of interest. "We didn't want to make you wait."

I offer her my arm, kiss her on the cheek and give the illusion of ignoring our companion.

"Let's not waste any more time, then. The pilot is waiting at the airport."

"Okay. Shall we go, Océane?" Sophia asks, softened.

"Yes… of course," stammers the blondie.

Does it confuse you to be transparent again? Perfect…

We go towards the Bentley. The driver leaves to open a door on the passenger side; I open the second to let Sophia pass. She gives me a smile and gets in. I have the bad idea of watching Océane going around the vehicle to enter on the other side.

Damn, I wasn't prepared for that!

The back of her outfit takes my eyes hostage and heats up my veins instantly. What the hell is she doing with that neckline plunging to the edge of her lower back? My mind is on fire. What could be underneath such a thing? Nothing?

Shit, Tiger, you can hardly take your eyes off her.

I end up turning them away. I get in and sit down. Sophia in the middle, Océane and I at each end of the back seat, I declare in a phlegmatic tone to the driver,

"Let's go."

"Yes, sir."

Seeing Sexton senior again under these conditions will put my nerves to the test.

You better behave yourself, Miss Temptation…

OCÉANE

Tiger didn't deign to make a miserable comment about my outfit. But I don't care what he thinks, do I? I really don't! I'm just too uptight. I don't dare turn my head towards the Sexton couple anymore. However, I notice Sophia's manicured hand resting on her husband's big, manly hand. In hardly a thousandth of a second, he releases his. Not to reinforce Sophia's embarrassment and pain, I quickly divert my attention to the outside.

Not even a loving touch between them?

I focus on the window, fiddling with my purse. With my mind full of guesses, I see the city of Sydney passing by, adorned with lights. The vegetation, the skyscrapers, and… the reflection of two intense eyes staring at me through the glass. Shit, Tiger Sexton is watching me from his side! Our eyes find each other; they don't let go anymore. The tension reappears in me. An unspeakable trouble settles in my belly. I don't know if it's the way he stares at me discreetly, with such insistence, or if it's the presence of his wife in the middle of us or his behavior towards me, which is impossible to decipher, but it causes unknown sensations. My cheeks start to get hot, my mouth to dry, and my pulse to accelerate. It is absurd!

Wake up, Océane!

We don't want Sophia to surprise us and think that... that what? That there might be something unusual between her man and me?

You're rambling, girl! Stop it right now! You can't stand this guy, period.

I tear myself away from his blue eyes and inhale. Sophia's fingers seek mine like a substitution for the tenderness refused by her husband. A little lost, I intertwine mine while smiling at her.

I hope that she did not see anything, I hope that she did not see anything

I intend to cheer her up, not leave her alone. Instead of getting emotional when her Tiger is... Stop!

"It's going to be my first flight in a private jet," I say to Sophia to defuse the pressure.

"I'm glad your first time is with us," she says, returning my smile. First times don't get forgotten, do they, Ty?"

He turns to us and captures my gaze again.

"Some of them deserve to be remembered," he says, looking at me.

No, don't read anything into it. There isn't, so stop feeling weird!

It's just a night out with them, we'll all behave, and it'll be fine. There's no ticking time bomb that's going to blow up in my face at any moment.

Is there?

14

Tiger

When we landed, I was much more on edge. We leave the Tarmac, our car heading towards our host's property. Look at the time. Holy crap! Twenty-one thirty! James is going to love it. I try to convince myself that nothing will get to me tonight.

With the press, celebrities, and other wealthy people present, we must not give anything to speculate about us. It's one thing for the financial press to give me their front page on a regular basis; making headlines in the tabloids is another. This is one of the reasons why I've been quietly working on the tracking. I alone decide what I want to expose, even for the battles I fight.

"I won't tolerate any mistakes, is that clear?" I say, turning to my two companions.

Sophia frowns. I hold her gaze before turning my attention to Blondie. This one doesn't know anymore how to adapt her reactions. I know now one thing: if my wife was not sitting between us in this vehicle, Océane would have taken out her claws again. Seeing a hint of irony in her eyes tickles me. Especially when she holds back from challenging me and nods her head.

"Of course, Mr. Sexton."

"Relax, Ty, everyone will be fine," Sophia says, bringing her fingers over me. "This goes for you too."

Is she calling me to order? No kidding.

I release my hand again and grit my teeth. And Sophia asks me to relax. Even though I know James will no doubt find a way to irritate me, as always. My better half knows this since the previous damn galas have all ended the same way for both of us. Going home alone or with a very personal assistant. And me, locked in one of my lairs with company…

Do you imagine that the presence of the au pair will change the scenario tonight, Sophia? Or will it be worse?

"I'm planning on it," I say.

During the rest of the ride, the two of them chat. I immerse myself in my thoughts. I remain impervious to the hustle and bustle outside. South Yarra begins to appear. Luxury boutiques and gourmet restaurants—including one by Sophia's—follow one another through my window. We drive along the street where some period mansions stand proudly. Soon, we see the Sexton's house. The driver enters the yard, maneuvers, and parks. Valets and bellhops are waiting, impeccably dressed in their uniforms. One of them hastily opens my door.

"Good evening, Mr. Sexton, ma'am," the employee greets us.

I nod to him and get out of the car, knowing that my uncle has surely been warned of our late arrival. A second bellboy goes around the car to open the door for Océane. My palm rests mechanically on Sophia's lower back. I wait until our au pair is at our level. With my other hand, I hold her for a moment and lean into her ear.

"You can't afford to make mistakes, Lily. Neither you nor I want you to be in the tabloids tomorrow morning… or online tonight, right?"

Ignoring a possible response from her, I begin to cross the green space towards the lobby with my wife. Sophia calls Océane and offers her free arm. I don't worry about it anymore. Soon a couple appears and stands at the entrance: James with an umbrella stuck in his posterior and his wife with a smile of circumstance plastered on her lips.

"Tiger! Finally! Thank you for honoring us with your presence," he burbles. "I was beginning to doubt you were coming."

I commandeer my phlegm not to respond to his sarcasm.

"James… Aunt Carol, sorry for the delay. We had a slight setback."

"Don't worry about it. It happens so rarely. You are all excused," Carol assures me.

My eyes lock with my uncle's, and he swallows his grievances. It is only a postponement. Sophia moves in for a formal hug.

"Nice to see you again, James, Carol. We've only just arrived, and I already feel you've outdone yourselves once again," Sophia says.

As a trained woman of the world, her flattery has the desired effect, especially on Sexton senior. His lips initiate an ersatz movement while his spouse joyfully reaps the rewards.

"You're adorable, Sophia; I can't wait to show you the extent of this beautiful work," she says proudly.

On my side, I guess the interest aroused by our silent blond girl. Even if nobody mentions her for the moment. I glance at her—she is quite quiet and a little too sublime—before continuing, "Sophia must have told you. We have an extra guest tonight."

"Yes, indeed," Carol agrees. "No worries, your wife gave us a call."

They don't hesitate to show their curiosity. Sophia and I look at each other; she adds, all smiles, holding Océane's hand between hers, "Let me introduce you to Océane Rousseau, a friend."

"It's nice to meet you… Mr. and Mrs. Sexton," completes the latter, a bit intimidated.

"Oh, but what do I hear? This accent, this name, it's got a French flavor, doesn't it?" Carol gets carried away.

James' attention shifts to Océane. Routine pleasantries continue for a few seconds. Paris, culture, mutual compliments on each other's outfits, and other blah blah. We finally get inside. Immediate immersion in the type of atmosphere that James Sexton loves. The music of a stilted orchestra lulls the conversations, and trays are passed around, garnished with glasses and *petit fours*. Handpicked waiters and waitresses slalom among the many guests. Too many tuxedos, too many evening gowns, and jewels were taken out of safes just for the occasion. Too many laughs and pretenses. Too much feigned lightness, too many fake smiles. One more party, exactly the same show as in previous years…

The greetings go on and on. James always uses this reception as a gauge of his pseudo-influence. He goes to a lot of trouble to gather as many important people as possible. In order to savor the moment, he struts around with me, trying to impress me.

I would almost laugh. I comply with the greetings and stop to chat. Carol takes the women on a similar ritual. Leaving me alone with the mayor of the city, her husband, and my dear uncle. Given how much he's frantic, maybe he has a surprise in store for me? I scan the audience to find out why.

So, who does James have as a VIP today?

Mistake! My gaze falls on Océane still from behind. The sight of her cleavage momentarily blurs my train of thought.

"Please excuse me, Mrs. Capp; I have someone to introduce to Tiger," James's voice seeps into my head.

The "no mistakes" goes for you too, Tiger! Staring at her… turn your damn filter back on!

Plus, there are cameras popping up from time to time. One of the reporters dispatched to the scene could capture an embarrassing, even compromising, image. I don't let anything of my distraction show as I turn my gaze back to my uncle. He seems proud of himself.

"Really? Who is it?" I ask him calmly.

"I don't think you've had the privilege of meeting him," he tells me meekly.

I sketch a half-smile and exchange a handshake with the mayor, who releases us.

"Please do! It was nice to see you again, Tiger."

"Good to see you too, Sally. Have a great evening, Andrew," I continue to her husband.

They leave towards another small group. A gray-haired man comes to meet us.

"My dear nephew, let me introduce you to Roman Prokhorov. A very good friend!" boasts James. "Roman, this is Tiger Sexton."

Intrigued, I greet the newcomer. Despite his name, this man is a stranger to me. His face and first name mean nothing to me.

"Good evening, Mr. Sexton," the guy spouts with a heavy accent. "Nice to meet you."

My lips curl; I immediately understood. Too bad for James' pride; he doesn't play in the big league anymore…

"Roman Prokhorov, right? Are you related to Mikhail Prokhorov?" I inquire, shaking hands with his find of the day.

James' smile freezes even before I even get to the next part. If he was going to blow my mind by playing the Russian oligarch card, he might as well pick one at the top of the hierarchy who wasn't already in my address books. However, James is unaware that I have made contact with the Russian oligarchy and other men of power during my extensive research around the world… Just to make sure that nothing is left to chance when my teams are meticulously tracking down in every territory those and what I am pursuing in secret and without respite.

But let's move on; this access will also remain locked, under control…

I smile when I understand that the one I'm being introduced to is just a distant cousin with no real weight in the business.

"I see," I reply. "How is he, by the way? I hope he's recovering from my last golf victory over him. Tell him that revenge is when he wants."

"Oh… uh… of course," the Russian says to me.

"Perfect. Have a good evening."

I grab a drink from a waiter's tray and take my leave. I barely take two steps when James grabs me.

"Underneath your air of an accomplished man, you haven't changed at all, Tiger! You're still that arrogant 17-year-old who thought he had all the rights," he accuses me between his teeth.

Self-control, self-control, breathe.

"You're in my house, and you're already throwing your insolence in my face?"

"No, your pathetic contest of which one of us has the most in our pants is just starting to get on my nerves, dear uncle."

I calmly free my arm. Letting him read my warning in my eyes: don't mess with me tonight. James begins to turn red. He ruminates on his old grudges, his anger, and surely what he considers an umpteenth humiliation. Fearless, I drink a sip, then empty the flute of champagne. I'm going to need something stronger than that.

"Nick would be disappointed to see this result, the man you have become," he begins as I turn on my heels. "And to think that Courtney—"

Hearing my parents' names, I tense up all over. Brutally. Inexorably. My breath goes out of control, and my eyes harden. I move closer and encircle my uncle's arm in turn, at the risk of creating a source of gossip in the jet set.

"Don't even finish that sentence, James. Don't say *her* name again!"

"You're under my roof, you brat! Your mother was also and above all, my brother's wife," he informs me as if it were possible to forget it. "So, I talk about Courtney when I—"

I hug his arm. Hard. We're not going to talk about this anymore. Never again.

"Shut up now, James, if you don't want to be embarrassed in front of your guests. That's fucking advice!"

My skin heats up, and my fists itch. If this old fart deliberately chooses to press where he shouldn't, I'm going to make sure I've made my point. My resolve to keep my cool threatens to crumble in a second.

I must not grant him the pleasure of leaving his reception immediately. For I hold on less and less, and this feeds the gossip every year. I take a long breath. Under his silence, I release him. I step back, looking around the room in search of a diversion. What I discover disintegrates the little phlegm I have left. Harry Carter, the stupid heir I will soon ruin in business, is chatting with my wife. And he's staring at Océane. He keeps touching her as they talk.

Great, this evening is taking a turn for the worse! Sorry about your memory, Father, my nerves are starting to fail me.

OCÉANE

"I love France. The vineyards, the gastronomy, the beautiful women…" list the guy with whom I have been chatting for several minutes.

Carol Sexton, the hostess, introduced Sophia and me to this small group before vanishing to other guests. This guy is the archetypal daddy's boy with a golden life who thinks he's irresistible. Even though the insufferable Mister Control Freak and his orders in the car pissed me off, I promised to keep a low profile. If only for Sophia's sake and to honor my contract as much as possible. So I smile at the heir's rotten jokes, I put up with his lack of originality, and I listen to him distractedly displaying his pedigree as if the fortune of his family dazzled me.

No, I have never had the soul of a Cinderella 2.0 whose only dream and hope in life is to catch the eye of Prince Charming. I'm not waiting piteously for a noble warrior, loaded with riches, to magically embellish my existence. And I'm not going to swoon, surely not!!

What's even more annoying is that this Harry Carter, besides being convinced that his sex appeal is increased tenfold by his money, manages to touch me when he talks.

He doesn't know my mind is wandering far from the yacht he says he owns in Nice. It's Tiger's warning that still eats my brains out. I do not want to rush into shortcuts full of clichés but in their worlds of heirs imbued with their person, do they really imagine that everything is due to them? And that a girl like me is easily enslaved? Especially Tiger, who has the nerve to treat me like a toy that his wife has just acquired. By the way, where is this psychorigid of an order giver?

Bad idea, Océane. Don't look for him in the crowd. Don't look for him. Don't look for him.

I have the persistent and insane impression of feeling her penetrating glance while the other one drank me with his flow of empty words. Sophia, on the other hand, displays her usual class and assurance. But she seems not to lose sight of her husband. When she tenses, I immediately understand that only Tiger produces this kind of effect on her.

"Océane, it's going to degenerate sooner than usual," she confides to me suddenly in the hollow of my ear.

"What is?"

She stifles a curse as she stares at a spot behind me. I pivot. Oh shit! No longer possible to avoid eye contact with him. Worse! He comes to meet us. I ask quietly, "Did something happen?"

"Old frictions between his uncle and him… James has a hard time digesting some things. Just like Tiger…"

"Oh."

I don't know what to say; the famous uncle also displeased me at the first second. I don't know why, maybe because of his haughty look. However, Tiger is also good at this little game. A gene passed on in the family, it seems. In a few steps, he dodges hands extended in greeting, pays no attention to the engaging smiles addressed to him, and quickly reaches our side.

"Well, Sexton!" launches my interlocutor with surprise. "I met your wife's friend. She is—"

"Get your paws out of here, Carter," he says with a calm that contrasts with the sparkle in his eyes.

Eye of tiger.

This warlike expression suddenly takes on its full meaning with that dark glow I remember all too well.

"Excuse me?" asks my annoying guy.

It clicks in my head; it's not Sophia that this Harry Carter is touching, but me. Once again, his hand remained posed on my shoulder. I'm not a fan of the guy's untimely tactile approaches, okay.

But who does Tiger think he is anyways?! He's a billion times more pretentious with me, too.

"You're making our friend uncomfortable; get your paws off of her," Tiger repeats.

Our friend? It doesn't sound friendly at all in his mouth. No, there is a note of… possessiveness. Contained anger. I can't believe it! Either it's the altercation with old Sexton that's got him in this state, or he thinks I'm not playing my "wise doggie" role well enough after his little threat when we arrived.

Calm down, Océane. The worst thing for you would be to make a splash in the Southern Hemisphere tabloids. Don't you think?

True. In a few lines, I would become the most famous "slut" in France, Australia, and even Zimbabwe and Bab El Oued because it would be circulated all over the world. Christine, the bitch, would wriggle in the depths of her social housing in Paris, all hatred increased tenfold. I don't need this; I should avoid it at all costs and make myself very small. But I start to rant in spite of myself. Sophia, on her side, curls up against her Ty and slides her hand under his arm. It is useless; he continues to perforate Carter with the same glance.

I bet he doesn't give a damn about the tabloids right now. Gutting Harry Carter has risen to the top of his priorities, and it brutally downgrades everything else.

"I'm not uncomfortable," I can't help but put him in his place. "Thanks for your concern, *Mr. Sexton,* and I'm big enough to tell this person or anyone else off if need be."

His features harden further. The other laughs, satisfied with my retort. Yet, the second my impulsiveness got the better of me, I realized my mistake.

"Well. Sophia, do you mind if I take Océane for a little dance?"

He grabs me without waiting for any response. He drags me to the opposite side of the huge room where there is a musical orchestra. Sophia's eyes beg me not to make a fuss. With aplomb, she smiles at Harry Carter, whose jaws do not loosen as we walk away. I think she offers him to go dancing too. I try to walk normally without ducking. Just to make the audience believe that everything is fine. We join the couples dancing on the dance floor in a blink of an eye.

"What the hell are you doing?" I finally revolt in a low voice.

"And you? What did you not understand in 'no mistake?'" he replies.

I can't believe it! What's wrong with this guy?

"I didn't make a mistake. It is you who has just dragged me against my will to dance with you!"

His large hands rest behind, on my bare skin. His irises take root in mine, and his breath caresses my face dangerously. He hugs me tightly, and a new wave of conflicting emotions overwhelms me. Confusion, fury, and neurons flashing. His body against mine, his palm gently consuming my back.

"Harry Carter is using you to go fishing for information. And that's out of the question! So, you're going to dance this damn tango to the end, and then you're going to send him away for the rest of the evening."

"Don't give me that kind of order!" I rebel despite my wavering voice. "Besides, he might just find me attractive, and I want to flirt with him. After all, I seem like that kind of girl to you, don't I? If I believe your attitude towards me."

"Stop it, Océane!" he warns me between his teeth.

"Or what, *Tiger*? You will put me in the corner and deprive me of dessert? I'm 20 years old, damn it! Employee or not, I'm tired of you treating me like a kid."

He frowns. Not another word from him. The dance continues, and he observes me with a kind of magnetism that, little by little, makes me lose my means. My synapses and hormones are messing around, and he's hugging me more. He directs me skillfully, grabs my thigh, and arches my body sharply, pushing my body towards an unexplored zone of languor. He straightens me up and presses me with a sensual masculinity against him. He stuns me, all in power and rhythm. I didn't know I was able to undulate, pulse, and move like this in a tango. As if my body guessed and abdicated each step and demanded gestures of my rider. He knows what he is doing; torrid, master of the tempo he establishes, he takes his pleasure in making me bend, molding me, and sticking me against him. His blue marbles wrap me in a cocoon. They devour me and warn me during this involuntary and volcanic osmosis. It becomes disturbing. My brain is softening second by second. My temperature is out of whack. The way he makes me—

Don't do anything stupid, Océane.

Shaken by the sudden anarchy in my body, my head, and my sensations, I try to react to free myself from this growing hold of Tiger on me. I move back one step, two, three. Motionless, he thrusts his hands into the pockets of his tuxedo pants. He stares at me as I escape. My back hits someone. It is Sophia dancing with Carter. Did she see us? Was it noticeable, or am I the only one who is so disturbed?

I stammer an excuse. In a kind of emergency, all I can think about is putting some distance between him and me. Lots of distance. I end up in front of the ladies' room. My heart is pounding as if I had just done something stupid. Everything becomes excessive with this man. My emotions are all over the place, including how he pisses me off. All he has to do is look at me, talk to me or touch me, and I forget to feel pain, shame, or fear of letting go. Suddenly, everything is blown away, and I am left with the consuming need to challenge him. To assert myself like never before.

It's terrifying to react like that, not understanding how he does it.

I have to turn things around. I have to slow him down. Not lose my footing. What if I… what if I bang the other heir tonight, just to piss off the one who's creating chaos inside me with a snap of his fingers?

Go out with Harry Carter to put Tiger in his place and take back my destiny?

15

OCÉANE

The reception is in full swing as if nothing had happened. I think…
I walk into the bathroom and grab the sink. My reflection reflects
back to me the image of my shining eyes and my rosy cheeks. I
finally escaped from the too-torrid tango and the too-directing tiger,
hypnotic and—

Stop, this is crazy! It's just that it makes you react quickly!

I know that, but I can't help it. My problem isn't just his
bossiness; his looks, his eyes, and that fucking charisma he exudes
also make me spin when I shouldn't. It's like my damn body stops
obeying my brain and makes me lose control of my reactions.

I take a slow breath to regain my composure. Tiger still
doesn't know one detail: Harry Carter gave me his card with his
phone number. I had no intention of calling this other flirty, boastful
specimen, but who knows? The door opens just as I'm considering
the consequences of this option. I expect to see Sophia walk in. I
discover a young woman in a red evening dress. I'm about to look
away when she speaks to me.

"You came with Sophia and Tiger Sexton, didn't you? You
were dancing with him earlier."

Be careful…

"Yes… You are?"

She stares at me without answering, comes to camp at the
nearby basin, and stares at me through the mirror in front of us.
Who is she? A journalist? Someone close to the family? We haven't
been introduced… My confidentiality agreement and Sophia's fears
about people's interest put me on alert. "The slightest trifle about us
is sold to vultures." I have not forgotten.

"Are you replacing Kelly?" continues the girl.

Uh, who is this Kelly?

"Excuse me, I don't remember your name," I dodge, facing her.

"It doesn't matter. The right question to ask is, what will happen when they are done with you? They're toxic, those two. Sophia Sexton is the worst. She uses you, wears you down, tears your relationship apart… And you end up like Kelly," she tells me, with a kind of bitterness in her eyes.

I swallow as I try to deal with the overflow of information. There were already names that stuck in my mind: Byrne and Annie mentioned in my contract and shrouded in mystery. But where does this third name come from? Are they all former employees of the Sextons? So, it wasn't all guys, as Tiger claimed…

I insist, getting increasingly uncomfortable, "I don't know what you're talking about. Who are you?"

"I'm Kelly's girlfriend… well, her ex-girlfriend since working for the Sextons. And you'll end up like—"

The door opens again. Sophia walks in and gets nervous the second she notices who I'm talking to.

"What are you doing here?" she asks my interlocutor curtly.

"Here! You see? She doesn't give you free rein; it's going to get worse and worse," spits the woman at us with more animosity.

"Get out of here! Our lawyers were very clear with the restraining order. I'll call security," threatens Sophia. "I don't know how you managed to crash into a private party, but it's over!"

In shock, I note the harshness with which they challenge each other, then the woman retreats. Then she pauses and says, "The truth will eventually come out about what you did!"

"Kelly left you of her own free will; stop with your defamations, go away!"

"Defamation! Pffff! You just have the system and the best lawyers in the country under your belt. But I won't give up. You hear me, you lavish bitch? I won't give up!"

Sophia's breathing goes out of control. She slides her trembling fingers through her hair and checks that there are no witnesses to this embarrassing scene. Once we are alone together, I turn to her for clarification.

"Who was that woman?"

"A hater."

"But what does she want from you? Who is the Kelly she was talking about? Who was she to you?"

"Océane, not here… And don't believe… a word of what she could have said to you," murmurs Sophia, very pale.

Does she intend to get away with that kind of trick? Just now, this beautiful, self-assured woman, owner of fancy restaurants around the world, has turned into a frightened little girl before my eyes. In the end, she drapes herself in her secrecy, but I'm too intrigued to let go of the case, either.

"What do we do? Do we go out, and I get a lecture from your husband if Harry Carter asks me to dance? Like this is normal?"

"No. We must go. Nothing is going well tonight; let's limit the damage," she says, trying to pull herself together.

"Sophia—"

"No, not here, Océane," she repeats. "Luckily, there was no one else in that bathroom. Someone could have seen… this," she says. "Remember the agreement; you'll get your explanations at home. I promise."

I hesitate, staring at her without moving. After the trouble caused by her husband, the tension in this room is playing on my emotions. After several seconds, I let out a sigh.

"Fine. But real answers, Sophia, with all the details. Do we have a deal?"

"Okay. Let's go home first, please. I don't want the situation to escalate, and I need you, Océane."

Sophia suddenly seems so weakened to me that I capitulate despite my doubts.

"Okay. I promised to stay by your side until the end, and I keep my promises."

Her boyfriend has pissed me off, but the flirting with Harry Carter to teach him a lesson is postponed until next time. Tiger Sexton will see! If he thinks he can use my contract to rule my private life! This part doesn't concern either of them. Obviously, they have a lot of shit to deal with in theirs…

TIGER

With a cold stare, I keep Carter at a distance. He'll know very soon that he is finished, that one. Financially and by reputation. No need to waste my time with him. Sophia slipped away to the bathroom to meet Blondie there. I swallow my scotch in one go while waiting for them. Neither of them returns, and no head, no discussion captivates me. I've kept my cool too long; I can't stand this place anymore! This room is filled with men and women from the top of society. These glittering chandeliers, these expensive alcohols flowing freely, the refined dishes that garnish the trays of the waitresses and waiters. Childhood memories are intermingled, other receptions where the hosts were my parents…

Conversations continue to liven up, and people keep on wiggling. Everything oppresses me, especially my uncle's face. Yes, everything annoys me! I do not want to reach the critical point in front of this crowd. The "almost mistake" with Blondie was already borderline. It's time to leave; I'm sick of it!

I empty my new glass and refuse the third when I finally see Sophia and Océane walking in my direction.

"Ty, can we leave?" my wife almost begs me.

She takes the words out of my mouth. Pale, Sophia tries to pull the wool over the gallery eyes; however, I know her too well not to notice it. She's not going to give me a fit for dancing with her *au pair*, is she? Okay, this little shameless girl almost made me lose my mind in public; this tango with her has more than made me hot. On many levels…

Nevertheless, I won't give James or anyone else the satisfaction of flinching again.

"Yes, we're leaving," I say calmly.

The goodbyes barely last. Aunt Carol obviously tries to hold us back longer; Sophia justifies our departure with an "I'm sorry, I'm not feeling very well." It's not a first; after our marriage, it took her a long time to adapt to my world, so this excuse has served her well…

The driver picks us up at the exit. A heavy atmosphere settles in the car.

"Where would you like to go, Mr. Sexton?" asks the driver.

Good question. I have a duplex in Melbourne. A bachelor

pad, as Sophia would say. Ordinarily, after a fiasco like this, I would have ordered a ride, and my wife would have gone "home," joined by Kelly or someone else… As for me, I would have used my usual outlets on my side. Instead, I growl, "At the airport, we're going back to Sydney."

"Yes, sir."

The journey begins in silence. I feel like smoking.

"Can we talk about it here, Sophia?" suddenly asks Océane.

I turn and look her straight in the eye. My dear and tender wriggles slightly. I feel her embarrassed; her pupils are riveted to mine.

"Océane was accosted in the bathroom by Kelly's ex," she informs me.

"I need to understand," says Blondie.

Argh! Is it the full moon or what? Everything is going wrong.

I inhale and tell the driver, "Stop the car."

There is no need to repeat myself. The vehicle instantly stalls on the side of the road. I pinch the bridge of my nose, open my door and get out.

"Leave us alone, Sophia."

"Ty—"

"What? It was your initiative this new hiring; now that we're entering a turbulent zone, it's up to me to manage as usual. Right, Sophia?"

She stares at me, sheepish, saddened, or… lost? Maybe she's sorry, but it's too late.

"Go outside."

"Okay."

She turns to the Frenchwoman to whisper something to her. I only catch the end of her sentence,

"… I'm sorry."

Of course, Blondie exits the car after her by opening the door on her side.

"No, it's not with him that I want to discuss this, Sophia!" Océane rebels.

Damn, I really don't need us to put on a show in the middle of the street. More lively, I rush to catch Blondie.

"You, you go back in the car!"

"No way! Stop this! I'm not going to take orders from you, Tiger!"

She tries to rebel, but I block her firmly and slam her against the front of a closed store. My body is a barrier between her and what surrounds us. Her delicate perfume instantly excites my nostrils; her quiver of revolt infiltrates me and awakens my lower abdomen. The effects of the tango are reborn in my veins. She tries to twist, to push me back, in vain.

"You're making it worse, Lily. Keep doing that, and you'll feel my erection."

My frankness shuts her up. Her beautiful eyes widen; she is outraged.

"What?!"

"Do you really need me to say it again?"

"You know your wife can see us?"

"So what?"

"So what?! Damn, do you have a blast hurting her? What are you playing at? This Kelly, you fucked her, didn't you?"

That's it; she gets her tiny claws out. I still hold her. Then amusement stretches my lips. I throw a glance toward Sophia, who observes us at a few feet.

"To hurt her? You are so far off the mark… Kelly is not my type. He was Sophia's last personal assistant."

"He? What do you mean?"

"That name is mixed, didn't you know that? Anyway, if someone was banging him at home, it certainly wasn't me. What exactly did his ex-girlfriend tell you?"

Stunned, Océane blinks. She can't find her words anymore.

"But I… I don't understand anything anymore," she whispers.

My face reduces the distance with her, and my eyes plunge into the bewitching green of her irises. Close by, I contemplate with lust her mouth. She moistens it uncomfortably, her cheekbones colored.

"Where…where is this guy now?"

"He was getting a little cumbersome, so we made him an offer he couldn't refuse," I summarize, keeping the details under wraps.

Lawyers, money, confidentiality, and obligation to leave the territory and never contact us again or make a fuss…

"He was… sleeping with Sophia? You knew it? Are you making her pay for it through me?"

I turn my head again to look at my wife. With a half-smile, I turn back to Océane. And I emit a small click of the tongue reprovingly while shaking my head.

She bats her eyelashes and tries to look for an answer in Sophia's eyes in the distance.

"I still don't… get it," she murmurs.

"To put it bluntly: my wife fucks with whoever she wants, and I do the same. In eleven years of marriage, we have had partners… The only rules are the other person must know about it, that he or she must approve, and that the affair must remain discreet and not last forever. I can cut Sophia's short; she can cut mine short.

"Oh, boy!"

I laugh out loud at her reaction. It had been a long time since someone had amused me so much. I take advantage of her stupor to affirm to her in the hollow of her ear, "Now Sophia sees this attraction between us. I'm not going to let you leave us, sexy Lily. Not right away. But I'll give you some time to think about it, and you'll tell me your conditions and whatever you want in exchange."

I step back, staring at her. Her breathing hitches. Her shock turns into a surge of ardor. Before I can anticipate, her hand lands on my jaws.

"You… you can't be serious! What did you expect, Tiger? That I would be excited and honored?"

"No," I reply, touching my cheek without feeling the slightest anger.

Her volcanic temperament makes her more attractive. Aroused, I persist. Since we're at the point of unveiling the possible program for the next six months, we might as well speed up.

"You said it yourself; you're not a kid anymore… From now on, you know how I feel about you. You may think I'm pretentious, but I can see that you're not indifferent to me either."

New slap out of her. Blondie massages her fingers and her overheated palm. Me, I only feel the manifestations of the desire that roars in me.

"Wow! Basically, I've been 'promoted?'" she ignites, miming the quotation marks. "Bravo, Océane, are you going from 'au pair' to 'sex toy to entertain Tiger Sexton?' Go jump in the lake!"

Feverish, she pulls out her cell phone. My half-smile fades when I see her pull out a business card to dial the number on it.

"What are you doing?"

"I'm taking the night off. Go home with your wife! Hello, Harry? It's Océane…"

Harry? Damn, is she calling Carter under my nose?

16

Words from my father reappear in my mind, the ultimate reminder of the deliciously archaic and chivalrous allure that lulled my childhood. I try to calm myself by using this wise advice he was so fond of. During our moment together at the stud farm.

My son, a gentleman, has a code of honor:

1. He carries on family traditions and honors the name he bears.

2. He always protects the people and heritage that matter to him.

3. He acts with nobility, heroism, and fairness to win and keep the respect of his neighbor.

4. He never kicks a man when he is down. But knows how to be ruthless with the enemy who deserves it.

5. He never raises his hand to a woman. Except… No, I'll explain that to you later, when you're older…

That you can do it under special circumstances, for the lady's pleasure, and with her consent?

Yeah, personal deduction. That, I learned on my own…

Right now, I'm not sure I want to play the perfect gentleman to spare the Sexton family name any stain.

"Yes, the Frenchie," confirms Océane to Carter.

Then she simpers and laughs at some bullshit that the other is probably telling her. I fume inwardly.

Usually, I don't care about the job of my security department or the work of a bunch of other professionals who are paid to handle their jobs perfectly. I know they are present, competent, and ready to handle various contingencies to cover my back. Discreet and proactive, they are non-existent, at a safe distance until I need their intervention. I pay them handsomely for this efficiency. At that very moment, this asset will serve me well.

A few miserable seconds of silent boiling ensue. I watch Océane challenge me with Carter on the line.

"… Actually, your suggestion to end the evening elsewhere suits me well," continues Océane, proud of herself. "We could me—"

Just those few miserable seconds and I snatch her cell phone from her and turn it off right away. I counter her protest movements.

No, sulfurous Lily. No more slaps, no more bravado. I'm back in control.

"Hey! But who do you think you are? Give me that back!" she rebels.

I take advantage of her agitation to grab her and hoist her into my arms. She struggles; I tighten my embrace and move quickly toward the car.

"Tiger, get off me! Let me go now!"

"Manage with this mess. No leak," I order the driver, who helps me when I put Blondie on the back seat by force.

I move to the driver's side, and the key is still in the ignition. Océane is trying to escape. My henchman blocks her, allowing me to lock the doors on us both and speed off.

"What are you doing?! I want to get out!" she cries while struggling with the latches.

I press the accelerator and see my staff miraculously appear in the rearview mirror. Cars with tinted windows. Seasoned field men. Sophia's silhouette—among them—is gradually reduced in my field of vision. I know my guys will put her in another vehicle and drive her wherever she wants.

We will have a chat later, her and I… Maybe in a trio with Murphy.

In the immediate future, the team will clean up after us. They will make sure to get any Smartphones that have witnessed this mess, buy the silence of possible witnesses, impose iron-clad confidentiality agreements, and do whatever else it takes to cover up this incident within the hour.

"Damn, what are you doing?! Stop, Tiger!" exclaims Océane from the back seat.

She moves so much, shaking the back of my seat, that we could crash in an impact. And yet, I speed up, beside myself, and whisper to her in a deceptive calm:

"You better put that little ass down and buckle up."

"NO! Where are you taking me? And Sophia, we can't leave her on the sidewalk like that!"

I speed off, my knuckles gripping the steering wheel.

"Buckle up, damn it! And for the last time, never tell me what to do again, Océane!"

Pedal to the metal, I split the night on the asphalt. I run red lights, slalom, and drive with one goal. Being slowed down by cops is not an option, and for the speed camera, that will be taken care of. I will first make my passenger understand how much she has exceeded the limits.

"On top of that, he's playing *Fast and Furious* now! I want to get off!" she insists, her cheeks burning, her beautiful eyes shining with adrenaline.

Very funny!

I increase the speed.

"You'll get off when I decide," I retort.

New shakes in my seat. She's going to cause an accident if she keeps going. The little composure I have left focuses on the road.

"Who do you think you are?! Do you really think you have absolute power over everything and everyone? I quit! Do you hear me? I want nothing more to do with you!"

Don't be so sure, Blondie…

Her speech stretches out on the way while my increasing speed intoxicates me as much as my impulsive reaction. Irreverent and fiery, Miss Rousseau managed to make me forget my basic principles. "No strong emotions in public, especially no bullshit that could lead to a scandal in the press, on the Web."

Damn, in one evening, she just dumped a monster job on my security, communications, and legal departments! It's going to take a lot of people to clean up the mess.

But meanwhile… my irises cling to hers, and my pulse is in overspeed. Her hairstyle has come undone. Her pink lips are cursing at me. And her doe eyes accentuate the fever in my veins.

"Calling Carter, despite my warning, was a mistake," I tell her calmly.

A control of me on the surface, which has the gift of pissing her off even more.

"And your revelation just before, can we talk about it? Kelly… The indecent proposal under your wife's nose and all. It's surreal! It seems like you're so used to always getting what you want, never getting turned down, that you don't even realize when it's too much!"

"Too much? Stop playing the outraged virgin; this is sex between consenting adults. Or even a transaction like any other. We will all be winners."

"All or you alone? Did you ask Sophia and me for our opinion? Do you even know what century this is?"

With a touch of sarcasm, I say over my shoulder, "I know my wife's tastes and expectations by heart, thank you for caring. You wouldn't be here if she hadn't liked you, if she hadn't validated you. This is how some couples work in the 21st century and even before…"

Great! Now she bugs, then shakes her head in disbelief.

"What does that mean?"

"Three adults. Multiple possibilities… Do you want a drawing?"

"I can't believe it! What does Sophia get out of it? Unless she's… Shit, she's bi? Did you plan that from the start?"

"You ask her. I take care of the part of the deal that concerns me. You—"

"No! I repeat, I am not for sale! I'm free and tell you loud and clear: no, Mr. Sexton!"

"Okay."

"Okay?" she repeats with suspicion.

"I've never had to force a woman to have her, and that's not going to change. But you, would you have gone so far as to fuck Carter to prove to me that we won't sleep together?"

She blows and forages in her blond mane. Disturbed by the turn of events, she stares at me through the rearview mirror. I take a turn too tightly; the steering wheel jerks her against the walls. This stubborn woman always disdains the belt.

"I told you to buckle up!"

"You're crazy!" she spits in my face, giving in, in spite of herself. "What's the plan now?"

"First, keep you from getting into the sheets of this little idiot Carter," I tell her, rushing into the underground parking lot.

"Don't you think this kidnapping is disproportionate to an ordinary phone call to Harry Carter?"

"There she goes with the fancy words," I quip. "Am I the

nasty billionaire who kidnaps his innocent *au pair* to have sex with her… even though she claims she doesn't want to?"

"That's the truth! I. Don't. Want. To!" she says.

"Really?" I reply.

I turn to her, my eyes glued to hers. Dilated pupils, shortness of breath, feverish skin… Looks like we have the same symptoms. No?

"I don't desire you, Tiger Sexton."

"Your body is screaming at me otherwise, sweetness."

"You… But what a shithead!"

"I won't touch you against your will. I would never commit such an aberration, but you know what? We'll end up naked, sweaty, you and I, pressed into each other," I promise her nonchalantly.

"In your dreams!"

"We'll fuck together, sweet Lily. No, I'll fuck you. Because there's this spark… You feel it too. The only difference between us is that I am direct. I'm pragmatic enough to admit it, and until we satisfy that desire, it won't stop growing. You're wasting your time denying the obvious."

"Bullshit!"

I unlock the car and cut the engine. Her fingers clutch the leather, and she opens the door.

"Is that it? Can I get out?" she wonders.

"You're free. Just like… the kind of couple I form with Sophia. A free sexuality, clearly assumed in our union."

"Yeah. Well, do what you want; I'm not a prostitute dedicated to spicing up your sex life."

Trembling, she pushes the door and leaves. I leave the vehicle myself. Océane spins around, trying to find her way around the almost empty parking lot.

"Are you going to give me back my phone?"

"No, I'm not."

"Why not?"

"Because you tend to act on a whim just to irritate me. I have an empire, a reputation, real battles, my couple, and our lifestyle to preserve."

Stunned, she licks her lips. They struggle to pronounce anything. We stare at each other for a long time under the artificial light of this closed door.

"You do what you want. I'm not at your disposal. I just want to go back to my old way of life," she concludes after an indefinite time.

I feel my tuxedo pocket and extract a magnetic key while advancing in her direction. She moves back with every step I take. I sketch a grin.

"Relax, I'm not going to eat you. Not now…"

"What… what are you going to do then? Your bulldog stole my wallet. I have no money, no papers on me, and no idea where I am," she summarizes, a hint of fear in her voice.

I stop my progress and hand over the object.

"This tower belongs to TS Naval. I'll leave you the keys; my card unlocks the private elevator that will take you directly to the penthouse. You will have access to what you need for tonight: think, eat, sleep, change clothes… An employee will bring you what you want. All you have to do is ask."

She seems to be looking for other options in her pretty little mind. How to escape from me, for example, or how to manage on her own in a city where she knows no one and with nothing on her but this delicious dress? I wait. I think logic ends up winning out over her independent temperament. Her eyebrows are furrowed, and a je-ne-sais-quoi flickers in her eyes. In any case, her anger and apprehensions turn into confusion.

"Océane, at least grant me this. We'll keep a low profile for a few hours to make sure I can handle our outbursts tonight and their probable consequences tomorrow."

"On your public image, you mean!" she says. "And what about me? All this falls on me, turns my stay into a kind of… I can't even find a word for it! That's not why I came to Australia. Do you understand, Tiger?"

Tiger. My name in her mouth sounds like an aphrodisiac. Why does it turn me on so much? Because she is the first woman in everyday life to stand up to me, to resist me? Because she has everything that a Domina, a call girl, or Sophia doesn't have: a mixture of candor that still resists my assumptions, my solid preconceptions, and sensuality which she doesn't seem to realize yet? Or because I simply like challenges? This passion for victory motivates me in business, in the balance of power. This challenge, more intimate, really tempts me! The obstacles will make me slow down even less.

Especially since you're not as smooth as you want to make believe, future bud…

"I understand better than you imagine…" I finally decided to open the trap door. "Actually, Océane, I know what made you flee France. It's not just the taste of adventure, am I wrong?"

Her attitude changes instantly. Her eyes widen. She swallows, withdraws into herself, and begins to turn pale.

"What are you talking about?"

"I know about it," I say.

"Knowing about what exactly? What… do you know about…"

About Victor, you mean? You can't pronounce his name?

Golden rule in the business world, Blondie: stay one step ahead, hold an important element on the opponent before facing him to be able to destabilize him at the right moment. I avoid getting involved in this field for the moment and tell her succinctly, "I collect the necessary information about my employees. Getting your visa at this specific time was perfect, wasn't it? With that Victor around… Sophia didn't know a crucial part of your life when she hired you. Luckily, I usually dig on my own to get all the information before playing.

"My… past isn't a game. Neither is this, by the way," she snaps, pointing at me and her.

"Probably… Look, game or not, I won't impose anything on you. I'll just let you consider my proposal and what it would bring you in return. Your real… ex—I guess—is on parole, according to my sources… Will he want to contact you, or has he already?"

She tenses up. Sensitive subject.

"I… No, we're no longer in contact, and he's not my ex."

I frown, waiting for her to tell me more. Which she doesn't seem willing to do.

"Fine," I say without insisting. "But you might need a powerful ally, given his background. I would put my resources and my contacts at your disposal, including your home in France."

"It's just… I can't fucking believe we're talking about this," she mumbles, frozen.

"Anyway. These places are yours. The choice is yours, Océane… Whether it's about your past or the present. And as far as I'm concerned, things are very clear."

Her breathing becomes unnatural. I turn on my heels, satisfied that I've advanced a pawn she wasn't expecting. Transaction in progress, nice distraction. Ready to put in the means to achieve my goal when I covet something.

And now, I want your ass in my palms, my cock nestled in your wetness, and your mouth chanting "yes" over and over to me.

I sense her gaze as I walk away toward the car. Motionless, lost, delicious.

"Tiger?" she calls me, with a different tone.

I stop and turn around slowly. She looks…confused? Cornered? One step away from letting go?

"Yes?"

"About… France… Did you really find out everything?"

"My staff are efficient."

She waddles uncomfortably.

"Victor hadn't… No, nothing, forget it."

I stumble on what she was trying to say. But at this moment, it's hard to trust my instinctive lie detector. Too many pheromones in the air to have a clear vision.

"What are you going to do, then?" Océane hastens. "Does Sophia know too, now?"

"No. Don't worry; your secret is well kept. Sophia has her own; let's not add more. Besides, you've become a bit ours, now."

Our secret, well, one of them… My wink embarrasses her even more.

"I won't bother you all night," I assure her. "Nor will you be left on your own in Melbourne. Whatever you decide, the jet will fly you back to Sydney tomorrow. I'll be back around nine-thirty. Is that okay?"

She doesn't answer; I think she remains stunned. I walk to the car, get in and start it. Our eyes weld together one last time. Deep, filled with all our dissimulations to which will be added perhaps heaps of others more burning… if she gives in.

Now, I desire too much to have you as my diversion. And my body could be yours if you are as I presumed.

PART II

WHAT IF THE FIRST LOCK BROKE...

A secret revealed can weaken when it exposes too much... Should we venture further or not? No guarantee of what will happen... Just this avalanche of sensations tinged with fear, questioning, and excitement.

Fuck, yes, such excitement!

17

Océane

Endless minutes later, I'm still rooted to the concrete floor of the parking lot, under the neon lights. Tiger is gone. Just gone, after this muscular and unpredictable James Bond-like intervention. Damn, he literally kidnapped me in the middle of the street in front of witnesses, in front of Sophia! Classy tuxedo, unwavering confidence. He dragged me across town to dump me here!

His home.

To add insult to injury, he managed to dig up some information about my less-than-glorious past. The ones I thought would be impossible to dig up.

He could have taken more advantage of the situation, but he didn't. I see only one explanation for this: what a man like Tiger Sexton is interested in is regaining the upper hand. He realized that was the case; Victor was the biggest mistake of my life.

And realizing that my employer knows about what happened disarmed me. My heart is pounding, my palms are sweaty, and my mind is racing. Towards Paris, the past. Then Australia, and this troubled present.

So, now, Tiger wants me, claims it, and assumes it. His wife knows. And he knows everything about my other life. It's a disaster!

My carelessness displayed so far, my pride in front of him, and my joy of living crashed miserably into his dilated pupils.

Have we just taken a weird turn in our pseudo-professional relationship? What will happen from now on?

I'm nervous. My fingers fiddle with the magnetic card. Do I have any other choices tonight? My steps guide me slowly toward the elevator. Very quickly, the penthouse floor button lights up, and the device reopens its doors on the luxurious entrance of a two-level apartment. Paintings by renowned painters hung on the walls, sober and masculine colors. Leather, midnight blue, black, pure chic. No flourish. I move forward and discover the dizzying dimensions of the rooms with their gigantic glass facades overlooking Melbourne by night. A masterpiece reeking of money, power, and perfection.

I'm in one of Mr. Sexton's dens!

Do I want to see this billionaire's trap close on me? No. No matter what the stakes are, tomorrow, at 9:30 a.m., I have to escape this gilded cage. He's taking me back to Sydney, and I'm ending my engagement with Sophia.

That's it; resolution made! We'll stick to it. Or…

No! You stick to it, Océane!

TIGER

I filter, dodging private calls and only handling business emergencies. I try to ignore the more insistent calls, almost as much as those from Sophia. Murphy's…

For now, I have no desire to rant. Too many things are buzzing in my head; I turn up the music and start my morning jog.

With "Sweet Thing" by Mick Jagger in my ear canals, my strides take me away from the Langham. My guys perform their duties from a safe distance. I need to think, alone at the controls.

The videos watched hundreds of times, the hunt, the last track followed in Paris by my team of mercenaries. I can't get it out of my head. It comes back to the center of my concerns…

Around seven o'clock, I come back sweating and with a clearer mind to manage the day-to-day. The missed calls have been piling up. I abandon the Stones to contact the concierge of the TS Naval tower in order to give some instructions. Océane is probably sleeping. Under *my* sheets, in *my* bed, her silky hair strewn across *my* pillows. Unless she's lounging in *my* shower, in *my* bathtub, naked, alone.

I kept imagining different pictures of her in my den. Where I usually receive other types of "guests…" Not to doze off, even less to leave a woman there without company. I had the whole night to regret my spontaneous decision, locked in an impersonal hotel suite with a view of my stronghold, the skyscraper across bearing my initials. I smoked cigarettes while watching the lights on in my penthouse…

Between the unofficial investigation that obsesses me and Océane, who excites my neurons for other reasons, I found it impossible to sleep.

Has she thought about my offer? Has she evaluated the option "booty call for whatever she wants?" Was my little allusion to her past enough to convince her? I have no certainty, Just my determination to get her into bed—this time with me—and for a period of time.

Take a bite or two and move on to the next recess… Like Sophia with her partners.

"Good morning, Mr. Sexton," welcomes the director of the establishment when I pick up my card at the front desk. "Did our housekeeper provide you with everything you needed?"

Yeah, they followed my list to the letter. I had zero luggage; I needed a complete sports outfit, a change, and some specific toiletries. Their concierge was up to the job; someone went out of their way to do my late shopping in record time…

"Perfect, thank you," I reply.

"My pleasure, Mr. Sexton. How was your jogging?" he lingers.

He needs to get off my back. I understand that he was thrilled to see me show up unexpectedly yesterday. Having my own place to stay in Melbourne, the palaces of the city are not used to counting me among their customers. As a result, this good guy bends over backward, hoping to make me a regular. It was a waste of time; it was a case of force majeure after having lent my place to *a young lady not really in distress*, the time to let her digest some things.

I quickly dismiss the director's bows. I continue on my way, my mind occupied by various elements. Work. Sophia. Océane, the past, and present of each of us… The elevator man opens the door and presses the button for my floor, silent, respectful. During the ascent, my thoughts suddenly branch out on a precise point. My stomach contracts. By improvising last night, I left Océane alone in my place. I hope she won't snoop too much and won't try to find the strong room. In any case, she won't have access to it and won't stay in our way for long…

OCÉANE

It's eight o'clock in the morning; I pace around. I couldn't sleep. This place is imbued with Tiger, and I have the disturbing impression of feeling his presence, even alone. Too much space; obviously, the apartment occupies the entire top floor of the tower. Plus, a rooftop terrace that makes you dizzy. I go back to the room where I hung out last night. Probably Tiger's because his things are stored there. With its adjoining bathroom and dressing room. Other rooms in the same manly chic style share the endless space. All have a sliding door, glass windows, or no wall except the one near the master bedroom. Why is its access locked by some sort of high-tech system? Some kind of crazy thing with a fingerprint scanner and everything.

Is this his office? With sensitive files, a safe? Or a Christian Grey's twisted rich private room?

You've been reading too many romances, poor thing! It would be a bit of a cliché. And it would really suck for your ass too!

For the tenth time, I stand in front of this impossible-to-open fortress. Valuable stuff abounds everywhere: expensive watches, designer shoes, and suits. The paintings. The furniture. Everything must cost a fortune, and yet nothing is locked. Except for this room. Why is that? Could I also discover secrets about him and…

And what? Feel less pissed off that he discovered mine so easily? Blackmail him into leaving me alone?

Argh, the lack of sleep didn't help! My head is heavy, and my thoughts are confused. I go back to the bathroom. A bunch of new pastel-colored toothbrushes are stored in one of the drawers. Who are they for? To the girls he fucks freely when he's not at home with Sophia? I don't want to become one of the fancy chicks that he then despises or rejects. Like Sophia. Even though she wears a wedding ring and his name as an extra… Why did she sink into such a life?

Do these kinds of plans bring them closer? Did he join her afterward, with that... erection that I'm having trouble forgetting? To please her? Damn, I don't know what to think anymore!

Maybe they talked about me last night. The only clarity now is that one or both of them wants to "fuck" with me. Tiger was clear.

"We'll fuck together. No, I will fuck you..."

Who could I tell such a crazy thing? I'm lost. His intense gaze and his raw words never left my thoughts.

A transaction like any other... You'll tell me your conditions and whatever you want in exchange... Need a powerful ally...

This possibility is on my mind too. When I testified against him, Victor swore to make me pay someday. So yeah, I freaked out when I was told he was going to be released soon. I did everything to speed up my visa process. To leave France before an inevitable confrontation.

I wish I could convince myself that I'm a new version of myself, just happy and free to live my dreams. To succeed again this morning in burying the past so far away that even in my thoughts, I don't go back to it. But Tiger has just dug up the roots. My fears and regrets are surging again...

And then there is this sneaky attraction that arises between us. Despite his pretentiousness and the thousand and one reasons to avoid him, he's not wrong: this guy puts my senses on fire with odious ease. How do I come to want to slap someone so badly, to send him packing when my body betrays me in his presence? Ready to liquefy when he gets a little too close to me.

Pathetic, right?

It is better to stop this rampage; the libertine functioning of the Sexton couple will only make things worse. A bell rings, cutting my thoughts short. Panicked, I look at the time.

I remember Tiger saying 9:30. It's too early! And I look like nothing!

No need for a mirror to visualize my appearance: crumpled evening dress, make-up blurred in clusters of ugly stains, hair in battle, and for the breath, let's not even talk about it... Defeat! It's ringing again. I'm not mentally ready to face the insolent face of Mr. Sex after a restless night by his fault. Nor to bark at him without fainting that he won't get me.

Third ring, panic on board! I am caught off guard. Fourth ringing. I end up understanding it's coming from the design thingy? Holy crap, it's the landline phone!

Why are you getting so worked up over nothing?

Exhausted, I go to pick up the phone and inhale. Okay, I'll pull myself together and get out of this convoluted contract. I breathe with a slight revival of combativeness, "Hello?"

"Miss Rousseau?"

"Yes, this is Miss Rousseau."

"Hello, I'm the concierge manager. Did I wake you up?"

"N… no."

"I'm sorry to bother you, but Mr. Sexton wanted us to bring you the necessities on time," the lady on the line explains.

"Excuse me?"

"Clothes, cosmetics, and breakfast, Miss."

Of course. The king of control makes sure every detail is taken care of.

"I see. Well…yes, very good idea," I say, grateful that he had thought of it.

"Would you allow us to go upstairs now?" asks the employee.

"Yes, of course. Thank you."

"You're welcome, Miss Rousseau."

"See you then."

About to hang up, I'm stopped by the girl's voice, "Wait! Would you… press the unlock button, please?"

"What button?"

"The one that allows access to the private elevator and the top two floors, Miss. It's located at the entrance. No other elevator in the tower can get up to the penthouse otherwise."

I was right; a real fortress!

"Okay… here," I stammer.

Five minutes later, the apartment is invaded by two bellboys and the woman with whom I spoke on the phone. The first one pushes a compartmentalized cart filled with food under a bell jar and hot drinks, various fruit juices for a regiment. It smells divine.

"Damn, I can't swallow a tenth of this!"

They smile politely at me. I hope Tiger doesn't plan to join me. Maybe with Sophia? New anxiety in my stomach. If they both show up, I'll need strength.

"Is it just for me?" I ask apprehensively.

"Yes, Miss. Don't worry about the quantity," the girl tells me. "Mr. Sexton didn't know your preferences, so he planned ahead and ordered as wide an assortment as possible. If you need anything, I'm at your service."

A glimpse of the mornings he could offer you if you accepted his special "deal?" A spoiled princess life. And what would he take in return?

I nod without comment and turn to the second guy in livery. He's holding a lush bouquet of white flowers, the same as last time, in a delicate vase. Is this also a mania with him? Shivers run through me when my eyes fall on the card slipped into the flower arrangement.

"I'm going to put the products, shoes, and clothes in the room, then we'll leave you alone, Miss Rousseau," says the Tiger employee.

Her boss has just put my mind back in turmoil with a snap of his fingers. And he's not even there yet. My mouth goes dry, and I watch them perform like good little soldiers. He orders and everyone obeys. And now he knows more about me than anyone else in this country—

"We have chosen L'Oréal for the types of makeup removers and other toiletries for women. Would you have preferred another brand?" asks the concierge.

"No, this will do just fine. Thank you."

Satisfied, she smiled at me.

"You're welcome. We wish you a beautiful day, Miss Rousseau."

"Likewise, thank you," I say, eager to find some privacy to deal with my tangled emotions.

They slip away. The elevator doors lock, and I think my legs don't hold up as well. I open the card, and Tiger's racy handwriting announces the color:

Hi, sweet Lily,
I hope you're hungry. Eat whatever you feel like.
See you soon.
TS
P.S. By the way, did you like my bed?

Involuntarily, a smile sprouts at the corners of my lips as I imagine him scribbling these words. Presumptuous as can be.

One more provocation; is he looking for slaps or what? He doesn't apologize or backtrack; he just goes for it. Nothing has changed. Tiger Sexton knows what he wants. My amusement evaporates very quickly. My stomach knots. I toss the card. My hunger is gone. I prefer to head for the shower. And hang out there in the hope of clearing my head.

This is not a life for you, Océane. The dream job is ultimately just a subterfuge to lead a sloppy life. Not that I'm a saint or a little naïve girl.

When I get out, I wrap myself in one of the big, soft bathrobes. Or is it rather his smell that envelops me? In this refined virile setting, I can't help but think again of the man who tries to lure me with the complicity of his wife. Was I so wrong about Sophia? I discover the packages deposited in the room. The size, shoe size, style, everything suits me. Did Sophia give my measurements to her boyfriend?

Damn, I don't know what to think about them anymore! I put on lace underwear, a playsuit, and derbies. I have at my disposal two large brand-new makeup bags filled with the best accessories and beauty products. But no, we must not feed Mr. Control Freak's fantasies of lust any further. I decide to tame my mane and stay natural.

I gulp down my second cup of cappuccino. Even coffee in the world of the great Sexton tastes special. This irony gets stuck in my head when the light tinkle of the private elevator sounds. 9:29 a.m.

He's here. Regulated like a Swiss clock.

I take a deep breath, close my eyes for a moment and turn around.

"I think Bethany deserves a raise," he says, glaring at me.

Who?

I squint my eyes, already confused by this introduction. He smiles as he walks forward. Tousled hair, hypnotic eyes, growing beard, gray T-shirt, sports jacket, raw jeans, sneakers, and the look of a Hugo Boss commercial.

For God's Sake! Self-absorbed rich people like him should not be allowed to be so volcanic. It's too many weapons in their hands.

I wet my lips; he stares at them. I concentrate as best I can and repeat, "Bethany? A raise?"

"The concierge. For orchestrating this delight in front of me."

His burning gaze wraps around my figure, going down to my feet and back up to crash into mine.

The clothes. He's talking about your clothes, silly!

"Yeah… not bad," I say casually. "It's nice and comfortable."

"I would have used other words," he laughs.

He moves towards me. I forbid myself to flinch. I thought that not wearing make-up would help me not to feel like a succulent dish under his hungry eyes. I failed!

"So, delicious Lily, did you sleep well? Ate well?"

Neither. Your life is too special, too intense, too disturbing.

"I'm fine, thank you. Shall we go?" I rush, putting down my cup.

He raises an eyebrow and stops.

"Are you in such a hurry to go back to Sydney?" he asks me.

Mostly in a hurry to escape from your cage as an experienced wildcat.

"Yes… To find my friends," I say. "My little habits."

His jaws tighten as he shoves his hands into his pockets.

"Your new routine from before this job or the one from before you came to Australia with your… *old buddies?*"

France, the past come floating back between the lines. Shit. Is it time to expand on the subject? I'd rather not. His hoarse voice doesn't betray any emotion; he reduces the space between us. My synapses are struggling. I breathe out; he's still devouring my lips with his eyes.

No, I'm not hot. He's trying to throw me off my game. He won't succeed.

"The habits I used to have here before I met you," I whisper.

He is calm, indecipherable, and does a few more steps.

"Noted," he replies. "So, I'm going to do something I don't usually do."

"Do what? Give up?"

"Apologize to you, sweet Lily."

Huh? Is this yet another strategy to bamboozle me?

"Apologies about what, Tiger?"

"About… this," he says.

He hugs me and… Oh, boy! The Earth suddenly goes off its axis. His intoxicating perfume corrupts my little vital plot, and his greedy mouth seizes my cry of astonishment. He rushes into my mouth and finds my tongue in an indescribable kiss. My world becomes foggy, my reference points vanish, and foreign sensations stir me from the inside.

He kisses me like the whole world is at his feet. No, as if I—despite the stop signs and my pride—could enjoy being at his feet too. A torrid, imperious, breathtaking kiss. The kind of fusion I've never known until this moment. My heart races and my breath dies; Tiger ends up deviating towards my cheek.

"You see, my sweet flower, our fucking spark is still there. Are you still burying your head in the sand?" he whispers against my quivering skin.

How can I deny it? My God, yes, I feel it! The "fucking spark," as he says. I would like to extinguish it or run away from it. It crackles between us. The evidence pins me to him. His sex appeal on me, this incandescent desire in his irises, me not so experienced, close to fainting so that he can devour my lips again, drink my moan and intoxicate my tongue. His hands slide over my waist; my head whispers to me to back off. But my legs and my body do not cooperate.

"If we don't see each other anymore, it'll disappear," I argue, helpless.

"You think so? I think you should reconsider the alternative I proposed to you… You will get what you ask for. I'm open to negotiation, Océane. I'm open to a lot of possibilities."

My palms touch his pecs. Damn, does this guy have a physical imperfection somewhere? I try to push him away and get my hands off his muscles before I act stupidly.

"I… I'm not trying to up the ante, Tiger. It's just not for me, although what happened in France might mislead you."

"No, I'm not mixing things up… We'll talk about that in detail later. But you were sixteen; you had time to grow up… And I'm not talking to this Océane. I just wanted to let you know that I had this data," he supports me.

Something to make me understand that you see me as I was too. A girl who was on a very bad path…

The maneuver works; I feel like shit. His index finger lands on my mouth as I half-open it to say the only word that common sense commands me, despite my shame. A no.

"We won't be alone on the flight home," Tiger tells me, breaking the awkward silence. "I promise to be as gentlemanly as possible. Consider it again until Sydney. And if you give a definite no, I will respect your choice. Do we have a deal?"

I search his blue eyes for sincerity or anchoring; I don't know. The indecent gleam is still there, lurking in his dilated pupils. However, for the first time, his innate arrogance that sets my nerves on fire is gone. As if Tiger Sexton is dropping one of his many barriers in this penthouse in front of me. Like he wasn't judging me…

Or his kiss and words are starting to create illusions in your mind. And that sucks!

"Okay?" he repeats.

Instead of answering him, I ask hesitantly, "Who else will be on the jet? Sophia?"

"No, she came home last night. The pilot is coming back to get us. I invited my CFO; I don't know if you met him at the party last night."

"Uh… no, I don't think so."

"We have some things to consider before an important meeting. He'll be joining us. So, you and I will refrain from doing anything impulsive; he teases me with a wink. Right, sweetness?"

"How could I?" I say. "I don't have my precious phone to call handsome Carter."

Instead of the reaction I expected, a smile appeared on his face. He comes back to me, pulling something out of his pocket. My cell phone? Yes, it's my cell phone. And he hands it to me without flinching.

"Knock yourself out," he encourages me in a gravelly voice. "If you prefer to play in the little league, I won't stop you. I know what I can offer you compared to Carter or anyone else. On any level, my sweet Lily."

Unexpected hot flash.

Tiger turns on his heels. His so hot butt taunts me under his jeans and his confidence saws at me. That's it; my stupid body sends distress signals in the heat wave. How long has it been since I got laid?

18

Tiger

This kiss was supposed to be an argument to convince Océane to give in to temptation. An unfair proof of our sexual tension, more powerful than words. I'm suffering the consequences now; her flavor excited my taste buds. I want more; I want her.

She wants it, I want it, and we are both free to explore this chemistry.

Since takeoff, my gaze has constantly been seeking hers and strayed on her pink lips. She has taken a seat opposite the chairs occupied by my financial director and me. Usually, I like to be given my space. However, right now, the idea of getting closer to the pretty French girl is nagging me. Talking about acquisitions while being constantly caught up in this delicious passenger is quite annoying. Difficult to stay focused; our eyes are locked, and hers are filled with questions and doubts. I think I see the reflection of a desire similar to mine for a fleeting moment. Then she looks away at her cell phone.

Is she ashamed of her past and some of her choices and actions? She's not the only one… It's even better that way. At least I know she's not all clean; she's not an innocent young lady who would be defiled. Well, she is less candid than Sophia imagined when she saw her. Neither of them having all the cards in hand concerning the other, I remain master of the game. Because some locks must remain closed and under protection: my asperities and those of my wife which exceed by far the skids of adolescence of Océane…

"I'm finalizing this," John continues. "All that's missing are the shares of—"

I switch off… What does Blondie think? Have I rushed her? Frightened her? What will she tell me when we arrive?

I grab my phone and listen with one ear to the progress of my CFO on the mission I've given him. I can't take my eyes off the back of Océane's neck for long, who has now turned her back on me, not to look at me again. That damn kiss obsesses me a little too much. It has fueled my hunger.

"Shanna transferred confidential data to me," John is still explaining to me.

My thumb wanders over my keyboard.

"I know. Everything has to be in place by the time Carter's takeover is announced," I say.

"Absolutely, I'm on it. You can count on me. We've already—"

My attention returns from the numbers on John's tablet to my phone screen, then to the blond hair on the other side of my plane. And vice versa. What could she be doing? Browsing the net? Checking her emails and social media to see what's going on in Sydney or in France? See if anything is getting to her? Or reach out to that little moron Harry Carter?

In the midst of the angle my employee is pitching me, I start texting.

Tiger: Favor number 1: Now you have permission to send me an eggplant.

I press the send button. The signal of reception of my message resounds in Océane's hand. Three seconds later, her pink face turns in my direction. I lose track of John's strategy. I'm waiting for the answer.

Océane: Pack up your "favor" and focus on your meeting, Mr. Sexton. Plus,I have no idea what you are talking about.

I take a glass of water and hide my amusement behind it. She has some repartee, the delicious temptation.

"Everything is going to speed up this week," rejoices John, misunderstanding my reaction.

It's not the prospect of smashing the Carter heir that ruffles my hair as my eyes once again lock onto those of the object of my distraction.

I mechanically punctuate the remarks of my financial director with "um, I see…" My finger flirts with the digital screen. Océane fidgets; I know she feels that furnace that disrupts the temperature in the jet. My lust rekindles. I write:

Really? You wouldn't know what is the female equivalent of an eggplant?

She stifles a small laugh. It's all over for discretion because John stops speaking and turns his head toward Blondie. Busted! And I don't care as long as I can get her to play my game. But Océane scrupulously avoids meeting my eyes. So, I persist by selecting the appropriate emojis, followed by question marks.

An avocado? A coconut? A jar of honey? A peach? It makes me terribly hungry.

Her response is slow in coming. I try to get back into the financial swing of things and briefly explain my point of view to John. Until there are new vibrations coming from my phone.

Océane: Very gentlemanly! How would this crucial question be useful for your meeting?

I smile at the baffled gaze of my CFO sitting across from me and reply:

I become more productive when I am sexually satisfied. You should try it... Shall I show you?

"Lady and gentlemen, we're almost at the end of our flight," the voice of my pilot interrupts us. "We will be landing in a few minutes at Kingsford-Smith Airport in Sydney. The sky is clear; the outside temperature is twenty-three degrees Celsius."

Océane puts away her smartphone. The back of her chair and her golden mane hide her face. Shit, is she likely to run away now?

Océane

In one hour and twenty-five minutes, we are in Sydney. My decision is made. Well, I think so...

Of course, Tiger has been de-zapping my neurons and libido during the whole flight. And he has a fucking sense of humor too! Who could have guessed that? I'm torn between my principles, my need to improve my image in my own opinion, and this sexual chemistry that is devastating my marks. I gave Tiger a convincing "no" earlier in Melbourne. I know that, and I wonder now what it is that weighs so heavily in the balance and makes me hesitate.

His money? I'm not a venal chick, but we can't pretend he doesn't reek of money!

His looks? I'm not usually that superficial, but when you watch him, who would remain perfectly indifferent to that?

His sex appeal? His burning gaze on me? His unwavering confidence?

Shit, no, I know what I have to do! I take a deep breath as I cross the Tarmac. Tiger is still talking business with his collaborator or whatever. But he keeps looking at me with an enigmatic look. His exchange with John Parker ends with a very professional handshake. The latter takes his leave to pick up his car at the airport parking lot. While one of the well-recognizable Bentleys from the Sexton stable awaits us at the exit. We are alone again. It would be a bad idea to ride with him, but my things and papers are at the Sexton's.

Besides, I want to have a discussion with Sophia before I submit my resignation. Yes, it's better to refuse the tempter's offer and get away from him as quickly as possible. I turn to him, repeating to myself this well-considered decision. Our gazes meet, and his wrinkles scrutinize me.

Tell him. Don't chicken out.

"Tiger, I… What you're offering scares me. I'd rather… No, I must, I… choose to refuse."

He comes closer, his eyes locked on mine. I no longer deny the attraction between us; however, I do not want to succumb to it. For my own good. We're in plain sight; anyone could recognize him and take the opportunity to steal a snap or two. He knows it. I don't want to end up in the tabloids. I don't think he does, either. He doesn't touch me, but his breath and his eyes do.

"I am quitting the deal. I'll let Sophia know."

"I see… I have a crucial appointment; I can't postpone it. Would you mind waiting for my return before leaving our house?" he bargains.

Mute, I try to hide my confusion. I am torn between these incredible sensations and my reason. He checks the time on his watch, then rummages through his hair.

"Let's have dinner together, a goodbye meal to make your departure less abrupt."

For who? For Sophia? I don't really understand, captivated in spite of myself by his long visual penetration.

"Tell me yes, Océane. At least for that."

"Okay… Why not," I find myself conceding.

"Good. See you tonight. The driver will take you back home," he says, stepping back slightly.

I'm a bit out of it when I get into the Bentley. The door is closed on me. Tiger stands with his hands in his pockets, staring at me through the window. The vehicle starts and drives away under his indecipherable gaze.

You did the right thing, Océane. Leaving is a reasonable decision. Because the new version of you doesn't want to get bogged down again for or because of a guy.

So why don't I just feel happy to be back to my usual anchor points soon? Why do I feel a kind of unmentionable frustration deep inside me? Alone in the back seat, I don't manage to admire the landscape with serenity. I fiddle with my cell phone, hesitating to erase the text messages exchanged with Tiger. To turn this short page and act like his indecent proposal, our kiss, all this had never existed. However, during the whole drive, other scenarios parasitize my head filled with "what if…"

No! I don't regret having refused. I have to convince myself of that.

The butler welcomes me at the entrance to the majestic Sexton's house.

"Hello, Miss Rousseau. Nice to see you again. Did your stay in Melbourne go well?"

"Pretty much, yes, thank you," I say, looking around me. "Actually, I came to pick up my things. I'm leaving."

"Oh… sorry to hear that, Miss."

This is the first time that this man has been so straightforward, and he seems to me disconcerted. Is it a surprise or something else? Does he have any idea what was going on with my arrival under this roof?

No, forget it; focus on your departure.

"But first… Where can I find Sophia?" I pull myself together.

"Mrs. Sexton is… She's gone."

Is it me, or did he hesitate?

No, she could also be in the middle of shopping or in one of her restaurants, running her business as if nothing had happened, like Tiger. A couple that makes money, looks intimidating and unapproachable on the outside, and lets loose in private by hiring human sex toys…

But why does Peter seem… uncomfortable? He suspects something, I suppose. Or is Sophia avoiding me and making this good man lie? No, it doesn't make sense since she's the one who "chose" me. So a priori, she and her sexy hubby both assume their unbridled and atypical intimacy. Her husband must have briefed her on his final hours without her in Melbourne, and she knows I now know their intentions about hiring me.

Yeah. So, I'll go check Sophia's wing to see if she's hiding there, just in case. If not, I'll call her. Either way, she and I need to have a final tune-up before I leave this house.

"While waiting for Mrs. Sexton's return, if there is anything I can do for you, don't hesitate, Miss Rousseau," the butler offers.

"Thank you, that's fine, Peter. I'll just… gather my things. Anyway, Sophia will be here for dinner, right? I'll wait."

Peter nods politely. I go straight up to my assigned room. Where do I start? First, I have to find a new place to live and start looking for a job. Louane had promised me that I could stay in their roommate's house if I needed to. I send her a text message to inform her that I would need her help temporarily. I receive her answer immediately:

Loane: Of course, girl, we'll work it out. What happened with your great host family?

If only you knew what "host family" they are. And what they want from me…

I'm thinking about what to say to Louane when I suddenly hear a noise in the hallway. I put my phone down and open the door. That voice? Holy crap, it's Sophia! Was she really there, or did she just come in? I open the door a little more, ready to face her.

But who is she talking to? Tiger? No, I only hear her voice. And… something is wrong. Her intonation is weird; it sounds like she's reciting a poem or something in English. I hear her say:

"'… Because I am special. I am pure in my faith.
I serve with happiness and devotion the Chosen of our temple.
I wait passionately for the day of Ascension, for our final Flight.
I only live for this.
I bloom, I invest in myself, and I give myself for this ultimate Privilege.
For my people, my true Family, for Alpha and Omega.
At every moment. Away from the impure seeds…'"

Lost, I'm not sure of my translation. Sophia suddenly switches from English to a language that is unknown to me. The same one she had used on the phone once. Intrigued, I go out and see her. She's… Fuck, she's in lingerie, breasts and bare feet, hair down. My eyes roam over her exposed anatomy and freeze for a moment on the tattoo revealed by her thong. Usually, it's a bit more hidden under her other underwear. A serpent encircling a red apple on one buttock and a lily with a Roman numeral on the other… Like some kind of… marking? No, I have too much imagination; it's probably a white ink tattoo? However, the aspect is special, different… Swollen like a burn? Sophia continues to spout I don't know what to I don't know who, in a monotonous voice. Another poem? The same one? Something else?

Faced with these unexpected enigmas, I stare at the pattern engraved on her skin while swallowing.

What does this thing mean? What is she telling? And to whom?

"Hi, Sophia, I just wanted to——"

She turns around; the rest of my words die in my mouth. She doesn't look good. Her eyelids are barely holding. She looks tired, absent. Disconcerted, I advance.

"Sophia?"

"Sister, there you are! Where is Ty?"

"He… he had an appointment. Listen, I wanted to let you know that——"

She smiles for no apparent reason as she approaches and cuts me off in the middle of my sentence.

"That's it, you're my family? He accepts that you are my sister?"

"Wh… what do you mean?"

She sighs and mumbles things in the sort of gibberish that comes back. Is she fucking high? Unlike her, I freeze.

"Have you guys…" asks Sophia. "He and you, all night long…?"

Is she lucid enough for this kind of discussion?

"No, I haven't slept with your husband," I reply. "I refu—"

"Sex will take on another dimension," she interrupts me, closing her eyes. "Besides, my Ty fucks like a… But I have to initiate you…" Sophia whispers as if speaking more to herself than to me.

Her words are disjointed, and I'm not sure I understand. She is definitely not in her normal state. Or it's a wake-up call for me to get out of here.

I bat my eyelashes, trying to come back to my initial feelings, my intended resignation, and how I feel duped by their "hospitality." Sophia baited me to put me in their bed; that's the only truth. This thought revives a new anger in me, this time directed against her.

"No, Sophia. I want—"

Here we go again for her incomprehensible monologue in this strange language. I get mentally confused as she gets closer. She's close enough now to notice how her eyelids don't hold any more; they flicker over her misty eyes. She smells of wine. And I don't detect a phone or hands-free kit. Was she talking to herself? She raises her impeccably manicured fingers to me, and I tense up. She caresses my cheek.

"Sophia… Have you been drinking? Or taken something?"

She smiles, her face meeting mine.

"Maybe," she whispers to me. "Or not… You want him too, don't you? Do you have his taste on your tongue?"

Her lips come closer. I step back and shake my head.

"No. That's what I'm trying to tell you; I refuse your—"

"No?" she repeats in a tone halfway between disbelief and disconcerting cheerfulness. "Don't you want him? You don't want to be my sister?"

Damn, she's delirious! She must be having a bad trip!"

"Sophia, I think you're drunk or maybe… drugged?"

"I am going to confide a small secret, honey…" she continues weakly, completely confused. "Ty wants to fuck you; he's going to—"

"Oh, my lord! Miss?" someone suddenly exclaims on the stairs.

A maid appears, cutting short this hallucinating conversation. She calls the butler and hastens to untie her apron to cover her boss with clumsiness. The latter laughs while refusing her help.

"Did you see, sister? Our man is not a saint, but he has surrounded himself with a bunch of prudes," laughs Sophia.

"Mrs. Sexton, come with me, I'll take you to the—"

"Let me go! Go back to the kitchen... Oh, here's good old Peter to the rescue. Relax, dear, your face is all red."

Sophia giggles. I saw the scene as if it was all unreal, insane, and incomprehensible. What the hell is happening to her? It's completely crazy; I no longer recognize the sophisticated woman who had previously made me complex. She looks like a different Sophia than the one I see every day. She doesn't really listen to me when I ask her what's wrong.

The butler is as rigid as ever. Jaws clenched, he quickly disappears into a room and shows up with a bathrobe. After several attempts and the unintelligible blahs of the mistress of the house, Peter finally wraps her in the robe and orders Mary, the other embarrassed employee, "Call Mr. Sexton! Immediately!"

Under my dumbfounded eyes, he embarks a recalcitrant Sophia in the direction of the bedroom. They leave me stunned, rooted to the spot. Many questions fly through my head.

What the hell was that? What's going on in this house? What is the reason for this sudden change?

Has living with Tiger "damaged" his wife too much? Or is she an alcoholic or a junkie, and he's the one who's doing everything he can to deal with it?

19

TIGER

"Mr. Sexton, it's Mary. Madam has… My God… Madam is… Peter, who asked me to call you… I didn't mean to… But…"

My knuckles stiffen on the phone, and I raise my other index finger to indicate that I'm taking a break. I straighten up, trying to keep my calm and order gently, "Mary, take a breath. And explain to me more clearly what's going on."

"Yes. Yes, sir," my interlocutor more or less resumes.

Her breath settles in my ear. I insist, "Is there a problem with my wife?"

"Yes, sir. I think she… is not well. She has…"

Mary begins to tell me, hiding her embarrassment badly. Worry is slowly building up in my gut.

"Where is she?"

"Upstairs with Peter and Miss Rousseau."

Shit, Océane!

"Did our guest witness the scene?"

"I think so, sir."

"Okay. You're going to hang up, pull yourself together and make sure you don't leave Océane alone with Sophia. I'm coming.'

"Yes, Mr. Sexton."

Tense, I go to get my jeans and put them on quickly.

"You're going? We haven't finished—"

"We're going to have to cut this short, doc," I say, grabbing my T-shirt.

"But it's been several weeks since I've—"

"I know," I say, almost ready. I only have my socks and my sneakers to put on. "I'll get back to you. That's it for today."

I don't expect any superfluous blahs; I'm already on the phone asking my driver to get ready. I grab my jacket and head for the door. I exchanged one last text with Sophia on my way to the appointment. I didn't feel anything unusual in our brief exchange. A pang of guilt nags at me as I think about it: I could have found out by having her on the phone. I should have called her before I started!

And, damn it, there's Océane!

How can I influence her choice and encourage her to stay after that? With my nerves on edge and my mind overheating, I get into the car. We drive fast, but not fast enough, in my opinion. Despite the flow of traffic, my patience is wearing thin. In the meantime, I trust Peter to handle this emergency as well as possible.

However, it's up to me to… Argh!

I squeeze my phone. It's no use to me if my butler is busy and Sophia can't talk to me. I hate this inactivity, this feeling of helplessness on this damn trip! Like that day…

My fists clench, and my jaws ditto. Sophia, what the hell did you do now? Counting the seconds and considering hypotheses only increases my anxiety.

We reach my property at top speed. As soon as the car is parked, I jump out and run the few interminable meters, climb the stairs, and curse the succession of rooms leading to Sophia's room. In the hallway, I come face to face with… the housekeeper.

And Blondie. Obviously disturbed. Rightly so…

My fists clench, and my thoughts race. Our eyes lock, and she guesses my question before I ask it.

"She… she's in the other wing. In your room, I think. Peter didn't want me to go with them."

"Thank you," I simply say, turning back.

I take the opposite direction without wasting a minute. We will discuss this later; Sophia is the immediate priority. I rush in, push open my door and discover her over the comforter. She's wrapped up in a bathrobe, pressing one of my pillows against her like a comforter. My eyes stop on Peter, who whispers to me, "She threw up and is starting to doze off, so I called Dr. Murphy and Dr. McDouglas. They will be here soon."

Okay. Good reflex on Peter's part.

"Was she drinking?"

"Yes, I think so. Mary had brought her a bottle or two of chardonnay."

"And did anyone check her medicine cabinet?"

"No, sir. I'm sorry, I had to deal with—"

"It was not a reproach, Peter. Thank you. Leave us alone now and go and check her room, the stock of pills, the last purse she used, if she left a note, etc. As usual. I want to know what and how much she swallowed."

"Yes, sir."

I sit up in bed and touch Sophia.

"Hey, it's me, Tiger. I'm here."

"Oh, my love," she mutters, her eyes heavy. "You're here?"

"Yes. Look at me, Sophia," I tell her, stroking her hair.

"I'm tired… I've been a good Lily; I've been good, right?"

"Sophia, did you take Xanax again?"

I think she's nodding. I make a mental note: pills + alcohol. But what the fuck did you do? Why? Because of the spat with Kelly's ex? Because of how the introduction of a third person into our relationship has turned out? No, Océane, it was her idea, damn it! I would never have proposed that kind of plan to her myself. Banging extras when I couldn't keep from cracking up was fine with me.

"You had recovered, Sophia… Why did you do that?"

Woozy, she manages to open her eyes briefly. I shake her, and she grumbles, "You. I… I want my flower crown, and I want you, Ty… You and me…"

She doesn't finish; she has no energy left.

"No, no, no, look at me! Sophia?! Sophia!"

Her artificial Morpheus draws her into the mists. I pull out my phone to bark in turn at each of the two doctors about how urgent it is. My regular doctor has virtually no contact with my wife; these are two very different things. And the prescription can't come from one of the specialists who follow Sophia. I would have been informed if she had had to be prescribed anything of this nature again. She has been off her antidepressant for a while. Has anyone else provided her with any? That—

Argh, I have to think!

I'm chomping at the bit watching Sophia's condition. The minutes are piling up. The clock is ticking. Finally, her doctors show up one after the other. Sophia's trusted private doctor to pump her stomach and make sure she's out of danger, and the therapist who will be on duty here for twenty-four hours. As a precaution.

Groggy, I leave the room. With the need to get drunk, too, to bury this brutal rise of old demons under waves and waves of whiskey. At eighteen, when we got married, I thought I could handle everything like a knight in shining armor!

Here I am, eleven years later, suffocating and wondering if it was all worth it.

I enter my private projection room, one of my best bottles in hand, and I lock myself in, alone with myself. No film on the movie screen or videos that I have been scrutinizing for the past few years. No sound. Only darkness, dead calm, and empty seats around me.

My fucking reality: owning everything and contemplating my choices and loneliness at the top.

I lean my head back to take a sip from the bottle. Unfortunately, I hold alcohol pretty well, and I don't really want to get drunk. That would be another form of loss of control, unworthy of a Sexton. My mind wanders to the responsibilities that this heritage requires, the maturity that I had to seek in myself to take over from my father Then I think about what my wife is asking for. A chaos made of ambiguities and duties, of hard fights and reputation, of stalking in secret and of objectives to be reached, laminates my brain.

I take a second sip. I can almost feel them again… Eve's fingers desperately clutching mine. Even if I am still to this day unable to measure her level of pain and disappointment at that moment, the emotional earthquake that overwhelmed her makes me rage inwardly again.

Damn, if only!

I swallow another long sip of alcohol, hit full force by a surge of images. They break through my shields and invade the projection room.

It's getting rough, too rough…

20

Océane

Pacing, that's all I've done since the scene with Sophia. The cook has been on my back all morning. With an excess of kindness and her damn devotion to the Sextons, like the others! My questions are not answered or are, but very vaguely.

What the hell is keeping me here?

I should get out of here, but the truth is, I still care about Sophia. And I don't understand what's happening to her. After a while, I get tired of being kept in the dark. In front of a ridiculous homemade smoothie in the kitchen, away from the sultry duo.

I don't want to be coddled; I don't want their embarrassed smiles to avoid talking about the hostess. Tiger didn't come back to talk to me; is it because it's serious?

If that were the case, they would have taken her to the emergency room, right? And above all, what exactly does she have? You don't go crazy like that overnight, so it's not new? Do they all know in this house? I put the smoothie glass down without tasting it.

"Oh, you don't like it? Do you need anything else, Miss?" Mary asks.

"No thanks. I'm not thirsty or hungry."

The butler becomes less imperturbable for a moment, and I stare him straight in the eye. The three of us in this big kitchen, this sort of omerta, it's nonsense! No one is fooled.

"I'm going upstairs, Peter."

"Of course, Miss," abdicates this good man who is as quiet as a grave about his masters' secrets. "Mrs. Sexton's wing is also yours," he says.

A polite and subtle way to remind me of the ban on access to the other part of the kingdom reserved for Tiger. Where he, she, and their "personal white lab coats" have been hiding for ages? Whatever!

"Yeah," I confirm without adding anything.

What's the point? My steps lead me upstairs. On the left, Sophia's deserted apartments. I head to the right, in "the forbidden city." I don't care about the rules anymore! I reckon Tiger lost that power the second his erection stuck to me, and his tongue went in my mouth! Wherever he's hiding, I'm going to flush him out since his accomplice is in no condition to listen to me!

I push the doors one after the other. My heart begins to race with each discovery. Empty rooms. An empty high-tech gym. Empty bathrooms. Spotless, empty rooms, drenched in daylight.

Where is the tiger? Where Sophia must be rambling right now with the invisible doctors and the big boss.

I continue and come upon a closed door. Oh! It is identical to the locked area in the penthouse in Melbourne. Are they in there? No way to open it. I end up giving up and moving on to the next one, the doors upholstered in black leather. What is this? Another bedroom? I enter, curious and apprehensive. In the dark, I notice the absence of windows, unlike the rooms before. I search the wall, no switch under my fingers. I'm about to walk out empty-handed when I hear a loud noise.

I turn around and try to probe the darkness.

"Is anyone there?"

"Damn it!" a voice growls.

Tiger? I flushed him out!

I walk blindly. The darkness accentuates the impression of infinite space until I bump into something. I stop my progress by cursing.

"Is that you, Tiger? Where's the light?"

"Not now!" he grumbles.

Is he kidding me? I take a deep breath. The smell of alcohol titillates my nostrils. I open my eyes wide as if it would help me to discern him better in this mass of shadows.

"Have you been drinking too? Are you all drunks or what?"

"I told you: Not. Now. Océane!"

His words echo; he moves with muffled steps on the obviously carpeted floor. I can't help but be ironic.

"Are you avoiding me so you can drink overpriced bottles in your private bar?"

"You're so stubborn! Okay, what do you want?" he asks.

"What do I want? What do you think I want?"

We're way past the point of being polite.

"You're not choosing the right moment, Océane," he reprimands me.

"It's never the time, Tiger! In fact, I will never get enough answers. There will always be more questions than explanations with you two. The deal was unequal: *I* agree to fuck and shut up about the rest?"

A sudden sound of breaking glass answers me, and makes me flinch. The smell of whiskey wafts up.

"You know what? I'm done. I'll go away and leave you with your fucking secrets!" I hiss as I gesture into the void.

Tiger lets out a curse in English, which tears through the darkness. Then he calls out "light." Instantly, spotlights light up. Embedded in the ceiling, they diffuse a shower of blue light. I blink and scan the surroundings. Big velvet armchairs turned towards an XXL screen… Holy cow, is this a movie room?

After the surprise effect, I swivel and take the full force of Tiger's enigmatic look pointed at me.

"You'll stay tonight," he says, looking grim but more lucid than I expected. "For dinner, as we agreed."

"Well, that's no longer happening."

I go backward; our pupils are locked, and my breath is turned upside down.

"I'm throwing in the towel, Tiger."

"No, wait! Please. What time is it?" he asks, checking his watch.

Instead of sending a scathing retort to his face, my eyes lock onto his hand. I hadn't noticed it yet…

"Shit, are you bleeding?"

Before I realize what I'm doing, I reach over and grab his wrist. Shards of glass are still stuck in his flesh; he hadn't even noticed?

"I expressed my nerves by slightly pressing my hand through the glass of the bar. It's nothing," he evades by tearing off the debris without care.

His palm is in a bad state.

"It looks painful. You have to disinfect and maybe do some stitches… Your doctor is still there, I think."

I move back towards the door. To go get him or just to restore some physical distance between us?

"No, I'll take care of it later. It's no big deal. I'm yours; I'm listening," he decides, taking a few more steps toward me.

On alert, I tense under his irises. I try to fight back.

"Really? You don't ask me to get out like a little doggie and come back with my tail between my legs when you want to see me again?"

"Anatomically, I'm the one with a tail," he reminds me. "Not you."

Very funny! I'm not about to forget it, especially with this intensity that emanates from him when he says it.

"Go ahead, Océane. Ask me the question that is most important to you at this moment," he urges me.

I take a long breath, try to regulate my emotions, and sort through my head. The first question comes out by itself.

"What's happening to your wife? I demand a detailed and truthful answer!"

He raises his eyebrows.

"You demand?"

"Yes. If you are so 'open to negotiation,' that means communicating with me. I'm not just a common sexual stimulant in your relationship. I also have a brain and need to understand what you were trying to get me into!"

He stares at me and doesn't say anything for seconds. Maybe nobody has ever given him an ultimatum, let alone a woman. Well, with me, he'll have to learn.

"And what exactly are we negotiating, sweet Lily? Your change of heart?"

Business genius to the end, even banged up and preoccupied.

"I didn't say that," I defend myself. "You're just not in a strong position right now. You want me, and you asked me to make my terms, remember?"

He bites his bottom lip and nods.

"You win this one. You've got something I'm interested in; I've got to give you something in return."

Fuck, is that how it would work between us if I committed? By considering everything as a transaction?

"Exactly," I say, crossing my arms.

"Ok, let me summarize. Sophia had… a particular childhood and teen years," he begins. "And… let's say that from the beginning of our marriage until now, we went through a few suicide attempts, and different phases of therapy, including a period under treatment. Then she became the person you met. Stronger, ambitious, serene…"

Suicide? Oh, boy!

"I guess you were the one who taught her to 'break free' from all that? Did you shape her, pull her up?"

"I did my best… I was barely of age, actually."

Okay, so he got engaged at a very young age. Either he must have been crazy about her, or he's the kind of guy who likes to save fragile young girls?

I whisper, "You seem to have invested a lot in yourself… I read somewhere that you also gave her her first restaurant and probably helped her start her business."

He doesn't express an ounce of arrogance, doesn't brag about it, doesn't comment on it; he just nods.

"What about the treatment? Is she still following it? What kind of treatment is it?"

"Xanax. And maybe something else… To deal with anxiety attacks, among other things… It was a passage, a temporary necessity. We always wanted to avoid a withdrawal problem, a dependency problem."

"Did she manage to stop?"

"Yes, for a long time. Well… today, she broke down and took pills again. What you saw is due to the interaction of meds with alcohol. The side effects are amplified, so she will be sleeping for a while. Everything should be back to normal by tomorrow… It's up to her to decide if she wants to confide in you about it, to reveal more, you understand?"

"Yes, I can understand that," I reply. "I… thank you for the effort."

I recognize that we are not always proud of the different stages in our lives or not necessarily ready to talk about them. I know what I'm talking about…

Tiger pauses; I try to assimilate the data, to fit them together: he has pulled Sophia out of a complicated past. Maybe she'll tell me later?

Right now, his revelations begin to change the idea I had of him. And of their relationship. And their couple. With his lineage, his wealth, and his good looks, he could have taken the easy way out. Choose any beautiful, rich, well-educated young woman with an unmatched pedigree. But he got involved with a girl who obviously had a rough start in life…

A modern-day fairy tale? He, the true prince 2.0. And she, who was his damsel in distress?

A strange feeling came over me because I realize something I hadn't realized before: Sophia means enough to him to have put up with these "complications" all this time. It moves me to finally get proof of the bond between them. But why does it shake me up so much?

No. Let's get back to Sophia. You're not concerned…

"You care about her," I say.

"You thought I didn't? I don't want to see her go down or make her unhappy, Océane. But I…"

"Yes?"

"I also have wars to fight."

Wars? Is that a way of speaking? Sure! Of course, it is! He manages a financial empire; he has the weight of a name, of a legacy on his shoulders. With the reputation, obligations, and responsibilities that go with it and that he must reconcile with his chaotic private life. And he is not even 30 years old!

Yes, I'm starting to see Tiger in a different way all of a sudden. And that's what hurts me inside.

"Your presence fills a void," he whispers. "I was skeptical about Sophia's initiative, but you did her good…"

He brushes my face. I am unable to push him away when he passes behind me.

"You're good for me too," he adds in a gentle tone.

My defeat signals turn on again, and my body temperature

rises a notch. Is it my back that goes towards him or his chest that joins me? I don't know, but, pressed against him, I soften. He plunges his nose into my mane and does not move anymore for a few seconds.

I don't know what I want anymore, what I'm doing.

A wave of heat seeps through my veins; my neurons shut down. Tiger takes the opportunity to gently push me into a chair. My eyelids close by themselves as he walks around me again. His hands come on my shoulders; I don't care if he smears my clothes with drops of blood from his wound. My chest fills with his perfume, his smell. He pushes with delicacy my hair to the side, leans on me from behind, and nibbles my ear. I feel myself succumbing, frantic thoughts stumbling through my mind… His fingers brush my temple, cheek, and mouth before sliding under my chin. His breathing changes tempo, and the bottom of my face is held in his palm. Slowly, Tiger's thumb encourages my moist lips to part and wedges itself between them.

"Stop talking about leaving. Don't go, Océane. Please stay."

In this whisper that implores me, I shiver. And without warning, I lose my footing. All I want is this virile voice vibrating with desire. The body that goes with it. The possible shit that also goes with it doesn't scare me as much anymore. I sigh against the pad of his finger.

"Stay," he begs me.

"Tiger…"

"Please, my sweet. Say yes."

"I… Okay, I… maybe I'll give it a try."

He sighs heavily, urging me to get up. We are face to face; he glares at me. His mouth is seriously starting to create a haunting hunger in my head. I spin when his sexy mouth reduces the space between us. Then opens to tell me, "For the next six months, are you offering me everything about yourself?"

"Maybe…"

Shit, what did I do?

21

TIGER

This "maybe" sounds like a yes and dissipates the indelible darkness that was unfolding in my memory. The compact clouds lighten a little…

I hold Océane close to me, using her soft curves to chase away the shadows in my mind. And I contemplate her pupils that widen.

"*Offer you everything from me?*" she laughs, leaning in closer. "What does that mean exactly?"

His hands become wandering, mine go down lower, grab her butt to squeeze it. Our breaths intermingle, and our lips brush against each other. My lower abdomen hardens.

"That, sexually, you and I are between consenting adults. And that you will be mine for these six months."

"It still seems a bit possessive to me, considering you're married. I'm not going to let it happen unless I can be as possessive as you."

"Hmm… do you think so?"

"Uh-huh…" she whispers to me, more and more enterprising.

My fingers slide over her hip, leaving her delicate rump to run over the fabric on her skin, looking for an opening. This tiny combination fits her divinely, but how do you get rid of it, damn it? Océane undulates against me and feels my cock bulging. My breathing saturated, I finally find a zipper. Eyes in eyes, I undo it and see this beautiful blonde flinch. She shudders. Even though she always tries to verbally challenge me.

"Six months is a long time… One of us might get bored before then, right?" she asks me in the hollow of my neck.

That's the moment I choose to open her suit and take it off.

She doesn't fight, sensual and malicious. Because she notices her effect on me. The more I discover her body, the more I am hot. I bend down to slide the clothes on her legs, then throw them farther as I get up. My attention crystallizes on her black lace set, her tanned skin, and…

For God's sake! Her breasts bewitch me under the transparency of the fabric.

I embrace Océane, press her against me with more ardor, and growl to her, "Six months can pass very quickly… When you are very hungry."

"Are you? I thought it was your super cell phone that I felt against my belly," she teases me "innocently" by feeling my crotch.

She compresses my stiffened member, and my veins heat up. That doesn't prevent me from whispering to her, "I don't know. Ask me to check if it's my phone you're touching through my jeans."

Amused, I don't wait for her answer. I grab one of her thighs, pull her on top of me and devour her mouth. I hold her in balance on one foot, like during that damn tango at James'. Except that there are no more photographers, gossips, or witnesses around. At my mercy, Océane clings to me. She moans. Our tongues find each other to not let go. While kissing her, my uninjured hand slides down on her, not to dirty her if the other one is still bleeding. She devotes herself anyway to maintaining my embrace.

Instead of warning her, my fingers flatter the curve of her breasts, and I deepen the kiss. Her moans reverberate through me. Her scent stuns me and exhilarates me beyond reason. Shivers rain down my spine as she lifts my shirt. Her nails wander over my skin. My fingers migrate gently to the south of her anatomy. They trail at the edge of her panties, on the delicate surface inside her thigh. They end up getting under the lace. She arches her back.

"An authorization? What's next?" she gasps.

Fuck, I love what I touch.

The beauticians have done a marvelous job… A tiny silky hair forms a triangle on Océane's pubic area, and everything else is smooth around it. I'll have to look at it closely… Later… For the moment, our eyes locked, and my index finger slowly invites itself into her wetness. Soft, wet, and so tempting. I touch her bud, and she arches her back with a long sigh.

"Yes, delicious ingenue. You thought you could get my cock so easily?" I say to her, going between her intimate lips.

She pronounces vague protests, which draw a smile from me. She abandons herself, her eyes as feverish as mine must be. Her face in front of mine, her mouth opens at the same time as my phalanges penetrate her in search of sensitive points. I search subtly in her femininity; I absorb her moans in a greedy kiss, then lose myself in her dilated pupils. I contemplate her blossoming under my targeted movements. My fingers sink in, come out, titillate her, and little by little, I begin to guess my areas of power on her body. The sensations expose themselves with indecency on her features; her eyelids flutter, and her breath shortens. Her leg on the ground is not stable anymore. And she continues to be wet. I kiss her again, captivated by her emerging pleasure. My gestures become more sure, more expert, and her shudders tell me her level of arousal. Everything of her testifies to it. I observe her in full lascivious surrender under my assaults. Her warm petals, pink button, and soaked confines drive me crazy. And to think that it is only my hand that is in contact with this wonder! My groin contracts in anticipation. Océane undulates her pelvis, claws at my back, and tries to stay on her feet.

"Tiger, I'm gonna… I… Oh, boy, you're gonna make me cum," she exhales on my mouth before I devour her mouth.

Yes, I feel her pulsating. The tension rises, I maintain it, then I decide to slow down. I take my time so that she stays at this level of pleasure. She liquefies and begins to beg for more. I avoid the places where she feels me most intensely inside her, and I lock eyes with her. We breathe in disorder. Loudly. We are electrified. I start tasting her again, running out of air. I flirt with the hollows of her neck, breasts, and ears.

And without warning, I again try to drag her to the extreme limit of implosion. Her arousal soars, unbearable. When I read in her irises that she oscillates at the edge of the precipice, ready to let go, a vicious satisfaction invades me. I stop exploring her and withdraw without haste while still scrutinizing her. My hand pulls out of her underwear, and I release her thigh that I was holding up. She wobbles a little, struggling to come to her senses for a few seconds.

"What are you doing? We're not done, Tiger," she complains, all languid.

"I know."

My thumb, still impregnated with her fragrance, slides over her swollen mouth; I coat her lips to eat them better afterward. I put all my hunger, all my thirst for her in this kiss by tweaking her nipple. To bring her desire to its climax again before interrupting me. I step back with a half-smile and decree to her, "You won't get any more right now, sweet Lily."

"What?"

"You have no idea how much I want this orgasm. But it won't come until I decide to," I tell her as I walk away.

She blinks, cheeks rosy, looking incredulous. Lost, ravishing, euphoric, and alluring to die for.

"Wait, are you serious?"

I first savor the sight of her naked body and cut off just as she is about to go into a trance.

"You'd better get dressed. Seeing Sophia almost naked is enough for my employees today. Let's not add to it with that adorable little ass.

Stunned, she feverishly runs her fingers through her hair. I fully understand the reason for this. I just got to know her better in depth while using her surrender against her. And now I'm stopping this delicious exploration with the sole purpose of preventing Océane from cumming right now. Some things deserve to be savored longer, a very long time before the apotheosis.

What I enjoy most is measuring her surprise and frustration.

"But what exactly is wrong with you?" she says.

A little sensory torture, and it's just getting started.

"I'll give you a taste of *edging*."

"Something sadistic? I should have known—"

"Sadistic? I intend to make you cum, you know… But not right away, and it will be my way."

"I can't believe it! Even for that, you are a control freak," she complains.

I laugh, satisfied with the result on her nerves.

"The control freak thanks you for this sublime… *mise en bouche.* See you next time? I think my… 'cell phone' needs a cold shower now."

On that note, I leave her there. On my way out, I hear her "what a bastard," and I hide my smile with my hand that just played in her. Her taste and scent are there. My member is still erect within my boxers.

This sweet flower will now populate my fantasies… During her long and slow blossoming.

OCÉANE

"I can't believe it!"

Still in disbelief, I see that he really did walk away. No, but this guy did everything he could to get me to agree to their open-couple thing—despite Sophia's condition, maybe largely because of it—only to leave me high and dry just when he manages to break down my defenses?

I am overwhelmed with confusion, annoyance, shame, and a small dose of anger. But it's the frustration that tops the list. I put my playsuit back on and retrieve my phone that fell out of my pocket, trying to figure out what just happened.

What was the word again? This subtly sadistic pleasure has a name, then? End or ed… something, I think…

No, first, I have to leave this movie room; it's impossible to think in this place where I was so close to sleeping with the master of the place. If he hadn't put an end to this foreplay that made me spin, I would be…

Damn, the defeat!

This truth pisses me off more than anything else. Tiger managed to make me amnesic, crazy with desire. Just crazy. Nothing mattered anymore; I just wanted more of him. And I find myself like… like a little idiot in need of something she never really knew…

This desire. Too dazzling, which consumed me, overwhelmed me, intoxicated me, and shattered my resolutions.

I go to the left wing without meeting anyone or succeeding in controlling this flow in me. In the room which was allotted to me, I get rid of my clothes and go under the shower. I can't stop thinking about it. About him, his mouth, his caresses, his perfume, his muscles under my fingers, and his dancing inside me. And that damn ed-thing.

The ringing of my cell phone pulls me out of my retrospective. I turn off the taps and wrap myself in a towel. Impossible to think about it. On the screen, Louane's first name and face appear. I suddenly remember asking her to let me stay at her place. I almost left here. Then Sophia took me by surprise. And now this torrid and abruptly interrupted rapprochement with Tiger is screwing up my hormones… Not just my hormones, by the way.

I sit on the bed. Louane's call goes through to voice mail. Something else comes back to tease my mind.

Edging! That was the word!

I type it into my browser without being sure. The results scroll through my phone and confirm my deductions. It's orgasm control.

Fuck yeah. He really wants to keep power over everything.

I lay down on the comforter with a long sigh. What do I do now? Do I use my frustration and confusing sensations to go back on my word and walk away for real? Or do I… find a way to make Tiger succumb to this erotic game? The second option brings a smile to my lips. Either way, this has gone too far…

He wants to play? We are going to play.

22

OCÉANE

A tantatizing idea pops into my mind when my yawn reminds me of my previous sleepless night. All Tiger's fault.

How much time do I have left before this damn dinner? I could always take a nap and get my strength back to better deal with "my potential future lover on a fixed-term contract." So good with his…

Heck, I still feel funny about all this.

His hand on me, inside me, with his fiery gaze almost pulverized me with pleasure. He saw me as a little player in the big league. I want to be more than that, to give him a hard time, to titillate his need for control. I pick up my phone on impulse.

Edging, huh? Let's show Mr. Sexton who decides when I cum, how I cum, and where I cum.

I loosen the towel, straighten up to grab some pillows, and get comfortable. I turn on the voice recording on my phone and place it on my stomach. My eyes close I slowly run my fingers over my skin. It's not even hard to let the longing that Tiger sowed in me resurface. It hasn't disappeared; it corrupts every nook and cranny in me. My nipples start to harden again, my flesh to feverish and quiver, and my sighs are back. My sensations bring me back to him, his magnetic eyes, his three-day beard, his big soft hands, and his muscles designed to make you crazy.

And that haunting erection in his jeans… I'm losing it…

I squeeze my breasts, squeeze my eyelids, and my thighs. What if that was Tiger's goal? Fuck me on edge, craving until I break down and beg him to take me? Is that how it works? I won't let myself be controlled. Determined and excited, I put my idea into practice. A sumptuous masturbation to claim my pure and simple emancipation. I just have to remember what Tiger did to me, what he said to me, to set me on fire. The beginning of a feeling of well-being is growing in me, free to grow and spread this time. I take ownership of my pleasure again. It rises to a crescendo.

"Yes…Fuck, yes! Yeeess…"

I rub my erogenous zones, intoxicated by these sensory memories. Him, me, and this euphoria which rises, rises, rises… Damn, yes! The orgasm finally springs from my depths. Lighting, disorienting. I shiver for a moment, shaken by spasms. My cell phone slipped near me. I grab it to check that the recorder is still running. Great, it is the case! I bring it closer to my lips and whisper in my most languorous post-fucking voice possible, "You're a free couple, okay. And *I'm* independent, liberated, and the sole master of my choices. I'm not an inflatable doll, Tiger… Nor your docile little toy… Orgasms, I get them whenever I want."

I stop recording, a naughty smile on my lips.

I'm ready for round two, Mr. Sexton. You and me!

TIGER

It's early evening. I stare at the bandage Dr. McDouglas put on my hand after taking care of Sophia. Next to nothing, he removed the remaining tiny shards of glass, cleaned the cuts, and did what was necessary. Above all, he had to ensure the emergency with Sophia and check everything before leaving. Murphy, however, is still here.

And my mind wanders; the kind of bliss that boosted me during my one-on-one with Océane has evaporated. Replaced by things I can no longer repress. Even at the bottom of my vodka glass.

The filter no longer works…

"Ms. Sexton seemed fine on her last visit," Murphy says. "How did she… Was she starting to show signs of recidivism? Excess? OCD? Was there anything specific going on?"

The questions of the man sitting on the terrace in front of me pull me out of my thoughts.

You want the truth, doc? I wasn't looking at her enough to realize it.

I was too busy looking for the monsters that stole her childhood, her life, and for a long time, her sanity. And I had a hard-on for women other than her…

"Not that I know of," I admit laconically with a surge of guilt. "Now that I think about it, yes, something went wrong again. I was blaming it on your… idea, which I still don't really buy into, even though Sophia was enthusiastic about it… Maybe there's another trigger that I missed."

The first clue was when Sophia changed her language when she spoke to me on the day Océane arrived. It had been years since she had used that language. But since she and Océane got wasted, I thought that was all it was. However, we had a second cue today. Her old demons seem to have really resurfaced. How and why? I have to dig. I have to figure out what the problem is. It's possible that it's not only due to the presence of our *au pair*.

Murphy scrutinizes me.

"So, my suggestion isn't necessarily the reason? Do you feel that there is a reason for the relapse that she didn't tell us about?" he asks me, intrigued.

"Sophia?" a female voice comes out of nowhere before I can object or confirm. "Are you talking about Sophia? Is she getting better?"

Argh! There's my other problem.

I turn around to discover Océane. Fresh, rested, even more attractive than the last image of her in my head. I'd better counteract the next unforeseen event. Otherwise, I risk losing control of this whole mess.

Murphy's attention is now focused on the newcomer. He stands up and holds out his hand to her with deference. I can practically visualize the curiosity lighting up his practitioner neurons. In short, one of the people I pay handsomely to manage our secrets and keep it shut meets the woman I want to nestle into to momentarily forget those same fucking worries. And meanwhile, my dear and tender VIP patient of Murphy is snuggled in the arms of Morpheus.

"Good evening. I'm Doctor Murphy," he introduces himself.

"Oh… hi, I'm Océane. We didn't get a chance to talk when you rushed in," she replies.

"Indeed. Nice to meet you, Océane."

She smiles at him, then turns to me. Our eyes magnetize. On the outside, I have become impenetrable again, even if I can't help eating her lips with my gaze. I can't make out what emotions she's going through. Still frustrated? Is she going to pout at me? Turn me on? Or just wait to see what happens next?

"Hi," I tell her before taking my last sip. "Don't worry about Sophia; she's fine."

A frown crosses her face.

"Is that all? Nothing more?"

Damn it! Can't she just wait for the doctor to get out of the picture to rebel again? Our intimacy is just between her and me. I don't want Murphy involved in this, especially when I've just told the doc again how skeptical I am of this unorthodox method. Even if, as the latter claims, Sophia may not break down because of it. And even though this option that I'm contesting excites me much more than I would have liked. Damn, this is actually complicating things!

Here's the problem: I don't agree, but this girl exacerbates obscene desires in me.

I pour myself another glass, and Océane grabs it under my nose. She sits down with my vodka and dips her lips in it while staring at me, waiting for a reply from me. The doc keeps silent, probably interested in this blond girl I'm staring at.

He is not stupid; he certainly establishes a correlation with Sophia…

"Nothing more," I maintain, watching Océane chugging my drink. "She's resting. The other doctor did what was necessary; everything is fine."

"If you say so…"

Her face disconcerts me.

"You look pretty well rested to me, too," I divert the conversation.

"Uh-huh. I took a little nap… with my phone. Thank you for checking, Tiger," she retorts, fiddling a little too much with the phone in her hand.

I cringe more at her choice of words. Océane nibbles her lip as she types on her phone.

"Getting back to Sophia, can you tell me more about her, Dr.

Murphy?" she asks with feigned casualness.

Murphy, perplexed, seeks my approval. He doesn't quite get it and will have to stick to confidentiality. Let him give succinct news without deviation.

"Well, she'll get over it quickly. Don't worry… Océane."

Really?

"I see," replies my Frenchie… "As I was joining you, I heard you talking about OCD… I would just like to point out that she is increasingly fidgeting with her wedding ring, in case that info is relevant. And she was reciting stuff in English, and in a language I don't know."

New exchange of glances with the therapist. Argh, Océane intercepts mine; it intrigues her.

"Thanks for letting me know," the other says uncomfortably.

Blondie probably hopes for more clarifications. She waits, details us in turn. No additional information is emitted. Murphy's silence and my calm end up exasperating her, I think.

"Great. I'm going to slip away, so you can continue to discuss 'Sophia's top secret file,'" she says, pushing her chair back.

I take a deep breath and wrap my hand around her wrist to hold her back.

"You can stay," I say to her. "Are we still having dinner?"

"Not interested anymore. Continue without me. I'm going to say hello to Sophia and opt for a meal tray in front of my computer."

Confused, I bat my eyelashes. Is she making me pay for the little game in the private projection room? Or the fact that Murphy respects confidentiality and hasn't told her more?

"By the way, Tiger, keep your cell phone nearby. You'll get a message in a few seconds…" she says as she frees herself. "On that note, good evening, gentlemen!"

I watch her leave in her little black dress, trying to remain unmoved. Without comment, I grab my glass, half whistled by Océane, and gulp the rest. I wait for my phone to ring to discover her text message. I don't know exactly what to expect.

Hum… An audio message?

23

TIGER

Breathing… Silence… Sigh… Tightness in my muscles. New silence… Rather suggestive? No? Is it?

A flood of questions in my head.

A deep breath in the hollow of my ear canal…

What is that thing?

I straighten up, my phone pressed to my ear, and walk away from Murphy. Seconds pass, tension builds, and things become clearer in the sound.

Moans… Shit, yes, they are moans. She exhales… She… Damn, is that…

I think I understand, but this deduction catches me off guard.

Damn, Océane recorded herself when…

My gaze meets the slightly too curious one of Sophia's therapist. The sounds turn into images in my retinas, and this sensual voice becomes the main thread of a story without words. An air tinged with voluptuousness floats around me. And Océane is… Fuck! I can't see her, but I feel her panting, touching me, entering my mind, and setting my imagination on fire. It's worse than a video, more insidious. Because it forces me to fill in the blanks myself, without limit. To guess, to suppose, until my senses boil. Her breath starts to take the tempo I had a taste of earlier with her before stopping everything. It speeds up, increases. Fuck, I hear her getting off live! Well, in deferred, since she has just sent me this bomb. My brain goes wild; my brain activity flows lower. In my pants. Océane is saying, "yes, oh, yes!" My knuckles tighten on the phone. With closed eyelids, I cannot put an end to this listening at the limit of the voyeurism. She "shows me" her pleasure and I absorb it without being able to lose a crumb. Until her apotheosis.

"You're a free couple, okay. And *I'm* independent, liberated, and the sole master of my choices. I'm not an inflatable doll, Tiger… Nor your docile little toy… Orgasms, I get them whenever I want," her breathless voice whispers to me, satisfied.

During the following seconds, I remain nailed in the same position. Flabbergasted, annoyed, stunned… hard cock to be bothered with.

"Is everything okay, Mr. Sexton?" Murphy asks.

I clear my throat, still clutching my smartphone. Is everything okay? Hell, no! I want to run into the house, find that little troublemaker, and… fuck her hard! Do everything to her that a gentleman wouldn't do, except with the lady's consent. Nevertheless, I try to control myself. I breathe in, breathe out, breathe in, breathe out, and hold on to the relationships I am used to. How they turn out is up to me. I am a master of my choices. Socially and professionally, I choose, I decide, I analyze, I deploy the means deemed necessary, I take if I want, when I want.

It's not up to you to control my appetites, sweet Lily. I prefer the opposite.

If Océane fights back every time, I will readjust my reactions accordingly. I inhale a new bowl of oxygen and start to pull myself together.

"Mr. Sexton? Are you okay?" Murphy asks again.

"I'm fine. Where were we again?"

I sit down again and change the subject, trying not to give the rebellious lady what she wants: to make me react right away. Yes, I want to possess her. Yes, she has just marked my mind. If I was just following my base instincts, I'd already be climbing the stairs into her room and ripping off her clothes. That's what she's hoping for. I know that now. But she won't lead the way.

I'm not going to improvise; I'm going to plan this merger-acquisition. Do it my way.

Murphy goes on with his blah-blah-blah. I mentally replay Océane's audio message, now engraved in my head. I can't erase it. I imagine her soaked, on edge, hungry, and more and more uninhibited… Ready to rebel, to cross the line to reach me. This little sweetness has not yet understood. Our little-by-little foreplay has precisely this goal: to push her to the limit. I won't stop there…

The arousal must become unbearable, your blossoming slower. You think you've filled the gap, all by yourself like a big girl, but this gap needs more attention.

"Tell me, Murphy, do you play poker?" I continue to stretch Miss Rousseau's waiting time.

I'm not going to run in like a horny doggie. Even with a stiff cock, my brain loves challenge and control too much to let anyone win. I like victories, only it is enjoyable for me only with obstacles erected on the road. And resistance…

"A little, yes," answers the doc, baffled.

"Good. Shall we play after dinner? Might as well brighten up your night on call to watch over Sophia."

"I'd love to."

"Perfect. We'll go into the small living room."

"That'll give us a chance to… chat, too. Maybe go over what to do about your wife?"

My jaws clench.

"We'll discuss it."

OCÉANE

The first ten minutes, rather proud of my shot, I watch. Hoping to see Tiger arrive. I'm gloating. I am overexcited by my disobedience. He's going to join me, to impose his power with his body, his sex appeal, and that volcano in his eyes. I want him to fight back! Wildly. Intensely. Until the end of the night.

And I'll be the one to push him away after driving him crazy. Great plan, right?

Twenty minutes pass. I go to see Sophia, so peaceful in the dark, nestled in her husband's king-size bed. Is he going to sleep with her tonight? What the fuck was I thinking? The blurred boundaries of this couple are unfathomable.

A half hour. Still nothing.

I go back to my room, less and less exhilarated. Maybe Tiger doesn't give a shit about my little incentive? His sublime wife is in a bad way, snuggled up in his sheets. He could very well have gone to bed with her. Or go out and fuck whoever he wants while a doctor he has to pay a fortune stands guard.

Forty-five minutes. Shit!

What if I had no more interest in his eyes now that I've liquefied in his arms? My surrender flattered his ego. God, I'm ridiculous! He has more impact on me than I do on him.

An hour of waiting. He doesn't react or even text me to comment on my little recording. I stare at my phone, dejected, then decide to call Louane. I tell my ex-roommate some nonsense to justify my change of mind about the accommodation.

Discouraged, I pick out my five-star dinner from a tray in the bedroom. I try to clear my head, to reconsider this unspeakable "relationship" with lightness, and take things as they come. I may claim not to be a toy at the disposal of Tiger Sexton, but my desires and my behavior may not serve me well…

And then, as if this mess wasn't enough, I start to feel a certain attachment to Sophia. And to worry about her in this ambiguous situation. The sexual chemistry between her husband and me affects my brain. I'm playing with fire, unprepared for the backlash. Turning on Tiger to teach him a lesson is one thing, but getting lost in the fire is another.

The arrival of an SMS stops my introspection. Almost two and a half hours have passed. It's from Tiger.

My first part of the evening with Murphy was boring. Do you prefer to continue your solo mini exploration or join me?

What's he doing to me now?

I try to guess the effect of my little special dispatch on him without success. At best, it entertained him for three seconds, and now I look like a kid not up to his experience level. At worst, it didn't even touch him because he's been in more challenging situations with hotties. Damn! My confidence is gone, and I don't know how to react. I start to feel like a loser and give up answering him. Let him draw conclusions; suppose I'm busy looking for the pleasure that his hands have distilled in me with my own hands. Let him imagine what he wants. I stay stuck there procrastinating until I receive a second text message.

I'm not a dessert person. But I'm in the mood for sugar and a night swim. Up for it?

He comes back to play the pyromaniac, and my interest is awakened against my will. I hesitate without being able to prevent myself from being moved. I wanted to arouse him, and he manages once again to disturb me without effort.

Pffff! Okay, but he doesn't have to know that. It's up to you to learn how to sharpen your game.

I think about it and end up writing to him:

Maybe I'm having too much fun to go hang out in a bikini with Dr. Murphy and you.

His response is slow to come. Have I managed to turn the situation to my advantage? He finally shows up.

I suggested to the doc to go settle down in a guest room prepared for him. There's only you, your little body feverish + me, one of Mary's pastry specialties and the pool.

Sexton almost naked, a carb-rich treat, and the moonlit infinity pool? My pulses race loosely, my free will clashing with my hormones. I look down at my barely started meal with a defeated sigh. I should make him wait in turn, give him a symbolic "no thanks, I'm not hungry anymore," just for my personal pride and the thrill of pissing him off. Not hungry for him, not hungry for food. Yes, I should, but unfortunately, my appetite kills my will and makes me send something else back:

The pool and the cake are your only convincing arguments. I'll come to see them more closely...

TIGER

I smile when I receive the last message from Océane. Thoroughgoing and vibrant. The disadvantage of this little temperament is that she easily reveals her strong and weak points. I will better prepare my offensive. I start a few lengths to clear my mind of Murphy's words and I feel impatient to see Miss Rousseau's pretty face again.

She appears a while later. She is my first sight when my head emerges from the water: standing far from the pool, her mouth full of cake, a small spoon in her hand. Her doe eyes are filled with mischief. Under the lighting of the terrace, I notice a white spot at the corner of her lips. I moisten mine.

"By the way, how's your hand?" worries Océane. "Maybe you should have avoided getting it wet, no?"

Shit, I forgot the wound! At worst, the bandage will have to be redone… later. At the moment, I don't care.

"Don't worry about it," I tell her. "So, this cake?"

Océane takes a bite.

"I was right; this cake deserved that I come down," she mumbles without having finished swallowing. "This chocolate fondant heart, hummm…"

She gulps down another piece. Mary, our personal chef, is quite good at culinary creations. My gaze tries to tear itself away from the mouth of this libido agitator to caress her silhouette. It lingers on her dress. What's underneath? Does she intend to swim or just stuff herself as a delicious little gourmet under my eyes?

Let's check that.

I press my palms against the edge of the pool, lean on it, and pull myself out of the water. Océane suddenly starts coughing. Well, well, it looks like she is choking on her bite. She tries to calm down her cough. I move forward, and her pupils come alive on my dripping body, stopping in the southern part. On my cock in my bathing suit, which struggles to make itself discrete. Her ogling goes up my thighs, up my chest, my torso, the tattoo crossing all my right flank. The marks… Her attention reaches my neck, my mocking smile, and my nose. She swallows, riveting her gaze to my pupils, which are certainly dilated.

Watch out, glutton. You'll swallow wrong.

Her cheekbones turn pink, and she tries to regulate her breathing. But she can't fake it; that's the most entertaining part.

"Aren't you going to give me a taste?" I say, approaching her without worrying about looking for a towel.

"No… And you're soaked."

"A very pertinent remark," I reply, amused to feel her suddenly less sure of herself.

She becomes as intimidated as at the very beginning, before her discovery about our expectations… Having revealed my desire for her and then having frustrated her afterward gives a new dimension to her disconcert. I take this opportunity to tease her even more closely.

"I'm multitasking, you know? I may very well be soaked and lick this—"

"Lick?" she repeats.

Too late, I hug her and stick her against my wet skin. The space is shrinking between her breath and mine. I stick out my tongue to lap up the cream on her. A note of passion fruit? I feel her quiver; I deviate and gently suck her lip. I confirm there is passion fruit.

"To lick you. Like that, you see?" I whisper to her while doing it again.

The taste of cream and hers mingle on my taste buds. Even her lukewarm breath tastes like fruity delight. But she tries to pull herself together.

"Stop… I won't be your… dessert tonight, Tiger."

"Who said anything about eating you tonight?"

She proudly raises her beautiful face; a flash of defiance is again lodged in her irises.

"We agree then. I don't need a *Touche-pipi*," she tells me.

"What?"

She raises an eyebrow. Her features light up. She regains her sense of provocation.

"It's a French expression. Didn't you learn that in the kind of elite boarding school and college you must have attended?" she mocks me.

She tries to undo my embrace, and I tighten her. Her hands move to my chest. There's no need to tell her about my schooling or share such personal details with her.

I'm not the kind of "customer" who pays to chat, as the luxury chicks I order from prestigious agencies know. Problem: this girl isn't "in the business" and she turns me on differently, much harder, and for more than one night.

Her cheeky little smile points me to the most likely translation of what she just said to me. Literally, that would be… No, I think I get it. My smile widens.

"*Touche-pipi* is your equivalent of play doctors and nurses?" I deduce.

"Bravo, Mr. Sex! So, we won't play doctor; the cake is much more satisfying. Chocolate is more enjoyable."

"Is it?"

"Uh-huh. Let me go now."

I release her with one hand to grab her fingers. Before she pushes me away completely, I place them on my lower stomach and slowly slide lower.

"Do you feel that, Océane? It's not a kid's game; I want a stronger orgasm with you. If you looked beyond the immediate frustration, you would see that I'm… courting your pleasure, taming it, fanning it. I will feed it, desire it to the very limit of both of us. And then, when we no longer hold on, when we can't hold it any longer, when it consumes us too much to be contained, it'll explode, and you'll understand why it was worth the wait."

She integrates my words, and her beads darkened. No more bravado, she sways. I press her palm against my erection, staring at her.

"No *Touche-pipi*, this is prolonged foreplay, sweet Lily. Why fuck in a hurry when I can revel in the lack, get hard for you until it hurts, and not have you right away so I can savor you better, implode when the finale comes?"

"Damn… Is that what you want?"

Her tone is eroding, and I think she's starting to look at things from a different angle.

"Yes, that's what I want."

"How long can you go on like this? Without… trying to cum afterward? Zero orgasm?"

"You thought I only liked to control other people? Maybe I overestimated you and your ability to keep up with me?"

My targeted jab works. She blinks, surprised, intrigued, but above all, ready to rebel again for the pleasure of braving me.

"If you can do it, I can too," she rebels as expected.

What was I saying… Barely masking my amusement, I counterattack, "I doubt it, sweet Lily."

"Why?"

"You masturbated at the first opportunity."

"Well, because I… Each of us is free to do what we want with our body, aren't we?"

"Right…"

My eyes are laughing, seeing her on the defensive. Océane moves back; I don't move. She puts on her insolent air and goes back to the table. Is she already giving up the game? She takes a spoonful of cake and puts it in her mouth, and I detect the change in her eyes. This glow…

She then begins a languorous stripping. When she starts to unbutton her dress, feel my heart rate quicken exponentially, seeing what there is underneath. I contract, salivate at the idea of touching her again, of kissing her, of dragging her in the pool, on a deckchair, on the ground or this table, and to—

"Prove to me how well you can control your erection, Tiger. Lust after me. Show me how you stretch foreplay to infinity…"

Holy shit!

24

TIGER

My gorgeous temptress thinks she's in control of my unequivocal erection. It's cute and damn stimulating to feel her so happy with herself…

I don't give up; I whisper to her, "Up for it if you prove to me that you're up to it."

A number of partners have come before you, my sweet.

Including my wife. Beautiful plants to gather, to make bloom, to ransack with ardor, to wither… Some had their methods. Océane is adopting a specific one of her own; it gives a delicate novelty to the thing…

"I do, you know that," she reminds me. "Otherwise, you wouldn't be lurking like a predator around your *au pair*."

"Maybe I'm just curious to see if you're worth my time. Is that what you want?"

"Maybe…"

"Well. I told you before, having me inside you is to be earned, beauty. All the higher steps, ditto."

My indecent statement hovers for a few seconds in the warm air of this evening. Océane displays an exciting false modesty. She refrains from replying. Instead, she sensually reveals her velvety epidermis to me.

"Uh-huh…" she notes, showing me the absence of a bathing suit under her dress.

Damn, this piece of fabric has a terrible effect on my lower abdomen. The curve of Océane's breasts under the transparency of her bra, the satiny triangle under that of her panties, and everything else captivates me.

"Come here," I tell her, my voice hoarse and feverish.

She drags on purpose and puts my nerves to a hard test. Her dress falls to her bare feet without the slightest sound. She moves forward and challenges me.

"Are you going to show me, Tiger?"

"Shut that pretty mouth and come over here if you want to know."

Smiles of complicity, my desire goes crescendo. Her mischievous look and her exposed semi-nudity consume me.

"I don't like to take orders," murmurs Océane.

I catch her. Our breaths come together. I circle her waist, pressing her against me.

"Too bad, obeying could be so much fun… Leave the controls to me, for your pleasure and mine."

Our lips play hide-and-seek, seek each other, flee from each other, open up, and touch each other. She fights. My tongue coaxes her, encouraging her to open her mouth wider. Our breaths mix. One of my hands slides on her neck and slips under her hair to tilt and hold her head. A light sigh escapes from her, and it intoxicates me.

"Um… try to convince me then, Mr. Sex."

"I'm planning on it, Miss Rousseau."

I lift her up, bust to bust.

"You're always wet," she complains for the sake of argument.

"You too," I say with confidence.

I am obviously no longer talking about drops of water from the swimming pool. The redness of her cheekbones shows that she has understood. Yet she whispers to me, "Not at all."

"Watch out. I punish for big lies like that," I promise her.

"You punish? Oh, I'm scared…"

Player! I moisten my lips and eat her with my eyes. I take her to the table and sweep what is there to install her butt, which looks good enough to eat. Her thighs spread, leaving me space to stand in front of her. Her arms on my shoulders, Océane tries to look confident. Even if I begin to detect the signals emitted by her body. My fingers pass behind her, unclasping her lingerie without hiding my lust. My irises speak for me while I slide her straps and reveal little by little her breast, partially repressing my appetite. The prospect of kissing her without giving in to this desire is diabolically motivating. A delicious torture, for her, for me. We remain in this contemplation for a long time without words or gestures.

Her arousal increases, her skin texture bristles, and the pink of her cheeks turn red. And her pupils, damn, they are fascinating. I observe her with a magnifying glass, memorizing everything about her without haste. The tension rises, suffocating, magnetic. I brush against her earlobe. She shivers, unsure. I push her hair and caress the discreet tattoo that I had seen in this area. Numbers. She tenses up; I ask no questions. I already have the answers in her file compiled by my security staff. She knows it now… And I prefer to avoid her questions about mine…

I come back to her pretty face and immerse myself in her green marbles. I go around her face, and my fingers brush her lips. Hers burn the epidermis of my back.

"Are you still hungry, sweet Lily?"

"It depends…" she says.

I barely move; time to grab the passion-chocolate dessert she started without me. And I say, "I'm terribly hungry. You didn't offer me a single bite earlier. Shall we start again?"

Her raised eyebrows and the gleam in her eyes increase tenfold the ardor lurking in my crotch. I grab her wrist, direct her hand towards the cake and tell her, "Give me a taste, Océane. Now."

"Have I ever told you that I don't like orders?"

"Do it," I say again, firmer, more convincing.

The surprise can be read on her face, her emotion too. I'm not screaming; I'm not forcing her. She is simply discovering her limited options. Lady Candice and the whole panoply of dominatrixes I used when I was eighteen would find her almost as indocile as I was. And it's all the more thrilling to push the limits…

"What if I refuse?" Océane whispers to me.

"Then you will be free to go. From this table, from my house. Tonight. Deal done. No bonuses. No more negotiations. No more contact with Sophia or me."

I stay firm and probe her. She swallows her saliva and takes a deep breath. Her chest rises and attracts my gaze. Océane tries to know if it is a bluff or pressure. Except for my desire, she doesn't perceive any more of my emotions. That, I know how to lock. Access is prohibited to anyone, business partner, sex partner, or anyone. I'm just going to turn things around, make things go my way in the future.

"I can leave whenever I want, Tiger. In fact, I'll play as long as I'm having as much fun as you are, as long as I want to. Got it?"

Her defiant face increases my pleasure tenfold. Okay, no power struggle, the balance of power, she'll feel it when I'm inside her… I'll find a way to keep full power over the essentials.

"Got it, Lily. I'm good with that."

Satisfied with her development, Océane ignores the spoons. Her fingers sink into the cake and return with a creamy piece in front of my mouth. I wrap her wrist and bring her closer to me, devouring her with my eyes.

"I want it… there," I tell her, gently leading her hand back to her.

The revamped, creamier lamington crashes on her lips. I continue. A trail of creamy foam slowly marks the passage I create on her body. Her neck, her areolas, the tender space between her breasts. The dessert crumbles on her, sticks to her skin down to her belly, and makes her shiver.

"That's better. And so much more appetizing," I comment before finally retrieving smudged fingers and stuffing them in my mouth.

I begin to taste, my irises locked in hers. My tongue wraps around each finger and licks delicately all along, then slips between them. Then gets between them. My lips stop in the hollow of her palm; Océane stifles a moan.

"I have some almost everywhere," she tells me, her voice hoarse.

My eyes slide for a moment on her nipples; I sketch a smile while going up toward her mouth, which she licks in return.

"That can be solved. What's on there is mine. You, you've already eaten, glutton," I warn her.

"Damn, Tiger… You…"

I capture her. The rest is lost on my taste buds in a voracious kiss. Each of us rediscovers the taste of cake on the other's tongue. I kiss her breathlessly. An eternity later, without being satiated, I fork on the sweet way which marks out her curves and her hollows.

To savor her skin, to suck it, to nibble it. When I reach her breast, covered with fruity foam, Océane clings to my hair. She gasps and arches her back, her tips hardening under my tongue. I devour all I have sown on her, patiently, at length. She loses her footing. I incite her to lie down and take advantage of it to take off her panties. I straighten up with the lingerie and caress her while turning back to her neck. Her last sigh dies on the red fabric when I push it gently in her mouth like a gag and whisper to her, "You may need it to keep from screaming…"

She questions me with her beautiful intoxicated eyes. I keep her lying down, take hold of her calves and pull them to have her pelvis closer to me. One of my palms presses on her lower abdomen, and my hunger spreads further south. Her "hum" of pleasure is muffled for a time. Will she hold and keep the lingerie in place? This is the first test.

"Holy cow, Tiger," she groans when she feels the freshness of the cream I spread on her pubis.

Gone is the gag. I have the answer to my test: she's not a docile one, and I like that. I smile in anticipation. I touch her big lips and coat her bud to better enjoy her moans and contortions. My index finger and my tongue venture into her soft perfumed sheath. Océane mumbles incoherent remarks, arches her back, and stretches my name. Hungry, I infiltrate between her folds. Her intimate essence sublimates the delights that permeate my palate. The more I penetrate her, the more the fragrances intermingle and make me insatiable. Her thighs against my temples, her small hands in my hair, she is invaded by jolts that amplifies, following the rhythm of my tasting. She stiffens and begs me not to stop, saying, "Oh yes."

I linger on a sensitive point, dragging her to the edge of sensory madness. Her pleasure threatens to reach great heights. It's time… I go up and kiss her groin, her fleece, her navel. I help her to straighten up on the table and lick her again while going back to her chest, of which I nibble the erect extremities. I knead her flesh, scratch her, nibble her from bottom to top. She suffocates, claws me, and sucks me in the neck when I join her mouth to absorb her complaints. Our moist and sticky skins heat up and rub each other.

Océane tries to slip a wandering hand under my bathing suit. My muscles contract, full of desire. She succeeds, and our tongues race as she massages my cock. I lose my breath in her throat; my eyelids droop, and my dick stiffens to the extreme.

"Fuck, it makes you want to have more desserts," I confide to her while trying to put a stop to it.

"We agree," she purrs, bewitchingly naughty.

"You know we'll have to put the brakes on now?"

"No… You're annoying," she rebels with a delicious smile on her swollen lips.

My forehead comes against hers, and just to recover some phlegm, I seize her wrist to prevent her from palpating my erection more. I finally immerse myself in her eyes with a teasing smile.

"Do you promise me you won't go on alone?"

"I don't know if I can promise such a stupid thing," Océane replies, her cheekbones reddened, her pupils dilated.

"I feel you can," I assure her in a low voice.

She smiles at me, her fingernails running over me.

"And you, what says to me that you won't break your own rules?" she asks me.

"I'll stick to it. You have my word. Besides, I don't know what time it is anymore, but…"

I check my watch. Shit! I only have ten minutes left now.

"Argh! I have a video conference. I will barely have time to clean up and put something on before I get to work."

At first incredulous, Océane widens her eyes and then ends up heaving a sigh.

"Are you going to work now? A meeting in the middle of the night?"

"Sometimes I have to bend to other time zones."

She doesn't move. Neither do I. We observe each other; the caresses bloom again. My fingers can't leave her curves. My irises dig into her, encouraging her to gradually trust me. The kind of confidence that one doesn't contractualize, which is created between two people… patiently, skillfully.

"Fine," she finally capitulates… "What am I going to do?"

I think to suggest her something to occupy her.

"Swimming, for example. Or watch a movie? Whatever you like. You have free access to my movie room now. The staff will bring you drinks and snacks…"

She pouts at me; I freeze for a moment on her mouth, trying to channel that still burning need to go down on her.

"So you're offering to drown my frustration," complains Océane, encircling me with her legs, her arms on my shoulders.

Amused, I dig my fingers into her disheveled hair. The clock is ticking, but I enjoy feeling her being a little more accommodating.

"You'll get a reward if you hold this time."

She wrinkles her pretty little nose, puzzled.

"You want to buy my cooperation?" she asks.

"No, I want to earn it. I'm going to win it," I say calmly. "And you will obey, just for fun, remember."

"Yeah…"

Then she laughs and shakes her head to contradict me. I steal a kiss from her; then I manage to free myself. I glance at the watch on my wrist. It's starting to get urgent.

"Sorry, Miss Rousseau. I really have to run. We'll resume negotiations tomorrow."

"You torturer," she reproaches me with a mischievous smile. "I understand better where your reputation as a tough and inflexible businessman comes from."

I burst out laughing as I bent down to retrieve my phone from a deckchair. She throws her panties at me, and they don't reach their target.

"Have a good laugh; I haven't said my last word," she challenges me.

"I hope so. I hate games that are won in advance. Challenges excite me much more."

I pick up her lingerie and head for the patio door with it.

"Tiger, give me that back!" she asks me.

"No, this piece of fabric belongs to me. It will sit on my desk tonight like a first trophy," I say to her as I walk away.

I hear a tiny noise. Turning around, I notice she has just sent me her bra as a second projectile. Missed again! She sticks her tongue out at me, unaware of the image she sends back. Under the insistence of my gaze, her arms try to cover her pubis and her breasts. Exposed, gorgeous under the moonlight. Then she shrugs her shoulders and heads back to the pool naked. Damn, fuck, she will get what is coming for her. Always eager for her, I struggle to take my eyes off her body when she jumps into the water. Her head reappears three seconds later.

"Who knows, you might find it hard to focus knowing I'm there," prophesies Océane in the splash of her midnight bath.

She doesn't admit defeat. I lick my lips and deny my turn. This picture will be engraved on my retinas for the rest of the night; I have no doubt about it.

But the arousal won't stop me from working, Blondie. You won't change a thing.

Before I rush inside, an idea springs to mind. I stop and turn around. She is still looking at me.

"By the way, I have another option if you will do me this favor."

"Like what?" Océane's suspicious, pushing her wet hair back.

"I'm going to work late… When you're sleepy, can you slip into my bed and keep Sophia company tonight? It reassures her when she is in this state."

Even at a distance, I perceive a certain shock on Océane's face. No more carnal games and other teasing. A different reality pierces the bubble: my wife.

"Uh… yeah. Okay, I'll sleep with her."

I wink at her as a thank you and disappear from her sight.

OCÉANE

Tiger's request freezes me for a moment. I realize with discomfort the paradoxical situation I have put myself in. Despite the complicity we have just shared, his wife remains the center of his preoccupations. Which makes sense. But a kind of mental cold shower named Sophia is also holding me back.

I am getting lost in them… One after the other…

I dive back into the turquoise water and exhaust myself by swimming a few lengths so as not to start thinking again and strain my neurons. About their relationship, about me, and where it all leads me. How will this end? Even if I should reactivate my brain high on pheromones and listen to my reason…

At the children's home, Myriam advised me to live my life freely and let go. But maybe not as much? I feel like I can't find the right balance.

Several lengths later, I get out and wrap myself in a towel. I get my bra and my dress to enter the Sexton fortress. Under the shower, my eyelids closed, I replay the caresses, the kisses, and the torrid cunnilingus lavished by Tiger. I was again close to the peaks, feeling the orgasm on the edge of my body. Strangely, having flirted with an orgasm without reaching it is no longer just a sensory frustration. But I can't identify the feeling or the sensations that it awakens in me. Why do I keep shivering just thinking about Tiger, imagining how far he'll go next?

Damn, I feel like I'm enjoying it!

I dry myself, dry my hair and tame it in front of the mirror. I barely recognize my reflection, this gleam in my pupils. As if a facet of me, titillated by vice, grew in contact with this couple. Everything is so singular, unconventional, and different from what I am and believe I have always known. I feel… different, excited, and not just physically. For the first time, I feel a nagging curiosity growing within me. The curiosity to explore other facets of my sexuality. It scares me to admit it. I freeze and contemplate my face, my neck still marked by the assaults of Tiger's passionate mouth. His teeth on my lips, his tongue… A sigh betrays me.

I spread a dab of moisturizer on my skin and put on a pair of panties and one of the nighties I bought while shopping with Sophia. Introspectively, I walk along Mrs. Sexton's wing to join her in her husband's. This is crazy. I feel weird sneaking into a bed next to a sleeping woman after pulsing in her husband's arms.

There is nothing conventional between the three of us anymore… They are blurring the marks and boundaries I am used to. My meager certainties are slowly crumbling under my feet…

I take pleasure in this disorientation of the senses and emotions. So carpe diem, even if a small part of me wonders if there will be a reverse side one day…

25

OCÉANE

The bed is huge and comfortable; nevertheless, I can't relax. I play on my phone and watch Sophia from time to time by the light of the screen. She seems so peaceful and vulnerable. She doesn't even suspect I'm there or what I've done with her man. Damn it! As much as I know about the liberties in their relationship, their out-of-line extras, it's hard for me to handle the facts with the same naturalness they do.

And then, there are still some gray areas…

When Tiger told me that having someone with her tonight would calm her down, he seemed to know what he was talking about. As if the situation was recurring… Is Sophia often in this state? Will I ever know the real cause? What does her husband usually do in these cases? Does he exceptionally accept her between his sheets and in his arms? For a moment, I imagine him touching her, making his wife's golden skin blossom with the burning attentions to which I was entitled…

You are losing your mind, Océane.

Gee, even my thoughts are getting lewd, straying from the boundaries and tingling my heart in spite of myself. I have a hard time minimizing that little inexplicable twinge when I remember that they are married. I'm just a distracting, temporary fixture. I have agreed to this. Nevertheless, the more my hosts integrate me into their couple, their daily life, and their intimacy, the more I have trouble finding my way in. The physical closeness between Tiger and me threatens to worsen this mess in my synapses and my emotions. Absolutely have to keep this in the "special sexual experience" box, a "fun adult moment" where no one will become permanently attached to anyone. I'm going to make sure of that... And never let this threesome shake some of my psychological barriers, turn my world upside down.

There are three of us... Even when I'm alone with Tiger... He and Sophia are an inseparable pair. Don't forget that.

By dint of repeating it to myself, the fatigue starts to soften my body and brain. I abandon my phone on a bedside table and sink under the comforter. I toss and turn, unable to get comfortable. The smell of Tiger without Tiger around and Sophia next to me is a confusing amalgam. I close my eyelids and find his eyes again. Filled with desire.

Damn, Océane, why are you still here?

My nose sniffs the pillow; my suppositions tumble around in my exhausted skull. Little by little, Morpheus gains ground in this chaos. Sophia mumbles and moves. I stop breathing when she rolls towards me and snuggles against my back. Oh, shit, she has no clothes on! What do I do? She emits a rambling gibberish, then something akin to a "Thank you..."

Who is it for? Her "new contract friend?" Or to the man she loves so much? I assume she is dreaming of her Ty and thinks she is embracing him, curling up against me. His manly body is very different from mine, but after all, I'm not supposed to be here, in Tiger's place. In his room, his previously impassable sanctuary. Sophia is light years away from my inner conflict. She presses herself against me and wraps her leg around me. My attempts to disengage myself delicately fail. She tightens me by mumbling words similar to "don't abandon me, my sister." Her woozy, imploring voice shakes me; I stop insisting on trying to free myself.

I can only hope to push her away a little later. Or count sheep to put me to sleep too. Is it possible?

TIGER

In my office, I started my video conference. Although another screen also captures my interest. The night vision one of the property's video surveillance cameras. At first, I turned it on to keep an eye on Sophia's sleep even though Murphy was keeping watch in a room in my wing. I wasn't sure if Océane would comply with my request; it actually confused her. However, here she is. In my bed. She doesn't know about the cameras, and I don't normally look at the images either. The ones inside are usually deactivated when I'm there to preserve our privacy. Except in case of necessity, like tonight. This is just a security precaution most of the time.

To prevent Sophia from…

Fuck! I rummage through my hair to tame my thoughts. They come back to focus on the bewitching source of distraction in my lair. Océane.

I saw her tiptoe in, using the light from her phone to navigate her way through. Her feminine figure in a satin nightie still distracts my attention. A… booty call in my personal quarters is unusual and destabilizing. For my head, and for another part of my anatomy.

My interlocutors are discussing a potential investment in Europe. On one side, those who work for me; on the other, the two directors of the tourist company who are trying to lure me. Each of them is trying hard to present their arguments. I breathe in and interrupt them.

"I could consider a counter-proposal… My final decision will depend on the opinion I will have during my visit."

"We'd be honored to host it," says the CEO of the tourism company. "Your date will be our date, Mr. Sexton."

My team is waiting for my answer. In order to prepare a future trip to gauge the whole. I take the time to think for a few seconds and exchange glances through the screen with John, my CFO. Despite my concentration, my eyes still wander to the computer next door, quieter, and plunged into darkness. Has Océane fallen asleep? My wife has snuggled up to her; this infrared picture is becoming obsessive…

"Good," I say without taking my eyes off the image. "John will book a time slot that will suit my team to consider this trip. My assistant will contact you shortly."

"Great, Mr. Sexton. Thank you for your time; we'll wait to hear from your assistant then."

This subject is closed for the moment; the tour operator's

representatives say goodbye and disconnect. Leaving me in consultation with the TS Naval heads to continue the discussion on our possibilities of expansion on the European continent. I study the alternatives. My guys dig for the best angle. Offering TS Naval the opportunity to diversify our activities and establish ourselves in other territories is a project that I think my father would have liked. My ambitions and our strength today are beyond his expectations. He made the shipbuilding company he inherited stronger. Unfortunately, he did not have the time to make it grow further outside our borders and outside our first sector of activity.

Now it does, yet this thirst for more still grips me. I still don't feel fully up to the lineage…

It fires me up to focus on the essentials, to excel, and to leave no detail to chance. The interview gets longer. I comb through the analyses made by my experts, demanding sharp answers to my questions.

In my left palm, I crumple a piece of red cloth. My rational brain puts itself on hold as my thumb caresses Océane's panties. I contemplate again her blond hair spread on my pillow. Does she feel Sophia close by, or does she not realize it? Would she be inclined to… What if I joined them afterward?

No, the filter, Tiger!

"… I'll send you a summary email, Mr. Sexton."

"Perfect," I say, seemingly unperturbed.

Seeing Sophia and Océane like this brings to mind Murphy's more or less subtle remarks about the direction our sex life seems to be taking. During the poker game at the beginning of the evening, Sophia's therapist ended up being curious about Océane. His patient, my dear wife, had obviously not confided this to him during their sessions… Deep down, we all know that a lack of control would shatter things.

This warning does not leave my mind during the rest of the meeting with John.

OCÉANE

How long did I doze? Because when I become aware of my surroundings, I feel a body curled up against mine. Then a second one.

Oh, shit, there are two? Sophia and…

"Were you waiting for me, sweet Lily?" confirms the husky sound of Tiger's voice in my ear as his large hands brush against my skin.

I recognize them on contact; I feel them embracing my curves. It's so sudden, and yet not surprising. Maybe because a part of me was hoping for this kind of outburst? Did I secretly want Tiger to come? For him to join us? To join me? God, I think so, and I quiver with pleasure. His bandage scratches me slightly and reminds me that I am about to go further into the intimacy of two people at the same time. Getting closer to him brings me inevitably closer to her. And vice versa. My hormones, my limits, and my thoughts become foggy. I am literally at the heart of their couple, sandwiched in their duo, caught on both sides by different sensations, emotions, and feelings.

What am I doing? What doors am I opening? Where am I stepping?

In the semi-darkness, in a bed haloed by the brightness of the moon outside, Tiger's greedy hands leave me to wander over other female curves. I guess that he touches Sophia. This one, finally rested, moves lasciviously; she rubs herself against me. Or against him, taking me in the vice of their embrace. On the one hand, I am relieved that she is well, but also very confused to be doing with her what I do…

This is going too far, isn't it? Where is the point of no return? Why don't I say stop?

I know it's going to turn upside down; Tiger makes me lose my bearings. It all shifts to something else, to a world that is unknown to me. Because he is there, he arouses me to the highest point. This body entanglement tastes like a drug, a bewitching flavor of forbidden fruit. The two together diffuse in me a je-ne-sais-quoi of euphoria.

I feel weak, tempted, curious…

"I'm glad you're feeling better," Tiger whispers to Sophia.

"For such a welcome, I should break more often," whispers Sophia.

Her breasts press against my back. Feline, soft. At the same moment, her husband's fingers sink into my hair and bring my mouth back against his: expert, passionate. He shakes me, takes me in a shivering voluptuousness, and opens wider this intimate door that he has unlocked. He erases the established limits, all that I clung to until then. A deviant pleasure and an intoxicating disorder germinate in me. My ambivalent sensations increase tenfold when I feel Sophia's lips spreading delicate kisses on my shoulders and neck. The situation is unusual, unexpected, and disturbing, but I find myself savoring this budding three-way connection. They form a pair of sensuality and lust around me. They make me shake, more and more intoxicated and lost…

What the hell am I doing?

Both of them touch me with such naturalness. Sophia suavely releases my hair; her gestures contrast with the raw desire of her husband. He devours me with ardor as if he had thought only of that for hours. Her, she caresses me through the silk of my nightie, kisses my skin, and whispers to me, "I'm glad you're here."

Is this for her man or for me?

My brain turns to cotton, and my senses give in to temptation. Tiger flips me onto my back and straightens up to kiss his wife above me. Breathing hard, I look at them without knowing what to do or daring to move. Intimidated by the turn of events, afraid to want more.

Tiger comes back to me, hungry and aroused, and he makes me feel it by lifting me up and pressing me against him. Kneeling, we are joined by Sophia, who sticks her bust against my back. Their hands brush me, massage me, and cross my body. I realize that I am the only one who is still dressed among them. Tiger's erection presses against my groin while his wife wraps her palms around my breasts and titillates the tips through the satin fabric. Her lover kneads my ass and presses me harder.

"What am I going to do with two women in my bed?" he growls in my ear.

"I have a small idea on the question," teases Sophia. "What about if you removed all that first, my darling," she whispers to me then.

Joining the gesture to the word, she slowly rolls up my small dress. Stunned by my own audacity, I let myself be taken care of. My arms are raised in order to help her. A sigh escapes me when Tiger seizes the opportunity to catch my nipples, one between his teeth, the other between his fingers.

Oh shit…

"We want you," says Tiger.

"Really want you," Sophia confirms to me.

He kneads my breast, sucks, blows, sucks. His avid virility and the liquefying subtlety of his wife are deployed together on me. Two mouths, four hands, bandaged muscles, and supple curves… The thesis and antithesis of an insidious euphoria in my veins, in my neurons. I should say stop; this is definitely going too far. I've never done this, never even fantasized about something like this. It's crazy and frightening. Yes, I should say stop, but I moan, "Oh yes…"

And that's when I lose what little control I had left. Tiger, nimble and skillful, drops me on the mattress. On my stomach. His rigid cock pulses against the crack of my butt, and his breath invites itself on my hair. He seeks my ear and growls to me, "Do you think I'm going to make you cum this time or punish you by only fucking Sophia while you watch us?"

"Punish her, my Ty," intimates Sophia, completely aroused. "No, come here and punish me first; I was very naughty."

He abandons me and grabs her to lay her in the same position as me. Then, his arm passes under her, between the sheets and the body of Sophia. Tiger pulls her towards him and penetrates her without bluntness.

"You are right, my dear wife. You were a very naughty girl," he says by assailing her a rough thrust.

Sophia hollows her back and stares at me while moaning, looking feverish and fulfilled.

"Argh, yes! Fuck me, Ty. Let her languish," she sighs.

He grabs the hips of his beautiful woman and sinks into her once again.

"Like this?"

"Oh, yes! I like to have you back."

"Me too. She played her part perfectly; your find rekindled the flame."

What's he…

This sentence gets into me, sly, and painful to hear. The sulfurous pleasure it has made in me in their arms gradually becomes an unpleasant impression. They are still as exalted. Tiger penetrates Sophia again, who arches her back. Their moans are echoed in my head. With a dry mouth, I become aware that they put me in the second plan. I try to free myself, not so sure of what is happening.

"Yes, I… I did the right thing by hiring her," Sophia says, shaken by her husband's powerful thrusts.

Their heads turn in my direction. I can't miss the intensity of Tiger's pupils bursting with arousal because that's the one I'm staring at. In shock, I wait, hoping for an answer from him that wouldn't hurt me so much. Maybe Sophia is still rambling a bit, but he knows he begged me to stay. He told me how much he wanted and needed me.

Say it, Tiger. Tell me again…

"I am not sure…" he says.

I blink, suddenly cold. What's he doing?

"She hasn't convinced me yet," he concludes. "We should extend her trial period."

"What?" I squeak.

"You're going to have to give us more, sweetheart," Sophia's moaning voice whispers to me.

A wave of suffocating heat invades me; I feel oppressed now. Tiger repeats; it sounds like echoes in my foggy brain. I close my eyes and shake my head. My heart is racing. My breath, ditto. I am agitated. Suddenly, my eyelids open.

The heat is still perceptible. It comes from Sophia's body, slouched over mine. I can't help but tap behind me, looking for the third member of our trio.

He's not there. Of course, he isn't. Fucking erotic nightmare! It was just a dream, and I believed it… or hoped it until the end. What's wrong with me?

Damn it; it's official: I'm going astray! And Sophia is too close, which amplifies my uneasiness. I am almost afraid to fall asleep again.

Fear of the barriers that are breaking down in me. It is the chaos in my head.

26

OCÉANE

Is that background music I hear? I stretch. A languid voice and clean instrumental notes seep into my ears. I keep my eyes closed to wake up gently. Far from the confusing dream I had last night, which seemed much too real at the time. I had a hard time falling asleep again.

Now I'm filled with doubts and questions. Not just about the Sextons. But also of my own… expectations?

Do I have any unacknowledged desires? Threesomes, another woman…

I don't fucking know anymore; I can't trust my completely broken-down reference points. Lost, I try to chase away these unheard thoughts by trying to identify the music I hear. It sounds like Sia's voice. This curiosity pushes me to open my eyelids to grab my phone to use the Shazam app to make sure.

I freeze at first glance in the dim light of the day coming through the blinds. Because I meet Sophia's eyes. Unsettling, contemplating me.

"Good morning, you," she whispers to me without an ounce of surprise to discover me near her.

At the same time, she seems to have been awake for several minutes. Arm bent, supporting her head, she is lying next to me and perhaps observed me for a while. I sit down, a little embarrassed.

"Oh… hi," I answer. "Sleep well? How are you feeling?"

"Headache, a little confused… You, me, Tiger's bed… Can you explain?"

"Erm…"

"Did we…"

Shit, I'm blushing. Her forehead wrinkles, her sentence hanging in the air. I flounder, then notice that the idea of the *three of us together* doesn't seem to unsettle her. New discomfort…

"Oh, no!" I pull myself together. "I was just… keeping you company. Your husband was working late, I think."

"I see."

I moisten my lips, embarrassed to show signs of my dirty little game with Tiger when Sophia was not operational. Or of the destabilizing erotic scene they both generated in my sleep.

My fantasy box has gone mad; you've smashed it.

"Relax, Océane," Sophia says before lying back down completely and closing her eyes. "A threesome wouldn't have been a first for Ty or for me."

Damn!

Okay, I could have guessed; their unbridled sexuality is no longer a surprise. But the naturalness with which they take on these types of multiple combinations is too new for me. The interference deep inside me, in my habits and certainties from before, is felt. I can no longer find the right attitude to adopt in my shaken "normality."

Originally, I would have left this residence yesterday if Sophia hadn't had this "drug and alcohol problem." And I wouldn't be here asking myself questions I never asked myself about them, about myself. Was it just my concern for Sophia Sexton that made me stay? Or was it the tempting muscular, charismatic sex appeal of her husband?

Our fucking chemistry.

Are you afraid it's all of these at once? Or something more licentious and confusing? Would the two Sextons make you feel something… different, each of them?

"Do you need anything, Sophia?" I ask, caught off guard by this questioning.

I think I'm having a hard time assuming and understanding my dream. My presence in their marital intimacy is like entering a secret and too-private bubble, intended for two.

Sophia doesn't move. The music fills the silence. And the silence doesn't help me.

"Dr. Murphy should be around here somewhere, I think," I add. "Can I get you a coffee, breakfast, or something?"

I may be confused this morning, but one thing remains clear: I am worried about Sophia. Her meltdown yesterday left a lasting impression on me. She asked me for some joy and needed a friend to be there for her. I really want to be her friend right now. I would like to know how she feels. But I don't dare push her to confide in me, for fear of being too invasive or of committing an error. Eyelids closed, she seems to me… absent. Is she having a bad descent? I don't know if that happens with the mixture she's taken. Maybe she's just trying to sort out her thoughts, her memories of yesterday.

What time is it anyway? And where is Tiger?

Darn! Thinking about Tiger brings back my own memories. It gets complicated… Demotivated, I lie down. Or rather, I fall backward like a mass. In Mr. Sexton's king-size bed, next to his naked wife. Everything's for the best in the best of all possible worlds, right? I was hoping to break my chains, to let go, and finally live fully despite the weight on my conscience. Now I couldn't have done any better. I am at the top of an emotional Everest, in a dense fog of unanswered questions.

I stare at the ceiling. The softness of the music does the talking for us. I am unable to do so. I finally recognize "Breathe Me" by Sia. I close my eyes and let myself get carried away. The sound is melancholic, heady, a bittersweet pleasure that echoes in the master's den.

Where are you, Tiger? What's next?

I am now entangled between the two of them, and I think that's what my dream was about. I love being there for Sophia. At the same time, I hate this irrepressible desire to see her husband again. I want him to smile at me again, to devour me with his eyes. This uncontrollable thing torments me, making me feel like a poor girl in need of a dope, too unique, atypical, and ephemeral to take the risk to shoot up with it. Unfortunately, I have hardly tasted it, and I still want more.

I would like special and radically opposite moments with each other. Mr. Sexton for sex and Mrs. Sexton for friendship. Is it really compatible?

Sophia's sigh sounds like an echo of my inner drift. She starts humming about Sia. This incites me to listen more carefully to the lyrics. I turn to her, carried away by the wave of sadness that comes from the song.

"Sophia? Please talk to me."

I implore her so low that she may not have heard me. I doubt it until she gently opens her eyes again.

"I'm good with you, Océane."

"I'm good with you too. And I'm here for you. Tell me how you feel, right now."

Silence. She brushes my eyebrows and my cheek, then drops her hand and sighs again.

"That song…" she whispers. "Sometimes you come across lyrics that seem written for you. Has that ever happened to you?"

The words I hear are so painful that my heart sinks. Because if she recognizes herself in them, it is because she has bruises anchored in her. Bruises in her heart, in her soul. Tiger revealed it to me between the lines. I remember her words about Sophia. "Difficult childhood and teen years…" Obviously, he couldn't put all the pieces back together to fix her. Is this what led them into this singular spiral, free sexuality in their union? How is Tiger affected by the situation on his side?

I will find out. I want to know everything about them, not out of unhealthy curiosity but because they really captivate me. Each in their own way. I take a long breath of air and whisper, "No, I haven't found my song yet. But I really like this one."

With a faded smile on her lips, Sophia brings back her irises to me.

"I'll lend it to you then," she says to me, almost jokingly, if she had had the strength. "I could listen to it on a loop all day long. We'll let it be ours."

"Thank you… I'm fine with that. I love Sia. How about breakfast in bed with her?"

Sophia nods and extends her arm toward me. I take her hand, and our fingers intertwine. I pause my questions and my brain; I just anchor myself in the moment with her. To be there for her. And that seems to be enough for her to emerge little by little. I touch the hollow of her palm; she pulls me slightly. I let myself fall back next to her. Lying down, silent, each one tightly clutching the other's fingers.

Never mind. We'll eat later. Time doesn't matter anymore. I enter with her under a kind of invisible tent, vaporous and nostalgic. It turns me into a lost, hypersensitive, overwhelmed with compassion for Sophia, who holds me almost desperately. At this moment, we look more like two girlfriends than two strangers discovering each other. She needs a friend; I perceive it with such intensity. She needs a friend, she needs him, and she needs so many things I don't know yet… She is touching, fragile.

"I'm a little slow today. Tomorrow we'll do lots of things, okay?" she promises me.

"Don't worry. We'll stay in a calm atmosphere."

Our phalanxes lock together, and our arms brush against each other. Regular breaths. Our voices are paired when I start to sing with her.

Normally, this is my day off. I could have gone for a ride in a Volkswagen van like I dreamed about in Paris. Hanging out on the roads and beaches of Australia like a good little tourist, with the Michelin guide at the bottom of my bag. But I stay in bed in Tiger's den… with Sophia, and I get used to it. With a naturalness that is difficult to explain.

Soon the sexual attraction between Tiger and me will fade, Sophia will become strong again, and they will eject me from their lives.

Why does this prospect frighten me so much this morning?

The opening of the door surprises us. I see Tiger. He is shirtless, with a towel tied around his lower abdomen and a second one with which he rubs his hair. A beam of daylight enters with him through the half-open door. His blue eyes rest on us, and a slight smile graces his lips.

"Hello, ladies. Sorry, I need my dressing room," he says to us.

Sophia sits down and covers her chest with the comforter. Tiger's indecipherable gaze goes from his wife to me and back again.

"Did you sleep well?" he asks us.

"Sort of… How about you, Ty?" Sophia replies.

"Not really, I've been… working," he finishes, staring at me. "Aren't you off at the beginning of the week, Océane?"

I fidget, embarrassed, terribly blushing, as if he could guess just by looking at me what I dreamed last night. And everything that's been going through my head since…

"Well, yes. But I don't mind staying with Sophia."

"No," protests Tiger. "Enjoy your two days. I got ahead of schedule so I could spend time with you today," he says to his wife. "You know what we do when you lose it like that, don't you?"

She tensed up; he didn't add another word. His natural authority modifies the atmosphere which reigned in the room. Their attitude too… He wraps his eyes around me, suddenly reminding me of all the sensations he brings out in me. Then he turns around and goes back to his adjoining dressing room as if it didn't matter anymore.

They murder my brains.

Sophia strokes my hair awkwardly.

"You can go, Océane," she whispers to me.

"Are you sure?"

"Yes, you can go. Leave us alone. You'll be back tomorrow night like we agreed, right?"

To tell the truth, I'd rather turn into a little mouse and hide in a corner instead of leaving. The urge to spy on them is so much more tempting than the urge to walk away.

"Yes, tomorrow night," I confirm almost reluctantly.

"By the way, Lily, you have a car and a driver at your disposal," Tiger tells me back in the room, wearing black boxers and a white shirt that is still open.

I try not to glare at him and murmur a "thank you." Even though I don't know what the hell I'm going to do with these forty-eight hours without them anymore. Tiger goes back into the other room. I exchange one last look with Sophia. Sumptuous, vulnerable, naked, sitting cross-legged in the middle of her husband's bed. She gives me a kiss on the cheek. I feel that I am too much. In the grip of emotions that clash, I get up and leave the room.

Part III

Door half open

Close it or open it wider? There is nothing more arousing than an emotional no-go area... When you know you shouldn't venture into it, but you are dying to explore it anyway.

To give up or to enter this garden with her?

Fuck no, I'm not ready... but she's sucking me in more and more.

27

OCÉANE

Louane and the other friends in her shared apartment are at work or in class. Normal for a Monday. So I find myself with forty-eight hours to kill, an indecent amount of money transferred to my bank account, a Bentley with a driver at my disposal, and no great idea how to use it all. What to do in the middle of the week, alone, in a foreign country? Sure, I can manage on my own, and there are plenty of things to see in Sydney, but it's so… tasteless to wander around alone.

I spend the day playing tourist, trying out random addresses on my walks. Visiting, snacking, taking pictures, and recharging my Instax. I do all this on foot, but Tiger's bulldog is never far away. It seems he has been ordered not to let me out of his sight.

In the early evening, I hesitate to call Louane to crash at their place. And hang out with kids my age who have similar concerns to mine. Well, the ones I had before this double encounter. Talking about their internships, their love stories, their little jobs, their good plans, and their night out. However, I'm a bit worried that I'm being asked too many questions to which I don't have a clear answer.

What's up, Océane? What are you up to? Where are you living now? Tell us about your job.

And Louane is a bit of a stickler about "my activities." And Garrett, the other roommate, a business school student, idolizes the Sextons. He might smell something… I don't know how I can continue to be around them and still keep my confidentiality agreement with my private employers. In the end, I end up in a hotel. A little lonely and pensive.

Sophia, Tiger. Tiger, Sophia. Get them out of your head!

Barely a day out of the Sexton bubble, and I'm disoriented, cut off from the world. I don't want this. I need to get back in touch with Louane and have fun with regular people, people like me. Otherwise, what would I use my damn free time for?

Almost twenty-four hours later, my Monday night can be summed up in a few words: room service, binge-watching series, and social media. Snooping in the virtual lives of some people from my past in France to maybe reassure myself a little bit… As I went to bed, I couldn't help but imagine what Tiger and Sophia might be up to on their side. They corrupt my thoughts, making me unable to step back even on my first few "off" days.

The ringing of my phone wakes me from a restless sleep on Tuesday morning. On the screen, the name of the one I wasn't expecting. My heart races and my thumb hesitates to press the green button. Is he at work? Or is he still with his wife? Why is he calling me?

I dither too long, and the phone call stops. Sigh. He starts again two seconds later. Insistent, impatient. I give in to the urge to pick up; I'm not going back to sleep anyway.

"Hello?"

"Hello, sweet Lily."

I am dead. Even his voice reflects this erotic je-ne-sais-quoi and gives me this dangerous dose of alchemy.

"Hi," I pretend to be casual. "Uh… how's Sophia? Are you calling me because she wants me?"

"No, I'm not. Sophia is doing better; she has work to do too. I dedicated my Monday to her and much more… We're handling it. Today, I want to forget the formal settings. I need to let go and… to see you again."

I hate to admit it, but his words do something to me. My heart starts to beat stupidly again.

"Océane?" Tiger gently urges me. "Will you give me the day off?"

My silence stretches. His caressing tone insinuates itself in the hollow of my ear.

"Just you, me, I need it," he whispers to me. "Please."

My willpower goes out the window. I push an umpteenth sigh and say to him, "Okay."

"Great. I'm downstairs, waiting for you."

Our breaths mingle.

"Thank you, Lily," he whispers to me.

He hangs up. Feverishly, I jump out of bed to get ready. Ten minutes later, I am fresh and ready. My heart pounding, I put my things in my backpack and go downstairs. I am both anxious and nervous about finding him. Far from his wife, far from the rest…

Yes, I will have fun. Because I have the right to. They are liberated, and I am a liberated girl in the air of time. I'm not hurting anyone. Am I?

I return the keys to the hotel room, almost motivated, and then I leave, feeling a little excited.

He's here. Right in front of the hotel, on the sidewalk, leaning against the Bentley that I refused to use until then. Except for the drive from their property to downtown Sydney.

He wears a cap and sunglasses. If he's trying to blend in, it's not working. A face and build like that, even in casual jeans and camouflage, can't go unnoticed. In any case, *I* recognize him immediately. I go forward under his attention stuck on me.

"Hi," he greets me, in too-male-for-my-good mode.

"Hi."

We stare at each other, neither of us making a move toward the other. We are outside, in a public place, and he is a married man. He doesn't forget it; it's me who tends to forget it when he devours me with his eyes. Even behind tinted glasses, I can feel it.

"Is your driver making a detailed report on my movements?"

His lips curve slightly. Insolent, attractive.

"Nice to see you too. You look great," he says.

Don't act as if he has an effect on you, Océane! You'll make it easier for him.

I cross my arms on my chest to give myself composure. During an interminable visual penetration, he spreads a nagging sensation inside me. His charisma and his sexual aura are dangerously unfolding.

"So, you decided to skip work one more day to follow me around?"

"Don't worry about my schedule, sweet Lily. As for your driver, he's just looking out for you."

"And as a bonus, it allows you to keep an eye on me?"

I glimpse his irises through his glasses. They are only more hypnotic and tenebrous. They devour me with indecency. Big problem: I think I love that. He is so close. His warm breath and virile fragrance are disrupting my defense systems.

I confirm you're getting a serious lobotomy, poor thing.

"I rectify: it allows me to… find you when I'm in need of you."

Damn, if he keeps looking and talking to me like that, I'll have monstrous difficulty making my reason work instead of my hormones. I keep quiet so as not to betray the emotions that weaken me too much.

"Come to Canberra with me," he adds, "to break down my already shaky barriers. This is not part of your contract; it's an invitation."

"I don't know if—"

"Do you want something in return? Ask, and you will get it," he haggles.

Damn, he's got it all wrong! We don't function in the same way. He reduces everything to the notion of desire and the price to pay to get what he wants. How can I make him understand that my attraction to him is not something to be paid for? If I accepted his deal, it is not to become a luxury chick that he maintains, but because I simply want it. I want him, and that's all. No man has ever disturbed me so much; that's scary.

I moisten my lips and blink for a few seconds as I search for my words. I'm afraid to put myself out there too much emotionally.

"This isn't a damn trade, Tiger. Especially if you show up on my days off. Don't think you can buy my time or…"

My body?

Do I need to point that out? With my senses in turmoil, I hold his gaze.

"… Or anything of me. I'm not for sale," I tell him. "I'm not a possession to be acquired, nor am I a… whore."

Even though my desires, reason, and self-esteem are not in sync, I try to show him the opposite. The more my body reacts to this closeness, the more I'm afraid I will not come out unscathed. If I'm going to play with fire, I might as well make sure I'm doing what matters most to me. Set limits, and make him stick to them.

"I know," he nods, his pupils intense.

"The situation is strange enough. There's Sophia, you, me, your Pandora's box, my past... So that chemistry and our contract aside, here's what I demand in return: your respect. I don't know what to call what's going on between us, but I want you to always treat me with respect."

He stares at me for a long time, unfathomable, sexy as hell. But I hold on.

"Do we have a deal, Tiger?"

That rare and ravishing smile that you never see in any press photo blooms. He finally nods his head.

"It's a deal, sweet Lily," he says.

His hand settles on my lower back and sends shivers down my body. Tiger then applies a little pressure to guide me to another car parked behind the Bentley. A dark SUV with tinted windows. He unlocks the door, opens the passenger side door for me, and signs to the driver.

"Take the day off. I'll take Miss Rousseau home myself tonight. And tell my pilot I may need him for the return trip."

"Noted, Mr. Sexton."

"Of course, my wife doesn't have to know."

"Naturally, sir," replies the employee with a respectful bow.

He slips away without further ado. I exchange a look with Tiger. Mine is surprised; he has become seemingly serious and unapproachable again. Once we are locked in the car, I feel awkward but intrigued.

If I'm off duty, if his wife doesn't know about this escapade without her, then what does this day together mean?

No, I have to keep my feet on the ground. It's probably not the first time; they have their habits.

"Buckle up," Tiger tells me.

"What?"

"Fasten yourself... please," he completes with a little complicit mimicry.

As if commanding was natural to him and that muzzling this trait with me was a favor. I press my lips together so as not to provoke him, and I do it. He starts the car, and the music from the car radio starts. Enveloping and languorous, it pours into the car. He looks at me.

"'Soldier,' a song by Fleurie. If you don't like it, we'll change," he suggests.

No, it is splendid, and this car has a sound system that sublimates the instruments' sound and the artist's soft voice. I didn't know it, but Fleurie might become the soundtrack of a special moment in my memories… Later, who knows?

"I like it," I answer.

"Make yourself comfortable; it's about a three-hour drive to Canberra. And don't hesitate if you don't like my playlists."

TIGER

Océane leans back, extends her seat a little, and closes her eyes. To savor the music, the ride. Or to wonder if following me is such a good decision. I contemplate her for a moment, my mind titillated by a thousand pros and cons. She listens in silence, radiant and so… different from the women I am used to.

I glide along at an increasing speed. To the sound of "Breathe," by Hurricane, and other pieces by Fleurie. An intimate cocoon settles in; we fly along the asphalt. Riding relaxes me. From time to time, I feel Océane's eyes on my profile. Our glances catch each other, and my hair stands up. I do not want to break this calm filled with temptations. She obviously doesn't want to either. So she admires the landscape, and I let myself be intoxicated by the horsepowers under my hood. And by… this feeling of need established by our unfinished preliminaries…

She ends up dozing. I'm eating up the miles faster. Almost three hours later, we are driving in the backcountry. The stud farm materializes on the horizon. I stop in front of the old black wrought iron gate and get down to open it manually. I chose it myself. This place was supposed to be "our spot for us, our den between men". A place where a father passes on his passion for horses and his philosophy of life to his son. Now it's just me, with more collected brumbies than thoroughbreds. However, I refused to replace this creaky old gate that has rusted over the years…

"Now it'll be our boys' road trip, son. You're six years old, big boy. So welcome to Tiger's Stud, young cowboy!"

He places a Lucky Luke hat on my head, my favorite comic of the moment.

"So cool, I get to ride a horse? Can I choose? I want the biggest, strongest, fastest!"

I can still hear him laughing. And me running far ahead, crazy with joy…

Ridiculous nostalgia. Back in the car, I discover Océane awake. She observes the surroundings, then my face.

"Have we arrived?"

"Yes, beautiful lady. Welcome to *Haras du Tigre*[1]."

She smiles and returns her attention to the name engraved in French on the thick stones of a wall.

"Just that!"

"I'm not that pretentious," I spontaneously contradict her in response to the amusement in her eyes. "My father chose that name… partly for me and partly as a tribute to his father, who was also named Tiger. But also because he loved France."

She nods, her mocking smile turning tender. Well, I guess so.

"It's gorgeous," she comments, directing her wondering eyes again at the surroundings. "You… you never mention your parents. I'm glad I found out a little something about your father."

But what exactly am I doing? I'm going to pull out the old family albums too?!

In the grip of contradictory feelings, I restart the car and move forward without adding unnecessary words. Océane looks at the trees, plants, and every element of this wild scene. I go out to lock the gate and come back. While the SUV goes along the wooded road leading to the groom's house, my passenger continues to contemplate the vast areas around us.

---

1 Tiger's Stud

"This flag is a kind of family coat of arms?" she asks me when I park near the flagpole.

I turn to her to explain.

"It's the aboriginal flag; it means: 'Us, black men on the red land, under the sun.' Anatjari, the man who runs the stud, values it, as well as his entire culture. I respect that."

Not ready to add that Anatjari and Peter are the closest things I had to a father figure at one time…

Océane comes out at the same time as me, her irises shining. I feel her fascinated and eager to learn more. It is no longer the Australia of the tourist guides but the green setting where a crowd of memories from another time are buried. Where a herd of horses and two fabulous people dedicated to their well-being now thrive. A piece of my roots…

In fact, this familiar duo from my childhood comes to meet us, alerted by the noise.

"Tiger!" shouts Anatjari, followed by his wife and our faithful Doberman.

The latter jumped on me, wagging his tail happily and trying to lick me.

"Hey, did you miss me, Sausage Two?" I say, giving him a scratch under his nose.

"Why Sausage Two?" laughs Océane.

"Because, as a child, I had named Sausage the one they gave me; that dog was crazy about it. So they took the initiative to perpetuate this tradition."

Kind of like my first name. Uncle James didn't have a child; it was his brother who had once again what he didn't have: the opportunity to honor the tradition in the Sexton family with a little Tiger…

Don't fucking lose the thread! This is none of her business.

The stud farm is becoming too special for my emotions today. They are coming in any way they can. I admit too late that maybe I shouldn't have invited Océane here. The context of one-on-one time with an employee who is "momentarily too close to us" doesn't really fit with her.

"We're all happy to see you again, Tiger. Well, you and…"

Our hosts' stupefaction regarding Océane would be almost comical if I didn't suddenly stress out that I was doing something stupid. Usually, I come with a future personal assistant of Sophia's to gauge him and keep him on a leash. No woman. Hence the astonishment of Anatjari and his wife Bindi, who discover this blond girl falling for the dog.

I hesitate to backtrack; memories come back and interfere with my phlegm…

"Sweet pea, we didn't know that your companion was, in fact, a young girl," Bindi finally completes. "Get over here, you!"

She pulls herself together and hugs me against her opulent chest. Océane stops playing with Sausage Two and laughs.

"Sweet pea?" she repeats, incredulous. "I definitely like the lightness of the names here. It's so unlike you."

Very quickly, her hilarity becomes contagious. Bindi releases me, looks at her, and starts to laugh in turn.

"Right," she confirms. "It was more appropriate for him when I was preparing the snack for this little boy. Can you introduce us to your… friend, Tiger?"

"Bindi, Anatjari, this is Océane. Océane, you have the honor of meeting the only people on Earth who never take me seriously."

"Nice to meet you. Sweet pea should have told me about you on the way here," she says as they give her a warm hug.

"I guess she doesn't take you very seriously either," the queen of the stud rejoiced. "I like this one. Welcome, honey!"

I lean towards Océane, too excited to see possible cracks in my armor, and whisper to her in French, "Take that mocking look off your face, or I promise to—"

"To what, sweet pea?" she challenges me. "Will you eat me for your snack?"

"Damn, you'll pay for that!"

She laughs; I have difficulty finding a damn balance to restore an effective filter between the effect of this young lady and what resounds in my depths since our arrival at the stud farm. I stare at her; she is pink and absolutely not impressed by my warning. It ends up causing me to smile in spite of myself. I am destabilized; I'm not sure I like it.

"Kid, when I got your call, I had the usual horses ready," Anatjari says in his native tongue. "I thought you'd want to take a look around to check on the actions taken to counter the summer fires. But your agenda seems… different this time, right?"

"We'll see about that. This girl needs to be taught a few things, I think," I say.

Anatjari frowns and scrutinizes Océane. Neither he nor his wife ask any questions for the moment, analyzing the situation.

"Good," he says to me. "What is her level?"

I probe Océane and decide to answer in English so that she half understands what we are talking about, "She's a beginner. But not for long…"

"What?" she asks.

The more I observe her, the more her mind—or perhaps mine—seems to take a more vicious turn.

"Tiger, what am I a beginner at?"

"You'll find out soon enough. I have… a lot to teach you, I think."

I take advantage of her surprise and confusion to hug her.

"First, we'll gallop as far away as possible from this charming couple and get into nature. Then I'll pump all your energy until you can't laugh anymore when we get back. Because… and I'll admit this to you very respectfully: I'm going to fuck you today, sweet Lily."

"Oh, shit!"

My lips stretch. Her words are derisory; the impact of mine on her overheated face is enough for me. I release her and walk away in the direction of the stables, Sausage Two yapping at my side. Mentally, I speak to a ghost that haunts me much more today.

What would you have thought of her? Of this lady with whom I fantasize about doing many things not worthy of a noble young man. I'm not sure why I brought her to our boys' den. The only woman invited to walk this ground, our ground…

28

Océane

Tiger has that indefinable thing in his eyes again.

We flirt, and my mind goes wild. He wants me, it's obvious, and it's definitely mutual. But even as I watch him walk away with that sexy ass, his long thighs, and muscular legs in his jeans, I'm not sure what we're doing.

Anatjari follows Tiger. His wife, obviously entertained by the whole scene, observes me with a smirk.

"Is everything okay, honey?" she asks me.

I don't know. Tiger's pyromaniac techniques catch me off guard. He makes sparks fly between us and then lets me burn out most of the time. But now, does he want to go all the way? What about me?

"Is it the riding that's stressing you out? Don't worry; Tiger is a great rider. He's been riding the most stubborn mounts since he was a kid; he'll teach you the basics."

Oh, if that's all it was… This woman has no idea what her "sweat pea" is up to, and he's no longer an innocent, harmless little boy.

Shit, maybe she does? Does she know things?

I turn around and meet her eyes. I can't help but blush like a kid caught in the act. Deep down, I'm a beginner at a lot of things compared to Tiger. Not just about horses.

"However, he hates wasting time," Bindi says, gently pushing me. "Come on, let's go! I'll take care of the picnic. Do you have any preferences or allergies?"

"I just haven't adapted to the taste of Vegemite yet. Otherwise, I'm not that picky about food," I reply.

"I'll take note of it. Go, honey!"

I'm not even dressed for this thing. Nor is Tiger, for that matter. Do we ride in jeans and sneakers? No, actually, I'm mostly panicking about the "after." I try not to show it and to play it cool while heading toward the stables. A characteristic smell titillates my nostrils when I cross the threshold. Hay, leather, spacious stalls, equines everywhere. Tiger is talking quietly to one of his superb specimens. Holding a brush, he strokes his shiny black coat. He seems to be in his element, in quasi-communion with this animal, all in muscle and height.

"There you are," he welcomes me. "Come closer."

Pretend you're not torn. You can do it.

He stares at me, the shadow of a smile on his lips. Playful. Confident.

"What's the matter? Are you chickening out, my little warrior?"

"Not at all," I say, not dwelling on his implication. "It's just a big first for me, and this one is impressive."

"Don't worry; you will have a mount adapted to your level. And I'll guide you," he answers me.

"Yeah…"

"Let me introduce you to Midnight. He's rather wild and unpredictable with most people."

"With everyone," corrects Anatjari. "Only with Tiger, he lets himself be tamed."

"Very reassuring… He's super tall! And beautiful, too," I whisper.

"He's mine. Anatjari, please, will you bring us the mare that Océane will ride?"

"Yes, of course. I'm going right now."

As the groom steps into a stall, Tiger holds out his other hand to me.

"I thought you were more adventurous," he teases me. "Come on; he's not going to eat you."

I grab his fingers, and he pulls me against him and puts both our hands on the animal. His hand envelops mine; he makes my palm slide on the horse's side.

"However, I am dying to devour you," he says in a low voice.

His breath comes to lodge itself against my ear, his body

against me, his heat in my back. Tiger continues to touch the animal with me, slowly, our phalanges intertwined.

"Are you ready for this, Océane? Do you want it?"

A double-edged question, we both know. We're talking about horseback riding. But also, above all, about the "next step," the one that follows the long and intoxicating foreplay. The one he was pushing away when I was craving in his arms. My head tilts back on his chest, and my eyes seek his. Maybe to read something.

Like what? That it's not a mistake? We're just two consenting adults, wanting to give in completely to our attraction to each other? Tiger turns me around and hugs me. The bulge in his crotch presses against me. His pupils dilate as we watch each other. His fingers are invading my hair. My body temperature is disturbed lasciviously; our breaths come closer.

"Maybe," I say, like a half-confession.

"If we open this trap door, I risk involving you on a ground filled with… vices," he whispers to me in my language. "Are you ready to go that far with me?"

Oxygen gets stuck in my bronchi. My horizon crumbles all around, caught by the deep blue of Tiger's eyes.

"Yes," I hold in a whisper.

He takes this surrender from my mouth and rushes himself into it. With an imperious, greedy kiss that weakens my whole body and fogs my brain. Anatjari's insistent throat clearing and the dog's barking surprise us, burst the incandescent bubble and leave us panting, craving, feverish. Tiger frees me and moves back slightly.

"Pearl is ready," the employee announces.

"Thank you, Anatjari. You'll see, this one is sweet and obedient, Océane. I'll help you," Tiger promises me, his voice rocky.

He grabs a riding hat, puts it on my head, and ties it up. Feeling emotional, I follow his advice. He introduces me to my mount and cuddles it with me, as we did with his. Four-handed caresses, him against my butt, leaning on my shoulder. Our fingers get lost together in the mane of the mare. He whispers, "Shall we go?"

I nod. Tiger encircles my waist and presses me against him to probe me for a long time. Then he helps me into the saddle, tells me what to do, and urges me to relax so as not to stress Pearl. With my feet in the stirrups, I am exhilarated by the height and a myriad of sensations. I straighten up when my irresistible riding instructor urges me to do so. And I hold the reins, squeezing the leather straps to try to release the tension in me.

"Remember the basics. You're not going to fall. I'm here, okay?"

I nod. In one smooth motion, Tiger climbs onto his stallion. Bareback, because Midnight can't stand equipment or restraints, from what I hear. Free and spirited, like his master.

"Are you going to be okay?" he asks.

"Yeah… I think so."

"Breathe, Lily."

He gives me a last look that looks like a furnace in his blue eyes with dilated pupils.

"You're delicious, you know that?"

My cheekbones catch fire. Before I can say anything, Tiger decrees with a wink, "Let's get out of here, beautiful rider!"

TIGER

Bindi is waiting for us outside with a backpack. Almost like before, when we went on a father-son horseback ride. I clench my jaws with bitterness, pierced by this uncontrolled flood of memories. I pick up the package and thank her with a smile. At a trot, we leave the place. I do everything to relax Océane. Little by little, she becomes less stiff. I follow her rhythm. Too bad, no galloping or obstacles for me today. She has to enjoy the panorama from the top of her mount, overcome her apprehensions, be in osmosis with her horse, and savor it.

The landscape scrolls smoothly. As a good little student, Océane focuses on her posture. I think she's still a little afraid of falling, even though Pearl is not the type to rebel.

"It's so beautiful, so pure and… amazing out here," she marvels. "Can you still appreciate it?"

I stare at her.

"Yes, I can appreciate it," I tell her.

Our eyes meet when she turns her head. She bats her eyelashes and moistens her lips. My desire soars again. Okay. We're not far enough away, but I don't care. I decide to ride towards the river to stop us.

"Break time, sexy cowgirl. I've reached my limit."

"Already tired?" she pretends to be surprised.

The color of her cheeks doesn't fool me for a second.

Nah, I can see your game, Blondie.

I smile as I get off my horse and tie it to a trunk. Then, I lend a hand to Océane.

"Who said anything about tiredness?" I finally reply.

"Well, my posterior and thighs are sore, and my back is a bit painful, to tell you the truth," she argues when I grab her waist to bring her against me. "I know that it is not very glamorous but that—"

I stifle her false protests with a kiss. Gentle at first. Then a voracious appetite takes over, making the reluctance in my head implode like locks that open. The complaints of Océane die in the bottom of my mouth, and her quivering body melts against me. I interrupt myself one second to untie her from the helmet of protection. When I resume our fusion, I deepen it, blocking her head between my palms to better taste her. Progressively, I unbutton her jeans and start to lift her top to slip my fingers in. While I kiss her to stretch my boxers to the extreme, I unhook her bra and take hold of her round, tender breast.

"Damn, Tiger…"

I stop temporarily to rid her of everything that bothers me. Her clothes ejected, she takes the initiative to remove mine. My mouth and my caresses return to the assault intermittently. Soon, my erection is released, exposed to the great day under the bright pupils of the one who is responsible for this state. I push her again against me and knead her pretty ass. While devouring her with my eyes.

"Is that where it hurts?" I say to her, the tone hardly recognizable.

She gasps, clutching at me.

"Yes, a little…" she whispers to me.

"I will take care of it."

I take back her lips and pull her on me. Her legs wrap around my hips, and her tongue drives me crazy. Mine drinks from her. My pulses go to my fifth member. We land on a grass carpet, Océane on her back. Me above her, still captive of her members around me. My attention turns to her ear. I feel her sensitivity in this area, which increases the intensity of her reactions and mine tenfold. My mouth lingers there before starting a sinuous way to the hollow of her neck. To hear her pronounce my name while squirming makes me feel euphoric. I reach her chest and stop for a moment to contemplate her.

Damn, she is beautiful! And receptive… That's not going to help me stay on track.

"Come back, Tiger," she meows, pulling me by the neck.

We kiss indefinitely before I can detach myself to explore her elsewhere. On her areolas, her hardened nipples. They stick out and remind me how much I am in need. I knead her breasts, hungry, and I press them against each other to access both. I bury my face there, smelling her scent. My tongue comes back. My teeth bite her between the suctions. She pushes small cries, contorts herself, and clings to my hair. I continue; her delicate flesh and her velvety skin intoxicate me. Interrupted curses and moans follow one another when I cross her belly, going more to the south. I play with the outline of her belly button. I don't know if it tickles her, titillates her, or both. But damn, she's blowing my mind! It gets worse when I discover her wet petals, murderously soft. My mouth is lost, a big part of my reason too.

Océane arches her back, calls me and moves her pelvis to meet me. Sensual, covered with dew. Her intimate perfume obsesses me; I no longer control the ardor of my comings and goings to the borders of her femininity. Her pink bud under my tongue, my hot breath in her wetness, her thighs which encircle me. My fingers imprison her to have her groin all to myself. To suffocate. I perceive a beginning of trance germinating in the depths of her delicious corollas. Her words become incoherent, her trembling unmanageable. Her pleasure is about to reach its apotheosis; I backpedal to calm the game.

"Please… No…" Océane begs me, her breathing jerky.

I move up again to catch her mouth; the taste of all her lips mixes and consumes my crumbs of self-control. I return to the conquest of her breasts, triturate the tips, suck them without moderation, lick them, knead them. Then I go back down to take care of the tender pearl nestled in the hollow of her femininity. Second round. More methodical. The first signs of her pleasure come to the surface, and she loses it again. I speed up, bring her to the edge of the abyss then I slow down again.

Time is suspended in eternity. A thread of sweat covers Océane's skin, and her arousal takes an unsuspected path. She rises, almost to the point of climax, before I block her at this stage, tame her to maintain her. For a long time, as long as my nerves manage to hold, I flirt with her orgasm at hand.

"It's… criminal… what… you do to me," she accuses me with anarchic breath.

She palpitates of desire, cracked up brain, and softened body. I give her a smile; I get an insult. And I start again to maltreat her. When I come to the same degree of sensory madness, I stand up. She leers at me completely.

"Tiger, I will kill you if you don't come back here!"

Her redness, her hair in battle, her curves decorated with my marks of attention, everything of her is of a devastating eroticism. Lying in the greenery, moist, weakened, magical. I bend down to pick up my pants and take out the condom set. I detach one and join her.

"You thought I was done with you, Miss Rousseau?"

"Good for you, sweet pea. Nah, actually, that nickname definitely doesn't suit you."

A naughty smile lights up her face, to which I answer. Her eyes wander over my chest and my abs, stopping their exploration at my erect cock. This simple glance makes me the effect of the torture of too much.

I rip the package and put on the condom. The next second, I am on my knees, between her thighs, lifting her hips. My dick slides over her clitoris in suave torture. Océane sighs and shivers. I lean over; she retains me and claws my butt. I slide between her petals and come to the edge of her intimacy. Our eyes find themselves.

With slowness, I penetrate her while looking at her. The more I progress in her, the more the manifestations of her pleasure merge with mine.

"Damn, I want you so much," I say to her in a last movement.

And I enter entirely in her. Trapped by a devouring need, I remain motionless.

"You're killing me, Tiger," whispers Océane to me without suspecting the monstrous pleasure that I am taking.

She struggles to breathe, and so do I. I lean in and kiss her for the thousandth time. But this time, the fusion is total. My sex stiffens in her. I take support on a folded arm; my hips move lazily withdraw, return, withdraw. In slow motion. I'm shaking; my muscles are getting hard. My comings and goings keep this tempo while I admire the woman under me. She embraces me in her sheath, compresses me, and drenches me with pheromones.

To feel again the orgasm coming and to repress it asks of me a superhuman effort. My sex leaves hers, always full of desire at its peak. Océane moans, calls me a sadist, and braces herself to make me let go. So I capitulate; I fit myself in her in a thrust. My assaults accelerate, binding me deeply in her with each return in this narrow wetness. Stronger, almost merciless. My neurons disconnect, and the primitive sensations take the orders and smash me relentlessly in the hollow of Océane.

I know that she wants to cum, that she will implode. I see it, I feel it, and I fan the flames. No more question of control, but rather of chaos of the senses. Let her let go! I activate myself. She takes off, screams, and violent spasms sweep her up before my eyes. My lower abdomen contracts at the moment when my cock perceives the orgasm of my partner. A torrent takes me with her... We rock for a long time before regaining our footing.

"Oh, God!" I say, completely blown away by her.

Damn, what a delicious secretive woman! I wouldn't have guessed it... I lie down on my back next to her, still in a trance.

"Damn!" she cries out.

I look for her glance. She is sublime and... distraught? Disoriented? Become shy again? My lips stretch.

"I think that... Shit!" she says again, now peony red. "No, damn, no!"

No? Could it be that this discovery that has just atomized me is also one for her?

I'm beginning to think so. Océane sits down again, puts her hand over her mouth, and looks down at her own body. I stand up, literally soaked with her, shot with endorphins.

"Why didn't you tell me? Because now we'll stop using condoms."

The way she stares at me with embarrassment makes my eyes narrow.

"I'm not sure I… understand," she hesitates.

"Which part do you want me to explain to you, little wonder?"

"I know you… felt that thing when we…"

"Oh yes, I felt it. That's why we're going to make arrangements not to use a condom anymore. Now that I've seen how you cum, I want you without a latex barrier next time. I want to feel everything about you."

"But that was… I didn't… I'm not…"

Shit, is she really ashamed?

"Wait, was this the first time this has happened?"

"You're talking about…"

Yes, she is unsettled, as if she just found out too. Stunned, I notice her unjustified embarrassment. The shock, we are two to take it.

"I don't know what got into me," she apologizes.

I wonder if I should laugh or kiss her.

"So, you're a squirting queen, and you didn't know?"

"Squirting?"

Holy crap, I can't believe it. No more doubts; she's finding out! I nod, trying to make her realize that this is not a problem. It's just the opposite. Damn, it makes me want to fuck her again. I try to verbalize gently, "What do you call that in French?"

"I have no idea," says Océane.

Her cheekbones are getting more and more flushed. She suddenly seems so inexperienced, disturbed by this unexpected and dazzling response of her body to the prolonged stimulation.

I grab her and pull her to me. If I had known from the start that she would be so receptive to edging, I might not have lasted long. The finale is more breathtaking than I am used to in delayed orgasms.

Delightfully stunned, the reason for this cataclysm in my fantasies tries to find its way back. An innocent flower has just bloomed, beaded with pleasure.

"It's a little embarrassing, Tiger," she mumbles in her confusion, reaching for her shirt to wipe herself.

Her awkwardness and emotion are adorable to watch… Touching too. Is she afraid she's made a fool of herself? With an asset like that?

"I've never… Good thing there are no sheets; that would have been a disaster."

"Hey. Put that down. And stop looking away from me. That was… awesome! You just gave me a woman's ejaculate; you should look up and show off."

This time, her tainted innocence turns into astonishment. Then little by little, in amusement. I stare at her until she starts to be proud of it. A gleam lights up in the bottom of her beautiful green eyes, like an awareness of her secret weapon, unsuspected until now.

"Is it you, or am I the one who's been great?" she teases me now.

"What do you think, little show-off?"

"I would say that my body has just reached apotheosis. And, yes, it was great; for once, I won't contradict you. Enjoy it, Sweet Pea."

"Scoundrel! Your body has finally found a partner capable of putting it into a trance, and I intend to prove it to you again under a shower of dew."

To make you cum again, to unleash this again, to taste this geyser of pleasure inside you, to be sprayed with it. Shit, I'm not going to stop getting hard anymore!

29

OCÉANE

Tiger describes in a classy and poetic way a crazy upheaval in my entire being. I still can't believe that such a sensory implosion happened to me at twenty years old! It's as if I were discovering sex and my body for the very first time.

He is talented; he bewitches me, and he confuses me to my core.

"I want you even more."

"You mean, right now?"

Do I have the strength right now? I'm too stunned, exhausted, and… fulfilled… to do it again. Not after this very wet orgasm.

Now, under Tiger's indecent gaze, and because he compared it to a dew rain, I feel like a rare flower that he has revealed and intends to feast on. Avidly. He gives me a carnivorous smile, sticks his lips to the hollow of my palm, and then stands up.

"Don't panic, little player," he taunts me in a hoarse voice. "We'll recover first, like any normal human being. Then… we'll check if what happened happens again or not."

"Normal?" A female ejaculation released in his arms?

The rough grass under my butt, my thighs still wet, and my body still euphoric indicate to me that "breathtaking" would be a better qualifier.

My body is flooded with oxytocin, and I realize how out of control I am. While my head is racing with this conclusion, Tiger grabs the backpack I couldn't even remember. He opens it, takes out two bottles of water, and offers me one. His eyes wander over my nakedness, making me even more aware of it. This lust makes me feel beautiful, desirable, and unique. However, I am not the only one for him. I will never be…

Shit, is it the intensity of the fucking that causes this heightened sensitivity?

There is a surge of this silly "attachment" hormone in every part of my body. It's chemical, just chemical, and it will evaporate. Tiger may be used to causing such strong feelings in other women. Only me, no man has ever… fucked me like this. I sit up on my knees, dusting myself off with my wet T-shirt. He doesn't comment; his dilated pupils are enough to reinforce my emotional confusion.

You have to take this lightly, relax and enjoy yourself… Live, Océane, live in the moment!

I try. But this extraordinary pleasure proves to me that Tiger Sexton can make me lose my mind just by touching me. A sensation that is at the same time doping, frightening and terrifying.

Without imagining the tsunami of emotions he has created in my being, Tiger takes a sip. I take off the cap of my bottle to give myself some space. I take a drink under his increasingly insistent attention.

He stares at me without a word; the teasing connivance in his irises becomes an enigma. The intensity of his gaze turns to something else when he lights a cigarette.

"Do you regret it, sweet Lily?"

"No."

This answer comes out by itself; then its truthfulness increases my fear and confusion.

"And you?" I ask in return.

A smile. That's all I get. I absorb this image. With his shaggy hair, his charisma, his scattered scars, his tattoos that snake down his side and back, and his intriguing knight symbol tattooed on his groin. I don't know why this one reminds me of medieval coats of arms. An old-fashioned emblem engraved in an intimate area with black ink, with letters tangled in his pubic hair.

Under normal circumstances, a guy like that wouldn't be interested in a girl like me for a second. That's obvious. God, I'm torturing my mind and losing my nerve.

"What's going on with your birth control?"

This question catches me off guard and pierces my thoughts. Tiger exhales his wisp of smoke, attentive.

"I'm… I'm fine," I stammer, running out of more elaborate repartee.

He ruffles his hair, the shadow of a smile on his lips.

"Okay, let me rephrase that, you delicious little Frenchie: you and I are going to do a lot of what we just did, and I want to… abandon any physical barrier between us. By that logic, I need a more concise answer on every important part of your health. Especially gynecologically. So 'I'm fine' is not good enough for me," he adds while coming back to my side.

Faced with his mocking air, his self-confidence, and his naked anatomy without complexity in the wilderness in broad daylight, I finally manage to swallow my complexes and hesitations. He is right; I don't have to blush anymore. It was unique.

I snatch his cigarette and take a drag to deal with the rush of "ifs" in my head before retorting:

"Considering the number of cunnis I've had, you weren't especially worried about my health. So, long story short: I'm fine and on the pill, Mr. Sexton."

I see his lips curve through the smoke I exhale.

"Indeed, we were a bit careless," he admits. "We'll work it out when we get back to Sydney."

He takes the cigarette out of my mouth and stubs it out. His comes closer and brushes against me. His pupils get bigger again, animated by an ardor that slowly seeps into my veins.

"The smoke break is over. Where were we already, my sweet?"

His hands slide on my skin. They diffuse a quivering along my spine and slide towards my buttocks which he seizes with a firm softness to place me against his budding erection.

"We wanted to check something, I believe," I answer him by scratching his chest delicately.

He kneads me harder and nibbles my lips without trying to kiss me. At least not for the moment, like a feline playing with its prey to whet its appetite. In this sensual game of our tongues, with his warm breath, I start to crack again.

Fuck, I'm screwed.

Without warning, the kiss becomes brutal and possessive. The sensations bloom in me again, invade me. My nails wrap around Tiger's muscles, and my fingers cling to his hair. When he drags me to the ground, I don't care if the grass scratches my skin again because this guy seems to know exactly how to liquefy me. It was as if he knew my body by heart and that it obeyed him to the letter. His hands and his mouth go through me, finding my sensitive points.

Stretched out under him, I twist; I take charge of making him as feverish as me. I manage to make us change position, me above him. My breasts in his palms, my hair flowing on him, he kisses me.

"You are a little monster," he grumbles to me.

He devours me and rocks me on my back. That turns into a kind of carnal duel which he wants to win. But I put all my ardor in my kiss, feel him growling with desire in my mouth. His sex beads point hard against me. His caresses lose their tenderness; he kneads my chest and triturates my nipples. I undulate my pelvis and moan while coming back to gather closer his sigh.

"I want you so bad," he reveals to me in his native language.

English has never seemed so sexy to me as at this moment.

"Me too, Tiger," I confide, mouth to mouth, straddling him. "I want you, Mister Sexton."

Hearing this, he captures my lips, making me dizzy. Before I fully realize it, he grabs a condom. I watch on my little cloud of lust as my stud rips open the wrapper and slips it on without taking his eyes off me for more than two seconds. His sex expands and stiffens once more… for me. I am all things, more hungry, more disoriented. He brings me back to him. We merge, our skins rub, our tongues challenge each other, charm each other, and our breaths merge. I collapse, and Tiger takes the opportunity to turn me around. On all fours, uninhibited, aroused. I don't have time to anticipate, to prepare myself for the ardor with which he wishes to quench this torrid desire which exudes from him. His rigid cock suddenly enters in me; a deep and sudden penetration propels me onto my elbows. My chest crashes to the floor, my hips held at the height of Tiger's hips. Our knees sink into the grass, and he into me. It is not any more the calculated control of our beginnings; the pleasure doesn't linger any more. It roars in my lower abdomen, swells, and electrifies me immediately!

His thrusts are violent, close together, frantic, and insatiable. I catch myself screaming.

"Yes! Yes!"

He pierces me with extreme shivers, shakes me, and fills me with him. My neurons spin out of control. My cries are repeated. My senses are exacerbated. My breathing becomes choppy. My whole being is monopolized by a kind of trance that germinates; it increases and spreads everywhere in me. Tiger redoubles his vigor; his comings and goings lead me further and further away. I lose my footing and scream his name. And the pleasure explodes in a liquid pleasure flowing between my trembling legs.

Fuck, he did it again!

Tiger's orgasm follows closely behind mine. He squeezes my waist until it hurts and lets out a long sigh. When he withdraws, I collapse on my stomach. Interminable spasms still assail me, replicas to the infinity of a carnal earthquake.

"Damn it!" growls Tiger. "We have confirmation."

Languid, I struggle to get my brain working again. We can set this in stone: I just lost another form of virginity in the arms of Tiger Sexton.

And boy, is it amazing! And scary intense!

TIGER

I stay floating in an orgasmic ocean for a long time, my mind scattered, my breathing anarchic and hot. How can I keep a cool head after that? I wouldn't want to spend the next few days considering locking myself in a suite with Océane and trying to get my fill of her. Because every time I touch her, I want her even more afterward.

I'm going to have to keep this sexual chemistry under control, or it's going to be a disaster. For her, and for us… That last thought manages to chill me slightly. I sit down and run my fingers through my hair. Océane doesn't move, still lying, wonderfully sexy, fragile, lost… wet.

I suddenly close up out of necessity. Tense, I stand up again and get rid of the condom. I hear her finally react behind me when I light a cigarette again.

"I believe that my body needs a respite," she announces. "I am going to bathe."

I swivel around; she goes to the river below.

Argh! Stop staring at that reddened rump! You haven't even completely lost your erection yet.

You're wasting your time. I inhale, exhale and crush my cigarette to follow her. She senses my presence, turns around, and our eyes lock. I perceive an ounce of indifference in hers, but she beats her eyelashes and continues her way. Her curves are immersed, and I swim to her.

"Squirter," she whispers.

In incomprehension, I come closer.

"Sorry?" I say.

"What I… What is…" she stammers. "This thing of madness that you make me," she finishes by summarizing with a pink face.

Does she know that this particularity risks to obsess me from now on? I don't dwell on that. I might as well stick to the sex and reduce the discussions. With a call-girl, this question wouldn't even arise; now I'll have to readjust my barriers… I manage to make her feel comfortable while sticking to the basics: it's all about sex. As exquisite and sensual as it is with her, it's a fad, an outlet. I only have to remember my wedding ring to change my mood. Océane's head resurfaces in a splash. She drips, unconscious of the walking fantasy that she represents.

Femme fontaine[2]… The French could not have found better than this assembly of words for such a sexy, torrid, surprising, and… unforgettable phenomenon?

The slightly puffy mouth of the object of my desires still attracts me. What I remember is that no other man has known this side of her. Not even the other one, or that Victor, the ex-con, we haven't really discussed yet.

But I don't want a rational discussion right now. I'm trying to channel my desire to kiss Océane. To fuck her soon.

I get out of the water to stifle this hunger of hers that is already coming back and causing anarchy in my routine. It will calm down; I will start to move away, at least mentally. I have to.

She is splashing around, hanging out in the river, lost in her thoughts. I put my boxer shorts and jeans back on and grab the bag.

---

2   Literally mean "Fontaine woman" this how French say squirter.

When I unpack the things prepared by Bindi, Océane goes back to the bank.

"Can I borrow it?" she asks me, picking up my T-shirt. "It's hot; it'll dry by the time we eat. I got mine… wet."

"Don't worry, I tell her. Keep it."

The cotton fabric hugs her curves and sticks to her breasts. I fall back on the Thermos of iced coffee to focus less on that. Usually, after having slept with a woman twice in a row, I am less attentive to her charms. This pattern should not change. Even if this blond girl is not a pro, even if there are things about her that blur the course I'm pursuing. Even if my dick and body are getting a little too excited to allow my brain to fully function.

The pattern must not change. The filter must not break down.

"Thank you," whispers Océane.

I notice a hint of shyness. I have closed myself off; she doesn't know how to behave anymore. This change helps me to build a safe distance on all other levels. She sits down on the tablecloth and accepts the glass I hand her. Her eyelashes bead with water, and she observes me. For an indeterminate time, we remain like that, eyes in eyes. I suppose we have a lot of questions in each other's heads. And two, three secrets in the guts of each one too.

Well, not really. I already know hers. Meticulously documented in a file.

Given my wife's schedule, Miss Rousseau's former life is a subject that will have to be reconsidered soon. Océane takes a bite of sandwich. She lets out a greedy "hmm." That simple sound, her fluttering eyelids, and the sight of her pink lips affect my nerve endings.

Oh, shit!

"So good!" she comments without suspecting the libidinous and chaotic turn my thoughts are taking.

"Do you like it?"

"I love it, I was starving."

"Bindi will be happy to hear that."

I decide to have a taste of my own. Watching her eat gives me more appetite.

To be honest, it's not my style to go easy on an… occasional guest partner in my relationship, to subtly bring to the table what I want to get or express. Not in the terms and conditions, not to listen to a contract, etc. However, this sweet little face and what we have just shared make the process go wrong. Our eyes keep meeting. Océane seems lost between the sexual complicity that we had and the distance that I try to take now. The attraction is always perceptible between us, but one of the subjects mentioned with Sophia during our private conversation yesterday concerns Océane. Not only one, by the way…

I have to get straight to the point.

"Is there a problem?" she asks.

My jaws lock up.

"Go ahead, I'm a big girl," she concludes. "You're not entertained by this whole charade anymore, are you? You got what you wanted, and you're thinking about how to fire me?"

"You're off beam, Lily. I'm trying to figure out how to handle the next step beyond the medical checkup… We have a little less than six months before us. I'm married. And since we're discreet about the fact that Sophia and I are in a free union, on the outside, no one has to know that I have a monstrous urge to fuck you again. Which leads me to rethink the logistics."

Océane's eyes widen, then she breaks into an incredulous smile.

"Wow! I don't even know how to take that. Basically, your life is planned down to the smallest detail, even the private stuff?"

"In my position, and with our lifestyle, there are always issues to control. I prefer to be a few steps ahead," I admit. "You'll get used to it."

She picks up her sandwich again and shrugs casually. Real or fake?

"So, what's the program? Your assistant will add me to your schedule for the next few months?" she jokes a little bitterly.

The program? In mine, there is a team of experienced mercenaries locking down targets in France right now for me. The hunt may be coming to an end, and this is of prime importance to me. For too many years now. I carefully sort out the words in my head because her program is different. I am hunting. She is running away from her country, her mistakes…

"In fact, I am taking you to France soon," I say. "We are taking you, to be more precise."

It was not planned, but I only say that to prolong a little more our intimacy. Océane stops chewing and stares at me.

"What?"

"A trip to Paris for three."

She fidgets. The T-shirt goes up, and it reminds me of her nudity underneath. Thankfully, mentioning Sophia and France puts some concerns into perspective. I put things back on track.

"I… I'll accompany you to France? I didn't think of going back there any time soon," she says with a less sure voice.

"Traveling with us was part of your… job description, wasn't it? Sophia needs a change of scenery and wants to meet a starred chef. I've also scheduled some business meetings in Europe."

"When?" worries Océane.

"I'll make the arrangements; you'll get the dates."

She turns pale, her eyes drifting toward the horizon under my gaze. The atmosphere is no longer the same. I'm starting to itch to find out more about the sources of her tension. What impact does her past have on her?

"Your reluctance is due to… this Victor?"

She is silent; my interest is more titillated. I insist, "Tell me, Océane."

"You… you already know the story," she says quietly.

"No, what really interests me is not in the file provided by my security team. Your experience, your perspective."

Definitely uncomfortable, she pushes her fingers through her hair. I wait, and she hesitates. I question myself about this discomfort and look at her for a long time, patiently, so that she stops hiding this part of her.

"Océane, normally, I would leave your past where it is. I have the information I need, but it's from third parties. But it's you I'm sleeping with, and we both want to do it again. Am I wrong?"

"No," she concedes. "I mean, I think…"

Shit, are we questioning everything?

"I'd just like to analyze the situation better," I say, a little on edge. "In order to prepare for eventualities to protect all three of us in case of necessity. Sophia, you, me… Do you understand?"

She shakes her head, walks away, and crosses her arms.

"It was a mistake," she whispers to me from behind.

What is she talking about? About sleeping together or about her past?

"Victor was the biggest mistake of my life."

Listening to her, I swallow the unpleasant feeling that the first eventuality has caused to germinate in me. I barely relax, but I don't intervene or rush her. I let her open up.

"Tell me more about this guy," I end up directing her.

"Where do I start?"

"Your meeting."

"Okay…" she abdicates by fiddling with her hair.

I notice the signs of nervousness in her. This state of unease shakes us both, but not for the same reasons… I need to know, to have confirmation, to hear it from her.

"My mother raised me alone," begins Océane in a sad voice. "When she died, I… I grew up in children's homes, in between two or three brief stints in foster homes," she says softly. "Never long enough to really feel at home. I felt bad about myself and met Victor in my last home. I was fourteen; he was sixteen. He…"

My eyelids furrow, and my gaze focuses on her.

"He was a kind of leader, leading a group of local teenagers. We hit it off, and I felt truly surrounded for the first time since my mother died. Integrated into a clan."

"I see," I say to encourage her to open up more. "Did you fall in love with him?"

"No. In fact, it was mostly the feeling of belonging to a group that I liked at first. We became friends. Without realizing it, the friendship took a certain turn as we went along."

Did he seduce her? I stiffen up at the thought that maybe this little jerk took advantage of her weaknesses…

"What turn, Océane? Sexual?"

"No. Victor was a ladies' man with lots of women. We flirted sometimes, but nothing more. I wasn't ready for that. Or maybe I was just being too romantic at the time and waiting for the perfect opportunity with the perfect boy."

She smiles sadly. Was the other guy mentioned in the file, the one called Lucas, was he the "perfect boy?"

"In high school, there was this guy, Lucas," she adds from herself. I realized that he was really attracted to me. It was not a game like with Victor. For me, it wasn't love at first sight either, but we got along well; I was good with him. Victor found out; I don't know how because he was a school dropout and didn't even go to our school. To make a long story short, Victor was the cool brother, who encouraged me to give Lucas a chance. I…"

Océane's breathing is getting worse. She turns around and briefly meets my gaze before dodging it for good.

"And then?"

"I started to date Lucas. We were seeing each other more and more, and I was hanging out less and less with the gang…"

"Let me guess; the other one didn't appreciate not being the center of attention anymore?" I try to deduce.

"In a way, yes. I was naive and in need of attention. Lucas and his mother became a substitute for… family in my eyes, well I don't know… Then I understood too late that there was some stupid rivalry between the young people of the neighborhood where Lucas lived and Victor's group. A stupid story of territory. The fact that this guy from the neighboring ghetto becomes my boyfriend in the long term is seen as a provocation in their eyes, a lack of respect on his part. I think that if Victor pushed me to accept Lucas's invitation, it was perhaps because he thought I was too much under his thumb and imagined that I would quickly leave him and come back to hang out with them. They would have made fun of him, and that's it."

"That wasn't the case; you got attached to this boy. To this kind of stability: him, his mother, a real family?"

"Yes," says Océane. "So, Victor decided to use me without my knowledge."

Her voice shakes and weakens. I join her and pass my index finger under her chin to raise her face toward me. She seems affected as if four long years had not passed since the facts.

I am anxious to ask the question that is burning in my mind now, realizing that the data I have does not reveal the most important thing. Nevertheless, I finally ask, "Without your knowledge? So, you didn't know anything about his plans?"

What do I really want? To dispel the doubt or to continue to use it? Because convincing myself that she's not as white as snow has made me take the plunge. And it helps me—selfishly helped me—not to have any scruples about her. Because if she had been capable of something like that, then it balanced the scales of my conscience a little bit about my own dark areas…

"No," she says.

Damn it! That's the answer I was afraid of.

Océane's confession of innocence brutally distorts all the conclusions I made in front of her file. My deductions no longer hold water, or at least they are wavering…

Far from guessing how much this disturbs me, Océane continues, "Even if there are still people—in particular Lucas's mother and the girl friends influenced by her—who are ready to bet the opposite, I was not an accomplice," she develops. "I didn't know that I was being used as bait and that I dragged my boyfriend right into an ambush. And that was ugly…"

Her eyes are wet, nothing like those of the sublime monster I almost wished she was. This truth, I don't take it well.

Mentally, I match her words with the results of my team's research: the irreversible wounds of this Lucas—the victim—then Océane's testimony at the trial against the other little jerk. The promises of reprisals made by him and his accomplices. Everything fit together and messed up my conclusions. My men and I had thought that Océane had probably escaped justice because she had agreed to rat out the others. So from guilty, she had become an assisted witness to help put them away. But it is possible that she was simply fooled and tricked. I did like the mother of this Lucas; I condemned her because it suited me… And now… shit!

I remain silent; she continues, "I was not charged; there was no evidence against me. But seeing how it happened, even if I didn't know what Victor was planning and didn't knowingly participate, I will never be at peace with it. And Christine, Lucas's mother, was constantly on social media to remind me of it. She played on this blur around my possible guilt… It was hell, but I'm not complaining; I don't have the right. It was Lucas who paid the price. I… My pain seems so illegitimate compared to what he went through. Christine hammered me so many times that I was abominable, that I was only that during the months, then the years which followed… I am at fault in spite of everything… In short, I worked hard, saved, and I left to try to move forward," she hurried to conclude. "There, you know everything."

I take in her words. So, trapped, Océane found herself muzzled in her own suffering, and in parallel, she was a victim of cyber-stalking. She is a collateral victim.

I look at her, stunned by this discovery. Her lips quiver and a glimmer of fragile strength flickers in her eyes. She tries to hide her emotions. In the dust of guilt that this raises on my own conscience, one element also manages to shake me up inside. My questions about the feelings she may have had or still has for this Lucas. Did she love him? Does she still love him? This pain she talks about and which is so vague to me, what exactly does it reflect?

My features harden. I have made a masterful mistake about this girl. Suddenly in a hurry to end our discussion, I proclaim, trying to be just pragmatic, "Okay. I had made sure that no one would dig up this case here, that the press would not be able to get into the breach and trace it back to you. That Victor won't get to you again."

Dejected, Océane stepped back and locked herself up in all the dignity she could muster.

"Because it would affect you and your public image?" she deduces herself.

"Yes."

I am not fooling her; she just messed up my head. I'm having a hard time dealing with this.

"Don't worry," she snaps. "We're sleeping together, but for the rest, I'm a big girl, Tiger. You wanted my version; you got it. I don't need to be overprotected."

I clench my fists and add nothing. I just can't do it.

For God's sake, she was innocent?! She didn't do it, unfortunately, but we've already gone too far because I believed otherwise.

30

Océane

When I close my eyes so as not to talk on the way back, it is this that comes back and swirls:

Lucas's swollen face, his nearly disjointed body on the ground. The blood. The smell of sweat. This hatred… And me, hysterical, shaking.

"Let's get out of here!"

"Fuck, move, Océane! Let's get out of here!"

"Oh my God!"

I push Victor violently away, push the others who try to bring me back with them. My face is bathed in tears, and my heart is pounding too hard in my chest. I shout for help, screaming at the top of my voice.

"Noooooo!"

"Shut the fuck up! COME ON!" Victor pushes me.

I fall to my knees in front of Lucas. They shake me, and I refuse to run away with them. I'm afraid to touch him; he's so… My God, he's a mess. I think he's still breathing; it sounds more like the grunts of a dying animal. I start to cry.

"Hang on, Lucas. I beg you, don't die…"

My phone, I'm looking for my phone. I can't think anymore. Calling for help. Yes, I must call for an ambulance.

Lucas tries to talk to me. He spits blood. Terrified, I don't know what's going on anymore. Time has stopped. I think my heart exploded in my chest at the horror.

The arrival of the ambulance, then of the cops… I speak in a confused way. Is he dead? I think he's dead. He's dead…

"She is in shock," I hear.

Why am I not allowed to get in the ambulance with him? Why am I being put in the back of a police car?

"What have I done? My God, what have I done?"

I cling to the present as best I can. Fleurie's "Soldier" still echoes in Tiger's car. In one afternoon, my damn mantra was swept away. No, I don't feel any better than I did four years ago. That fucking mindset I tried to cultivate to move forward is gone. Yielding to a melancholy as strong as the euphoria that preceded it. The more minutes pass, the more I feel exactly the same as before. When I found myself isolated, excluded from the circle that I had long considered a second family because the others all supported Victor, their leader. And I was demonized by those who believed I was in league with him.

I remain this "good-for-nothing."

If only Tiger hadn't laid me bare, only to become distant and hermetic, I'd feel a little less… monstrous. Is this how he sees me?

Guilty and addicted to making bad decisions. A magnet for trouble that is now fooling around with a married billionaire.

This is how I would look if I showed up in Paris with the Sextons. Yes, in theory, things are more complex than that; this "relationship" is supposed to be discreet and consensual by the couple. And there is little chance of running into anyone from my past in the prestigious places that Sophia and her husband certainly go to in France. But in practice, the mere prospect of accompanying them makes me question everything.

I close my eyes, completely lost. Tiger doesn't say anything to me anymore, and that kills me. It gives me an idea of how he must feel about me now. As if I wasn't there anymore, he makes short, directive phone calls and ends up with someone named Shanna.

Is this another "partner?" Even his wife has no hold on him. How could I think for one second that I was a "good-for-nothing" who would matter in any way? With my disgrace. I almost regret the whole day…

"As soon as I get to Sydney, I'll give you a call," Tiger promises this Shanna on the phone.

I can't control the twinge of sadness this causes me. More and more pitiful; in fact, I feel weakened. But I hide behind my wounded self-esteem. Neither of us makes an effort to talk anymore, even when he has no more calls to make. The music fills the car, and my moods oscillate. The time passes, the drive drags on…

Our arrival interrupts the foggy nap in which I sank by spite.

Tiger parks; he doesn't cut the engine. The butler opens the door for me, straight as a ramrod.

"Good evening, Mr. Sexton, Miss Océane," he welcomes us.

His boss nods to him, perfectly distant. While driving, it seems he erased all the things that don't have any more importance in his eyes. Our getaway, the fact that he showed me his less formal relationship with the employees of the stud, and especially the moments he offered me all cease to exist when we enter his property.

It was just sex. You don't expect anything from him. And he doesn't expect anything from you either.

I'm about to leave, trying to keep a minimum of dignity, as much as to say crumbs, considering the circumstances.

"I'm going out again, Peter," Tiger says calmly. "Don't make any dinner plans for me, and don't bother me."

Great, access is locked to all! He'll be with the famous Shanna, and you don't care, remember.

"All right, sir."

"See you later, Lily?" says Tiger, against all odds.

Our eyes lock on each other. I think of my descent after having touched the summits with him. Unchanneled bad vibes run through me from side to side.

"I don't know, Tiger. Am I supposed to stay at your disposal and mope around like Sophia? No thanks."

His jaws tighten, but he doesn't comment. The chasm widens. I pick up my bag and walk out.

"I hope that you benefited well from your days of rest, Miss," continues the butler, impassible.

"I have mixed feelings, Peter…"

I know that *monsieur* heard my reply before the butler closed the door behind me.

"Anyway, everything is fine here?" I resume as Tiger leaves us with a sudden roar.

His departure and the look on my face momentarily make the old man uncomfortable. But he quickly pulls himself together and puts a respectful smile on his lips to answer me.

"Yes, everything is fine here; thank you, Miss."

Of course! Everything is still under control on the surface of the planet Sexton.

"Where is Sophia?" I ask, following him inside. "How is she?"

"Fine, Miss Rousseau. I think Mrs. Sexton is taking her bath. I will inform her of your return as soon as she is available."

"No, don't bother, Peter. I'll drop in and say hello."

"As you wish, miss."

I thank the good man and go upstairs to put my things down. Not so eager to be faced with Sophia, I make a detour to the bathroom next to my room.

I just had sex with her husband. I spent most of that day with him, on him, under him… In osmosis, until it all turned sour in a heartbeat. I don't know what to make of it, let alone how to behave now with Sophia. Should I walk in with a big smile and act normal? For the moment, I am unable to do so.

I'm too upset, too confused. Tiger's reversal, his coldness after the heat wave, is killing me.

31

Océane

Facing the mirror, I stare at my reflection. My lips are still marked by merciless kisses, feverish to disintegrate everything in their path. Will Sophia see a change? After all, I'm not the first to be caught up in the middle of them. One of the endless parade of Sexton's partners…

Something clicked in my head: Tiger asked the driver this morning not to tell his wife about our program. Does this mean that I will have to keep secrets from Sophia? Is it because of this Xanax story?

I have doubts about what to do next; now that I find myself back with Sophia in this huge house, my reason conflicts with my emotions. Like me, in her own way, this woman is also lonely. She was beginning to open up, to become attached to me. And vice versa. Sophia moves me more than I would have imagined at first. Very sincerely. It probably would have been easier if I didn't feel tenderness and compassion for her.

The traces of my lonely childhood and my need to be surrounded by others probably alter my judgment of her. The question of the day is: what kind of friendship could be built in this convoluted three-way relationship?

"Océane?" a female voice suddenly calls out to me.

My reflection freezes. My questions dissipate, interrupted by the arrival of the object of my introspection. I hear her in the room, heading in my direction. I don't have time to mentally prepare myself before she knocks on the door, then slides it open. It unnerves me to see her again. She is radiant; she seems to have found her energy while I…

I feel awkward. It's she who defuses my embarrassment by taking me in her arms.

"Hello, my beautiful! Welcome back home!" she enthuses.

"Thanks, Sophia. How are you doing?"

"Much better, let's forget it!" she evades.

Yes, she's sparkling… It's as if the episode of the stoned chick wandering naked in the hallway never happened. Nor that wave of sadness I left her in when I left their property yesterday. Alone with her Ty. Whatever the latter did, it was obviously effective.

This realization stirs something inside me and increases my inner confusion tenfold.

"And you, Océane? Tell me everything, did you rest? Did you have fun? What did you do?" Sophia continues, not noticing how stiff my neck and back are.

Rested? No, I slept with your man, and he is anything but restful.

I think back to the post-battle discussion that left me with a bitter taste, then repress it all. Why is it up to me to get out the oars or inform Sophia of what we did while the male of the house is maybe banging another one right now? After all, these are their codes, their habits. Me, I became the girl between them, confused and who feels guilty. I run my hand through my hair, looking for an idea about what to tell her.

"I did a few activities… I wandered around a lot," I say, turning away. "It was… nice."

No. "Nice" is clearly not the word to use for a day with Tiger.

Sophia comes closer and brushes my cheek. I tense imperceptibly. Nothing in her indicates any animosity, suspicion, or anything like that. It's with my own conscience that I'm struggling with. Faced with this woman who has become classy and perfect again, I remember how intimidating she was during my job interview. And also how well we got along afterward until the balance tipped.

"Just 'nice?' We'll do better than that!" she declaims. "I, too, in between meetings with my managers, have been bored the last few hours. What if we went out for dinner?"

Say something, Océane. At least look excited.

"Why not? Where would you like to eat?" I manage to say with a little enthusiasm.

"Cool! We'll improvise. A girls' night out will do us good, won't it?"

"Of course, but does your… husband know that… Well, does he…"

Boy, you've got it all mixed up; she'll suspect something.

My embarrassment amuses Sophia. I don't think she knows… And if she found out, would she mind? After all, she "chose" me, right? What the hell am I doing?

"Is Ty still impressing you?" she misunderstands. "Relax, honey. He gave me twenty-four hours of his time this Monday. You can't imagine what kind of hole that is for this workaholic to fill."

In fact, he lost almost forty-eight hours with the two of us… Don't fucking digress, Océane!

"Yes, I bet," I reply.

"I got him on the phone. He's with Shanna; I'm not likely to see him again soon," the wife tells me.

Okay, so he keeps her informed of what he thinks is necessary to communicate to her? I was dumped in front of the property before he disappeared without any explanation. I swallow the flood of comments this raises in my head and try to continue naturally, "I see. Is she a… friend? Do you know her?"

I hate this misplaced curiosity that has been nagging at me. Or maybe I'm just offended by the way my time with Tiger ended today. I'm on edge, and my brain is a mess. I hate all these petty thoughts that I can't control anymore.

"Shanna? She's sort of the female version of Ty," Sophia tells me without a hint of concern… or jealousy. "She works for him."

Sophia is already changing the topic, now talking about fashion. So why am I still bugging about this? Besides, what does a female version of Ty mean? That she's hot? Charismatic and confident?

This whole situation is insane; I don't recognize myself anymore in this kind of polygamy bullshit where each new female name awakens something involuntary in me. On the one hand, I still haven't recovered from today. On the other hand, there are still unanswered questions about the Sextons…

I try to let go of it. In "it doesn't affect you that much" mode. I shower and then join Sophia in the dressing room to get dressed.

On second thought, maybe it's a great idea for both of us to get some fresh air.

Two hours later, we were escorted into the VIP room of Velvet & Diamonds, a beachfront lounge bar I had never heard of. Considering the standing, it's not surprising. Valet parking, no line, escort, and immersion in a few seconds in an intimate, chic, and hushed atmosphere. We settle into a comfortable sofa draped in velvet. Sophia smiles at me while playing with the strap of her black dress. I put on an outfit just as sexy as hers; I thought I would feel better by making myself beautiful. Bullshit! My brain is still running at full speed.

"Do you like it?" Sophia asks me.

"This place is sublime," I answer her, conquered all the same by her choice.

"They make aperitif dinners to die for; wait till you taste it," she promises me.

We place our order. The cocktails and small refined appetizers do not take long to appear as if by magic. I realize that I was really hungry. We discuss everything and nothing, and I relax almost totally.

"The other particularity of the Velvet & Diamonds is that they have a nightclub in the basement," denotes Sophia to me while sipping her luxury margarita.

"So, I stuff myself, and then we burn the calories?"

She nods and laughs. My apprehensions are gone for good. It's much easier when neither of us mentions Tiger, and I try to avoid thinking about him. The minutes go by, and my budding complicity with Sophia takes over. After the meal, she takes me in the elevator to the lower level. Like her, I want to dance and clear my head. So, no need to ask twice when she pulls me onto the dance floor. "Blood in the Cut" by K.Flay resounds, and Sophia intertwines our fingers. Our eyes lock together; she begins to sway her hips. Slow, sensual, a smile on her red lips. Slightly tipsy and in a better mood, I gradually settle on the rhythm. I close my eyelids and move with her.

Little by little, I absorb the notes of the music. My body undulates, and my hands sink into my mane. I don't look at anybody anymore; I want to release the pressure and sweep away my suppositions, shames, and doubts.

TIGER

Shanna refills our glass of bourbon; I barely look up from the numbers on her computer screen. She continues to tell me how the next financial operation prepared with her traders will inflate the capital of TS Naval at the opening of the Sydney Stock Exchange tomorrow morning. The beep of my phone momentarily catches my eye. One of many text messages to be read later. No, this one is from my communication department. My eyelids wrinkle, and I grab my phone. They only signal me when necessary, so there is probably a problem.

I breathe slowly as I first discover the message left by my butler earlier in the evening. I hadn't paid attention to it.

Peter: Mrs. Sexton and Miss Océane prefer to dine in town, sir. They are going out without a driver. Mrs. Sexton drives.

Shit, Peter warned me! The second message was from the head of my communications department. My fingers tighten on the mobile as I read:

I'm sorry to bother you, Mr. Sexton. Your wife and Miss Rousseau have just been tagged online. The link is attached.

I click on it and begin to boil. Shanna interrupts.

"Ouch, I know that look," she says. "Who has just incurred your wrath?"

Before my eyes, a story on Harry Carter's Instagram account. This little jerk is still having fun stepping on my toes. I see him on live, sticking to one blonde who is dancing. Oxygen closes off in my chest. The jerk filming for him comments off the record, "Velvet & Diamonds has never been hotter!"

My jaws clench. I imagine that if my staff is alerting me, there is a valid reason. This one materializes on the image: my wife wiggling. I hear music; I see Sophia exposing herself in the nightclub. Chanting the lyrics of "Blood in the Cut." Right away, I'm thinking of kicking that jerk Carter's ass for being around at the wrong time again. In theory, on a weeknight and in this select club, there are few people. But he had to be there. My fist clenches and my vision blurs.

Fuck, breathe!

Another story. Carter is pressing against a body. The one of…

…*Océane.*

I know it; I know it for sure before she even turns around. I know this body by heart now… I still have a burning memory of it. A few hours ago, I couldn't think about anything else. Our return from the stud farm, what we shared there, and her reaction to the announcement of the trip planned for the three of us, all this mess was taking up too much of my neurons. I needed to step back to see things more clearly. And working was the best way to do it.

Well, that was the case.

The camera changes angle, giving me confirmation. Eyelids closed, dressed in a tiny dress, Océane hums the chorus of the song. What the hell is she playing at? She doesn't push him away when he hugs her. On the contrary, she…

"Tiger?" Shanna calls me back.

I get up and pick up my key. My pulse is racing.

"Is there a problem?" insists my collaborator.

"You'll have to do a follow-up later; I have an emergency."

"Is it Sophia?"

Before Shanna expands more, I head for the exit of her apartment, contacting the head of communications to find out her plan of attack. I call the elevator and finally rush into the stairwell to gain time. With my mind in turmoil, I run down the stairs. I do not know which of the two heats up my nerves more. Sophia, who lets off steam in public with videos in support. She can draft off course at any moment, without an escort, without a net… Or Océane who…

What the fuck is she doing?

32

TIGER

I get a speed violation on the way, being way over the limit. We'll deal with that later; for now, I don't care. I pull up in front of the Velvet & Diamonds and throw the keys to the valet, who catches them on the fly. I rush inside the establishment, ranting.

They might both be drunk and potentially out of control. Damn it, was Sophia going to drive again afterward? Two of my guys join me in the elevator.

"What are the instructions, Mr. Sexton? A quick exfiltration without a fuss?" one of the bodyguards asks.

"For my wife and Miss Rousseau, yes. You clean up the area and leave me alone with Carter," I reply.

"Copy that, sir!"

The elevator reaches the basement, and the doors open. My two escorts coordinate their actions, and in just three seconds, we enter the club. The music and the ambient joy bother me instantly. I spot them; they are still dancing. That jerk Harry is still hovering around Sophia and Océane. Especially Océane. Harry Carter may be provocative, but he knows that one finger on my wife—in public— and his dentist will have trouble putting his teeth back in place. He'll have to find them first. That said, he's ignoring a new fact: from now on, I won't tolerate him touching that blond girl, either.

Not as long as she...

In fact, Océane turns around laughing; her beautiful green eyes widen with surprise when she sees me.

"Tiger?!" she exclaims.

This alerts Sophia, who turns in return. My wife blushes like a kid caught in the act.

"What are you doing here? Don't tell me that—"

"We're not going to talk here," I tell her.

One of my staff locates Carter's friend. He snatches his cell phone from him to prevent another video leak. Immediately after, my bodyguards catch Sophia and Océane to incite them firmly to leave the place. My wife complies; she knows that I hate to attract attention for bad reasons, and she is not going to make the situation worse. No, the one who could cause a scandal is my Frenchie. She struggles and forbids the bodyguard from touching her. Inevitably, the probability that other cell phones will start filming the scene increases.

Why didn't she do the same with Harry Carter, for God's sake? She should have pushed him away with that same vehemence instead of sticking to him!

"Let go of me! I don't want to go home! I'm free, Tiger!"

"Damn it, stop it, Océane! We won't make a spectacle of ourselves. Follow my employees and shut up!" I shout in French while Carter looks on.

I don't want to catch this one in front of her. No violent outbursts in her presence, but taking it out on me while Océane resists is wearing on my patience.

"Sounds like she'd rather stay with me, Sexton. Your friend and I will finish the evening together. Why don't you go home with your wife," says Carter, proud of himself.

This is the final straw that drowns my phlegm for good. I run into him. Océane lets out a scream that fades away as she is taken away by force through the back exit. My team pulls her out, with or without her cooperation. And my fist finally smashes into the jaws of the daddy's boy. I keep him from collapsing; I'm not done with him. He's in too much pain to talk. Great, I'd rather hear him whimper than come up with more nonsense.

"Last warning, you clown," I say, bringing my face close to his bleeding face. "Stay out of my way."

To conclude, my forehead violently hits his. At the same time, I feel something vaguely on my neck. I release Carter, who collapses. I hear his acolyte exclaim, "You'll hear from our lawyers, Sexton! Do you know who I am?"

"No. And I'm already shaking with fear," I say as I head for the emergency exit.

Outside, I take a breath in and breathe out to regain my composure. My cell phone vibrates, and I pick it up.

"Mr. Sexton, I can confirm that we have them both with us. We are on our way to your residence."

"All right. I'm on my way."

OCÉANE

I can't believe it!

I'm pissed off at Tiger. Who the hell does he think he is? The arrival at his property in Sydney happens in a hurry. His bulldogs are dumb, loyal, and border on bullshit! They didn't give up and didn't hesitate to treat me ruthlessly to make me give in.

Sophia gave in too quickly; I don't understand, damn it! Maybe she is docile by nature. Or too into him to dare to upset him. He can probably do whatever he wants with her whenever he wants, but I'm not his thing! There's no way I'm going to silently obey a man who thinks he's above everything. And of everyone! I don't take offense; it is obviously not the case for Sophia, who takes off her shoes on the terrace and speaks to one of the employees.

"Bring us two mojito ice creams," she demands before looking at me. "Are you up for it, Océane, or do you want something else?"

Is she serious? Is it her routine to have to leave parties escorted by some kind of military commando?

"No thanks, I'm not going to have an ice cream. I'd rather rip apart the macho bastard who is your husband! Why aren't you angry? Why do you let him act like that?"

A gleam lights up in her eyes.

"It's exciting to see him overreact," she says. "It's been so long since I've seen him so possessive."

Okay, so it got her excited that Tiger would come in and act like he owned us. While I'm chomping at the bit to jump down the bastard's throat.

He appears soon with a dark face, glass shards on his shoulders, and stinking of champagne. He looks like a guy coming out of a fight during which a bottle was used as a weapon. Sophia rushes to make sure that he is well.

Seriously!

I cross my arms and look at him without moving. He dispatches his wife while mumbling, "I'm fine, stop!"

"No, Ty," resists Sophia. "It is time to go to your private room. Me, you brought me there after my small excesses of the last time. I'm going to call your—"

"I said stop, Sophia!"

He boils, but she braves him, "Why's that? Because Océane doesn't know that detail yet? She doesn't know why you have a secret area in all your properties? Or you're doing everything you can to avoid it?"

"What are we talking about?" I ask.

"That's not the point, Sophia! We've got another topic in mind: what the hell were you doing tonight?"

"A girls' night out," his wife maintains without breaking down. "We were having a great time until you burst in, weren't we, Océane?"

I am overwhelmed between my anger and this thing that Sophia almost revealed. Tiger shifts and walks towards me.

"Isn't that right, darling?" insists Sophia.

"It's true," I maintain. "And I needed that breath of fresh air."

"Interesting… With Carter?" Tiger asks me in a husky, low voice.

"With whoever I want," I reply. "Need I remind you that Sophia is your wife? Live by your rules if you want, but I won't ask your permission if I want to have fun!"

He stops close, too close, dripping with authority, arrogance, and… sex appeal.

No, you won't flinch, Océane, you certainly won't! Fucking him won't make you a possession among others; let him understand well.

"I warned you, Lily—"

"Stop with the 'Lily!' And I told you I wanted your respect, Tiger."

"Respect works both ways. How is letting a loser grope you in a nightclub disrespectful to me?"

No, but this guy is phenomenally in bad faith!

He stares at me, his eyes darkened and too magnetic for my armor that has become too permeable since our afternoon… I swallow. His warm breath and the heady scent of champagne mixed with his own shake me up. Even if I try hard to hide it.

"No," I say. "I repeat: officially, I am single and free of my actions! I'm here because I want to be. Outside of your house, I can date Carter or a bunch of other guys, and you won't interfere."

He squints his eyelids.

"I'll set the record straight," he whispers.

The next second, he pushes me against him. I try at first to push him back, to persist in playing the proud one, but his tongue rushes between my lips, and his hands press my hip. I can feel his bulge hardening against my belly. Does he want me or just to establish his male dominance? His kiss is violent and furious; he cuts my breath.

"No one else is going to get their hands on you for the duration of your contract. My lawyers will add an additional clause because your behavior tonight won't happen again," he hammers against my swollen mouth. "Never again, you understand?"

Outraged, my legs wobble, and I manage to back away. My body and my mind are fighting; one is getting dangerously soft, and the other is trying to rebel. Backward, I continue to challenge him with my eyes. I pass near Sophia, and my arm brushes hers.

"Nobody else?" I repeat, the nerves in effervescence. "We'll see about that, Tiger! We're equals; you don't have to demand anything from me!"

Deciding to teach him a lesson, an impulse crossed my mind. I don't give a damn about his social status compared to mine; servitude is clearly out! Before he anticipates my retaliation, I embrace his wife. My hands go up toward the face of Sophia. She and I look at each other, a spark of complicity in the bottom of our eyes. Feminine solidarity, the desire for rebellion. We are in the twenty-first century, damn!

"My body belongs to me; I do what I want with it. And you, Sophia? Are you as free as he is?" I ask, ready to push her man to the limit. "After all, I'm here mainly for you, right?"

Careful, Océane, you'll do the wrong thing again.

Let's rectify: I've already been doing nonsense for a while. I might as well keep going and set the pace. And when Tiger looks at me like that, it makes me feel good and encourages me to assert myself now. My initiative disconcerts Sophia for a short time. Then I feel her ready to play the game; I see it in her half-smile. Conscious of making a mistake, of reacting out of pride, I savor the pleasure of proving to Tiger that he won't be the center of our universe. At least not mine. Even if I have to push the boundaries and leave my comfort zone. My boldness takes a winding path, out of control…

"Absolutely, my darling," Sophia whispers to me, starting to brush my hair.

"Don't play with fire, Lily," Tiger warns me.

This nickname and this warning increase my complicity with Sophia. My lips touch hers with delicacy. I stifle the hesitations which swell in my head, the warnings that light up. The beautiful woman caresses my face, and our mouths meet again… Slowly, they open for an unexpected kiss, confusing but consensual. A brilliant claim of my freedom.

At the end of this little demonstration, his wife and I are caught in a fit of laughter, staring at each other incredulously. We just kissed! A real kiss!

"I had forgotten that kind of sweetness," says Sophia, the delicate intonation. "Well, thanks, Ty. We'll find another way to have fun."

And I add, "Without you, of course."

Sophia winks at him as she takes my hand to drag me inside. At the same moment, I dare glance in the direction of the tiger. Inscrutable, he observes us without a word. The look he gives me makes me shiver. He has never stared at me like that…

Shaken, I do not capitulate. Once up there, Sophia locks her door on both of us and laughs like a proud teenager to have finally behaved against the rules.

"You're very surprising, you," she says to me. "I love it! Do you want to go all the way?"

One of the warnings in my brain suddenly materializes: she is bisexual!

Creating the illusion seemed to get to her guy; that was my only purpose. I shake my head, my cheeks on fire. My whole body

shudders. Not for Sophia, not because of our kiss, well, I think…
But because of what was in Tiger's blue eyes when I transgressed his
prohibitions. Did I manage to upset him? To piss him off as much as
he did to me when his gorillas took me by force?

"I… Sorry."

"Don't worry," Sophia reassures me softly. "I have an idea; we
are going to be convincing."

"How?"

"In the living room area of my suite, there are video
surveillance cameras. The other rooms don't have them for my
privacy," she whispers to me.

"Oh."

She hugs me and encourages me in the hollow of my ear,
"Relax… We're just going to make him feel like something hot is
happening under his roof, over which he has zero power. Just sound,
no images."

"Make him feel left out of the fun? I like it a lot," I affirm,
tempted.

Sophia releases me, steps back, and delicately undoes the
zipper of her dress. She sends it waltzing over to the other side of
the living room, waits a few seconds with pink cheekbones, and then
starts to moan, "Oh, yes, Océane! Yeeeees…"

I place my palm over my mouth to stifle my amusement.
Sophia continues her stripping, her underwear joins the dress, and
she makes objects fall knowingly to the ground to simulate a burning
effusion between us. I finish by imitating her by biting my lip not
to laugh. Just to spice up this comedy, I throw my pumps, then my
clothes. He'll certainly hear us moaning upstairs.

A splendid simulation of orgasms later, we spread out in the
bed. Hilarious. I pull the comforter to cover myself.

"It was completely childish but so jubilant!" I laugh.

Seconds pass. Mrs. Sexton's breathing returns to normal, and
she turns to face me, propping up her head.

"Since when do you sleep together?" she takes me by surprise.

The effects of our shared joke die abruptly, my stomach
twitching. The intense marbles of Sophia don't leave me anymore,
and I have difficulty looking at her.

"I…"

"There's no need to deny it, Océane. I know Ty inside out."

Damn it!

"Your reaction… and his outburst tells me he's fucked you, enjoyed it and intends to do it again."

An uneasy feeling explodes in my brain, and a swirl of questions assails me.

"It's not… Sophia, I…"

"Don't give me a lot of lip service, Océane. Technically, each of us has free rein with you without any secrets if you want to. And I can see that you and Ty… Anyway, I need to know if we're all on the same page," she persists. "Are we, honey?"

"Wh… what do you mean?"

"I don't want you to forget that this is temporary. You're like a flower that will fade and that others will replace… Don't get attached to him."

A warning: sudden, unexpected, and destabilizing. I try to regulate my breathing to appear calm, but my palpitant is getting a little excited. I look for my words, and I then say, "As we are finally at the moment of clarifying this mess, I, too, have something on my heart."

Sophia blinks, all ears and disconcerted too.

"Yes?" she says in a tone of concern. "About Ty and you?"

"No. About you and me. I think you weren't very honest with me from the start. Your life, this 'job' is like Pandora's box with more in it. Nothing is as harmless as it seems…"

"I… I know what you mean," she admits without elaborating.

Is she walking on eggshells? Is she afraid I'll delve into her past, her secrets that even her husband hasn't revealed, to get answers? What kind of childhood and adolescence did she have? Why does it still weigh so heavily on the functioning of her marriage?

"I owe you an apology for that," Sophia adds. "But honestly, if I had laid my cards on the table from day one, would you have agreed?"

"I don't think so," I say. "And, in fact, if you hadn't blacked out the other day, I would have left."

I'm not so sure about that now… Looking back, my chemistry with Tiger and my compassion for Sophia skewed my opinion and influenced my behavior.

I notice the surprise in her eyes.

"You... you stayed for me?"

Sophia probes me. Deep down, I don't know what's holding me back. I just know that I got too close to the flames instead of away from them. I swallow and nod.

Sophia probes me for a long time. She nods and sighs.

"Then, I don't have to worry about what occurs between my husband and you," she deduces. "As long as you're a friend, a sister, it won't be a problem. I'll be willing to show compersion."

"Can you explain?"

"It's a kind of pleasure that one feels in sharing one's partner without feeling jealousy, a pillar in free couples. Compersion and trust. As long as the boundaries are respected, everything is fine."

"Oh, I see."

No, I don't see it. It's another Pandora's box that is unlocked without me really knowing what it contains.

"Of course, this discussion remains between you and me," she says.

Caught off guard and a little uncomfortable, I murmur, "Yes, of course."

"And can you make me a promise, Océane?"

Hesitantly, I whisper, "I listen to you?"

"Will you promise to slip out of Ty's life when I ask you to?"

This request slips into my brain, pernicious and incomprehensible considering that she's the one who drew me into this mess. Unless...

"I... Of course, Sophia. But I have a question: did you take the initiative to hire me, knowing what the outcome might be, or did Tiger force you into it?"

"No, it was my idea... We both agree, but this is the first time I've been involved in Ty's choice of a temporary partner."

Interesting... How does he usually do it?

It's to him I want to ask this, so I look at Sophia.

"Okay," I say. "So, does Tiger do this kind of setting up with your lovers when he invites them to the stud?"

She fidgets with her wedding ring and gives a half smile.

"Yes. We've always made sure to preserve our marriage, no matter what..." she says, "we are okay?"

Inexplicably, I feel a ball in my stomach. I inhale, exhale and nod. It's her husband, and she sets limits, normal. If there is at least one thing I can understand in this agreement, it's this.

"We're okay," I say in an unrecognizable voice. "And you, do you promise me that there will be no more incidents of alcohol and antidepressants?"

As tactfully as possible, I give her the opportunity to finally tell me her story if she wants to. But the subject is perhaps too painful, too heavy. Imperceptibly, Sophia closes up. She is embarrassed by the evocation of this episode, still vague for me, and prefers to smile at me.

I don't insist; she comes to me and takes me in her arms to whisper in my ear, "I'll do my best… It's good that you stayed. It's good to have a friend."

An indefinable feeling settles in the pit of my stomach. She oozes this fragility, loneliness, and need for affection from everywhere…

I am drawn into a singular story of friendship and sex between three consenting adults. There will be no more surprises; everyone knows what to expect now. I convince myself of it internally. At the end of this atypical exploration, I will leave on my own. And Sophia will live her secrets with her possessive, arrogant, and control freak husband. For this incandescent attraction between Tiger and me will fade.

Tomorrow, the day after tomorrow, or very soon… Yes, it can't work otherwise.

The silence falls again, full of contained emotions. What can I say? Suddenly, thinking about Tiger, a question comes to my mind: Sophia almost told me something new about him earlier.

"By the way, what's in these private rooms?"

Sophia bats her eyelashes. Does this have anything to do with her worries, this past that she obviously doesn't want to tell me about?

"These are medical areas with all the high-tech equipment necessary for regular check-ups," she confides to me.

Shit! I stiffen up and stare at her.

"For you? Are you sick, Sophia?"

"No, not me," she maintains. "These rooms are for Tiger."

A wave of anguish invades me. Is it him?

"What's wrong with him? How bad is it?"

"Ty has congenital analgesia. In fact, he is totally insensitive to pain. Even the most intense, the most unbearable. Any pain, physical, even emotional."

I take it in silence, in a state of shock.

"It is true that I have some problems," Sophia recognizes evasively in front of my amazement. "But to be in love with a man insensitive to certain things—however basic and natural—can sometimes push a person to drink or to abuse pills," she explains to me as if to justify herself. "Anyway, now that you know it, I count on you to keep this secret too and to support me in case of need if it is necessary to oblige Ty to see his trusted doctor. He's been following him since childhood."

"That's crazy! I… Yes, but concretely, if he never has pain, how does this disease show up in his daily life?"

"It's complicated when it comes to emotions. In general, he is stoic and cold-blooded. It's up to his loved ones to be more attentive to the possible physical injuries he may have unknowingly… Whether Ty loses a loved one, breaks a bone, or gets burned, he continues to move forward as if nothing had happened. Suffering doesn't get to him; he doesn't know what it is. Not like us, anyway."

Stunned, my mouth opens and closes in the void. That was the secret of the tiger.

33

TIGER

The moans, their kiss… During my stretching at the end of the jog, my head is filled with moans. Not those pushed by Sophia and Océane yesterday evening.

But those even more private of the beautiful Frenchie, lying in the grass and wet, make me lose my mind. It's getting in the way, and it's succeeding in dethroning the endorphins provided by the sport. I take off my headphones.

It is early; they are still sleeping when I reach the floor. What could they have done together? Where are we? Where are we going?

Fuck, that's all I could think about! As if I didn't have more burning issues on my plate.

My detectives in France have formally identified our targets. Buried in a nebula called *La Confrérie*, a vast closed club: of sex, of perversions. And one nickname obsesses me more than the others in the file: the One-Eyed Man…

Impossible to sleep; it devours my brain. I'll have to plan what to do next. At some point, I will have to find a way to inform Sophia.

I put off this realization. Océane comes back to excite my neurons. Because she stays despite everything… Angry and in full rebellion, but she stays. Damn, her anger and her rebellion were even sexy! In my shower, images come flooding in. My eyelids close, and the fantasies and desires soon mix in my head. The shampoo foam is dripping, and my desire to fuck Blondie is growing to the point of considering some misconduct… My cock is awakening; I imagine Océane doing… doing…

"Argh, what the hell am I doing!"

I calm my erection under the cold jets, teeth clenched. And I leave the bathroom, which has become a minefield for my heightened libido and my scattering mind.

I swallow my first dose of caffeine on the balcony in a towel. To better repress my unfulfilled desires, I immerse myself in reading the financial press and my important emails before going to my dressing room. I leave my quarters, knotting my tie, and meet my chief servant.

"Have a nice day, Mr. Sexton," he says.

I interrupt my phone call to reply, "Thank you, Peter. Good day to you too… By the way, there will be a delivery in the morning. My assistant will call to check with you."

"Okay, Mr. Sexton."

Outside, near the car, an intuition pushes me to raise my head towards the windows of Sophia's wing. In her robe on her balcony, my wife is watching me. She sends me a flying kiss. I probe her for a moment while the driver opens the back door for me.

My thoughts are swarming. Is Océane still in Sophia's bed? Naked? Filled? Wet? What if I…

Damn it, lock this!

"Good morning, sir. Your office?"

"Yes," I confirm to my driver.

Focus, I must take back control of my body and mind. Rigorously. I join Anaïs, my personal assistant, while settling in the Bentley. It's a struggle for my self-control. Océane chooses this moment to appear. A cigarette between her delicious lips, her soft silhouette draped in a silky kimono of Sophia's. It's fucked; she turns me on too much; restraint, it becomes complicated.

"Wait a few seconds before starting," I say.

"Yes, Mr. Sexton."

The dark tint of the window of the vehicle prevents Océane from seeing my face. A guilty pleasure: it leaves me the leisure to undress her with my eyes during a time that is suspended. Blondie's eyes stray to my car, which finally moves away.

My phone is still in my palm; my index finger is looking for the letter S in my phonebook. Sweet Lily. It's itching me to call her. Does she have her phone on her? I crack. The first two rings make me doubt it; after the third, her voice disabuses me of any doubt.

"Hello?"

Mine whispers to her, "Hello, you."

Océane's delicate breathing seeps into the hollow of my ear.

After their… little show the day before, I understand her hesitation. In broad daylight, I suppose she may be measuring how far she's gone. I can't wait to hear what she's going to say to me now.

"Did you sleep well?"

"Yes… And you?" she answers me carefully.

Me? I didn't sleep a wink.

In my hypothesis, I wondered if they were going to talk in private to dwell on my particularity. Sophia sort of hinted at it instead of keeping her mouth shut, and Océane probably ticked. This detail about me was strictly personal. They've overcome an obstacle—on a few too many levels—and it will have an impact. Quite different from the one my wife expected when she agreed with our guest's provocation. I am not one to accept defeat or loss of control of a situation.

Sophia has always known that. Your turn to learn it.

I elude and get right to the point, "Can you tell Sophia that my doctor came by in the night? Superficial wounds and subject closed."

"Uh… okay."

Océane is silent. I perceive the acceleration of her breath. I dread the questions that are slow to come out of her mouth.

"Why don't you tell Sophia yourself?" she finally asks me.

My breathing starts again. She skirts the subject.

"You have apparently become very intimate," I say, taking care to remain neutral. "So, I assume my wife has made a confession or two to you on the pillow."

Océane doesn't deny it. I continue, "Now that you know about this particularity, I think you know enough. We can both proceed with the serious business."

Océane's new silence seems to last so long that I glance at my screen to check that the call has not been cut off. My lips curl up; she is on the line but unsettled.

"What serious business?" she pulls herself together.

"Let your imagination wander, little sweetness."

With satisfaction, I hang up without waiting. I think for the next few minutes and then write a text message to the lawyer who established the au pair contract.

I want to add a clause with a kind of pari passu to the contract of Océane, Lilia Rousseau. Study the question to make me a proposal in my office in...

I look at the traffic, estimate the time on my wrist and continue:

...fifteen minutes.

Last night she claimed the right to be treated as an equal, didn't she? It costs me nothing to offer her this frail illusion. Giving her things in black and white will allow me to cunningly make a little push in the negotiations. She lets her guard down and gets off her high horse, and I get what I want.

I want her without restriction, sharing, barriers, or respite.

Océane

I take a drag on my cigarette, my mind in turmoil.

So, Tiger Sexton is insensitive... at least to pain. I'm still stunned. What does this imply for the man he is, for the adult he has become? All night I imagined how he would react to me this morning. In the end, he is more enigmatic, which turns my brain and my senses upside down as soon as I wake up. What is he up to? He said, "proceed to serious business." What should I expect when a guy like that comes up with that kind of agenda right out of bed?

Based on everything I know about him now, I'm sure he doesn't like to lose absolute control over his surroundings. Fuck, in a way, he has it over his own body since he can endure anything without being in pain... Crazy that thing! And as through my bravado with Sophia, I reminded him that he won't control me, that I was still free to make my own choices, I think to myself that he's going to fight back.

Won't he? But in what way? Is he going to—

"Give me one?" Sophia surprises me by joining me outside.

My assumptions disperse in my volute. I take out the cigarette pack from the pocket of the kimono that Sophia lent me so she can help herself. She pushes the cigarette between her lips. Her fingers slide on the nape of my neck and draw my head towards her. The blazing end of my cigarette sticks to hers, and she aspires to light it. Her eyes stay plunged in mine. The seconds and my thoughts fly away as we start smoking side by side. Neither of us breaks the silence for a moment.

"I need a latte," Sophia finally declares. "I'm going to have breakfast by the pool. You coming?"

"Yes, let's go."

Following her lead, I hesitate to pass on her husband's message. I don't want to be the middleman between them. As a perfect control freak, maybe that's precisely why Tiger played it that way. It could be some kind of twisted strategy to punish his wife for her deviation from me… Or to torture my brain at the same time? He puts me in a delicate situation because, obviously, after having shared so much complicity with Sophia, I fear offending her. I think her husband hasn't said a word to her since last night. But Tiger makes sure to let his wife know one thing: he preferred to talk to "the fling" that I am supposed to be.

He's too smart. And Machiavellian. But seriously sexy too, and… Damn, I'm getting off track!

At the end of my fourth sip of coffee, turning everything over and over in my head, I say, "Sophia, have you heard from Tiger? I mean, he seemed to have taken a magnum of champagne during a fight yesterday, right?"

"Probably, his hand was bleeding again too. But no, I don't know more. Neither about his possible injuries nor about the possible legal consequences of an altercation with Harry Carter," sighs Sophia.

I swallow and blurt out with as much innocence as I can muster, "Uh… as far as I know, he's been to his doctor. It's nothing serious, according to Tiger himself."

Sophia sticks her fork in a piece of pineapple and takes her time before answering me by directing the fruit towards her mouth.

"Ah… and when did he tell you about this?"

"This morning, on the phone. Quickly."

I smile at her, hoping to clear up any misunderstanding.

"I see…" she says.

I feel her suddenly acting strange, or maybe it is me? She seems to be studying me. I pick at my croissant and give her another smile, a little embarrassed. To which she ends up answering.

"So much the better," she rejoices while starting to eat again.

I dip my nose into my coffee, convinced he did it on purpose. Tiger knows his wife and their "limits."

"What are you up to today?" I ask her after a while to rekindle the conversation and relax.

"I have some work obligations to fulfill and a little private thing… Do you have plans?"

"No, I don't. I'm at your disposal," I say. "Do you need to have me around when you work? How do we do it?"

Technically, I'm not her assistant. And other than table service, I don't know much about the restaurant business. Besides, there's no question of shopping, a girls' night out, or a party in the middle of the work week, so I don't really see what my day job would be.

"Well, on the outside, as you know, you're very useful for the social events and invitations I have to go to. And often without Tiger. With my schedule today, I'll be able to manage just fine," she says with a hint of mockery. "I'll call you if I have a gap in my schedule for a bite to eat or a drink?"

"That's fine with me! Do you have any nice places to recommend if I ever go out for a walk?"

Obviously delighted, Sophia gives me an enthusiastic listing of the must-see spots in Sydney. And me, I put away in the corner of my mind the words pronounced by her Ty on the phone.

I don't know what he is planning. Maybe I should take a walk and make sure that Mr. Sexton's bulldogs don't track me all day. That way, I'll be home at the same time as his wife in the evening.

An hour later, Sophia has left the house for work, and I'm here, idle, still not dressed after my shower. Expecting I don't know what. Tiger's promise continues to cloud my thoughts. It nags at me until two sharp knocks on the door bring me back to reality.

"Who is it?" I exclaim, a tad feverishly in spite of myself.

"It's Peter, Miss Océane. I'm sorry to interrupt you. You have a visitor and a delivery," he informs me.

I go to open the door, not expecting to discover three other pairs of unknown eyes in addition to those of the butler.

"Uh… hello. It's for?" I stammer.

"Hello, Miss Rousseau. I'm Anaïs, Mr. Sexton's main assistant; it is he who sends us," announces to me a preppy chick all dressed up.

I shake the hand she politely offers me.

"Oh… nice to meet you, Anaïs."

"Let me introduce you to Saïf, Mr. Sexton's stylist and personal shopper. He will take care of your clothing needs and other jewelry, shoes, and beauty care."

"Anything you wish, Miss Rousseau," finishes the guy who gauges me by touching without embarrassment my wet hair. "I will doll you up, my dear!"

Stun, I beat my eyelashes, and then I shift with a hesitant smile!

"I don't understand. Sophia has already put me in touch with her staff for this kind of detail," I say. "I have everything I need; I'm afraid that you have come for nothing."

The assistant and the stylist exchange a look of connivance. As if they knew something I didn't. Peter takes a step back. The third stranger next to him still hasn't been introduced.

"I know, Mademoiselle Rousseau, but… would you mind giving us just five minutes in private? We won't bother you for long; I have to get back to the office anyway," insists Anaïs.

Curiosity is a very bad flaw, Océane…

Argh, I give in, though. I'm too intrigued by the famous "we can both get serious." The door closes on Peter and the other woman, who has remained in the hallway. Tiger's personal shopper places a cover and boxes on my bed, then both of them scrutinize me. I feel like a special task that has been given to them. Exactly what order did they receive? I tighten the cord of my bathrobe and try to regain some confidence. I invite them to tell me more, "I'm listening. What exactly did Tiger ask you?"

"To get you everything you need for tonight," says his assistant.

"But what else?"

"Honey, we are following Mr. Sexton's instructions with discretion, period. So, I got you an Alex Perry… I hesitated for a long time between her and a Lagerfeld, but my final choice is just perfect! A real gem," the guy says in excitement as he starts to open the case. "You absolutely had to have a piece from my favorite Australian designer."

He pulls out a cloth holding the hanger in front of me, proud of himself. I freeze. Did he say Lagerfeld, like, Karl Lagerfeld? And this Alex Perry is his equivalent on the fashion planet in Australia, I guess?

No, but why am I going to end up with a new overpriced thing with a wardrobe already full of haute couture splendors previously chosen with Sophia? And why are they talking about discretion in the first place?

My eyes stop on the dress in question, and my mouth goes dry. Black leather, low cut, laces running along the whole back it seems. In short, an outfit anything but innocent.

Oh, shit! Is this the next level? "The serious stuff?"

"What… what instructions did you get exactly?" I ask in a less sure voice.

The stylist smiles but doesn't answer. Neither did the chick.

"You also have a choice of matching shoes. I know some jet-setting women who would kill to wear these Jimmy Choo's. One of a kind, honey!" the personal shopper enthuses as if the exceptional quality of the products he presents would make me swallow my questions.

It is bad to know me, "honey."

I cross my arms without taking a step toward the fashion items on display and stare at the assistant.

"Can I talk to you alone, Anaïs?"

"Of course. Can you give us a moment, Saïf?" she throws to her companion, whose eyes do not cease shining with admiration for his purchases of the day.

"No worry, my beautiful," capitulates this one. "Anyway, I finished my mission. I have all that I needed," he continues by looking at me. "I had your measurements, but I absolutely had to meet you, honey. To better determine the hairstyle and the make-up to recommend to my team when my guys will come to help you to prepare you at the end of the day."

What?!

"I have a fabulous idea; you're going to be gorgeous!"

"What? It's not finished?" I ask.

"Of course not, honey. Mr. Sexton appreciates my perfectionist side; we won't disappoint him, will we?" declares the stylist.

With that, he leaves and closes the door, obviously delighted. I inhale for a long time, then exhale, more and more lost.

"Why should I put these…" I start before sighing. "No, actually, get those things and tell your boss I'm turning down his gifts."

If this is his way of apologizing for treating me like his thing yesterday, he's got it all wrong! Or worse, he's not apologizing; he's retaliating by putting the means to…

Yes, to what? To win this round? Teach me a lesson in his own way?

The employee doesn't move. She opens her purse, takes out a luxurious, off-white envelope decorated with golden arabesques, and hands it to me.

"This is for you," she whispers. "It will help you understand."

Perplexed, I grabbed the envelope and gave in to my curiosity. An elegant invitation card in the same tones is slipped in.

Miss Rousseau,

La Péniche is honored to welcome you and Mr. Sexton this evening at seven o'clock.

Please accept our respectful greetings.

An illegible signature is affixed at the bottom in fountain pen.

What on earth is going on?

I direct my suspicious irises at Anaïs.

"La Péniche? Will you explain it to me, or will I have to Google it?"

"You won't find anything about it on Google, miss," she says. "The place is too elitist and confidential to be listed there. Mr. Sexton prefers to give you the explanations you want."

How about that?

"A car will pick you up at 6:20 p.m. sharp. Saïf's team will come at 4 p.m. to do your hair and makeup and help you get ready," she says, tapping away on her phone. "Mr. Sexton will call you in a few seconds. If you'll excuse me, I have to get back to TS Naval."

Great! Another efficient soldier in the Sexton army. She obeys orders and slips away to complete other missions. Eyes glued to her screen, Anaïs is typing as she walks away. I don't have time to hold her back as Tiger's promise of a call comes through in a minute. Synchronized. Everything clicks into place with surgical precision.

"Hello?" I say as I pick up the phone. "What's going on, Tiger?"

"You'll find out tonight. I can't wait until seven o'clock."

"And you think I'm going to look forward to it too, don't you? What makes you think I'll come?"

"Nothing. But I know you're curious… Actually, I am too. We're both players, right?"

I think I hear a hint of amusement in his voice.

What the hell is he planning?

"You… Is there a connection with my night with Sophia?" I try to figure out, suspicious.

"Should there be?"

"You tell me, Tiger."

"We're not going to argue about it. I have to go. I won't be reachable for the next few hours. However, Anaïs will pass on your messages to me," he continues. "See you later; I'll think about it all day… Be ready, Lily."

With that, he hangs up, leaving me even more titillated. It's official; he's playing with my nerves.

34

Océane

The stylist and Tiger's assistant go back to their occupations. However, the second round of their boss' plan of attack arrives very quickly: my last visitor, the lady who was waiting with Peter. She introduces herself as my new gynecologist.

"I'm Dr. Viviane Collins. Can we get to know each other better, Miss Rousseau?"

Damn, he was serious…

And those famous arrangements Tiger mentioned at the stud obviously couldn't be delayed. I should balk at this feeling of being some kind of woman-object or billionaire-on-legs fantasy.

"I'm not sure I need it," I reply.

She doesn't back down; no, she smiles gently at me as if she had prepared herself for my refusal.

"Do you already have a gynecologist in Sydney?"

"That is not your concern. Is it?"

Right after I had turned on her, I try to correct the situation.

"I'm sorry; it's nothing against you. But woman to woman, you can understand that it's not up to the guy I'm sleeping with to choose my gynecologist, right?"

To my surprise, Dr. Collins bursts out laughing.

"I agree with you," she says. "But woman to woman, I've never seen a man so… willing to do whatever it takes to… get more intimacy with his partner."

I bat my eyes, confused. Okay, I admit it; I'm kind of proud of it. It's intoxicating to know that he wants me so much.

"You know what I mean, Miss Rousseau?" continues the doctor.

I think I'm blushing. The situation is quite particular. Like the rest of the world, she knows that Tiger Sexton is also a married man. Unless… Fuck, does she…

"And how many of his partners have you examined? Do you follow Sophia as well?"

"No, Mrs. Sexton is not one of my patients, and you are the first, the only one that Mr. Sexton entrusts to me," she declares from the start.

"Did he pay you to say that?"

Dr. Collins' smile widens as she shakes her head.

"No, I assure you. There was no precedent. I didn't hide my surprise when I was contacted by Mr. Sexton's assistant, who put him on the phone. It was important enough to him to speak directly to me. He wanted the best for you, and without false modesty, he was not wrong."

She winks at me. I relax a bit, I like her, and my curiosity is more titillated.

"So Tiger told you about me directly?"

"It was quick, but yes. He's keen on discretion; obviously, doctor-patient confidentiality is sacred to me," she says. "I know what he wants, but you're my patient—that is, if you agree—and I'm entirely at your disposal. Tell me what you want."

The doctor stares at me frankly, professional and pleasant. I don't feel any judgment. And deep down, my choices are my own business. This thing between Tiger and me, the sweet insanity his sex appeal diffuses into me, and the kind of phenomenal orgasm I've had in his arms, it's all seriously starting to make me lose my mind. My little heart is racing for no reason. Dr. Collins doesn't need to give me any details about her conversation with Tiger. What he wants is me.

"Now that I've seen how you cum, I want you without a latex barrier next time. I want to feel everything about you."

He told me straight up, and his actions prove it. It wasn't empty words, despite the coldness and distance he set up afterward. He comes back to me, more determined. How can I remain reasonable in the face of such burning arguments? The simple fact that he takes things in hand, that he invests himself so much, gives me the measure of his desire for me, in spite of the rest… And I want as much from him without falsely playing prude. More attention, more of him, even more naughty bends to propriety in his muscular arms!

"Well, I aspire above all to remain an independent, liberated girl. While preserving my health and avoiding an accidental pregnancy. So, okay."

We'll also have to address the recent upheaval that was initiated in my body during my orgasms. My cheeks are overheated, considering the far from ordinary circumstances, I begin the consultation…

Later, I feel as eager and impatient as my lover. Will we meet again in private? Or maybe not? I still don't know what this "Péniche" is.

Oh, shit! He's not going to show up in public with me dressed like this, is he? No, no way! Anaïs specified that it is a confidential place, and anyway, I will veto it when I want.

Independent and liberated is my new mantra of a girl who assumes her sexuality and this parenthesis of lightness.

Tiger Sexton is as much my man-object as I could be in his mind. His body and what he does with it with me, all of it intoxicate me to no end. And now, wearing this subtly indecent dress inflames my mind. Dressed and in expectancy, I have difficulty recognizing my reflection. The flattering cut of the dress highlights my figure. The midi length makes it chic in the front and the lacing in the back adds an incendiary touch. The result is enhanced by feminine sandals that are super hot. Saïf's team gave me a complete makeover with my hair, makeup, and everything else.

Result: the mirror reflects me the image of a femme fatale with a smoky look who has no idea what she's doing but whose senses are titillated by all this. Reason on hold and full headlights on my feelings. I think I have guessed the probable turn of this evening. Fantasies surge in my head.

I need to feel all over me that Océane, the little tourist passing by, manages to arouse an irrepressible attraction in a man so powerful and unattainable in ordinary times. And not to think of anything else. Not even about what the text he sends me at the end of the afternoon might imply.

**Don't worry about Sophia. I asked her to have fun
without you tonight. Can't wait to see you, to touch you…**

Maybe that's why Sophia didn't come home. Everyone will enjoy their evening in their own way…

TIGER

No answer from Océane to my text message. I hope she won't brake before the jump. I really need these few hours with her. And everything is okay with the staff and Dr. Collins.

I am informed when the driver hits the road with my guest. A knot loosens in my gut; she's coming… I check the time. With a drink in hand, I watch the waves gently move through a porthole. This peaceful pace would almost make me forget the fires that are starting to burn parts of the country and the catastrophic weather forecast.

No. We turn everything off, even this.

The only thing that comes to mind as I clear it is the envelope placed prominently on the bed with a single white lily on top. I try not to think about work anymore, about the Ares operation being set up, about the reports of the mercenaries in France, ready to strike soon with my authorization… I don't want to think about this rage inside me anymore. Nor the fires wreaking havoc in Australia and the unforeseen costs associated with the current hazards. TS Naval made a donation to help my compatriots who saw their homes go up in smoke. Now that was urgent.

And great for the Sexton image… See, Dad? The ship's captain who succeeds you is on all fronts.

Hell, no, I don't want to think about him! Goodbye to the overwhelming responsibilities and everything that had to be done to get to this point: my mindset, the numbers, the meetings, and the press releases. Goodbye to my usual concerns and other professional or personal duties.

I want a break! Unplug the machinery, and enjoy the calmness of the surroundings while waiting for Océane's arrival. It's already a small pleasure in itself that she answers this invitation.

I pour myself a second scotch and mute the phones. I'm not there for anyone in the next few hours. The minutes stretch, and I turn on the music.

"Love and War" by Fleurie plays on a loop…

My eyelids close, and the melody fills the spacious cabin. The Péniche has perfectly managed my instructions and privatized the place. Everything is ready; only she is missing. I know that the thick carpet put for the occasion protects the floor and will mask the sound of her steps. I won't hear her coming. This is part of the service I requested—that my guest doesn't take off her shoes when she gets on board—so that I can look at her from head to toe before undressing her. This anticipation stimulates me more than a powerful aphrodisiac.

Come to me, sublime bud. I am becoming addicted to your dew…

I swallow a sip and settle down on the club couch in the corner, with a breathtaking view of the entrance. Time doesn't matter anymore. Just this exciting wait. Until the doorbell rings discreetly. The door opens, and my fantasies come to life before my eyes.

It was worth it.

Océane stands in the doorway to the sound of Fleurie, dazzling in a black leather sheath dress. My gaze stops on her pretty feet perched on several centimeters of heels; her ankles adorned with knots. I go up slowly along her tanned legs, partly hidden by the dress which hugs her body and underlines her forms. My attention is focused on her breast. No flirtatious cleavage; on the contrary, it's all in suggestion… Pure, classy, and sensual enough to give me a hot flash.

Damn, they nailed it.

"Good evening, Tiger," she greets me with a voice that sounds like velvet.

I stand up and walk towards her, my irises glued to hers. I don't know if it's the high ponytail clearing her beautiful face, the dark makeup around her eyes, or her hypnotic pupils, but there's something about her. I can't stop staring at her anymore.

"Good evening, sexy lady."

My deep voice resonates differently, betraying the bestial and instant hunger that sprouts in my depths.

"You're splendid."

My compliment causes a slight coloring on Océane's cheeks. She smiles at me, and my interest shifts to her mouth, pink, natural, too tempting for her own good.

"You're not bad either," she banters while examining me in turn.

White shirt, different from the one this morning. No more jacket or tie.

"It's pretty convenient to be able to shower and change in the office."

"I can see that."

Inches apart, I breathe in her scent and caress her with my eyes. She glances around us, ticks off one item—the ebony BDSM pillory—then another—the beams with ropes and pulley systems. She blushes more before replacing her beautiful green marbles in mine.

"And now you're going to tell me why I'm dressed like a…"

She stumbles over the word, blinks, and still gets flushed. I pretend not to understand.

"A what, my pretty bud?"

"You… you know what. You've got an idea in the back of your mind, don't you?"

No, not one; I have a lot…

Her question floats in the air, and my desire too. Océane shifts. I smile, guessing the hypotheses that must have blossomed in her beautiful head. The music switches to "No Hesitation" by Marian Hill. My guest walks, deepening her exploration of the place. I let her and head for the bar. Her fingers drag on a string.

"If you intend to tie me, not even in your dreams, Sweet Pea," she says.

I laugh, then stare at her while moistening my lips.

"We'll see… But first, maybe you're thirsty?" I ask her.

I take a second glass and turn to ask her what she wants to drink. A "damn" escapes me when I discover the back of her dress. She also turns her back on me to look at the pillory. My neurons crack, and my gray matter definitely migrates lower.

To note: Saïf deserves a big bonus for his choices. This dress on her is to die for.

An interlacing of straps goes along the back and the rump of Océane. This arabesque goes down in a straight line and reveals her delicate skin. A long strip of temptations surrounded by black leather. No bra or panties visible, nothing but her skin through the laces. She continues and leaves to collect the envelope which awaits her. The suggestive lacing assassinates me, and its effect on my fly increases. Océane turns around and whispers, "Another contract?"

"An additional clause, as promised."

"Uh-huh…The doctor's visit with a gynecologist just before, my outfit, this invitation, this place, these particular objects I don't even know what to do with," she lists as she returns. "Are you planning to turn me into a sex toy, Tiger?"

"Interesting assumption…"

"Am I wrong?" she tries to grill me, dazzling, sexy.

Instead of starting to read the clause, she searches for her answers in me. I join her without confirming or denying her statements. Our glances hook again. More intense. "Breathe Into Me," with Marian Hill's languid voice, takes its place in the vibrant silence that spreads.

"Tiger, what do you want? What's in there?"

"How about you read it, little bud?"

The word bud, far from irritating her as she claims when I give her a little name, seems to grow on her. Not only does she not take offense to it, but it even sends a gentle shiver through her. My excitement is reaching a critical point.

Of course, she probably tried to read my intentions today… She had a choice, either she freaked out and put the brakes on, or she gave in to the urge to know more. However, I also detect an ounce of stress and hesitation in her irises. She is there, but nothing is won. For the moment.

As they say, you must be wary of what you wish for because it could come true.

Here we are, one of us will actually get what he or she wants. I'm willing to take the risk to see that…

And you, are you, attractive little player?

Océane tries to pull herself together. She takes my glass, finishes it in one go, and gives it back to me. I was too distracted to offer her one. Her defiant look is back, sexier than ever.

"Very well," she says.

She goes back to the sofa to sit down. The height of her heels and the tight leather make her walk with a sway. She offers me a new glimpse of the tempting back with the laces.

Damn, I almost want to ask her to keep this dress on as much as I want to take it off myself right now!

But I have to control myself. I have to remember that it's not Lady Candice or another Domina whose performances have quickly made me jaded… It's not a call-girl either, able to get into the skin of a docile submissive with whom I can forget to restrain certain things. Since these partners, as long as they are paid and held to confidentiality, I have never had a problem with them.

It's her. Partly a lady so innocent—especially sexually—that she didn't know she could have more violent, wetter, more intense, unforgettable orgasms… So, fuck, it costs me, but I try to channel myself. I don't move one iota, although I don't take my eyes off her. Attentive to her reactions. Her reactions show on her features as she reads. I need to know her opinion on this and start our deal on a more advantageous basis… Will she cooperate or chicken out? I have no certainty except for the contraction of my hungry belly.

Her eyes rise finally, confused, interrogative.

"Where's the trap?" she says.

I smile, get rid of my glass, and push my hands into my pockets.

"What trap? I'm simply rebalancing things in a formal way… to avoid future unnecessary mistakes. That's what you wanted, too, right?"

She takes a long look at me. Then she reads aloud:

"Respect will be mutual between the two parties. Mr. Sexton accedes to Miss Rousseau's demand for equal treatment on the condition that Miss Rousseau agrees to share fully in Mr. Sexton's intimacy and to grant him complete exclusivity."

She awaits my comments; I decide to summarize, "As long as this contract is valid between us, I won't have to have my people drag you out of a place where you shouldn't be. You'll get the respect you deserve and the rewards you want if you honor your end of the deal. No more parties that go off the rails, nobody's dirty paws on you, and no more moaning under my roof or anywhere else if I'm not the one fucking you."

She jumps to her feet. I suddenly realize I might be screwing things up…

"I can't believe it," she sighs. "And to think that part of me was hoping for an apology. But, of course, your thing is to get the upper hand."

Her disappointment and anger hit me much harder than I expected. To be honest, I hadn't anticipated them enough.

"I see," I say calmly. "Ask me again, Océane."

I tell her this with a half-smile that has the merit of disarming her. She bats her eyelashes.

"What? What's this change of subject? Are you evading?"

"No, I'm coming to that, sweetheart. Ask me again why I wanted to give you what you are wearing tonight."

"It is not necessary; it is obvious."

I insist by coming closer, "Are you sure?"

Our breaths merge, and her subtle perfume revives my appetite, whatever my brain does. I skirt around her by reformulating:

"This outfit on you… What does it remind you of, Lily?"

"That you want to turn me into a fantasy ready to meet your expectations, to obey you without flinching. I don't accept being reduced to this, Tiger."

"I know that."

I step back, unbuttoning my cuffs. She probes me, confused and suspicious.

"In that case, let's get it right."

My statement makes her eyes widen.

"I don't follow you," she says.

Unfathomably, I open my shirt, one button after the other, before continuing, "You are partly right. I rarely apologize, especially when I feel I'm in the right. So, no way am I apologizing to you for… the incident last night. You owe me one, but never mind."

At these words, I see Océane oscillating between two instincts: rebellion against what I am saying and desire for what I am methodically exposing.

"I won't beg your pardon either. You have crossed the line," she protests.

She is stung in her pride. Still, her eyes stray to my bare chest. An amusing dilemma that pushes me to continue by unbuckling my belt.

"Okay. Let's move on to the next point, then. About my sexual fantasies about you. I want you to know that no matter how I fuck you, I know I'm going to get off and make you come. There's no doubt about it now, is there?"

"Pretentious!" she says to me without being able to dispute or hide her emerging smile.

"Nevertheless, I propose you a compromise. Are you still angry, my little bud?"

I open the sides of my shirt, and my pants slide slightly over my hips. Océane's attention is lost; I take the opportunity to add, "Would you like to teach me a more effective lesson than hanging out in my wife's bed? Do you want to take real control?"

I pull my belt from the loops in front of my disconcerted partner. I hope she is as tempted as I am.

"Maybe… Convince me," she mumbles.

"First of all, a small rectification. You are dressed as Domina, not as a submissive. Secondly, as you know, I have enough confidence in my virility; I know what I am worth. I don't need to tie up a partner to prove it. Third, pain is a very abstract thing for me, so as a precaution, I never physically inflict it on a woman. To conclude I'm offering you a unique opportunity to get back at me, to show me how much I pissed you off."

"It's crazy," she contests, uncertain.

I take off my clothes, and my cock distorts the front of my boxers, which is quite real. Our thirsty glances and our hair stand up, ditto. This fucking chemistry pulses through me from everywhere. I say, "No, this thing between us is real. And you have my word. I'm giving you your only chance to take control, Océane. To seal our contract as equals. Right here, right now. Because then…"

"Then?" she whispers, on edge.

"Then I'm going to take you apart for everything you screwed up yesterday. And I'll show you how much you pissed me off."

"Oh, shit!"

My smile widens; I pull off my underwear and look at my Rolex before taking it off.

"You have one hour, do what you want. Unwind on me, my little bud!"

OCÉANE

My pulse is going crazy! Did I hear right? Is he giving me control over him? For an hour?

My mouth goes dry. Paradoxically, in "submitting" himself, Tiger has never been as sexy, intimidating, and confident as he is at this very moment. My eyes dart over his manly anatomy and that gravity-defying erection. Damn, I didn't expect this! For several seconds, I am paralyzed, tetanized by the living fantasy he projects in my face without losing his usual arrogance. My feelings are blurred between an ephemeral power, an unleashed libido, and immense confusion.

Tiger takes a look at me, and he puts me in all my states. He is the naked one, with muscles, old and recent injuries, tattoos, and assets exposed without complex. Sure of himself. And it's me, all dressed up and free to impose what I want, who loses my means.

"You're fucking amazing," I murmur.

His blue eyes become warmer and warmer. "Revolver eyes" as in Marc Lavoine's song. Fabulous, intense, pointed at me to disarm me, and I am touched. I'm screwed.

"I know," he throws me, too hot and full of confidence.

A mimic half-amused, half-excited on my features, he measures his impact and challenges me. I give in to this sudden vital need to touch him. My fingers rest on his chocolate bars.

"In short, I can do whatever I want with you?" I say to convince myself.

"Yes, exactly."

He grabs one of my hands and slides it slowly towards his erect cock, sticking his lips to mine.

"Just remember, I always hit back, and you'll get what you deserve. But for now, you have free rein, power, and zero safe-words from me to stop you."

No safe word, no doubt that BDSM would be outrageously risky with him… As "Master" or "Slave," he has abilities that escape me. His dilated pupils soften me up completely.

"Does this inspire you, my bud? Because I know exactly how I'm going to fuck you next," he warns me.

On this warning, he grabs my mouth in a violent, greedy, devastating kiss. My legs are already wobbling on my expensive shoes, and my body is liquefying. My mind is fogging. Holy cow! Tiger Sexton is turning all my previous perceptions of sex upside down. He propels my desires and my sensations towards unknown, sulfurous, murderous lands…

"Are you mad at me? Do you want me?" he provokes me, mouth against mouth.

He clasps my fingers around his erection, his eyes on fire.

"This erection, my whole body is yours, here and now. Let go before I fuck you up, little bud!"

Yes, I have a severe crush on him.

35

Océane

I feel the warmth and rigidity of Tiger's sex in my hand as his fingers tighten around mine. I am rooted to the spot, immersed in his gaze. My temperature rises a notch. My reeling brain tries to remind me that this is surely a trap. A clever, twisted, torrid, hard trap… so hard, manly and…

Damn, I surrender!

Nevertheless, I try to reignite some neurons. It's complicated with this taut column of flesh I'm holding. And obviously, Tiger intends to use it to smoke my mind even more. My free hand ventures onto his muscular buttocks. Our lips part together.

The most vicious part of me is pining for Tiger Sexton's superpower: the power to literally liquefy me when he makes me cum.

"I'll take you up on that," I warn him, grabbing his buttocks.

"I dare you, my delicious Lily. Let go," he tells me again.

A dangerous gleam dances in his eyes, the one that abolishes the limits. His or mine… Odiously tempting, he lets go of my hand and raises both his hands in the air as a sign of cooperation. At least, I think so. But it's just impossible to believe for one tiny second that this charismatic male is capable of leaving me in charge. Tiger Sexton is a man of power; absolutely everything about him says so. Even here and now.

Especially here and now.

He turns and offers me an indecent view of the other side of his anatomy, covered with inscriptions and patterns in black ink, as he leaves to get another drink. He knows he has my full attention. I am glued to the ground and a little panicked inside, in addition to the desire that burns in me.

Can I enter his disturbing game and… enjoy an hour of power over him? Well, if he really gives it up.

When he turns around, I have serious doubts about his intentions. But that's all the more reason to use my own assets. Even though I have no idea how to… tame a guy like that. And I know that this is just a way for Tiger to get his sacrosanct control back and make me pay for my audacity yesterday. I don't kid myself about that. The truth is, I'm having a blast making things difficult for him…

To excite him more than he excites me. But remember to protect myself if his taste for play and lust starts to overtake me, to make me drift too far.

But will I want to put the brakes on? For now, no. I want to enjoy this carnal power I have.

"Very well," I say in a slightly veiled voice. "I want you on the bed, Tiger."

Happy to note the hint of astonishment on his features, I come towards him to grab his drink again. Under his bewitching look, I dip my lips in it. In order to draw there more temerity to take up the challenge that he throws me. During a long visual penetration, I swallow two sips, then give him back his drink. His mouth settles on the print of mine, and he drinks the rest.

"On the bed? Okay," he obeys.

He puts the glass down and does so with that cheeky look that tells me he's not taking me seriously.

"And now?" he asks.

We go on the attack. Set the fire, Océane!

Tiger sits down. I join him, stop between his thighs and present him my back. I hear him swear softly, and I repress a satisfied smile. This dress is to die for; I could see it in Tiger's eyes as soon as he focused them on me.

His hands come to my hips, his breath on my skin through the lacing. I knew that following the stylist's advice and putting nothing on underneath was daring, very daring. I hesitated. Now, this detail that I was stumbling over—because I thought it was objectifying me, turning me into a submissive luxury chick—gives me confidence. Especially when I turn my head a little and see the raw desire in my partner's blue eyes.

"Hands off, Tiger! I decide when and where you touch me," I

say with a touch of authority.

He raises an eyebrow, amused, but withdraws his hands.

"Good," I pretend to congratulate him as I face him again. "Now, get rid of this dress."

"With pleasure."

While devouring me with his eyes, he finds the zipper under my arm and opens it. I step back a little, starting to trip at the sight of him waiting and still excited. His fingers venture over me again, brushing the leather on my thighs all the way down. With unbearable slowness, he rolls up my dress, and reveals my legs, then… my pubic bone.

"My God," he growls.

His breathing becomes disordered, and his breath caresses my bare skin as he pulls the black sheath dress up over my stomach. Then higher. Without a word, pupils exploded, he straightens up while continuing my undressing. He moistens his lips by discovering my breasts, also naked. I raise my arms, more and more electrified, and let Tiger remove me completely from the dress. It covers my face for a moment as if he was dragging on purpose to better watch me. Or to make me feel that he has more and more control… This power play with such a powerful man is an aphrodisiac… Tiger finally takes the dress off me and sends it waltzing.

He is no longer teasing; he is volcanic and hungry. A fearsome beast that tries to play the lamb. I shudder. He eats me with his eyes without touching me.

Is my femininity the fatal weapon that can put you down?

I take the measure of the ascendancy I want and will be able to take over him for the next sixty minutes.

"Tell me what you want, sweet Lily."

What do I want? A naughty smile blooms at the corner of my mouth, and I bat my eyelashes as I try to think about it. My hands press against his pecs to push him onto the bed. His erect column taunts me, indomitable, proud of not lying down.

"Lie down!" I declaim while climbing on him. "My turn to control your orgasm."

An eye for an eye, Mr. Sexton. You've driven me crazy with your methods; I'll turn your expertise against you. The tip of his tongue appears to moisten his lips, a lustful gleam in his eyes.

"I wait to see that," he braves me with a rocky voice.

I put myself astride him, lean, and say softly, "Keep your hands off my body. It's my time and… I'm going to fuck you, Tiger."

He lets out a sexy laugh, always too sure of himself. I lean in further, determined to provoke him. My nipples brush against him; it shoots us both under the epidermis. He takes the opportunity to capture me and kiss me ferociously. A dizzying kiss, a duel that I do everything not to lose. A leader at heart, even in bed, Tiger Sexton does not intend to follow me without going on the offensive. I am consumed by his contact; I disinhibit myself and squirm above him. He influences dangerously on my euphoric body. I am on the verge of flinching with him. But a delicious pride overcomes the carnal pleasure. I manage to free myself from his hold as he wraps my breasts in his palms.

"I said to you: do not touch," I tell him by seizing his hands to place them on the bed, on both sides of his head.

I hold his wrists, overhanging him. It is exhilarating to take me for an amazon on his stallion and to feel the level of pheromones soaring between us. Tiger lets out a moan.

"I think I'm starting to regret it," he admits to me while looking at my breasts close to his mouth.

"Sixty minutes, Tiger… You promised," I say, pressing my chest against his. "Prove to me that you are a man of your word."

Only his smirk answers me. This time, it's me who melts on him. I titillate him and make him hope for another kiss before dodging it. He bites his lip, a spark lurking in his eyes. I know he's holding back; I want to see how far he can control his instincts and let me believe he's the type to give up control to someone. I'm not fooled; I enjoy it. My curves caress him, my fingernails crisscross his muscles, and I move lower and lower. My lover's abs contract on my passage; he is breathing hard.

And I reach the climax of his manhood. Just looking at him gives me hot flashes.

I force myself to hide the fact that I am both conquered and intimidated. My fingers wrap around his member, and I lock my gaze with Tiger's. Burning, conquering, but he remains silent. My hand slides to the base of his sex, and he clenches his jaws.

"I am going to beat you hollow, Mister Arrogant," I promise

him by pressing him gently.

With my other hand, my index finger wanders over his glans, and he beads with desire. Deployed, hardened, perfect.

"Please… Torture me, pretty bud," Tiger challenges me, his tone more obscene. "If you have the guts."

Really?

My grip tightens, my touches spread along his dick, on his balls. At times feline and all claws out, at times excruciatingly delicate and teasing. My nails and fingers go and come back on his skin.

There are different methods of torture, right? You may be insensitive to pain, but I want you to feel me in every possible way…

I try to find his weak points; I track them down, brush against them, find them. Tiger watches me manipulating, cuddling, and kneading his sex. He is stingy with words, and everything happens in his intense beads aimed at me. And in his muscles that tense and react, and his male attribute that pulses. I bow and lick my own lips as I stare at him.

When my tongue tastes him, he lets out a long moan. I smile and start again. I lap him delicately, just the tip. I play with it, blow on it, put my mouth on it, all closed. For a slow torture, that he feels me, that he wants with all his strength this blowjob. Without knowing if he will have it.

The music intoxicates me unless it's mainly to have Tiger at my mercy. I am all about it. My kisses multiply, teasing his groin and his testicles. I breathe him in, crisscrossing this whole area of massive attraction for my boiling hormones. When I finally decide to lick him, he lets out an "argh… fuck!" between his teeth. At this precise second, I suddenly feel powerful, lifted to the top of my femininity. I weld my glance to his, sensual and mocking.

Who is the strongest, Mr. Sex?

"I forbid you to ejaculate," I order him before opening my mouth wide and taking him in the moist heat.

"You'll pay for this!"

My taste buds go wild; I taste him thoroughly, lasciviously, finding his dilated pupils at each rise. Tiger's fists clutch the sheets, and he loses his breath. I fan the flame in every possible way, to mark his mind, to blur his bearings as he does with me as soon as he puts his hands on my body.

I go there gently; I booty him, leaving no respite at any strategic place. Then I alternate, and I become firmer. He says a series of swear words in English, his head straightens, then falls back on the pillow. Feeling encouraged, my movements accelerate.

"Argh… fuck!" complains Tiger again.

I devour him; my fingers keep him on guard, and my tongue is active. For an indefinite time, I give everything; I feel him contract.

Petty and satisfied with myself, I backtrack, laze, stop and get up again.

"After all, I'm a little thirsty," I announce to him with nonchalance.

Tiger devours me with his eyes, boiling with a contained ardor. His beautiful, frustrated face and his choppy breathing boost my girl power. I leave the bed and walk with a rolling gait while going to seek his bottle of scotch. The atmosphere is charged with electricity. I know he's checking me out, and this silent examination, while he enjoys my nudity, instills more confidence in me. I take a swig from the neck.

"Satisfied?" he asks me in an indecently hot voice.

"What about you?"

He smiles at me, but it looks more like an obscene warning.

Not even afraid, my tiger…

He shifts, ready to get out of bed. I stop him with a snap of my tongue, falsely severe.

"You don't move; I'm not finished with you," I warn him.

"You're enjoying it, aren't you?"

"You have no idea," I answer him straight off.

His lips curve, and he sits still, checking the time on the clock.

"This is going to be the longest sixty minutes of your life," I say, sparkling with pride, as I stare at his cock.

"I should have known better," he says as he fumbles through his hair.

I drink again, passing a hand in my hair to undo my ponytail. I shake my mane and run my fingers through it in "keep getting hard by looking at me, I love it" mode. And that's exactly what he does. Then his attention turns to alcohol.

"Are you going to drink the whole bottle, or are you going to share it?" he asks me.

"Um… I don't know if you deserve me to be nice."

"Technically, everything in this cabin belongs to me, little bud."

"No. Technically, I still own you, sweet pea, and I decide."

He bursts out laughing. I move closer and swish the amber liquid in the bottle.

"So, do you deserve my kindness, Tiger?"

TIGER

Stubborn, hot, and sassy as hell.

I could leap in, neutralize her in no time, rip that seventeen-year-old scotch from Océane and drag her pretty ass back to that bed. But she's having a blast. I notice it, and her little maneuver sets me on fire from second to second.

I want to feel her mouth on my cock again or some other part of her. I want to sink into her, and… Damn, she has to sign the contract! There's no chance of her slipping through my fingers anymore; I want to stuff myself on her. She comes forward, delighted to tease me, in a birthday suit perched on heels.

Much too seductive for her own good.

"Your arrogance, your control freakery, your refusal to apologize," she lists close to me. "Are they worth a reward, Tiger?"

I examine her anatomy in detail, keeping silent. My rigidity that she abandoned when I was on a full trip starts to palpitate again with desire, with need. I won't miss her when she's done playing, I'll…

Shit! What is she doing?

Under my nose, Océane presses her breasts against each other and directs the bottle neck downwards in the hollow of her chest. My erection increases tenfold as I see her drip a small amount on her. Stunned, I follow the trajectory of a drop that escapes to her navel.

"No answer?" she taunts me. "You're not thirsty anymore?"

She smears her belly and her breasts with it. When I replace my eyes in hers, my breath is disturbed. What took me, damn it? This girl is driving me crazy.

"It'll be on me or nothing at all," she murmurs, teasing.

My gray cell goes out. I abdicate, "On you."

I hardly pronounced these words that my mouth left to the assault of her breast. I drink, eat, lick, bite, and knead her. Feverish and thirsty of her, I end up tipping her onto the bed. She gives a small cry of surprise at her fall, and the bottle falls on the floor. We don't care about the damage! I don't know how much time has passed, but my patience has limits. Limits that this blond girl has largely exceeded. My teeth and tongue meet her erect nipples. The taste of my Scotch whisky combines with Océane's flavor, and the intoxication of desire makes me voracious. She squirms and moans. I block her underneath, rush on her belly, her breasts. I go up, kiss her on the neck and suck her weak protests in a devastating kiss.

And she returns it to me. Feline and bewitching, she arches her back and claws me. Her legs wrap around me. My pleasure swells and starts to go out of control. Océane moves her hips and contorts herself to try to tame me. My sex brushes against hers, and I feel how wet, warm, and succulent she is… It drives me crazy. I grab her wrists, plate them on both sides of her body, and I search in her eyes.

"What if you let me take over now?"

"No," she resists, out of breath." I'll go to the end of the time limit. For now, I'm still in charge, Tiger."

"You want me to let you go? You want me to stop?"

We stare at each other for a long time, caught up in each other.

"I…" begins Océane.

I hang on her delicious lips with an intense boner.

"No," she sighs. "Take me, now. Make me come like no one has before you… But you, you hold back. You're not allowed to cum while I'm in control."

She's not…

"Yes, that's an order: fuck me, Tiger!"

36

OCÉANE

The eye of the tiger revives. Without a word, Tiger stands up off the bed. He grabs my thighs, pulls me toward him, and lifts my hips toward his. With a lightning thrust, he invades my intimacy. Saturated with endorphins, I try to protest, "The con—"

"The gynecologist briefed me. We're both fine; my test results are in the envelope with the additional clause. No more barriers, little bud," he states.

Feel everything from you.

My reason breaks down; euphoria radiates through my body. Tiger is now well embedded in me. His hands knead my hips, and our eyes lock. I could cum at this moment so much I am aroused. He slides out of my cocoon and returns there abruptly, drawing out of me a lascivious complaint. With a hypnotic look, he starts again, thrusting repeatedly, one after the other. Deep, powerful until intoxication. His measured cadence kills me because I see that he has to be stiff of arousal; he tries to control himself and uses it to make me crazy. Gradually, it is me who loses it. Tiger's fingers press me; his thrusts devastate me with pleasure. As if we collided at each sudden thrust.

I can vaguely hear the music. "Falling Down" by Muse, I think. The purity of the melody in the cabin and the magnetism of my lover start to make me high. He makes me sink into a madness of the senses. Our jerky breaths, the visual and carnal connection between us, and the jolts he generates trigger an ever-stronger wave in my lower abdomen. I am undulating with delight. It is at this moment that he withdraws.

"Come back," I moan. "I did not say to you to stop."

"The power is going to your head, little bud," he scolds me, his tone hoarse. "And you have no idea what your—"

"Of my?"

The answer is made desire; his head disappears between my legs. He murmurs on my clitoris.

"Of your effect on my erection," he continues.

Shivers.

He is going to end me.

His tongue slides into my confines, and what he whispers becomes inaudible. His fingers and his lips explore me, make me crazy, shoot me. I undulate, and my crotch sticks to him to better feel his kisses in the hollow of me. He holds me and spreads a myriad of shivers all over me.

"Tiger… I'm going to… I…"

Impossible to formulate a complete sentence; he does something sick to me that escapes my understanding. I start shaking, moaning, and chanting his name. My hands sneak into his hair and cling to it. My calves are on his shoulders, and my toes tighten. My feelings surpass all that I expected. The shivers intensify to the point of being unbearable.

"Damn, Tiger…"

"I know, Lily, you're going to cum… Then I take over," I hear in my early trance.

I don't care. My gray matter is out of order; it doesn't analyze anything when Tiger does the thing that's driving me crazy again. His lips move away from me, and he looks for my eyes.

"Do we have a deal?" he whispers to me.

"What? Don't stop, please…"

He moistens his upper lip and gives a little smile.

"I don't intend to; you're much too delicious. But you'll give me back the orders afterward."

"I don't believe it. Are you negotiating? When I—"

"When you're in a weak position?" he teases me. "I plead guilty."

Incendiary and sure of himself, he uses his weapons. His fingers still penetrate me, finding without hesitation the point that makes me feverish. And his tongue coaxes my bud again. I will dislocate with pleasure. He knows it; he knows exactly what he is doing. I lose my breath and my words. Tiger climbs up and hovers over me to kiss me.

"Give it up, sweet Lily," he whispers to me. "You were right: an hour of obedience is too long for me."

His hand returns to my secret folds as he haggles, his mouth against mine. My intimate fragrance is added to his own taste. The intimate caresses come back while he offers me a simultaneous kiss that lobotomizes me. I am too hot; I am dying.

"Now it's your turn to be docile," he insists. "Is it a deal?"

"You… Damn, you're evil."

"I know just when to turn a situation to my advantage," he replies, moving slightly over my body.

Enough to rub his cock against my wetness.

"You'll have my dick, my mouth… whatever you want, but you'll let me handle it," he persists.

"No…"

He penetrates me little by little to complete the torture.

"Wrong answer, sweet Lily."

"Unfair negotiations, Tiger, "I complain.

"I know," admits this sexual tormentor as he advances into my womanhood. "Just like it's unfair to be so bewitching and ask me to hold back."

I exhale a protest that he sucks in a kiss and our hips weld. My legs cross on him; my nails scar him. My desire reaches its paroxysm.

I want him with all my strength. Him, his leadership, his sex appeal, and his arrogant smile.

"Two," I manage to counter-attack in a whisper.

"Two?" he repeats.

"I want two orgasms in a row, Mr. Control Freak. Then you'll be free."

The gleam that reignites in his eyes sets me on fire. I feel like I'm influencing his erection nestled inside me. Then Tiger takes a long, hard look at my surrender and my mouth.

"Perfect," he concedes, with a satisfied tone.

I press on his buttocks; he smiles at me while making controlled movements with his pelvis. The first back-and-forth makes me moan. He repeats by looking at me. First gently, then the tempo increases by one notch, two, three… I lose the thread. His rigid virility fills me and sinks me more and more into the mattress. He digs me, possesses me, and causes me spasms and interminable sighs.

I don't know what I say anymore. I ramble; I take off. A horizon of voluptuousness inspires me. My supreme pleasure spurts, uncontrollable, intense!

TIGER

The orgasm of Océane soaks me. Her eyelids flutter and close. Her petals tremble around my sex. Her nails mark my back, plant themselves there. I don't have pain; I savor. I savor her contractions of pleasure. Her lips open. The dew pours over me.

Watching and feeling her come is a pure wonder for my senses. My muscles tense up in a titanic effort not to sink with her. It is long, exhausting, and hard to bear. I sweat. When she finally empties herself of her energy, I withdraw and collapse next to her. Frustrated, hungry.

Think of something off-putting. Think of something off-putting. Control the pressure.

"Holy cow!" she comments, prey to the aftershocks of her shaking.

The sheets are soaked, and I... I only think of fucking her! Not anything else. I clean myself up in a hasty way and run away, just to tame my instincts. Thankfully, she doesn't have the strength to protest. I go and get a bottle of water to at least quench this thirst. For a few seconds, our chaotic breaths almost cover the music. Then, Océane stirs lazily.

"I have to go and wash up," she announces to me.

I indicate to her the door without missing the spectacle of her small ass, which leaves. And which fuels the inferno which smolders in me. I divert my glance from the glass of the porthole, but I fail to erase the lustful image in my head.

The sun declines outside, and the waves darken. I don't care what time it is on my Rolex placed next to the contract. I stare at the lonely lily abandoned next to it... then I turn around when Océane returns.

Her blonde mane flows over her shoulders. A towel tied over her, she puts down her shoes. The terry cloth barely hides everything I know by heart now. This is going to turn into a priapism in this story. As she returns to bed, she catches my salacious and amused look.

"What's so funny? The fact that I've been knocked out?" she asks me.

"No, I was thinking about my doctor's face. He's seen so many suspicious marks and wounds on my body over the years. But I haven't needed him yet because I can't lose my hard-on because of a girl."

Océane's laughter bursts out. She's even cuter when she lets loose, irresistible.

"The poor guy, he wouldn't get over it," she laughs. "We are not going to wake him up for a nightly consultation."

Her irises sparkle, her cheekbones, and the base of her neck are almost as pink as her mouth blistered by my passion.

"I agree; you'll have to devote yourself to saving the doc from that," I conclude by coming back to her.

"Dedicate myself?"

"Yep. I know exactly where to stick that erection when you get your second orgasm."

Her eyes widen. My gaze lingers on her blushing cheeks, then slides over her. The challenge will be to continue taming my cock while I'm still working on hers.

"And can we know where you think?"

Would it be a point of concern that I perceive on her face? Interesting…

"You will know it… when I decide it," I say to her to destabilize her in my turn.

Soon, you will see.

"You think I—"

I don't let her continue. I gag her with a kiss while untying her towel. And I lay her back down, climbing back on top of her, before straying lower. Her breasts still have a faint taste of scotch, and her now ultra-sensitive nipples harden against my tongue. I suck them, nibble them, sniff them. My hunger increases tenfold. I walk more to the south and cross her belly. Her intimate parts open. Certain zones are still sensitive, which incites me to go there delicately. To play differently with her pleasure. The desire manifests itself, takes root delicately in her, and furiously in me. However, I take the time to court hers. Even if seeing her wet and offered again nibbles the little phlegm I try to keep.

Her moans give rhythm to this new bloom of my flower. Her flavor spreads over my taste buds, and her smell intoxicates me and pushes me to my limits. She stirs as she says my name and tests my patience.

"Fuck, I'm going to—"

She moans and wriggles against my mouth, which tastes her. The dew beads on her petals grow. And the magic moment occurs; her pleasure sprays me.

Damn, I can't get enough of it!

I give her a break. I held beyond the reasonable. And this desire too long contained shoots definitively my reason. My last barriers fall. As soon as Océane takes a breath, I get out of bed.

"Come here," I tell her.

She wipes herself and abandons the towel to join me.

Océane starts to realize the deal she made. She becomes the blond girl again without artifice, less experienced, and less reckless. This makes her attractive in a different way. Too attractive for me to keep a clear head. I grab her by the waist and press her against me. Smaller without her heels, more natural, she looks at me, a little fearful.

"Then?" she inquires softly.

"I want you terribly; I want your…"

"You want my?"

Is she thinking about sodomy? Maybe we'll come to that; I'll initiate her if need be… For the moment, I tease her lips, picking at them. Her fingers wander over my skin, almost shy. It kills me.

"Your mouth," I answer her.

Joining the gesture to the word, I suavely incite her to go towards the proof of my arousal. She lets herself be guided without leaving my eyes. What she does not know yet, is that I do not want to take the blowjob again where she stopped. She has tortured me; now I want my revenge.

When Océane starts, I already know how it will end. I first try to be a gentleman, letting her graze, kiss, and lick my beast as she feels it. Then I totally lose it. Her delicacy is too much torment. My fingers cling to her hair, and my sex spreads her lips, embedding itself far in her mouth. I maintain her like this, and she loses her breath, her eyelashes are lined with tears. My eyelids fall to better feel this moist heat. Her small fingers seize my ass. Her nails embed themselves in my flesh. My cock palpitates and gorges itself. The pleasure. The boundaries blur. I think she's lacerating me, slapping me. I open my eyes again and meet hers. I feel her… Shit, I feel her fainting, running out of air, begging me. In spite of myself, my mind has no filter, and my desires are no longer on a leash and under a muzzle…

The escort girls in my princely suite shortly before my wedding. Four voracious mouths, four deep throats, four pairs of agile hands.

Then, I ramble more sternly in my head.

Immaculate fabrics… Softness of silk… Smell of fuck, of crushed petals… Fevered bodies, at my mercy… She, naked at my feet…

Océane is shaking, clawing at me desperately. But this muffled sound of a person asphyxiating and fighting against something obstructing her throat and spreading her mouth shakes me. It snaps me out of my daze like an electric shock.

Damn, the misdemeanor!

I withdraw; Océane inhales brutally, suffocates, and coughs. I rub my face, stunned. That's it; I've freaked her out. Panic springs up in my insides.

I ask her, anxious while leaning to help her to get up:

"Are you okay?"

"No, fuck! I was… choking," she huffs. "And you were blocking me!"

She pushes me back to get up on her own. She tries to regain normal breathing to deal with the regurgitation reflex that can occur when a woman is not used to such a deep and uncompromising blowjob.

I forgot, fuck I forgot she's not familiar with this kind of road!

"I… don't know how you… usually get laid, but I… damn," she takes offense, backing away.

I run my fingers through my hair and blow out slowly. I screwed up! The explosion of pheromones, the dopamine, everything suddenly evaporates. Jaws sealed, I try to adopt the right reaction to decant this situation that got away from me in a split second.

"Did I hurt you?"

"Damn it, Tiger!"

"It won't happen again."

She wraps herself in a snatched sheet and looks at me.

"No, it won't," she replies.

I look at her wet eyelashes and clench my fists.

Fix it, and fast!

"Okay, let's stop. I'll take you to dinner," I offer.

Océane blinks, confused. She examines me for a moment. My hard-on is gone. Although the notion of pain is unknown to me, it's not difficult to notice that I've just inflicted it on her somehow. In any case, it scared her.

"I don't know," she doubts as she touches her neck.

"Please, Océane. I shouldn't have; I'd like to forget about this incident. Let's leave this place."

She hesitates, then nods.

"That's better, yes."

I don't dare go near her anymore; I feel like I've lost my shell, and I look like a monster. She gets dressed. I leave to wash and do the same. Muse melodiously furnishes the embarrassed silence. I blame myself, and I begin to blame Sophia. She knows my shortcomings; she must have suspected that things could go wrong if I let myself get too involved with… a novice who attracts me too much. Océane made me so crazy that I forgot that she is not comparable to my usual screwing partners. And… she is not like Sophia…

I put on my shoes and pick up my cell phone. Missing calls and a text message from my wife greet me.

Ty, where exactly are you? I can't reach Océane. I want you to come home. And her too.

I grit my teeth, trying to channel the emotions that are churning inside me. Then I write my answer.

Like I said, I won't be coming home tonight. Neither is Océane.

I send it and then make a brief phone call, ignoring my wife's incoming call. My caller picks up.

"Mr. Sexton?" he says, surprised to be contacted so late.

"Yes. You open for me tonight. I'll come by in about half an hour."

"Of course, see you then, Mr. Sexton."

I hang up and turn around. Océane, uncomfortable, smoothes her dress over her thighs, scrutinizing me.

"Are you ready?"

"Uh-huh."

I take my watch and the paperwork and hold out my hand to her.

"Come on."

She hesitates for a moment and doesn't take it. It breaks my morale, but I take it.

"Was it a restaurant who called?" she asks me.

"No."

"Where are we going?"

"We'll go wherever you want."

An indecisive pout appears on her face.

"The way I'm dressed, I don't want to show up in a crowded place like this," she says. "Besides, you… you wouldn't show up in public, alone with me."

I wouldn't be ashamed to do that, far from it. But it's… complicated. Too complicated…

What I am ashamed of is that this trap door opened with her. I hold her gaze and bite my lip. None of these words pass my mouth.

"I will, but I don't admit that another look takes advantage of this splendor," I contradict her. "We'll go and eat wherever you want. Without restriction."

Disconcerted, she stares at me. Simultaneously in my mind, a buried voice taunts me, *"Whatever you do, wherever you go, in the eyes of your fellow creatures, you will remain on the wrong side, baby tiger…"*

"Shut up!"

This laughter… cold… mocking, impossible to silence. This insistence. This discomfort in me.

"Never being in pain creates a twisted relationship between you and pain. You are 'abnormal,' baby tiger. It's exciting, isn't it? To be in a dark zone closed forever to the rest of the humans, to not feel everything like them. Me, it gives me pleasure!"

The violence of this memory strikes me. To have frightened Océane revives this flaw that I took years to fill. To lock it up, put it in a box. Now, things, too many things, break the barriers and invade my mind…

Until, with my irises locked in hers, Océane finally nods.

"Sounds good. I'm not sure I can swallow any food right now, but... I'd rather we get out of here."

"Okay. I'm at your service, Miss Rousseau."

She barely manages to smile at me; something has cracked between us...

OCÉANE

What the hell just happened?

Tense, confused, my heart beating too fast, I can't wait to get out of this place. This evening has taken a turn that neither Tiger nor I had anticipated. At least, I didn't plan this. Was this the game: to commit to sharing fully in Mr. Sexton's intimacy?

His sexuality is a new fortress that has just opened up before me in a truly profound way. And this glimpse leaves me with questions... and also with fear. I don't know what to think anymore. Deep down, I don't know this man. Until a few minutes ago, he was just the best sex of my life and the unlikely relationship I wanted to enjoy while it lasted.

But now I... I feel weird. Clueless, overly sensitive.

What the hell happened?

After we get off the boat, he guides me to a black car. I've never seen it before, but the personalized plate tells me it belongs to him. And there's no driver in sight, nor the Bentley that drove me here. Tiger opens the passenger door for me. I get in. It stinks of money. As he walks around the car, I discover the camel leather interior and a sort of *B* embedded in the heart of the steering wheel. What other luxury brand starts with that letter?

Tiger sits down, turns on the ignition, and asks me, "So, are you feeling better? Are you a little hungry? What do you want to eat?"

I can see his tension in this series of questions. He doesn't really know how to deal with me anymore. To be honest, food was the least of my worries; he's got me too shaken up.

"Uh… I feel like fries," I say mechanically.

A smirk appears on his features. He looks at me, trying to restore the contact and complicity short-circuited between us.

"Is that all? he tries to tease me. You are not very demanding, Miss Rousseau. But your desires will be satisfied," he concludes with a wink. "Buckle up."

I do so, a little amused, though. Tiger starts the car, turns his phone back on, and instructs the car's voice command to call someone. During the ensuing ringing, we drive into traffic. My thoughts get bogged down in the last fifteen minutes that have just passed.

"Good evening. Hubert's restaurant, Sophie speaking," a female voice rings out in the car.

With a French accent recognizable among thousands.

"Good evening, this is Sexton. Could you prepare a meal for two to go? Something quick," he says in my language, turning his head towards me. "With fries," he adds.

"Yes, of course, Mr. Sexton. The chef will take care of it right away. Are there any other dishes you'd like to include?"

Tiger questions me with his eyes. I nod, then whisper to him, "A chocolate dessert!"

I smile again.

"Surprise me. And add a dessert for two, with chocolate!"

"Very good, Mr. Sexton. I'll pass on the order."

"I'll be in your parking lot in about fifteen minutes."

"You got it. We'll bring it to you."

He hangs up and says, a little less seriously, "Do you promise not to play with the dessert, you little foodie?"

"Me, play with food? Never! You don't know me very well, Mr. Sexton."

He bursts out laughing. I think a kind of relief washes over us both; the ice is broken again. Tiger disconnects his mobile; I think he turns it off. Because he wants to be quiet with me? Maybe even a kind of complicity other than sex is emerging. Unless I'm imagining things. Shit, am I fantasizing? This uncertainty reignites my inner warning. I keep quiet and divert my attention to the outside.

What the hell am I doing?

The chaos takes place in my head and stretches my silence.

Between the naughty date, the misconduct of the blowjob, and… all this, I have no reference point anymore. My mind tells me to run away; only part of me is like… fascinated.

Damn it! It's screwed up, I'm spinning out of control, and this intoxication scares the hell out of me.

37

OCÉANE

Why am I still here? No, why do I manage to feel good with him again when I don't belong?

"My kingdom for your thoughts," murmurs Tiger.

My eyes return to him. He studies me, looking serious. Unreadable. I frown, hesitant.

"Are you quoting Shakespeare now?" I try to evade him, teasing.

"In this Shakespeare play, Richard III is willing to give up his kingdom for a horse. Your thoughts are worth a lot more, Miss Rousseau. Especially if they concern me," he argues.

"Well, I…"

He stops at a traffic light—still green—to probe me. I fidget with the hem of my dress, embarrassed.

"About…" I begin. "You know, in the cabin, when you had me… Can we… can we talk about this?"

"I… drove off the road," he pleads. "I shouldn't have treated you that way. It was a mistake that I deeply regret. Like I said, it won't happen again. Can we just get this over with?"

I breathe out slowly, immersed in his blue balls. Something tells me not to push it. Not right now. Too touchy to bulldoze through…

"Let's not talk about it anymore, okay?" Tiger insists.

I nod because right now, I need to untangle my own feelings. But he'll have to explain… Sure, he knew how to stop. But this dark side, I will never again be able to pretend it doesn't exist. Tiger starts up again; I stare at his profile.

I try to put it aside as we pull up in front of a restaurant. Tiger parks and checks the time. Like clockwork, a bellboy shows up with packages. Tiger gets out of the car, pays, and gets his order. The smell of food immediately wafts through the cabin as he returns. Finally, I am hungry. Even though my mouth and throat remain scarred by torturous sexual play, this more basic need finally shows up. And I begin to loosen up almost completely.

"Can I nibble on a fry or two, or shall we stop for a picnic somewhere?" I ask him, nosing through the wrapped food.

"Please, you little gourmand. Gobble up your fries."

"What if I stain your seats?"

"The Bugatti will survive," he replies casually. "I like to see you eat…"

Double meaning? Relax, Océane.

I breathe in, breathe out and try to let myself go. I take a bite.

"Hummm… delicious," I comment, my mouth full.

I offer some to Tiger. He takes the opportunity to grab and lick my fingers.

"Indeed, it's delicious," he confirms, looking at me.

I'm not sure if he's talking about the fries.

The desire is still present in his eyes. Reminding me that I was the only one who came. Twice. And he hasn't. Even though he still eats out of my hand while driving, I know that appetite is reviving too. He doesn't hide it. I become awkward, maybe a little afraid of this insatiable passion and of what it almost led me to.

Besides, where are we going now? Not to La Péniche, I don't feel like it anymore. To his place?

Shit, Sophia!

I don't know where my cell phone is anymore. I'm starting to feel panicky when Tiger suddenly pulls up. We're in a posh street, judging by the architecture and the illuminated signs of the big brands on the front.

"We're here," he announces.

"Where is 'here'?"

"Get out, you'll see," he tells me, doing the same.

I wipe my hands and stand up. He opens the door for me as an older man rushes out to meet us.

"Good evening, Mr. Sexton. Nice to see you again," says the gray-haired man in the suit.

As Tiger embraces me, the other's attention stops on me.

"Good evening, miss Sex— miss," he says.

He has just realized that I am not Sophia Sexton. I sketch an embarrassed smile without understanding the reason for my presence or his.

"We'll follow you," declares Tiger simply.

"Yes, Mr. Sexton," the man obeys.

"Follow him where?" I whisper to Tiger. "Who is he?"

"He's the Australian representative of some big luxury dealerships."

He puts his palm on my lower back to follow him, but I freeze.

"Huh?" I gasp.

"Car. By the way, what's your favorite color?" he asks me instead of explaining.

"Wait, I don't quite understand. He sells cars, is that it?"

"Yes, and he has exceptionally opened the store for us tonight," he confirms. "So, do you have a preference of brand or color?"

Stunned, I can't move anymore. My saliva gets stuck in my throat, and I cross my arms.

"You… you want to buy me a car? Just like that, on the spur of the moment?"

"Very perceptive," laughs Tiger, obviously not measuring the extent of my stupor.

"Do you realize that? What exactly is this? Overpayment for a hooker or buying my silence for the… thing at La Péniche?"

"Damn it, Océane!" he snaps, raising his voice. "What are you saying? I thought we had clarified these two points: I don't think you're a prostitute. If that had been the case, I would have continued what I started at La Péniche."

"So why did you suddenly decide to spend a huge amount of money on me?"

"Because I can. And I want to."

"Well, I… I can't accept that!"

He takes my face and stares at me for a long time.

"You don't refuse a gift of apology," he maintains. "I hurt you, and I want to make amends."

With a car worth hundreds of thousands of dollars? Is he really fucking serious?

Scandalized, I am baffled. The salesman is watching us, which accentuates my impression of the chasm under my feet, the one that separates my world from Tiger's. Our two personalities too.

"So, it's easier for you to pay me for something overpriced than to apologize to me?"

His mouth comes close to mine. My body, that traitor, softens, trying to reduce my neurons to mush too.

"If I say sorry, will you accept my gift?" Tiger haggles against my lips.

"No, I won't. You're not going to… I don't want or need you to buy me a car. I take public transportation and don't even live in this country. What do I do with it when I go back to France?"

His eyelids crinkle for a moment. Is he thinking?

"Who cares," he finally objects. "You can do what you want with it. It's only scrap metal and four wheels."

"Oh, no! That's insane! I don't even want to negot—"

It ends in an indecent kiss. The proof of his unfulfilled desire presses against me. Damn, he's really horny.

"Come on, sweet Lily… If we don't hang out here too long, I can take you somewhere else."

"To La Péniche?"

Does he see the return of that slight tension in me?

"No. I regret having made a mistake there… I suggest you finish the evening at another place. I'd like to keep you with me until tomorrow morning."

"Maybe we'd better go home," I say.

I haven't heard from Sophia since this morning; she's probably been trying to reach me. And I still can't remember where I left my phone. In the Bentley that drove me to La Péniche, maybe?

"But we're going home, sweetness. I mean, we're going somewhere I almost feel at home," Tiger tells me, looking mysterious.

"Where?"

"This will be the second step of the improvised program. Shall we finish this one first? You have to accept my gift first."

"No way! It's ugly to blackmail me like that, Tiger," I reply, pretending to be very outraged.

He laughs, although his eyes become more gloomy.

"In my defense," he replies, "I still have this need of you, and

I would like to erase what happened earlier. Say yes, Océane. It's only a few horses under the hood…"

He's minimizing, but we're talking about a car that costs, I don't know how much! There is no way I'm taking such a huge "gift." Excuse or not, in my world, this is still disproportionate, downright hallucinating even! So, I persist, "No."

Stunned, I wonder if my refusal is about the car, about sleeping with him again, or both? Maybe he's wondering that too? However, Tiger is an opponent who only stops when he's won. I'm beginning to realize this fully.

"Stubborn," he scolds me quietly. "You know that in some cultures, it's a serious offense to say no when someone offers you a gift?"

I try to stand my ground and walk away.

"Nice try, but it's still no," I say with a laugh. "And I have a delicious chocolate dessert waiting for me. I prefer this kind of gift… If you want it, I strongly advise you to put your credit card away and get your beautiful ass back in the car."

He raises his eyebrows, surprised then amused by the last sentence. I take the opportunity to move away, encouraging him to throw in the towel and follow me. I see him exchange a few words with the salesman. For a moment, I fear that he is going to go through with it. But he finally turns around. Phew!

Watching him come back makes my mind race. Despite the… incident, our attraction hasn't evaporated. But what do I want? I can't help but wonder what would have happened at La Péniche if I had let Tiger continue… Locked in, lips parted, his sex down my throat.

That should scare the hell out of me and make me run away. Actually, that was my first instinct: to say stop and get out. For good. So what the hell am I doing? It confuses me when we get back on the road, as if nothing had happened. I pick at the food a little. He doesn't talk about an oversized gift anymore. He just asks me for bites as we drive, looking like he doesn't care for a second that I might ruin the interior of his fancy car.

Soon, we enter the CBD in the heart of Sydney. We enter the underground parking of a skyscraper with the TS Naval logo. I turn to Tiger.

"Were you fantasizing about bringing me into your office, or are you trying to intimidate me, Mr. Sexton?" I tease him.

He tries to suppress his amusement but doesn't deny either possibility. We get out. He locks his car and devours me with his eyes.

TIGER

My palm rests on the lower part of Océane's back; I guide her towards the elevator without answering her assumptions. She's not running away from me anymore. Fuck, she's let her guard down, and it doesn't help me fight this growing desire for her. As soon as the doors close, my mouth sticks to hers. She's mouthwatering, with a bonus flavor of French fries. We won't talk anymore. I won't spend any more time on superfluous blahs. I want our bodies to fit together, so I can finally cum inside her. To release all the pleasure that this sublime creature prevented me from releasing during these last hours.

This unique objective animates me when we reach the penthouse and reach my company apartment. The one I use when I have too much work and no possibility of going "home." Océane and I are staggering; I keep kissing her. The bag from the restaurant escapes from her hands; her fingers sink into my hair. And this sign of cracking reassures me, damn it. I was afraid she wouldn't want it anymore, that something had gone off after my...

Eager, I knead her buttocks and snuggle her up against my erection. The sofa blocks us in our progression. Very quickly, I don't hold any more; we will never arrive in the room at this rhythm. I turn her over and tilt her bust on the back of the sofa.

"Damn, this dress..."

Crazy with desire, I start to roll up the leather without taking away this marvel. Just to clear a way for me... I open my fly, seize her rump with one hand and immerse myself in her. A wet, delicate, and velvety furnace envelops my stiffened member.

Arf, she is killing me!

I grip her hips firmly to accelerate. Her moans fill my control tower and reverberate in me. It embraces me and numbs me of pleasure.

And the climax takes me by surprise when I feel her first spasms around my cock. I finally release the pressure in a guttural complaint. Her orgasm flows over both of us, and my cum into her.

This is all I fucking needed!

At a quarter to seven, my eyes open. For a moment, I try to find my bearings, to know where I am and in what time zone.

Sydney, my apartment in TS Naval, and this warm, soft rump against me that belongs to… Océane. I've worn her out, and I don't feel guilty about it. On the contrary… She hardly moves when I get out of bed. The memory of last night floods my mind. The couch, the shower, the chocolate dessert, the carpet… Then I carried her to my bed. She was down. A smile blossoms on my lips as I think about it.

It was a perilous idea to force me not to ejaculate at the beginning of the evening, Miss Rousseau. I believe that you will not do it again, considering my outburst afterward.

I'll need at least a gallon of coffee today. I leave to take my shower and renounce to shave my incipient beard. After getting dressed for work, I come back to the room. I watch Océane for a long time, lying on her stomach. Her long, tangled hair partially hides her face, and her almost completely uncovered body is askew with the comforter half fallen on the floor.

I would pay a lot of money for such a splendid painting.

I avoid waking her up and choose to write her a note. I make a few phone calls about her before heading back to my office. No traffic jam, no commute, just the floor below.

"Good morning, Mr. Sexton," Anaïs greets me. "You… you have a visitor. She said you…"

"Ty? Finally!" Sophia cuts her off.

Damn it! I haven't had my first dose of caffeine yet. I nod to relax Anaïs and ask her to bring me a double espresso.

"Very well, Mr. Sexton," says Anaïs.

Sophia precedes me into my office, clearly on edge.

"What are you doing here?" I say to her once the door closes on us.

"What am I doing here?" my other half snaps as I press the button that makes the glass walls opaque. "Only at your work can I be sure to flush you out. I didn't even know if you had left the city or the country for a getaway."

"Well, you see, I'm still here," I reply calmly.

"What exactly is going on, Ty? Where is she? Why haven't either of you bothered to answer my calls?"

I stand in the middle of the room and shove my hands in my pockets while my wife glares at me.

"Answer!" she says, irritated.

"This discussion is not appropriate, Sophia. Not in a couple like ours, not when it is you who literally brought this woman to me."

With these words, she dashes to the lounge area of my office and smashes a vase to smithereens on the coffee table. Great, my employees are about to witness a scene.

"Yes, it is! Because there are limits, remember? And you're breaking every one of them at breakneck speed. You're doing it on purpose, aren't you? She doesn't count; it's just to hurt me, right?!"

"Are you kidding me? *You* hired Océane… probably under the assumption that she was no risk to you. Contrary to what you told Murphy, you were going to use her to sway me. Am I wrong? A third element that would be as close to you as to me… No, you probably hoped she would *be closer to you* so that she would be easy to manage."

"Indeed, I hired her. So where is she?" Sophia snaps without admitting my assumption. "Did you stay with her all night? Or did you leave her bundled on the bedside table of a hotel suite after you got tired of her?"

What, from her point of view, must have been a "handicap" for Océane—her inexperience and simplicity—now terrifies her? In any case, there is no question of giving Sophia a detailed report of what I do or don't do with the "other woman."

"It doesn't matter," I maintain without giving her any clarification. "She'll be home in the morning. Now I have work to do. You too, right?" I shorten calmly.

"No, I want to know… What's so special about her, Ty? She's just a little blonde. Pretty, okay, but too different from what you—"

From what I what? Keeps me in the dark zone as it would be with prostitutes?

Exasperated, I rub my beard to moderate what I'm about to say. I inhale, exhale and let go as I head for the door:

"This is getting ridiculous. We're done, Sophia."

"No, we're not. You may be unattainable in the eyes of everyone, but don't forget that I know your weak spot… And does Océane know?"

My jaw seals, and my gaze hardens.

"Get out of here," I order.

I don't like the smile on her lips, but I refuse to bend, to show any sign of emotion.

"Of course, she doesn't know," Sophia enthuses. "You fuck, you don't give yourself away. Right, Ty?"

Breathe calmly and control yourself, Tiger.

"Perfect!" she decrees. "You're not in control; I am. And I can make this whole thing implode if you don't start weaning yourself off of her."

"Are you threatening me, Sophia?"

"No, I'm warning you, my dear husband. I've changed my mind; I was wrong to invite Océane to join our couple. The trial is not conclusive; she must fly away."

My eyelids wrinkle, and my fists clench. A dull anger growls in me that only the arrival of my assistant with the coffee allows me to contain. Anaïs and Sophia cross each other; the one shifts while stammering excuses and the other raises their head proudly and hammers the ground with her stilettos while moving away.

Indeed, Sophia could jeopardize a lot of things if she broke down for good…

Her threat takes root in my head. I take it upon myself. Even if I suddenly feel like smashing something. And to save Océane from all this shit.

38

OCÉANE

I stretch lazily. Damn, the aches and pains! Tiger pulverized me! My body is a mess. Wonderfully fulfilled too. Is it wrong to feel this fullness after such a night of debauchery? Every bit of my skin bears the visible or invisible imprint of his fingers, lips, tongue, and skin consuming mine. Every little muscular pain reminds me of his ardor surging through my body and into my heart.

My leg goes in search of him under the comforter. Maybe he is tired and deeply asleep?

The place is empty beside me. Where is he? What time is it? Do I have to open my eyes? I am so good…

"Good morning," Tiger's husky voice rings out.

"Why aren't you in bed?" I mumble, stretching again. "To give me a long massage, for example…"

My eyelids lift up to look for him. All his attention—burning—is focused on me, even if he is dressed and a little too serious for my taste. My cheeks start to heat up again, and I straighten up while hiding my chest. By pure reflex of modesty which doesn't have any more reason to be. It's a little unsettling to wake up in my birthday suit in Tiger's sheets, at the top of his skyscraper, and to discover him in a suit and tie, staring at me for I don't know how long. He's full of charisma, fresh and ready, too sexy…

Damn, I'm going to be a nympho?

My naughty thoughts blush in my cheeks while he doesn't show himself as enterprising as he usually is. I repress the tiny hint of disappointment that titillates me. The instantaneous desire between us seems to work in one direction. Disconcerted by this observation, I try to appear casual.

"Already ready to go to work?" I say.

With his hands in his pockets, he briefly closes his eyelids and nibbles his lower lip. I tense imperceptibly. He looks at his watch.

"Actually, I'm coming back from my office."

"Oh… what time is it?"

"Five minutes after eleven."

"Darn! I overslept. Did Sophia—"

I don't finish my sentence. Tiger's polite distance affects me more than the likelihood of having missed a text or two from his wife.

"Where's my phone?" I murmur.

Tiger steps forward and hands it to me.

"An employee brought it to me," he says, his demeanor still confusing. "As for Sophia… You don't have to answer to her anymore."

I widen my eyes.

"Wh… why?"

"Because I am revoking your contract, you are no longer our *au pair*."

"What?"

In incomprehension, I stare at him without being able to make another sound, my heart beating wildly.

"You are no longer under contract, Océane. No more commitment to us."

"I don't understand."

This unexpected emotional elevator dries up my mouth. A ball forms in my stomach. A pitiful yet real reaction; I'm confused, in the grip of budding regrets. Is it my ego that takes a hit? As if I had let him use me, and he was now throwing me away. I didn't see it coming. On the contrary, his ardor last night made me feel more wanted than ever.

What has changed in the meantime?

My self-confidence is faltering, and my brain is going crazy. A kind of tumult is starting inside me. Tiger runs his hand through his hair, and his features harden. He erases all the passion that might have been there to leave a kind of unbearable indifference.

"It's just over, Océane," he maintains.

No. No, it can't happen so suddenly.

The contradictory signals confuse my neurons. I repeat, "Over? Just like that?"

"Yes. We had a lot of fun, but now you can tear up your contract and ignore the additional clause. You won't be living with us anymore, either. I can offer you an apartment as compensation. Anaïs will contact a real estate agent."

I stay frozen for a moment before jumping out of bed, draped in the comforter. I rebel in my confusion, "Stop! Are you serious?"

"I had to tell you in person," Tiger continues, unperturbed, "hence my return to this room in the middle of the day."

"Wow! So, you can forget to be a gentleman when you fuck, and choke me during a blowjob, but you have to dismiss with class?"

The mention of his error seems to have the desired effect; he digs his fingers into his hair and takes a few fractions of a second to digest. Only it doesn't make me feel better! No, I am boiling. My anger sweeps away the incomprehension in front of this brutal and inexplicable rejection. I feel like shoving him to erase this fucking phlegm he displays.

"Are you kidding me, Tiger?" I exclaim, pressing the comforter around me.

Weakened, scorned, used, and thrown away in a snap of the fingers. Damn it; this can't happen to me! Not even by a hot, debauched billionaire.

I hate this shock that screws me up inside. I still remember their insistence to Sophia and him and their efforts to attract me into their life. I remember the objections my reason would whisper to me not to give in to their indecent offer.

And I gave in. I let him take me for a… Holy shit! I don't even know!

"So that's how it is? There's no more challenge? You got me, and that's it? I was a trophy for a guy who needs to win, and nobody ever says no to?"

"Look, Lily, I—"

"Don't call me that anymore! Do you hear me? No more Lily, bud, or any of that crap! No more being a hobby for some arrogant rich guy's wife who's bored in her golden cage! Or a plaything for your libertine couple!" I shout as I go to brave him more closely.

My tone rises to a high pitch to try to hide the tears that threaten to overwhelm my voice. I don't want to break down in front of him, not like that. I am too hurt in my self-esteem for that. Jaws of rock, Tiger does not move one iota. As if he were impervious to my fury.

"Don't get yourself into this state," he tells me without breaking down.

This self-control finishes me off. My slap leaves me all alone, burning, enraged, unable to erase the painful feeling of betrayal which germinates in me. I move back, stunned. I do not understand. I don't recognize either the girl I became when I came into contact with them or the one who suffers from admitting that she suspected something like this. One day, sooner or later, a part of me knew it would end. Only I didn't anticipate this turnaround the day after a wild night out with Tiger. When he spent hours coating me with chocolate to eat me up, taking me with an ardor that was constantly reactivated, multiplied. As if he always wanted more from me, and…

But yes, that was it!?

The Péniche, the makeover, the luxury car, it was the final bouquet! A sneaky sorrow pierces me, adding to the tsunami that devastates me. So the so-called "additional clause" was nothing but a trick to make me feel confident and to fuck me in every sense of the word?

"I can't believe it!" I say.

He tries to touch me. I dodge him, stung to the core, and scream, "Don't come near me again! I can't believe I fell so low. It is me who made it easy for you. I gave myself…"

My throat becomes knotted at these last words. I move away from him. A sob rises in me; I'm afraid I'll explode in front of Tiger. I won't give him this pleasure. I swallow my tears of defeat, and I look at him for a long time. The poor fool in me still hopes that he will defend himself and contradict me. I only have the right to his silence, controlled, hurtful.

He doesn't care. Actually, he doesn't give a damn about me! The game just doesn't excite him anymore.

"You…" he starts.

Then he interrupts himself and tightens his jaws.

"Anaïs is going to bring you a more… suitable outfit," he spouts to me. "A driver is waiting for you in the underground parking lot. They all remain at your disposal if you need—"

"Shut up! If you're going to give me such banalities without any justification, shut the fuck up!"

Tiger Sexton is too powerful to give explanations to a girl he doesn't want to fuck anymore. I haven't been so fucking humiliated since I was a teenager. It hurts too much!

I turn on my heels and rush into the bathroom. I lock the door and press my trembling hands to my chest. What the hell is happening to me? I shiver all over; I can't think anymore.

TIGER

Time slips away, and I root myself in the penthouse, trying to keep my nerves of steel and myself from reneging on my decision.

"She has to fly away…"

I exhale and take another long breath. I grab the additional clause. Luckily, Océane didn't have time to sign it. My fist clenches on the papers. I leave this place before I make a wrong move and go back to my office. I finally have to catch the sons of bitches I've been tracking and break the chains! This is the first and biggest obstacle…

My assistant is busy picking up the broken glass and stuff I sent flying earlier after Sophia left. Now I'm in control. To feel nothing more than to keep my head cool. I announce, "Cancel all my appointments, Anaïs. I am unavailable until further notice."

"I'll take care of it, Mr. Sexton."

She hastens to accede to my request without asking any questions. I go back to my car, keeping an apparent calm. I start the car, but the lingering smell of French fries in the car doesn't help.

The pretty French woman eating them invades my mind.

My breathing gets out of control, and I increase the speed. Too many things clutter my thoughts. I have to sort, classify and move on. Always.

I arrive at my property. Sophia is not back. Good, I'm not in the mood. And I hope that by the time Océane comes to pick up her stuff, I'll be long gone.

"Ty? Océane? Are you both back?" Sophia trumpets down the stairs.

Shit!

I grab a couple of things, including my passport. Her steps come closer. She calls our two first names without success. A housekeeper seems to answer her something. She is now heading in my direction. I go out and intercept her on the threshold of my room.

"Ty, you're here."

I dodge her hand, encircle her wrist and give her a piercing look.

"Is your little crisis over?"

"Ty, I just wanted to—"

"I'll do all the talking now, Sophia. Don't you ever threaten me like that again."

My face comes closer to hers, and our breaths mingle.

"Never again," I tell her in a whisper. "Because I will act accordingly, even if you bear my name."

I advance, pushing her to do the same, backward until her back is against the wall and my body is a barrier.

"We understood each other well?" I ask.

Sophia tries to go up against me, but her glance is blurred. She cracks; that much is visible on her face. This varnish of strong woman, which is kneaded of insurance, doesn't work with me. She knows it because this layer of protection exists only because of me. I only have to scratch the smooth surface to find what's underneath: the girl, among many others, that I used to fuck in orgies.

A sexual object, devoted and without any will of her own at a certain time...

It was me who decided to take care of her, to take her out of that existence, to keep a fucking promise... In my darkened eyes, Sophia realizes how much I am trying to control myself at this moment. She swallows and finally nods.

"I'm sorry I had to do that, Ty."

"No, you're not. You were trying to manipulate me to get what you wanted. That said, this is my only warning: don't ever do what you did in my office this morning again."

"I wanted..." she complains, her tone low. "I hoped to make you change your mind, to revive our couple, to give you again the desire to..."

I was right, and Murphy has masterfully screwed up! She finally confirms my hypothesis.

I let her continue without comment.

"I don't want to… I miss it, Ty. It was so much better. Byrne, Annie, you and I… I miss you. We're out of sync, and I'm lonely, excruciatingly lonely."

I abruptly release her, putting distance between us. She clings to a part of her past that is completely gone.

"I want you. And you promised, Ty," she reminds me.

"I haven't forgotten… And believe me, I'm doing my best to keep that fucking promise. I'm even close."

"What do you mean you're close? You… you mean Annie? About Byrne? Did you find out anything?"

"I might have. You'll know in due time; I'm waiting to put all my pieces in place before I can act. In the meantime, you and I are doing what we've always done: we're sticking to the expectations the other had when we got married."

"But expectations change, Ty. Yours have gone one way, and mine have gone another… I want us to start over, to—"

"Stop it! Damn it, stop it, Sophia!"

I refuse to go down that minefield today. But Sophia's years of therapy and all the effort invested in this damn marriage push me to play it smart. I might as well give her at least one victory: if she's so obsessed with getting rid of the one she now feels threatened by, with wanting this new *sister* she's been trying to make fly away, then I have to get Océane out of the picture. Urgently. I tell her in the most detached way possible, "I have terminated the au pair's contract."

Surprised, Sophia bats her eyelashes. Today, we are stuck in this damn promise and this marriage. This freedom granted to the other, this assumed libertinism will never be enough to totally hide it.

I will keep my word.

"She reminded me a little of Annie… I wish it would have worked."

Stiff and mentally exhausted, I complete, "But you can't do it."

"No," Sophia admits. "When did you fire Océane? Last night? Today? Did I worry about anything?"

"It doesn't matter. It was destined to fail."

At least for you. Because she made me feel good. So fucking good, this girl.

I refrain from driving Sophia crazy by telling her that. She is already oscillating between the relief of not seeing Océane get from me what she herself has been struggling to get for years and the sadness of losing the one who was starting to fill another void in her.

Everything becomes unlikely to be reconciled, so we might as well face the facts.

"She'll pick up her things later today. I don't want to be there when she does," I conclude. "It would be better if you weren't there either, Sophia. Let's not make any more trouble. Just let her out of our lives, okay?"

"Okay. Where are you taking me then?" she haggles, hopeful.

Nowhere!

I need to go on a solo retreat, get out of here, call my pilot and take off within the hour. I need to take stock and avoid making another mistake. And see for myself what my mercenary staff has found for me. Reports and phone calls are not enough; I want to get my hands dirty.

But there's a hitch. I received the results of the research my team started after the recent changes in Sophia's behavior and my discussion with Murphy the other night. Since Sophia's last two episodes, a TS Naval computer expert has been monitoring her movements. Phone, computer… Because if our bodyguards didn't see it coming, as I did, it's because the problem is lurking elsewhere. Online, maybe? Everything leads us to believe that someone from her past has managed to get in touch with her without my knowledge. A dangerous prospect that I am still trying to gauge.

Who? How? For what purpose? And above all, why now?

It's as if a time bomb had simultaneously gone off as I was closing in on the bastards my mercenaries were tracking. Océane's arrival just aggravated this underlying flaw. It becomes an explosive cocktail.

Anyway, leaving Sophia alone now would be a very bad idea. Between the drug/alcohol mix she tried again, her mood swings earlier, and the language she used regarding Océane, I can see that she is fragile again. Far too unstable and vulnerable.

I don't want this to get any worse. Especially not now, when I'm so close. I reluctantly admit to her, "I'm going to move up my appointments in Europe."

She pouts, then relaxes a little more.

"Europe! Yes, I will find something to occupy me there," she raves. "It will be perhaps the occasion to pass to see the exhibition organized by Lilac Hood if you have time to accompany me?"

It was clearly not on my agenda. I have other priorities. No social events. No obligation to be a good husband in front of the press while hugging my wife, whom I haven't really touched in ages.

No. What I wanted was a particular blond girl. I would have preferred to have her with me in Europe, as originally planned. To fight fiercely, okay. But to have my respite with Océane when my nerves would be put to the test.

But it's crucial to keep an eye on Sophia… And to know if someone is working to upset her balance and ruin years of therapy, as I'm beginning to suspect…

I moisten my lips and nod silently. Sophia thanks me with a small smile.

"Give me five minutes to get ready," she enthuses. "I'll hurry."

I take the opportunity to contact the shrink. Dr. Murphy will be there; I'll need him to channel my wife's current and future reactions.

As for me, I'll have to get Océane out of my head now. If the last lock was to blow at the end of my war, it would be too violent for her…

PART IV

Damn fragments! She doesn't belong in this rubble. My brain knows it. Other parts of my anatomy just don't manage to respect this precaution. What can I lock now?

39

Océane

Keeping my head up. Keep my head up, whatever it takes.

Escorted by Anaïs, Tiger's assistant, I repeat this new leitmotiv over and over again. Not to capsize, not to make a fool of myself. I could almost hear Lucas's mother giggling with a "Serves you right, slut! It's your karma." No, no one needs to know that I have just suffered a second bitter humiliation after the one this lady gave me when I was sixteen. This one hurts me in a different but equally unbearable way.

But I won't show it. I may have cried in the shower, and I may still be wading through incomprehension and pain, but I won't make a spectacle of myself in front of one of Mr. Sexton's dedicated employees.

I can't wait to take everything that's mine, leave everything that this couple paid for me, including the spare clothes I'm wearing, and get as far away from them as possible. Then I can scream, blame myself and learn from this messed-up experience.

In the underground parking lot, the assistant gives me a polite smile. A driver opens the rear door of one of Tiger's Bentley with tinted windows. I don't say a word. My throat is too knotted. And then, to try to keep some crumbs of dignity requires all my strength.

To keep my head up. Not to break down.

Unfortunately, once I am sitting in the car that starts, my tears flow. Of rage, of regret, of… sorrow too?

What the fuck is wrong with me? Why did I accept this?

I close my eyes and see myself again in Paris, the day I left for Australia. This trip I had been dreaming of for so long. The luxury of no longer carrying my past around, of freeing myself from the weight of my teenage mistakes.

"You're lucky to be going to a sunny and exotic country," Myriam, one of the few educators at the home who supported me during the trial and afterward, told me. "Everything will be fine; you are a good person, Océane. You have to forgive yourself and stop punishing yourself for what happened. You have the right to happiness too, and to have fun, okay?"

I nodded without being convinced. Then little by little, during the endless flight, I started to hold on to it.

Myriam kept pushing me to live life to the fullest and to enjoy my youth instead of brooding over my missteps. That's where it led me to let myself go. I always have to make disastrous choices; it's distressing!

I've missed it all again!

I wipe my tears away angrily. Some words leave as much or more damage than the blows. Lucas is in a wheelchair following a most barbaric beating, and I am struggling with the weight of his mother's words and my guilt. My own mother would probably be disappointed with my choices. All of my choices. I still hung out with the wrong people and made stupid mistakes to feel… surrounded, integrated. For a little affection, friendship, attention… This stupid need to matter to another person has too often pushed me to believe in the impossible, and I do anything.

Like in Paris.

I sniffle and watch the traffic go by through the window. Because of my closeness with Tiger lately, I misread the signals. I saw myself as "better" in his eyes, important, desirable, and worthy of their trust in Tiger and Sophia. Sophia's loneliness was echoing in me. I know that feeling of emptiness, having few people to attach to without fear of losing them.

No! Pull yourself together, damn it! It was too good and out of line to last. And maybe you have bad karma after all.

In fact, I blame myself as much as I blame this obtuse couple. No, I blame Tiger in particular. Yet no one forced me—like before—I just had some silly illusions! All by myself!

I try to dry my tears and pretend to take it in. We approach the Sexton's property. Upon arrival, I struggle to deal with my apprehensions as I go upstairs to get my things. What if I run into one of them? Will I manage not to flinch? Fortunately, no, everything is silent. Even Peter is even more discreet than usual.

Does he know that his boss slept with me and can't stand the sight of me? Has he been told to kick me out if I hang around?

Damn, I feel like I've become a nobody again. Put down, rejected after having invested too much.

"Hello, Miss Océane," Peter greets me, always respectful, at least. "If you need help or anything, I—"

"That's okay, Peter. Thank you," I reply with a faded smile.

I swallow my bitterness and try to armor myself again. Like at every stage of my life when it was necessary. To learn to detach myself once again and to change my horizon. In the room, I find the strength to make a phone call to Louane. I leave a message on her answering machine, "Hi, girl, it's Océane. I just wanted to say hello. Sorry I've been a little unavailable lately…"

Because I let myself be impressed and lured by a dream existence. But it was ephemeral and without an ounce of sincerity.

"We had fun," as he said. Now I'm back down to earth, back to normal life, with ordinary people and my disgraces.

No.

I shake my head, censor myself and continue my monologue on Louane's voicemail.

"I… we can see each other soon if you want. I don't have a job anymore and am a bit freer. See you soon, miss. Kisses."

I hang up before my voice cracks. Depressed, I begin to collect my belongings. I change my clothes, anxious to get rid of any element from these people. However, I don't know how to erase the traces inside me, the ones that can't be seen. And that Tiger has sown all over my skin. Under my skin.

I wish I didn't feel anything anymore. I wish I didn't have this twinge in my heart when I think of his indifference earlier when his smell was still permeating me.

Stop, damn it! Don't make yourself suffer, not for this! It's not worth it.

Unfortunately, my brain is out of sync with the rest of my body. The pain and humiliation are too strong to be silenced. I hurriedly finish packing my bags to leave before bursting into tears.

Never again will I allow something like this to be done to me!

TIGER

Océane… Is she holding up? No, focus! I can't backpedal. Not anymore.

"Mister Sexton!" suddenly shouts Anaïs, all out of breath.

I crush my umpteenth cigarette in the ashtray offered to me by the steward while my assistant catches up with me on the tarmac. Smoking to contain my nerves doesn't really work. And Sophia is waiting for me in the jet, hanging on her phone to warn Lilac Hood of our next stay in Paris. Of course, it is necessary to have Sophia with me, even if I have no desire to be behind closed doors with her. I need space and distance before I make one too many mistakes with Océane. This abrupt breakup is eating away at my mind. So many other things are colliding in my head that I am afraid of my own reactions now.

And to make matters worse, Anaïs' call at the last minute delays our flight! She joins me by trotting. I signal to the steward to leave us and belch impatiently, "What was this emergency? There was a problem with Océane?"

"No, sir. Miss Rousseau was taken to your home, and she was quite calm. It wasn't because of her that I did everything I could to catch you before you left."

For a moment, I considered that my blondie had… fuck, no, what exactly did I expect?

"Okay. So, what happens?" I ask, annoyed by the turn of this insane wish and by all the wrong notes that punctuate this shitty day.

"The head of security at TS Naval gave me this for you," my employee justifies himself by handing me some documents in a closed envelope. "He says he has solved the mystery: the IT department has made a discovery. And you urgently needed to know about it."

Frowning, I quickly realize. The only thing on the stove that Anaïs mentioned to her collaborators and that was worth shaking up my schedule was "the Sophia subject." I wanted to understand what trigger might have come into play. Why is she talking about *Flight* again? How did she get the drugs that none of her doctors prescribed, and why is she getting more and more out of control?

So, I finally have answers to this problem?

My fingers tighten on the sealed envelope.

"Good. Thank you, Anaïs… And about Océane, if she ever…"

I abruptly cut short what I was about to say. I'm so fucking on edge and impulsive; it's almost reckless!

"Yes, Mr. Sexton?" asks Anaïs, all ears.

"No, nothing. Forget it; keep the course in my absence. Océane Rousseau will no longer be part of the picture."

"I'll take note of it, sir. Count on me. I wish you a good trip," concludes Anaïs, gumming up the ounce of curiosity which shone for a brief moment in her eyes.

Now closed, I recover my apparent phlegm, nod, and board the plane.

After takeoff, I unseal the fold. As I take in what's written in the envelope, my jaws tighten:

We've been looking at someone in Mrs. Sexton's inner circle. Mike Woods, the manager of The Sexton's restaurant in Sydney. An unofficial inspection of his apartment revealed that Mike Woods has an unhealthy admiration for The Garden, presumably for some time. Press clippings about the event accumulate in his home; he compulsively collects everything that has been said, written, and published about it…

Damn it, how did we miss this particular "hobby" when we hired this guy? My annoyed eyes meet Sophia's curious ones on the other side of the plane.

"Is everything okay, Ty?" she asks me.

"Yeah, just work."

"Okay," she answers without worrying further. "I can't wait to stroll around Paris."

"Good, I'm glad."

I look at her for a moment, perplexed. Did she reveal information to her manager, even without doing it on purpose? Not wanting to tip her off about my employees' find, I turn my attention back to my reading.

So, in light of this discovery, I put Henry, our little IT genius, on the case. Henry hacked Woods' laptop, cloned his cell phone, and snooped around in everything he could over the past few days. It turns out that Mike Woods, by dint of hanging out on dark web forums of fans of the Garden, ended up being contacted by a mysterious internet user. Since then, the communications between him and this individual have multiplied.

I don't know if there is a link, but it seemed disturbing enough to alert you.

If we follow the chronology, on the date you first noted the incidents, Mike Woods received a cryptic message in an unknown language via email to recite in front of your wife when he is alone with her. According to our findings, it is a coded phrase. It is written below. Also attached is all of the data we collected from Mike Woods' apartment and appliances.

I am at your disposal for any further information, and of course, we will continue to investigate in case you are not satisfied with these answers. I also await your instructions as to what to do with the manager.

"Holy shit!"

My spontaneous reaction makes my wife flinch.

"Ty?" she says anxiously this time.

I try to pull myself together. I moisten my lips and reassure her calmly:

"Everything is fine, don't worry."

But no, everything is not fine. It could be that the bastards I'm tracking have found my wife long before my mercenaries have located them. Either way, this fact has an impact on the changes in Sophia. They've targeted her…

Almost feverishly, I pull out my laptop to notify Terrence and put him in touch with the talented TS Naval computer scientist who found the breach. Let them work together to find the common point between these two cases, the bastard who managed to shake everything up on the sly.

Shit, maybe Omega was a lot closer than I thought! And he obviously has a plan too. But the Ares operation must not fail, not this close. I'm going to make a massacre!

❋ ❋ ❋

One… Two… Three… Four days later, London.

I digested the last news and re-classified my priorities. On the surface, I'm in London to finalize the new negotiations for the post-Brexit agreements with TS Naval's English business partners.

But unofficially, I'm making it the last operations HQ to catch the degenerates playing with my nerves and Sophia's sanity. All have now been located in France. I'd been waiting for this moment for so long that there was no more vital objective than this one in my eyes. I am almost there. It is both exciting and nerve-wracking. There's everything I've imagined, ruminated on, and planned for years; my promises to myself and Sophia. And there are the facts, the data collected, and what I can do with it now.

Something concrete. And so many things are reacting in my head, knowing that I have the power to finally step in, to act. On my morning jog in Regent's Park, I wait for the right man. Terrence, the leader of the hand-picked group of mercenaries hired as soon as I took over TS Naval. Right after I got my inheritance and was able to release the funds needed for the search. No amount of failure, no side wins, and no distractions have altered that desire. The desire to find these bastards and fulfill my promise to personally destroy them.

Discreet and punctual, Terrence arrives at our appointment and joins me in short strides. I take off my headphones while continuing to run beside him.

"So?" I tell him without preamble.

"The French police raided The Brotherhood. They arrested Omega, who called himself Sir Alistair Sinclair on his papers and whose pseudonym in this club was the Shadow. They also arrested his housekeeper, ex 'Child of the Serpent.' As well as the Executioner, alias the One-Eyed Man now. For kidnapping, sequestration, rape, acts of torture in an organized gang, and prime suspects in the series of assaults and murders perpetrated in France with markings."

Including that of the starred chef Angèle Moisson? I read that in the international press a while ago… My breath quickens. Damn, it's them!?

"It's certain?" I assure myself, my mind racing.

"Affirmative, sir. They also have Typhoon and Echidna, twins, former 'Child of the Serpent' for one and 'Lily' for the other. Among others, for acts of cruelty and sexual nature towards animals…"

That makes five confirmed among them. Five survivors, two of whom I particularly wanted to find: Omega and the Executioner.

"The identity of Aaron Denis is also confirmed; it's Byrne Hamilton."

Holy shit!

I stop running in shock.

He is alive. Byrne is alive and located!

"Byrne Hamilton?"

"That's right, sir."

Images storm my head. Those damn videos numbered, just like each follower was—marked—like cattle. Videos I've watched countless times. The initiations, the ceremonies, the special prayers, and the preaching of Alpha and Omega. The face of that tall half-breed, Byrne Hamilton, appears on many of them. In the middle of a fuck or in contemplation. Just like those of other kids, teenagers, adults…

"And Annie Hamilton?"

"For the moment, no trace, sir."

Damn it! Bad sign? She is nowhere to be found…

My fists clench. My source remains at my level, factual, calm, and without emotion. I slowly resume my run, thinking Terrence is following me. I try to assimilate what all this implies. I have the cards in my hand…

"What do the French authorities want with the prisoners? Have they discovered that they are Australians and that they are wanted?"

"Affirmative, sir. No extradition agreement negotiated at this time, according to our sources," he continues.

"Okay," I reply, regulating my breathing.

"We know the location of each of the targets now. We're ready to strike when you are, Mr. Sexton," my investigator reminds me.

The truth is, he knows I don't care if France wants to hold and try these scumbags for what they've done to their territory. Whether they send them back to the country or not, what I want is not going to be settled in a law court.

I clench my jaws tighter, petrified of rage. A quick glance sideways lets me see that my mercenary is reluctant to add any more information. I ask apprehensively, "Is there anything else, Terrence? Something that stops us?"

"A certain Samuel Durand was able to spot one of our guys, and he… he wanted to give you a message."

"Let's hear it."

"During the good haul, he took a closer look at Byrne Hamilton."

"Why?"

"It seems to me that this guy's brother was stuck in The Brotherhood with Byrne. They were obviously close and helped each other."

"Go on…"

"This Samuel Durand wants to keep his brother out of jail. They are French. According to him, the kid and Byrne are victims who played vigilante to avenge certain members and blow up this organization that Omega and the Executioner had integrated in France."

"I see."

"And that could backfire on both of them," my employee explains.

"What is his brother's name?"

"Morgan Sinclair."

Sinclair? As in Omega's alias? Why? Who was he to this freak? A new replacement toy or his equal in vice?

"I want to know everything about this boy before I decide. We'll see if I help him or if he's one of the enemies to fight."

"Roger, sir. You will have a detailed report later today."

"Perfect."

"Okay. I'm going back, sir. We're waiting for your green light to execute the final mission," my contact concludes. The equipment is ready."

"Great."

The next second, our paths separate. Terrence goes into the park while I turn back. End of the jog. It's time to go refine my strategy in the shower.

I've got them, damn it! I've got them!

40

Drying off, I go back to my computer to unlock it. Not to watch another video; this evidence was stolen before the police arrived on the scene on that fateful evening and is permanently undermining my conscience…

On my computer, my eyes remain frozen on the photos of the aged newspaper published the day after the tragedy. More than a decade ago now. I know its contents by heart—like the videos of their methods—yet my feelings are intact at this umpteenth rereading of the story revealed to the general public:

"*The Garden*: Macabre discovery yesterday morning.

A mysterious community seemed to have built itself up in the Australian outback for several years. Discreet, self-sufficient on a very large farm, and seemingly harmless, the members called themselves 'The People of the Garden.'

Unfortunately, what we thought were a bunch of dreamy ecologists wanting to get away from the nuisances of the modern world turned out to be one of the most opaque and worrying cults that Australia has seen since the dismantling of 'The Family.'[3]

Indeed, the long-standing infiltration of our investigative journalist Steve Kidman tried to clear up the followers and sectarian aberrations of this community. Unfortunately, the introduction of our colleague among them ended in a horrifying way last night.

Everything leads us to believe that the leaders of this nebulous

---

3   The Family is a sect that was active in Australia since 1964 for about twenty years. It was founded by Anne Hamilton-Byrne (whose name served as inspiration for some first names mentioned in this novel: Annie Hamilton, Byrne Hamilton…).

cult—having discovered that their mode of operation and their practices were about to be revealed in broad daylight—accelerated the accomplishment of their goal.

Thus, yesterday morning, the police arrived at a chilling scene. A mass suicide and no trace of possible survivors of the cult.

'The Garden' made its Final Flight with dozens of men, women, teenagers, and children forever asleep after having their last drink together.

The body of our reporter was also found under circumstances that have yet to be clarified. According to the first elements, Steve Kidman would have been tortured to death: tongue cut off, eyes chemically burned, and other unspeakable atrocities.

What happened on that farm? Who in the community committed these abuses? Did all the cultists die during the mass suicide? Will we soon know the full truth about what happened on the members' last night? And of every day the recovered victims lived there?

Unfortunately, Steve Kidman's notes are still missing. But the investigation is just beginning."

I abruptly close my laptop and reach for my phone. After a single ring, my contact picks up. I breathe in, breathe out. This is it.

"The moment I officially leave Europe," I say, stiff-necked, "I'll send you a simple 'OK' by text. That will be my green light."

"Yes, sir. We're standing by."

I hang up, extremely tense. But we have to move on…

I get ready and go out to honor my professional commitments of the present. The day goes by between work and the remote follow-up of the preparations of my guys in France. I receive the report on the famous Morgan Sinclair. When I join Sophia in Paris, I will take the opportunity to meet this young man's brother to see what I can get out of him. And see Aaron, well, Byrne Hamilton…

For the moment, my wife is with a couple of friends, the Hoods. Tonight, it will be four damn nights that I put my solitude in London to good use. I will wait until the mercenaries exfiltrate Omega and the Executioner and my lawyers simultaneously handle the transfer of Byrne to Australia to have a discussion about this with my wife. And to talk about her shady manager, Mike Woods, too.

Do you remember my promises, Sophia? Well, we found your "brother" and those who killed the rest of your community…

It took a long time, but I got there.

The endless psychoanalysis, the effects of antidepressants in abundance, and the long-term efforts to get Sophia out of indoctrination may be jeopardized again in the next few days. Her little fit of possessiveness about Océane and Omega's attempts to regain control of her mind through Mike Woods will be nothing compared to this ticking time bomb.

Stop! My brain is under pressure.

I need an outlet right now. To refocus, to feel less oppressed, to calm my nerves. Normally, I would have booked one or more experienced call-girls within my selection criteria and fucked like crazy to let off steam. With pros, it's easy. I fuck them and forget about them in the process. They don't demand my respect; they are content with my money. They don't make me laugh; they don't challenge me. And they don't make Sophia jealous…

Unfortunately, the pretty blonde-haired Frenchie has outdone the best of them. Her trembling voice during our breakup comes back to haunt me. The memory of her smell, the softness of her skin, her whole body, her mouth, her teasing way…

Never has a girl had this almost permanent effect on my thoughts. I don't like it…

I even caught myself thinking about her at the worst moment. In the middle of a business lunch, I lost the thread of the discussion when I saw the waiter bringing fries to the next table. It was as if, as I went along, the stalking was taking up less and less space in my head because it would soon be over. And that Océane was infiltrating me to occupy all this empty space. My lack of her reminds me of everything I gave up from the day I promised to take care of Sophia.

I miss her, damn it!

Locked in my hotel suite after a busy day and an evening of boredom despite my London hosts' efforts to entertain me, I hesitate to call my ex "au pair." Too many irreconcilable facts are swirling around in my exhausted head.

"She has to fly…"

I am not the man for her, and there was nothing to look forward to in this relationship. It was only sex. Alone, I set my sights on the Jacuzzi and a bottle of scotch, with "Baby Did a Bad Bad Thing" by Chris Isaak playing in the background.

When my eyes close to try to relax, it comes back to pierce me. That too rough ending in the penthouse in Sydney.

But I still want you, little bud. Your sass, your sparkling eyes, and your deliciously special way of cumming in my arms.

To drink from her as I had planned before Sophia threw her ultimatum in my face. Until I no longer felt this need to touch her, this destabilizing lack.

Suddenly, my phone rings. I straighten up and reach for it. Of course, it's not Océane. I've hurt her pride, I know. She will never call me, and I thought it would be easier this way. I look at Steen Hood's name on my screen. I'm not in the mood for a civilized conversation. And there's an impulse that's bothering me much more.

OCÉANE

What's it been? Four days? Five days? A century? Anyway, time seems so much longer and duller. My umpteenth day of solitude feels like the previous ones. Living in this small unpretentious hotel doesn't help me. Even if I often hang out with Louane and her gang whenever possible, there is no more room in their shared apartment to live in. And coming back alone in this impersonal room inevitably screws up my morale. Despite all the trouble I go through to try to forget—cocktails, animated discussions, group parties—nothing helps.

I always fall back into this deep feeling of isolation. Confined to myself, lonely. No more Sophia and those lovely moments of complicity with her. Which seemed so strong, so real, so sincere.

And no more Tiger and those hours of trembling in his arms. Intense. Too real, too sincere at the time...

There is only pain and anger left. Against me, against him.

Will it ever fade away? I'm starting to doubt it. I should just hate him instead of blocking out memories. It's hard to admit that I...

No, I don't miss him! I don't miss either of them. Him, least of all!

It's seven o'clock in the morning, and I've just come back from a party. I go to bed completely exhausted, hoping to fall into a deep sleep. To silence my gray matter which is trying to stir up moments still fresh in my head. But my eyes remain wide open in the darkness of the drawn curtains and this cold bed. I try to restrain myself from picking up my phone; I risk doing something masochistic like calling Sophia or snooping online. And discover pictures of them at parties. To find out that I already have a substitute.

Tiger works like a madman, a robot. He has no feelings and no time. But I know his appetite.

Stop right there, Océane! Why the fuck are you torturing yourself like this?

No, I don't want to be the pathetic chick who wastes her time thinking about this and spying on their digital lives. Besides, now I know better than anyone else that with this couple, the juiciest stuff happens in private. Their public image is managed with an iron fist, a locked communication that wouldn't let the existence of a new fuck buddy slip through. Or "friend" of Mrs. Sexton. Obviously. I benefited from this too. Despite all the "incidents" I caused, nothing appeared on the internet or in the press.

Thankfully, in fact. Because in France, some vipers' tongues like Christine or Victor would have jumped on the occasion to relay my little slutty drifts. Even on the other side of the world. I took too many risks, and I crashed into the wall.

This anxiety pushes me to check the Web… An excuse? Irrepressible masochism? Or lamentable weakness? I crack, I snoop. Nothing unpleasant appears about me. Absolutely nothing. At first, a tiny gasp of relief escapes me. Then, one thing leads to another, and I find it difficult to resist another temptation. Insidious, strong, destructive. I rummage around in stalker mode on Sophia and Tiger. Even if I hate myself for giving in to this unhealthy curiosity, I type Sexton in the search engine. The news is flying. One headline stands out and catches my attention:

"A glamorous wind blew through Montmartre today."

I swallow. A photo accompanies the headline of two women coming out of the Sacré-Coeur… According to the article, a redhead—Lilas Hood, wife of filmmaker Steen Hood—and Sophia look complicit when a paparazzi captured this image. This is from this morning, local time. I'm ten hours behind, but the obvious is clear: they are in Paris!

Holy crap! They made the famous trip where they had included me in the beginning. Without me…

Why does it hurt so much? Why do I keep putting myself through the torture? I scroll through the pages… Mrs. Sexton and Mrs. Hood photographed over and over… Tiger is nowhere to be seen. It is mainly these two women, happy to be in the French capital, who inspire the Web. Between the allusions to their husbands, the blahs of journalists on each of them, and other descriptions of their looks of fashion icons, I see only that. Influencers take advantage of this to offer themselves pieces almost identical to theirs and transmit them to the public.

What am I doing to myself? Sophia lives her life. She has obviously moved on very quickly. And so has her husband.

I have the inexplicable feeling that I have also lost a friend. Overwhelmed, I stop. This proves that I was not indispensable. I never was. Tiger and Sophia certainly don't torture themselves thinking about the insignificant tourist who distracted them; they do their own thing in France. I have to do the same: cross them off too. Get a new job and an apartment and prove to myself that the Sextons don't count anymore. That I can move on without…

Shit, my phone rings!

I stare at the name on the screen in amazement. Oh my God, it's him!

What do I do? Should I ghost him? Should I pick up the phone? I guess my desire to insult him and to evacuate my anger is stronger because I press the green button and let go, "Forget this number, delete it!"

"Good evening, Océane. And, no, I can't."

"What do you want, Tiger?"

"To see you again and apologize to your face. I know giving you gifts wouldn't work."

Is this a joke? Five days ago—a decade in the making—he blew me off without the slightest emotion, and now he's bored again? Or is it just to test his insensitive collector's attraction to me again? I'm getting annoyed.

"I don't give a damn about your excuses! The bond is broken, if only there was ever a bond between the three of us. So, stop it, don't call me anymore! And you're right; I don't want anything from you."

I can hear his breathing. Not a word for what seems like an eternity. I have to hang up before I let him disturb me further.

"You see, I gave in," he says. "Even though we're no longer under contract, I had to talk to you. Lily, I had no choice; it was a necessary decision in a rather delicate period... But... I want to see you again so much."

Damn it, do something! Send him away!

I open my mouth and close it again without being able to flinch. What's going on with him?

"I propose you an alternative."

"No," I say with a firmness that is, to say the least, convincing.

This instant weakness irritates me. I'm not "his sweet Lily," his "little bud," I won't be anymore!

"Meet me in London to discuss it. We're not going to do this over the phone. Anaïs will take care of the travel arrangements so that—"

"I said no, Tiger! Now I'm going to hang up. Keep your money, your jet, those nicknames you used to call me, your wife, your flowers, and your twisted ideas! You always get what you want in life, right? Well, you won't get me anymore!"

"Océane, wait! Let me—"

Too late, I cut the call, very angry, and I turn off my phone. I don't even want to know. I don't believe it! Does he really think he's going to snap his fingers like that and get me into bed again? That I have no self-respect?

Starting tomorrow, I will do everything I can to hurt him in one way or another and prove to him that it's over.

Because I have decided it! My turn to show you the effect of painful rejection, Mr. Sexton. And if the pain never gets to you, taking out your ego will!

41

Océane

I can't sleep anymore. Even that, Tiger has ruined. A little voice in my head keeps telling me:

He's in London, not in Paris with Sophia. And he called you.

This little voice insinuates itself perniciously in me. Why did he come back? Does he enjoy playing yo-yo with my emotions, like with numbers on the stock market? This isn't finance, I'm not a fucking number, and I won't let him! I need to shut the doors… I need a big counterattack. Something that will stop him for good. But what?

Suddenly, I know! Harry Carter. Daddy's boy, that heir apparent that Tiger never could stand to have me around. I still have his number.

No, bad idea. Or maybe yes? Pfffff! I have to rest.

I close my eyelids, hoping to tame the multitude of tumultuous things that are dismantling my mind. I'm exhausted and far too shaken by the phone call from Mr. Control freak insensitive. My fists clench on the sheets. I need to sleep—if I can—then I'll figure it out.

I wake up in the middle of the afternoon, still a mess. I should find something to do so that I don't have to endure this situation anymore. But what exactly do I want? Revenge?

If so, I have the Harry Carter option.

If not, I always have Louane's gang to party with whenever I want and help me forget. Putting a stop to it.

Right now, I mostly need to work to feel useful and strong again. I won't become that again by locking myself in a hotel room. By spending the Sextons' money for my "services rendered." I'll have to go back to square one: resumes, cover letters, canvasses, unsolicited applications, and interviews, if possible. And stop thinking about Tiger!

That I can do!

After a long time in the bathroom, I got dressed and dolled up to camouflage the traces left by my break down of the last few days. Here I am ready to make better use of my freedom.

I join my friends at King's Cross, a hype district. I have decided to put my life back on track. Louane welcomes me, drunk. We kiss each other's cheeks. I can tell that I'll be drunk before the end of the party. There's a crowded bar, a trendy, festive atmosphere, and several nightclubs around. It is perhaps what I need to get back on my feet?

"So, beautiful, what do you drink?" asks Trevor, Louane's boyfriend, obviously a little tipsy too.

"Uh… the same thing as your girlfriend?"

"A strawberry mojito!" he says. "Don't move, French girl; I'll bring it to you."

I let myself be carried; I chat and try to get drunk on the ambient joy. It doesn't work too well. Very quickly, I find myself on the sidewalk, taking drags and thinking too much. The past, the present, my crappy choices, my attraction to a married billionaire who dumped me after "having a good time."

Isn't my life great?

Garrett shows up to cadge a cigarette off me and dispel the dark clouds that are gathering over my head. Garrett, the guy who lives with Louane and the others. The business school student, an inveterate fan of the great Sexton for his business prowess and of Mrs. Sexton for her supermodel plastic. Basically, I end up with a guy who dreams of being a future Tiger.

If only he knew what it means to be a Tiger…

Deep down, do I even know? Okay, I have known Tiger intimately. He is sexually very open, but other aspects of his life are complex, padlocked, or very limited in access. And he's the only one who can take or throw out anything he wants. Including me.

Damn! Let's stop stirring things up. I'm pushing back my negative vibes. And I start thinking again about Harry Carter's number, right there in my cell phone, just in case… If Tiger ever insists, but he won't; I was just an ephemeral way to get off. Between two conquests of the world, as a powerful and invincible man. Always richer, always more inaccessible.

I smoke in silence with Garrett, depressed by this conclusion. Around us, the bursts of laughter, the echo of music coming from inside, and the snatches of conversation resound.

Little by little, I meet the eyes of a guy. A little too often for my taste…

Do we know each other?

That would astonish me; his face doesn't tell me anything. Maybe he is a womanizer on the hunt, and I look like a lonely prey. But I'm not interested in anything. At the moment, I am unable to flirt or have fun. I don't even have enthusiastic mantras to boost me anymore.

Behind my wisps of smoke, I avoid the dork and contemplate the surroundings. Let's focus on the animation of a beautiful night in a sublime setting. However, even if I put all my good will there, this effervescence doesn't reach me. On the other hand, Garrett is ogling a girl going out to make a phone call not far away. I turn my head in the opposite direction again, feeling the other guy's gaze.

Give it up, man! I'm not interested in you. And it's not like I'm some irresistible hottie. Tiger wouldn't have sent me packing so quickly if I was…

Damn, here I go again! Disgusted, I would slap my face. Now it's Garrett who's watching me with a little smile as if he's trying to follow my morose thoughts.

"By the way, what's up, Océane? Do you like it here? Don't you miss France too much?" he asks me.

His questions are simple, yet they awaken complicated answers in my head. No, I don't feel so good. Am I still happy to be in Australia? Am I suddenly homesick? Despite everything that made me leave? Not being able to chat with Myriam and the few people I could rely on when I needed them leaves me sad.

But it's not my roots and France that I miss; it's the people I was supposed to go back with.

Because with them, it would have been different: intense, fabulous. They became my illusion of "family": her, him, me. I would have rediscovered my country from a more magical angle, sheltered and cherished in their cocoon of luxury and lust.

For a moment, I imagine Sophia in Paris. I would have had a blast taking her to non-touristy places in Paris, strolling with her outside her lavish comfort zone. We had a pretty good laugh together, didn't we? Like "sisters?" Friends? The qualifier had no value. What was valuable was how much I loved showing her the real me, without barriers, to better discover her. I became light, carefree, free, and young again. We would have gone to nightclubs, between girls, as she did with me here. And then I would have let myself go into Tiger's arms for…

What the hell is wrong with me?

I shake my head and gasp. I'm so fucking confused! Garrett gives me a mocking pout. Damn, I didn't answer him?

"What enthusiasm!" he teases me. "You don't like Sydney anymore? What happened?"

"Nothing!" I defend myself a little too quickly. "I mean, I still love this city; I just… have some work issues."

"That's nothing; there are always jobs for waiters," he encourages me before exchanging a glance with the girl on the phone, whom he starts to follow with his eye. "Do you mind if I go…"

"Are you kidding? Go ahead, go!" I say to him, understanding that he wants to hook up.

Garrett, all excited, doesn't hesitate. I find myself again alone in the middle of anonymous people with my second cigarette. The guy from earlier takes this as an opening. Feigning his look doesn't prevent him from coming to accost me.

"Hi," he says.

Damn, I didn't send you any flirting signal. Go away!

"We've already met, haven't we?" continues the stranger.

"No kidding? Does this technique really work?"

Destabilized by my breaking tone, he scratches his temple. Then he gives me a big smile.

"In my defense, I'm gay. We have other methods," he laughs.

"Phew, I'm fine with that. Even if you did check me out a little too much for a gay guy."

His face lightens.

"Your French accent... That face... You look like Sophia Sexton's friend," he says. "And pretty funny, too, I see."

Oh, no, not that. A scoop stalker?

"Excuse me?" I say again, tense.

"The Velvet & Diamonds," he adds as if that would make me feel a little better.

I tense up, staring at him. That's the name of the club where Tiger and his staff came to get us out. Did it spread? What the hell, maybe it leaked? Videos? Photos that escaped me when I checked? How did this guy recognize me? What if that was the reason Tiger fired me afterward, to control his communication and...

My mind races in spite of myself.

"I... I have no idea what you're talking about," I say suspiciously.

The guy looks conspiratorial and glances around. He comes closer.

"Don't worry, I know... I signed a non-disclosure agreement and received a nice financial incentive," he tells me quietly. "Mum's the word!"

"I... don't know what to say. You must be mistaken; I'm sorry," I deflect.

I crush my cigarette in a rarely dedicated ashtray—it's not always easy to be a smoker here, especially in public places—and I'm about to turn and run away into the bar.

"You have nothing to fear, Miss. I am rather physiognomist; in my job, it is useful..." he throws me to stop me.

And it works. He tickles my curiosity.

"Can we just get to know each other?"

"Why?" I say, intrigued but not reassured, turning around.

Just because my contract ended abruptly doesn't mean I'm not supposed to keep quiet forever about what I shared with the Sextons. Even if I'm hurt, I won't betray that. First, because I don't do that, it would be small and petty. Second, because Tiger's lawyers would certainly grind me down if I leaked compromising information.

"I'm the manager of the Velvet & Diamonds," the guy explains. "I'm used to dealing with the press corps, celebrity agents and lawyers... well, that sort of thing. I'm sorry if I sounded suspicious."

"Okay. So, then?"

"I wasn't eavesdropping on purpose, but I think I heard you say you were having work-related problems."

"This conversation wasn't meant for you, obviously," I say.

"Indeed, sorry again. However, I would like to take this opportunity to make contact, if you don't mind? I often need staff; we could see if it fits?"

Like this? Like, the most innocuous coincidence?

"Absolutely not gullible," I frown and cross my arms.

"So, you just happened to be there and offered to help me? For a job?"

We stare at each other, and his eyes light up. He bursts out laughing.

"I can see why you seem so close to… well, you know who. You're suspicious and able to send a snooper packing. That's good; I love that!"

He pulls a card out of his pocket and hands it to me.

"There's no trick, Miss, I assure you. Yes, sometimes I go out of my little kingdom to explore the competition, gather ideas, etc. Your face looked familiar… If you're looking for work, call me. If not, it was nice to meet you."

"Uh-huh. I can't help but wonder why you would do that," I say without picking up the card.

"What do you mean?"

"Why would you offer a job to someone you've only seen twice, whose skills you don't even know?"

I've had my job handed to me before, after all.

"Okay, I'll be honest. If I smell a bargain, I'll take the chance," he admits. "Of course, I have my usual recruiting circuit, but right now, I realize something: you're a friend of powerful clients, and having you on my team would be a plus. A good network is important, right?"

"Yeah, I guess so."

"I won't bother you any longer. Please take my card. If I don't hear from you, it's okay. Perhaps you'll come as a customer some other time?" he concludes, slipping the little card into my hand. "Nice to meet you, miss!"

He goes away, leaving me doubtful. I can't analyze; I can't tell if it was all spontaneous. How can I not have doubts? Am I going to have to walk on eggshells here, too, because I had the stupidity to get involved with a major business tycoon in Australia?

Damn, I'm a magnet for trouble; it can't be otherwise! Ruminating on the twisted twists of fate and my stupid karma, I keep the guy's contact information. Just in case, although I don't plan to do anything with it for the moment. My job searches and queries can wait. I decide to join my buddies and try to clear my head.

My freedom, I'll do what I want with it.

Because I still have the damn right to have fun! To assume myself as a woman. To live, to be happy! And you won't be a drag, Tiger!

42

The next day, Paris

I come back to sit at the table after having read and answered an important email and made a phone call. Soon, my field troop will have free rein to execute my orders…

"Is everything okay, Ty?" worries Sophia again.

Does she suspect Mike Woods? Hell, that guy's been working with my wife for years, and he's a big fan of Omega. He's been used as a pawn by Omega to… To do what, really? Reactivate something in Sophia, like a sleeper agent? To control her? To manipulate her? To achieve what ends? I still wonder. I still haven't figured out how to talk about this with Sophia. Nor have I told her about the progress of my research or the imminence of my strike…

"Great," I reply without elaborating on the subject. "Sorry for the interruption. Work…"

Steen Hood, leaning toward his wife, barely notices my return to them. He kisses her as if there were nothing more important around. It seems to me that they have been married for a long time. How do they maintain this impression that they are constantly a honeymoon couple? I suspect Sophia is daydreaming about that detail. She gives me an envious, nostalgic look.

But a mouth other than hers obsesses me. A face framed by a blond mane…

"You always get what you want in life, right? Well, you won't get me anymore!"

Océane is cluttering my synapses and I hate it. After she hung up on me yesterday, I struggled to fight my primal instincts, screaming at me to jump on the jet and head back to Sydney. But to do what? Creating unnecessary complications? My life is already too full, with filters to keep in place.

So, I ended up doing what I agreed to, and following my reason, I joined Sophia in Paris, accepted this dinner, and tried to channel the rest. We arrive at the end of the meal, seated near the large windows of the Hood apartment. I stare at the landscape of the sixteenth arrondissement under the light of the street lamps through the glass.

What if Océane had been there? With us… At that moment… Damn it, lock it!

My eyes return inside; Steen finally breaks away from his redhead's lips. Cheeks pink, Mrs. Hood runs a hand through her hair.

"Uh… what was I saying again?" she asks us. "Ah, yes… Does anyone want a digestif?"

"With pleasure," I answer.

I exchange a half-smile with her husband before adding, "But maybe we should leave you alone?"

Getting a little more flushed, our hostess assures us how delighted they are to receive us and that they would like us to stay a little longer. Steen simply devours her with his eyes without contradicting her. Equipped with our glasses, we settle down in the living room. After a while, the women talk to each other. Hood and I get together to talk about our mutual acquaintances, current events, travel…

"We need to take a vacation from the Lilac Foundation exhibition launch," he tells me. "And I think Sophia is trying to lure my wife to Australia."

How about that? Predictable. Sophia knows that when we return home, she will feel even more lonely after Océane's departure. It will be worse…

The fact of depriving me of the company of our ex-guest also deprives her of her presence and of the complicity they shared on a daily basis. On this point, we both lose. I have alerted Dr. Murphy; the therapist will be back to help her with this turn…

Since the Hood couple represents an ideal in my wife's eyes, I don't want her to think that by seeing them more often, their marital happiness will rub off on us.

There is no way that our union will ever resemble theirs, for a thousand and one reasons…

However, I don't get flustered.

"I can see that," I respond to Steen's words, thinking of another option.

The possibility of acquiring more freedom, of taking back the hand concerning my desires… While keeping Sophia busy and under good supervision… I catch the attention of my companion and say, "Why not? You are welcome! Sophia will soon leave for Sydney. Go ahead of me and enjoy your stay in the meantime. I will finish my other appointments in Europe and then meet you there for the rest of the program."

Steen and Lilac consult each other. My *other half,* taken by surprise by my suggestion, tries to read me. Impenetrable, I turn my attention back to our friends. I insist, "We'd be happy to. Wouldn't we, Sophia?"

"O… of course," she confirms.

"Oh, yes!" enthuses Lilac. "What do you think, Steen?"

"If that's what you want, I'll line up, sweetheart," he tells her. "Thanks for the invitation, Tiger."

Perfect!

I crack a smile. No matter what stratagems and strength of persuasion it will take, I plan to use this time to get over my lack of a certain blonde girl. I have strong nerves, and so far, neither the weight of responsibility nor my commitments and desire for revenge have made me weaken.

But I can't manage the carnal magnet that is Océane.

I want, I need to sink into her again with all my might.

Three days later. Kingsford Smith Airport, Sydney

Sophia is in France with the Hoods.

My return home is being arranged with discretion. I need to master the timing and publicly protect my cover when the Garden's bastards are in the experienced hands of my boys. The targets are locked down; they won't escape me again…

Only Shanna, my ace trader, and Anaïs know about my whirlwind trip to Sydney. Most people—including my wife—still think I'm on the old continent, somewhere between London and Berlin.

When I arrive, I take a seat in Shanna's car.

"Harry Carter is dying," she tells me as soon as I close the door. "His failed takeover bid is no longer a secret in the financial world; they say he has his back to the wall and will do anything to save the furniture."

I had almost forgotten about him. This white boy is so insignificant on my current chessboard…

"Well, I've had a few echoes," I answer with barely a hint of satisfaction.

Shanna pulls the car out into the traffic and gives me a sideways glance.

"I would have bet on more gloating from you," she comments. "But apparently not."

She has a point. In my predictions, I thought I would savor this moment more. I had an old score to settle with the Carter Family. It is different today; some objectives seem more ridiculous now… Nevertheless, I get a semblance of a smile from Shanna while remaining silent.

"Besides, are you going to explain to me why you are trying to go incognito?" she asks me.

"No, not really… But I thank you for giving me a little help to attract less attention from the press."

The reporters are watching; I torpedoed Carter's takeover—the other heir to one of the area's former big fortunes—and they don't know my plans for the future. I haven't spoken publicly since the big announcement and the blowback just after the Carter Family business imploded. I'm basically still overseas and unreachable. My communications department is waiting for my instructions.

Privately, I have something else on the go that is my own business… The Garden and one woman in particular. These two perspectives are, to date, more enjoyable than my acquisitions.

"Don't worry," Shanna tells me with a wink.

She is used to respecting the limits I set. Just as I respect hers. Besides each other's skills and our professional complementarity, we also value each other for that. That's probably the closest thing to friendship I've ever seen. Suddenly, I remember the last words I exchanged with my father about friendship. The importance of distinguishing the kinds of people around you. The ones you know you can count on in times of need. Especially in my position.

He had a few loyal friends, including my mother. She was even more important than the others; she was his precious friend, his wife, and the mother of his only child. In his last father-son speech, he told me: "One day, it will be your turn to steer the ship Sexton, my boy. Love it as I have loved it. Only then will you make it prosper, protect it… When I inherited it, this empire became the most important thing in the world to me. Right after you and your mother… You know? And one day, I hope a young woman will make you feel that way too… I wish I could have been there to see it…"

I rub my face to bury these memories that resurface at the wrong time.

His cancer didn't give him the time. Chatting man to man, as he said, was his thing. I listened. His affection was also evident in the proud looks he gave me for my school results, my sporting prowess… And in our trips to the stud farm. Until he lost the energy to take me there.

How can you understand that at 12 years old? To accept the degradation of the state of a man whom I considered as the strongest in the world, whereas I, nothing succeeded in weakening me since I was a child?

Nothing was ever painful. Not a burn. Not a blow. Not a fracture. Not a split lip bleeding from a fight. I was never in pain, and damn it; I wanted to understand. I wanted to feel what he felt so I could feel in sync and accept this decline. My father was wasting away, dying of invasive chemo. My mother was devastated by grief.

And me, nothing. Just anger. And the impossibility of digesting something that I couldn't explain to myself…

Since then, I have learned other aspects of life and human relationships. My father had forgotten to tell me about all those ways in which one could be disappointed too… He failed to tell me that invincibility only lasts for a time and does not protect from everything.

Today, I have reliable and solid people like Shanna at my side. I have a wife who knows me better than anyone and vice versa. But blindly trusting and letting myself go completely with someone like my father did with my mother is out of the question.

And yet, out of the blue, uninvited, misty green eyes, a mane of blond hair framing a beautiful face in shock come back to mess with my head.

Shit!

"Since I'm playing cab, where can I drop you off?" asks Shanna, pulling me out of my introspection.

"TS Naval, my apartment will do."

She probes me, intrigued, but swallows her questions.

"Okay."

For the rest of the trip, we don't chat. Once I'm alone in my control tower, a suspicious feeling comes over me.

Océane. Again.

Even though the housework has been meticulously done several times since my night with her in this apartment, I can feel her everywhere. And I don't like the idea of her barging into my head, into my intimacy.

Anytime, anywhere. Especially here.

I need to see her! The ending has to be different, so I can get her out of my head. I need to control this lack like I control everything else. My security service in Australia has not lost track of the little Frenchie. They gave me the address of the friends she hangs out with, the address of the low-end hotel she chose to stay in, probably while she waits to find her own place, and her room number. Her comings and goings were recorded. And a bunch of other details.

And while security is busy neutralizing the threat Mike Woods poses to Sophia and dealing with his unhealthy fascination with monsters he doesn't know are really ugly, I'm dealing with a badly suppressed addiction. Since I can't get rid of this obsessive desire to see Océane again, I have to plan this reconquest project differently.

I'm in the middle of a fucking earthquake, but I'm not done with you, Miss Rousseau.

43

Océane

This is my first beach party since I arrived in Australia. On the surface, I should be overexcited, with my Instax or my cell phone camera to immortalize every moment.

But I don't feel this euphoria. I can't feel this carefree feeling anymore…

Melancholic, I remove my sandals to better walk in the sand in the direction of the happy crowd around the campfire. There are many people; I know very few among them. I exchange a few smiles with the guests I meet while looking for Louane. Luckily, we spot each other quickly and at the same time. She raises her arms while shouting in French, "This way, girl!"

We kiss each other on the cheek. Her boyfriend Trevor does the same while already putting a bamboo eco glass in my hand.

"Bottoms up!" he says to me, his eyes shining.

"Wow! Not even a 'hello, how are you' first?"

"No! We want to erase this sad face," Louane encourages me cheerfully. "No way you'll be bored tonight. Enjoy!"

I throw them an amused glance before sniffing the alcoholic cocktail. Normally, alcohol and tobacco are forbidden on Australian beaches, right? Everyone seems to be having a good time. No fear of fines, being put in a cell under escort, or what have you.

"What is it exactly?" I ask, unable to give in entirely to this ambient casualness.

At the moment, I feel like I'm too serious, too uptight, and too much of a party pooper. But I'm not really like that.

"These are the healthiest cocktails," Trevor tells me. "But everyone is free to add the little extra that comes in some bags."

Freedom, contraband, and risk-taking, then.

"How many did you swallow?"

"When you love, you don't count," laughs Louane. "Do yourself a favor, baby, and I hope you have a bikini under your clothes."

Oh shit, I forgot! My chaotic thoughts made me totally forget to put on a swimsuit before showing up at the beach party.

I shake my head no. Louane rolls her eyes theatrically as if I'm a hopeless case.

"Okay, so you have two options, chick. You can either take off that vest, shorts, and tank top when we go skinny dipping, or you can go in the ocean in it," she decides.

Uh… no, I don't think so…

I take a sip so as not to look like the uptight one, something I'm not normally when I'm happy. Louane also brings her glass to her mouth.

"Damn, it's empty," she complains.

She minces to Trevor to go get us more drinks. I resolve to drink more. Not bad their stuff, fresh and fruity, as long as it puts me in half as good a mood as them. I wouldn't mind a little lightness.

"Bottoms up, I told you!" Louane reminds me, her cheeks quite pink.

"Hey!" I pretend to revolt. "I am not Trevor, me. Only your boyfriend lets himself be led by the rod."

"You should try it. He loves it!" says this little dictator with a wink.

Conquered, I down my drink in one gulp. To please her and to feel in phase with the warm atmosphere surrounding us. A huge bonfire is blazing a few steps away from us. Some dance to the sound of guitars and hits sung in unison by others. Some Queen. It is fantastic; I measure my chance to live a similar parenthesis at the end of the world.

Even if my dream stay is less perfect since Tiger has… Shit, Océane!

I don't want to think about him anymore! I'm going with Louane and her lover on the next round of cocktails determined to put the tiger to rest. I'll drink and mingle, nothing else.

Little by little, it works. I relax enough to butcher the lyrics to "Bohemian Rhapsody" as I wiggle. I don't even mind a guy with a postcard surfer look. When he comes over to dance with me, I play along. I gobble down appetizers and drinks to let go a little. I try to enjoy it.

With Louane, we improvise a puerile choreography, and soon others imitate us, which leaves in lollipop a kind of spontaneous flashmob under the impulse of the nostalgia of this former fashion. Then follow improvisations of Tik Tok challenges. Everyone has fun; other hits follow, and we chant the chorus of "Ur So F**king Cool" by Tones And I in acoustic and percussion of fortune. Many get rid of their clothes. Continuing in a bathing suit or underwear.

Damn, the night swimming begins!

I barely have time to take my vest and phone out of my pocket and put them in a corner with my sandals when Trevor lifts me up and takes me on board in the general jubilation. I end up fully dressed in the water. Trevor maintains to me that it is necessary to let go before the cops arrive. Louane laughs. They are almost all knocked back, happy to savor an assumed immaturity. This is exactly what I am sorely lacking these days. They are laughing, agitating, and shouting with joy. I get splashed, and I splash back.

Some people play silly games in the water; others take the opportunity to grope their girl, guy, or booty call. When Louane and her lover start to kiss, I decide to go back to the fine sand. Suddenly, I feel only that: my solitude.

My clothes are dripping, sticking to my skin. I twist my hair to remove the excess water. I rummage to find my things in the clothes that litter the beach. At the moment, the atmosphere is heavy in Sydney with the heat wave and the fires that burn vast spaces in different cities. But tonight, it is a little less hot and heavy than during the day. Even if the rain so desired is still missing, the warm ocean remains refreshing. I find my vest and use it to dry myself briefly.

"You're not going to let us down, beauty?" the stud from earlier calls me.

He shows up and adds, "I thought we made an impression on each other."

He seems to me quite tipsy. In the kind of one-night flirtation plan, he could have suited me. He's pretty cute. But here I am; none of the guys here have any effect on me.

I shake my head.

"You won't have any trouble finding somebody else," I tell him. "I'm going home."

He comes closer anyway.

"It's you and your little exotic scent that I'm interested in today. I'm sure we could…"

He leans in and caresses my cheek. A part of me would like to break down my reticence, to push me to flirt to prove myself I don't know what. But when his mouth lands on mine, I don't feel an ounce of desire, not the slightest desire to have fun with him.

Neither him nor any other. Because there is this tiny part of me, that feels uncontrollable things. A wound and a passionate anger against a rich and arrogant, handsome man surely stuffed between the legs of a splendid woman in Paris.

Defeat! You're hurting yourself.

"No," I refuse, pulling away from the surfer's embrace.

"Argh, you're rough," he grumbles without taking me too seriously. "Why are you so rough, baby? Don't you like me?"

He tries to touch me again. I hold on, my emotional confusion and need to get better dissipating in a flash. I regret having encouraged him a bit; now, I don't want to flirt anymore, and I have no physical contact with him.

"Look, I… I'm not in the mood for this. Someone recently… hurt me; it's still too fresh," I try to justify myself.

"I see… Well, you can always use me to get this poor guy out of your head," my flirt offers, showing himself to be enterprising again.

"No, I—"

He is suddenly pulled back.

"She said no! And the poor guy is advising you to get out now," a voice orders.

Electroshock! Stunned!

I feel hot. The newcomer wears a cap that plunges the top of his face into the darkness, but his appearance is not unfamiliar to me. Neither is his rocky voice.

Tiger?!

"Shit…" I gasp, dumbfounded. "What… What… What are you doing here?"

The other guy cowardly retreats, staggering in the sand. And grumbling, "Not cool, man."

I almost want to beg him to come back now. Not to be alone with Tiger Sexton standing in front of me. With his darkened eyes staring at me. Where did he come from? Wasn't he supposed to be in Europe for several more days, according to the media? How long had he been back? How did he find me in this particular place?

He gives me no explanation. He stares at me intently until I realize that my soaked clothes are revealing a little too much of my curves. My cheeks flush with anger or with bitterness toward myself. I don't know anymore.

"What are you doing here?" I say, crossing my arms over my chest to cover my nipples and regain some semblance of confidence.

"If that's how you're going to forget me, set the bar higher than that," he says, pointing in the direction the surfer has gone.

His arrogance stings me to the core. I uncross my arms, step forward and slap him.

"What right do you have? Who do you think you are, barging in like that and interfering in my private life?"

"Your private life is my business, Lily," he says.

He takes my slap as if it hadn't hit him while my palm burns. I'm so stupid; he doesn't feel a thing! I refrain from slapping him a second one, even if it itches like hell.

"Surely not!" I say. "Get out of here!"

"Will you come with me?" he resists without getting out of his seat.

"Not even in your dreams! Go away, or I'll scream and let a crowd of drunken kids know that Tiger Sexton is on the beach with us," I threaten him. "You'll be toast in no time."

He clenches his jaws, silently challenging me.

"Try a little to see?" he encourages me after a few seconds.

"Oh yeah? You think I'm bluffing?" I warn him. "Get away, Tiger!"

He doesn't make a single move. I take a deep breath and open my mouth to moo, "GUYS? TIG…"

Suddenly, his hands grab me and smash me against his body. One slides into my hair and grabs my neck. The other squeezes my hip. His mouth melts on mine. Merciless, determined, greedy. He stifles my words and sucks in my breath.

Red alert. I don't want to. I don't want to open Pandora's box anymore.

44

TIGER

When I arrived at this beach party, I didn't plan to get so out of control, yet I couldn't stop myself. The sea salt and the taste of Océane seep into my mouth. I know she's mad; she's scratching me. But instead of ending my kiss, I deepen it. Her anger, her fiery temperament increases my ardor tenfold…

What am I doing?

Why can't I stop kissing her? She was splashing around in the Pacific with a bunch of drunken little pricks, for God's sake! Knowing that one of them was still drooling for her, ready to override her refusal a few seconds ago, is driving me crazy. Her denim micro-shorts and wet, see-through tank top make it worse.

On her side, Océane delivers me a passionate battle that I intend to win! I redouble my ardour.

Damn, I missed it! This mouth, this body, this smell.

It doesn't last as long as I would like, but she manages to free herself from my embrace. Out of breath, horny as hell, and pissed off. Her eyes are pointed at me like a weapon. Her puffy pink lips still attract me and prevent me from restarting my brain.

"You boor!" she throws me.

"Nice to see you too, little bud."

"When are you going to stop giving me stupid nicknames? And believing that you just want something and I'll do as you say?"

"I'll stop when you help me stop feeling this greed for you."

"Are you out of your mind or what? I'm not after you. I was just stupid enough to give in to your advances, and it's not happening anymore."

"Is it? Because I can still feel it, this thing between us, even from a distance, even after I terminated your contract. The sparks still fly. That feeling is there, with the same intensity, breaking all records."

"No, you're wrong."

"As long as I get that kind of erection just from seeing you, I doubt it. I almost gave it up for Sophia and a bunch of other reasons, but the point is…"

I point to my zipper. Her attention deviates there. Then she realizes her error and replaces her green balls in mine by blushing. I sketch a smile.

"You make me this thing, Océane. Not Sophia, not another one. You."

"Stop," she murmurs, trying to mask her confusion.

"You want to check?"

"Please, go away. I don't want to play this game anymore, Tiger."

"It's not a game. And I… realize that I've hurt you. I pushed you away to prove—and to prove to myself—that I was in control."

At first disconcerted, Océane runs out of scathing retorts. She swallows and crosses her arms. Maybe it's not the right time to admit to her that her breasts still turn me on? No, she reads it in my pupils and is annoyed to decipher clearly my desire. To be sensitive to it despite her pride.

"I see… So you want to 'get me back' to prove the same to yourself? To reinforce your power over everything and everyone around you? Except that I don't feel anything anymore, Tiger."

I shake my head, and my smile widens. I move forward, and Océane moves back, disconcerted.

"Nothing?"

"*Nada.* I'm not attracted to you anymore," she persists. "It was only sex. The only one who has power over my body is me. You, it's over!"

"What a delicious little liar. So, if I touch you again, you won't feel anything?"

"Don't you dare, Tiger," she says, running away from me a little more.

"What are you afraid of? That you'll feel exactly the same as the last time we fucked? Don't you ever think about it, Lily?" I say teasingly.

"Not at all. It's over," she says.

"I'll believe you if you take the challenge."

"What challenge?"

"If you stay cold and show me that you're no longer receptive, you'll never see me again. I give you my word."

She hesitates. I reduce the distance between us, and she establishes a new one by nodding. Less sure of herself, a bit panicked. I try to coax her, to reassure her, to negotiate the turn…

"But you are right; you have the power, my sweet rebel. Over your choices and also over my cock since a little while ago."

"Tiger…"

"Okay, I wanted to cut this short. Wrongly… My relationship has some nasty little secrets that make me less free than you right now. But, yes, I do like having control over certain secret areas of you, Océane. And being the only one with the keys."

I wrap my eyes around her with a look of lust. Here is where I am. From the total absence of sexual attraction for Sophia to the fleeting pleasures I bought from women I forgot after each ejaculation, to this desire that doesn't die out, never stops growing. For this girl who stands up to me, who devours French fries in my car and sprays me with pleasure during orgasm.

"No," protests Océane.

I move forward; she freaks out. Probably frightened by her own reactions… and by the voracious desire she inspires in me.

"No. Don't come any closer, Tiger."

"Because it would be hard to keep lying to yourself?"

"I just refuse to go along with this nonsense again, that's all."

"And I refuse to ignore this damn fire that's still smoldering between us."

She turns peony red. Her pupils dilate even though she tries to erect a makeshift barrier between us. She's mad at me because she's still attracted to me. Am I wrong? My rejection has affected her because she, too, cannot control this fire in us, in her.

I know it; I see it. And it makes me hard.

"No…" starts Océane before clearing her throat. "Nothing more will happen between us," she insists.

"Very convincing," I tease. "I love challenges; the fun is less exhilarating when you're not fighting for what you want, isn't it? I don't like easy wins, I don't like conventional; neither do you, Océane."

"No, shut up, Tiger! I have a feeling of déjà vu," she says. "This time, it's for good."

I pause, then nod.

"All right, I'll never force you, sweetness. I've told you that too. I'll give you time to convince yourself about this 'nothing more.' I don't believe it. Otherwise, you might have let that other idiot kiss you earlier or even more."

"I don't have to explain myself. I'm not going back; I'm moving forward. Without you, without Sophia. Go away!"

With a stubborn air, she proudly defies me. I detail her figure and caress her arms, thighs, and wet mane with my eyes.

"Leave me alone, Tiger," she orders me, more shaken than she would like to show me. "Find another hobby!"

"Fine," I conclude. "I'll be around when you can't hold on to your lies."

She bats her eyelashes and tries to pull herself together.

"I forbid you to appear again or to watch me," she rebels.

"A ban? Sorry, I set and follow my own rules. As long as I am sure I will soon sink into you and see you quivering beneath me, you will see me again, Océane."

She puts her palms on her face and blows out a long breath, not knowing how to counter me anymore.

"In that case," she pulls herself together, "I'm going to enjoy banging the next guy who tempts me enough to replace you. Because, you see, Tiger Sexton is not irreplaceable."

I nod.

"We'll see about that, my bud. I'm up for the challenge."

The higher the goal, the harder it is to achieve, and the more it motivates me. Failure is not an option. It never is. I turn on my heels. Océane shouts an angry "fuck" behind my back. I relish this manifestation of her anger, for it proves to me that I have upset her.

So, I occupy your mind as much as you occupy mine.

OCÉANE

"He's… Aaaargh!" I exclaim.

I watch Tiger walk away, my breathing ragged.

What the hell just happened?

I'm shaking. Completely sobered up, I stare back at the path he took. He disappears in the night, as he appeared. Leaving me prey to a multitude of ambiguous emotions.

What does he want in the end? To drive me crazy, completely irrational?

On that crowded beach, we could have been strafed with photos by a bunch of smartphones. Being exposed on Insta and Snapchat accounts in abundance. Everywhere! I brush my lips that he savagely devoured.

I'm so stupid! I shouldn't have let him kiss me and realize that I…

…capsize easily when he looks at me or touches me? He still affects me. Too much effect. And a stolen picture could have immortalized this defeat. I, as a starry-eyed girl, posted on a married billionaire's hunting list. Maybe he doesn't give a damn. But Sophia, what would she think? It's not just my image that would take a big hit.

My brain is flashing in every corner. Damn, he kissed me! And I was unable to resist fiercely.

"Aaaargh!" I'm still angry with myself.

"Oh!" jumps someone passing by not far away. "Are you okay, miss?"

"I'm fine, thanks," I grumble, picking up my things.

My reason wanted to reject Tiger; I should have done it with more conviction. This man has started a vicious game with me, and I won't be his toy anymore. I don't want to end up lost and without will because of such a man. I'll lose all esteem for the throbbing Oceania no matter what Tiger does.

It's up to me to do something about it so I don't feel powerless to do what he wants or doesn't want, and when he decides.

Ah, but yes! I also have a considerable asset in the game to barricade myself and defend myself. Determined, I enter the phone book of my phone. I look for the letter H and find the name that interests me. I press the call button.

No more yo-yo-ing with me, Tiger. I will no longer bow my head to the vagaries of life. I'm taking full power and taking responsibility for MY choices!

The phone rings, and the recipient of the call is slow to pick up.

"Hello?" I finally hear the caller.

Don't chicken out, don't chicken out...

"Hi, Harry," I say. "It's Océane, the French girl, remember?"

He doesn't react. Damn! His silence is a bad sign. This guy probably doesn't even remember me.

"Océane?" he repeats. "What a surprise! Of course I remember you... Sophia Sexton's hot blonde girlfriend."

Well, it's not a bad start, after all. I mean... his voice still sounds... weird. Is he drunk? Unsure, I ask him, "Uh... yeah. What's up, Harry?"

He lets out a confused, instantaneous laugh.

"What do you think, baby? Let me guess: Sexton sent you to make sure I die?"

"Huh?"

Why do we have to take everything back to Tiger?

I'm starting to doubt my plan; I don't know what Harry is talking about. He's still laughing. Now I'm pretty sure I'm interrupting him in the middle of a drink. Or worse?

"Why would you say that, Harry?"

"You're buddies with this scumbag's wife, and he's been very protective every time he's seen me with you. So..."

"I... don't have much contact with them anymore," I stammer, confused by the resentment I feel oozing from his words.

Of course, Tiger can't stand him, and it seems to be mutual. Professional differences? Rivalry? Anything else? The row at Velvet & Diamonds is probably stuck in his throat. But on the other hand, this animosity between them would be useful to put this control freak in his place. Wouldn't it?

Tiger challenged me to raise the bar. Well, he'll get it!

Let him do what he wants with Sophia. Reject her, take her back, shower her with gifts and indifference. She loves it; otherwise, she wouldn't still be so addicted to him. Not me!

"Sure?" growls Harry.

"Yes, Tiger had nothing to do with this call. He doesn't tell me what to do," I say, pulling myself together. "But obviously, this is a bad time?"

My backup plan seems to hesitate, and I scratch my head, wondering what he imagines. On the face of it, he thinks I'm just "friends with Sophia" so he has no way of knowing my motives or past ties to the one he can't screw.

"No, it's cool," he replies. "It's just… I didn't think you'd call me back."

"I figured that we… were free to see each other again if we wanted to, right?"

"Totally. That can be arranged," he says in a soothed and… a bit pasty voice. "Shall we have dinner together… tomorrow? Let's say eight-thirty?"

"Why not?"

"Top!" he gets excited. "Send me your address, and I'll pick you up."

"You got it. Good night, Harry."

I hang up and give a victorious "yes." I got the date! Almost effortlessly.

Okay, things are going faster than expected, but I'll manage. No more hesitation. Tiger's appearance tonight and my pathetic reaction will not happen again. I will remove any illusions he has that I'll fall back into his arms.

Even if it means showing up in public with a rich kid who might have the same flaws?

It's up to me to make sure I lead the way. With this decision, I followed my intuition and typed Harry Carter in my search engine. Just to be better prepared this time. On the front page, I find:

"Tiger Sexton and his financial empire, TS Naval, have struck again! The heir to Carter Industries is in deep trouble."

Damn! That's why Harry sounded weird.

Tiger screwed him too. In a different way.

The financial press, stock prices, and their fluctuations have never been my cup of tea. Now I find out that the Sydney stock market is in turmoil following a series of strategic actions by the finance tiger… against Harry Carter.

And I'm going to dinner with this guy who's probably more bitter than I thought? Boy, what have I done?

45

Tiger

TS Naval, Sydney. Tiger's apartment. Three o'clock in the morning

I'm tired of working so hard not to think about anything else!

After an intensive sport session and processing everything, I'm back at ground zero. That moment when I need a distraction to block out the crowd of ghosts in my head. They… they never go away; I just manage to keep those images permanently under control. I pull them out when I need more drive, more rage, and more fury to win.

Having the final goal in the corner of my mind. Always.

But it's serious if Océane takes up more and more space in there. The more she resists me, the more she stirs up another need for victory in me. While theoretically, this should set off my alarm bells. Make me slow down instead of counting on her surrender. Her skin, her lips, her moans, her pleasure…

Shit! There's another way to relax if the fuck option is off. Go back to your "box." It's been a while…

Okay. The box. I turn off my computer and get up. I take off my watch, put it down, start to undress, to take off all my clothes. The images come back to me. Immaculate, and flowery, they try to spread chaos. Océane, Sophia, the victims.

I have to get this under control, damn it!

I try to think of Sophia. She's been texting me; she and the Hoods are taking the jet in two days to Sydney. I need this time to get my house in order. Put the filters back where they belong. In my head, in my fantasies. Because this will be the start of the last action in France. Since extraditions have been negotiated between our two countries, my team must act before.

Omega, the Executioner, the return of Byrne, the continuation…

My neurons can't rest anymore. Overexcited, crazy with stage fright, they run at full speed, going from one emergency to another. Under the shower before immersion, eyes closed, I try to calm this storm. The image of Océane on the beach in her wet clothes resurfaces. If I could at least satisfy this desire, I could sort out the rest easily. Fuck her. No longer allow this confusion to take hold. Not to be haunted by my promise and everything that led me to it… To exhaust ourselves with orgasms, Océane and me, to regain control of the situation.

But I've only got my good old-fashioned second option tonight.

I get out of the shower, grab a towel, and head for the room whose door is closed. I position my eye in front of the scanner to unlock it. A beep sounds. The door closes behind me. The lights come on. The space reserved for my medical check-ins is here. However, this is not what I am interested in. I only go this way when I finally agree to let my doctor check me out to make sure I don't have a fracture, a serious injury, or some other bullshit without being alerted by any pain stimulus…

I am supposed to follow this protocol on a regular basis. As a kid, I was forced to do it every week. Now, I am the only one to decide.

About this, about everything… Even if it gets boring.

I throw my towel on a chair. Since I can't use sex, I open the relaxation tool: my box. A sensory deprivation box. Equipped with my earplugs, I program the duration of the cycle. I step over the box. The warm liquid on my feet awakens familiar sensations. There was a time when this was the only thing that could soothe me for an hour or two.

To float… to put myself on top of everything, to regain control over myself.

I lie in the water, and the box closes over my floating body. My eyelids fall back.

The calm. Nothingness. No more sound. No more visual disturbances. No more contact. I am isolated from the world. My senses annihilate, pause. I am looking for a kind of inner peace, trying to relax completely and reach the theta phase: my favorite. This long break during which I have full power over my brain, my thoughts, my memories, and my concentration. The quest for absolute well-being. More and more relaxed, I let the images seep into my head; I let them come.

Snippets of videos… Offered girls… Orgies… Sexual rites… An infinite number of perversions…

I don't see the time passing; the clock doesn't matter anymore. I float, disconnect, and get rid of all the weight. An eternity later, a discreet beep indicates to me the opening of the sensory deprivation chamber. I feel the air on my wet skin and the temperature contrast again. I lie in the salty liquid for a moment, my mind alert.

I head to my bathroom to shower again and remove the salt from my skin. I toss the towel across the room as I pass.

The past has flashed through my mind, and everything is back in its place. In order of priority. Today…

Today, I want to get Océane to let her guard down. I want her to become my decompression chamber again, the bubble of normality in my matrimonial secret garden. This blond girl, so independent, hot, and stubborn, has been my haven of peace in times of war and heavy compromises.

Today, more than ever, I want to return to that haven.

Océane

Dating Harry Carter? I messed up big time!

At least I hope the radio silence from Tiger's side is a good sign. He hasn't been pestering me with messages or calls, and he hasn't shown up here. What makes me nervous is that he's not the type to give up on a loss.

But maybe dinner with an opponent he's beaten wasn't such a great idea. I turn around in my room, analyzing the situation for the umpteenth time.

What should I do? Cancel?

Harry Carter was humiliated in public. He's bound to be more pissed off at Tiger. Much more than I am? Is he taking advantage of my initiative to get revenge in some way by dating me?

No! No? Is he? Geez, think about it Océane!

I keep pacing. Maybe Harry was too stoned to remember the call after he'd finished drinking. Yeah, chances are he won't remember it by now. Besides, why would he use me to get to Tiger if I'm just a "friend of Sophia's" who no longer has contact with the Sexton couple? By that logic, it would just be a mundane dinner to cheer up. Well, I hope so.

Ugh, I don't know what to assume anymore!

The memory of Tiger's kiss and his unwavering certainty that he'll get me back into bed stings my self-esteem again. I let out a sigh and let myself fall into bed. Wouldn't I be better off living my life away from the Sextons' social and professional networks? Instead of further complicating my already rotten life.

That's exactly what I was trying to do until last night on the beach.

I was kicked out of their world, and I was about to move on. Unfortunately, there's no guarantee that Tiger won't continue to act the way he likes. Just as there is no guarantee that I won't be easily riled up if he does it again.

I write and delete the text message I'm writing to Harry once again to cancel.

Decline the invitation or go through with it, measuring the new stakes?

Suddenly, fate decides for me. My phone signals the reception of a text.

I want your address, beautiful Parisian.
I can't wait to see you tonight.

Shit, he remembers it very well, and he's really looking forward to it! I start writing him a reply. Then another one replaces it, a third one, and a fourth one, quite different. I breathe in, convince myself and finally write down the address of my hotel with a seemingly casual "See you tonight, Harry."

The die is cast. Tiger may have the world at his feet and "nasty little couple secrets," as he put it, but I'll win this last round to turn him away. And claim my freedom! Determined, I put Icona Pop and Charli XCX to the fullest on the track "I Love It." Chanting, "I don't care, I love it!" I start going through my wardrobe to find the perfect outfit for this dinner.

8:40 p.m. The front desk still hasn't informed me that my date has arrived. He is not punctual. Not everyone is a clock-watching psycho like Ti—

Shit! Why do I keep thinking about someone I want to run away from? Let's stop this right now!

I leave my room ten minutes late to wait in the tiny lounge of my hotel reception. I don't know if Harry is just running late or if he's going to stand me up. At eight-forty-five, my doubt grows. Maybe he's been thinking about it and regretting his invitation? What if he didn't believe me and still imagines I'm in Tiger's service to approach him? The pressing need to discipline my nerves and thoughts prompts me to step outside to smoke on the sidewalk.

It's heavy. It looks like it's going to rain after weeks of devastation caused by fires in various parts of the country. The whole population is hoping for this rain; I look at the sky and feel as gloomy. My conscience is bothering me…

Latte after latte, I face the facts. No, it wouldn't be fair to Carter to bring him into this. Besides, I have no desire to spend the evening with him. I pull out my cell phone to call him and back up. He picks up on the first ring.

"My Frenchie!" he enthuses. "Sorry I'm late; I'm pulling in."

Damn!

"Where are you?"

"Gray Audi… I see you."

I look around, embarrassed. Suddenly, I freeze. Yes, Harry is there. And like a creepy remake of my own life, I see someone else I wasn't expecting.

Tiger Sexton. Fucking karma, Océane!

A violent memory strikes me. Two men I've been "dating" suddenly find themselves in the same place. The ambush, the blows from Victor and his buddies raining down on Lucas. My cries of terror. The surprise effect. My fear. My appointment with my boyfriend, which turns into a settling of accounts, and me, petrified, losing control of the situation… Everything comes to the surface and mixes with the present. The eternal beginning again…

Of course, it is not totally the same. We are not in France. I'm not a 16-year-old anymore, and these two men are not little thugs from a working-class neighborhood. But even in the big leagues, with a movie set and the weather getting worse, the results are similar.

One guy wants me, the other hates him, and because of me, their paths will cross again… Here and now…

Only three vehicles separate them. They will discover each other in a few seconds. My heart palpitates, and my hands become sweaty. One of them must leave immediately, and Tiger will not obey.

I know it. He's the most stubborn of them all.

"Uh… Harry," I stammer into the phone, my eyes caught by those of the tiger leaning against a car in front of the hotel.

It was as if he had been standing there for a while, wondering if he was going to enter the establishment or not. Was he waiting for me? Did he know Harry was coming to see me? My synapses slow down.

"I…" I start again. "I don't feel very well. I'd like to… postpone our dinner."

"You look good, though," Harry doubts. "Is something wrong? Wait, I'm coming, you can tell me."

He hangs up without waiting for my answer. Tiger is still staring at me; he senses my panic, I think. He scans me and devours me with his eyes. Then his head finally turns in the same direction as mine when my date gets out of his Audi and locks his doors.

Oh, God, please don't clash.

Harry Carter blushes as Tiger's gaze hardens.

"Sexton?!" shouts the former. "The bastard is back!"

Tiger walks towards me.

"What the hell is he doing here?" he asks me, his tone dangerously calm.

"So, I was right; you did set me up," Harry growls. "Your call was for Sexton to come and brag!"

Tiger wrinkles his forehead. In control. The more the other spits his venom, the more the tiger stares at me like a predator slowly advancing on its territory. His blue eyes become cold, and he tells me, *"Did you invite him? You were about to go out with that little prick after you said no to me?"*

"Ah, no, the asshole decides to ignore me," Carter still fumes. "Look at me, Sexton!"

Oh, shit, he's charging at him! The fist of my "suitor" of the day smashes on the corner of Tiger's jaws, still too posed. A scream escapes me. Not because I'm afraid he'll hurt my ex-lover, but rather for the opposite.

I remind myself that one of them doesn't know what it's like to be in pain, and I'm sure he'd punch much harder if he fought back. Harry, oblivious and blinded by his rage, repeats. Tiger's palm blocks his hand. He clenches his jaws, his eye threatening. I yell in French, "Tiger, please! Don't do that!"

His irises panic on me.

"What exactly is she?" he is still looking for his opponent, who is no match for him. "Your little maid?"

That's the word too much. Tiger picks up his collar, dark with anger, and neutralizes him in his ridiculous agitation. Then he asks Carter in maddening coolness, "Apologize."

"What?" my date yells.

"You. Apologize. To. Océane," Tiger slowly repeats in English.

"Are you kidding me, Sexton? You're the one— Aaaah!" Harry suddenly groans.

Tiger's grip compresses his neck. And that's when I feel the first drops of rain falling on us.

"Apologize, Carter. Now or I'll trash more than your legacy," Tiger persists, unperturbed.

Their visual duel sends shivers down my spine. The other turns scarlet, his neck in a vice in front of the intimidating face which overhangs him. Harry flinches very quickly and spits an apology at me while coughing. Tiger releases him, nods, and commands him, "Good. Get out of here!"

He pays no attention to the rudeness and threats that Carter starts to belch again. Now Tiger's eyes focus on me with more intensity. While the flood welcomes the sudden departure of Harry's Audi.

Tiger comes closer, takes off his jacket, and puts it on my shoulders. My hair is dripping now, and I can't help but shake from the backlash. I was afraid it would get out of hand; I was so afraid. Like a boomerang, the scene with Lucas violently hits my panic-stricken mind…

Collapsed on the ground… The thud of the shoes on his body… His spine bursting under the redoubled violence… The hoarse sounds of agony coming out of his mouth… And me, numb, crying, screaming, and living the nightmare live.

"VICTOR, NOOOO! Stop, please!"

Here and now, Océane. Here and now. Stop shaking; pull yourself together.

I don't succeed; I remain as if frozen in an in-between. The dangerous gleam in Victor's eyes, his rictus of hatred. The blows, again and again. He is uncontrollable, and I am powerless. Confusion, I can't hold on to anything anymore.

"Lucas? Help me! Help me!"

Tiger's big hands come to my shoulders. He squeezes them, reconnecting me to the present, to him.

"Hey? You're soaked, come on," he offers.

I don't know why… Something in his voice? In his look? The pressure that falls? Suddenly, I break down, and I am shaken by unexpected sobs. Tiger, caught off guard, swears under his breath and hugs me.

"I am sorry. Don't cry, my sweet, please."

Words come out, choppy, my mouth pressed against his chest, "You… you didn't hit him… Even though you did… And I'm… here, shivering under… the water. I'm… ridiculous."

"No, you're not," Tiger whispers to me.

He lifts me slightly to lift my chin to his face. He, too, is wet and obnoxiously sexy. His lashes bead with water, and his deep gaze confuses me. There's no more anger, no more arrogance, no more… rejection.

His mouth… No…

"Thank you," I say in a whisper.

"Why?" he says, hesitating.

"Of… You could have been even more violent, more brutal, but you controlled yourself. Is it because I asked you to?"

His eyes go from my eyes to my mouth, then vice versa. He liquefies me in spite of me and under the raging rain.

"For once, with this jerk, I stuck to one point of my code of honor: don't hit a man when he's down. At least not with my fists. But yes, in this particular case, I held back mostly for you," he admits. "You were terrified."

His words make me lose my mind even more. He wipes away my tears in vain. When he leans in again, I don't push him away. No part of me wants to reject him or has the energy.

"Allow me to kiss you," he begs me.

My lips open. He smells good, and he has the smell of the most delicious nonsense. Virile, heady, unforgettable. Our breaths mix and his tongue bewitches mine. An obscene kiss, voracious, incendiary under a celestial shower. I give myself up; he takes me. Without concession.

"That will not be enough for me," confesses Tiger to me against my mouth. "I want to feel you come for me."

He kisses me again, allowing me to gauge his level of arousal, largely at the height of mine. He manages to erase little by little the horrible memories that had flooded me until they became too precise, too real. In Tiger's eyes, Victor finally evaporates, this unheard-of violence too.

"Say something, Lily... Please."

"First... you owe me an apology, too."

An irresistible smile stretches his lips, and his dilated pupils stare at me.

"I humbly apologize to you, Miss Rousseau. I'm sorry I hurt you. I miss you too much, and I want you terribly; you must forgive me."

Stunned, I can't believe that he agrees to my request. Just like that, now, in his own way. What the hell? Tiger Sexton just apologized!

46

TIGER

"Wow," says Océane.

I wonder if she's touched by what I've just said, moved, satisfied, or amused. She remains hesitant, obviously still upset by the altercation with Carter.

I cuddle her against me, and she doesn't reject me. Are we on the right track?

An obvious fact appears to me: I had just had proof that the aggression she witnessed when she was younger traumatized her. She is not guilty, but she is marked for life.

Her stigmata, well hidden behind her volcanic temperament, I see them with hindsight. Océane was pale and panicked. Her pretty pink lips no longer quivered, but her misty doe eyes struggled to clear the irrational fear that had shaken her a few moments ago.

I knew a little bit about the strong, proud Océane most of the time. Discovering the frightened 16-year-old inside her who implored me not to hit Harry back swept away my anger and now generates a strange feeling in me.

The desire to reassure her? The need to protect her?

I ask her gently again, "Do you forgive me?"

She still stares at me, almost lost, then she undoes my embrace and moves back.

Shit, her little proud and determined look comes back.

"What are you doing, Océane?"

Without a word, she continues to walk away slowly. My certainties are wavering, taking on water under the heavy rain. While scrutinizing me, Océane goes around my vehicle. She flees from me, escapes from me.

"Unlock it," she suddenly tells me.

Surprised, baffled, I bug.

"What?"

"Unlock your car, Tiger. You just blew off my date," she accuses me, getting mischievous. "You'll have to feed me and keep me company instead of Harry."

Damn! What's imploding in me right now? Relief? Just a surge of desire?

"Do I have to?" I pretend to protest, almost unperturbed on the outside.

"Oh, yes," she confirms to me. "It wasn't planned, but congratulations, you've reached the status of… substitute. A backup plan, a stopgap… Well, you know what I mean?"

"Ouch! Very hard on my ego, Miss Rousseau."

"I know."

Her cheeks turn pink, and I open my car. We rush in, wet from head to toe. Enough to ruin the leather of the seats. As if I had a damn thing to care about. She is coming with me! That's all that impacts me. In the car, I lean toward her, irresistibly drawn to her.

But she stops me.

"Tututut! I never said to you that I forgave you or that you had the right to that," rebels my passenger by pointing out her body. "My instructions are: to feed me and keep me company. Nothing else."

What the fuck is she doing to me?

Incredulous, my smile widens.

"We're getting ready to row, Mr. Sex," she warns me before fastening her seat belt.

"Are you putting me to the test?"

"Maybe," she admits confidently. "Get out the paddles to earn my forgiveness, and don't get your hopes up for… the rest."

I burst out laughing, and she challenges me with malice.

"Okay, delicious Lily. Got it."

I start the car, tormented by the need to lock myself in with her. Whatever she's planning.

During the drive, the sexual tension is difficult to manage. Feeling the queen of my fantasies so close and out of reach fuels the fire. The slightest of her movements, each scent of her perfume, and each of her breaths become a spark of desire that can set me on fire. While driving, I am constantly tempted to touch her. It takes a lot for me not to brush her knee, her thigh revealed by her dress, not to catch her neck to devour her sighs, all that makes me crazy from second to second. The pressure rises, she feigns innocence, and she becomes even more attractive. I smirk because I'm sure she feels the temperature rising inexorably.

Are your thoughts as hot as mine?

Finally, the TS Naval underground parking lot! I park, and we get out without talking much. Keeping my distance becomes more difficult when we take the private elevator back to my penthouse. This place where the intensity of our orgasms still reverberates in every nook and corner… Her moans, her screams, and her pleasure have left an indelible imprint, like an erotic ghost designed to haunt me and never disappear.

Only, tonight, she is there in this closed space, and my cock can't put itself to rest. Our eyes meet again, the final spark, and everything ignites. I press the emergency stop button, block the elevator and capture Océane. Our lips collide, force each other, give in, and magnetize. Her tongue against mine, her curves under my fingers…

"Okay, I give up. I want you!" I say to her in a hungry growl.

Océane emits an intoxicating complaint which is lost in my throat. I press her back against a wall, and while kissing her, I caress her breast. My hand drifts lower and lower, going astray on her smooth thigh. Her little dress is rolled up on my passage, and soon I feel the softness of her fine lingerie. Océane moans, and I continue to devour her. I touch her intimacy through the fabric. This humidity is not due to the storm, which rumbles outside. Fuck, no. This one drives me crazy; it gives me proof that she wants me. I get harder as I brush against her pubic bone, her secret lips over the light lace barrier that covers them. Her little noises die in the depths of my being. Her thigh wraps around me, making her veiled femininity more distressing under my index finger sliding along her slit. The soaked panties stick inside her, her bud pulsing under the pulp of my finger.

Our kiss deepens, deviates towards her neck, the hollow of her breasts, then goes up. Thirsty. Magnetic. While I play with the forbidden fruit with my other hand. Océane arches her back, grabs my fly, and kneads my erection.

Critical moment, imminent breakdown.

I moan while inciting her to open my jeans.

"I want to feel you."

Her soft palms rest on my pecs, and she gently pushes me away.

"Nah… You won't feel me, my tiger," she decides, trying to re-establish distance between us.

"Her" tiger?

I wrinkle my forehead, disconcerted, frustrated, one step away from breaking down and unable to determine what this possessive little word is doing to me. I whisper to her, "We both want this, don't we?"

"Feed me and keep me company, remember? Thanks for the appetizer, but I'm still hungry, and it's up to me to decide what I want to eat. You, hands off!"

Argh! I begin to understand: she's going to torture me.

OCÉANE

The look on Tiger's face delights me to no end! I smile at him, take advantage of his confusion to sneak to the side, and press the button that stops the elevator.

No clouds nine for you, Tiger! Let's go up to your 2.0 den now.

He takes it with class, a smile on his face. Torrid, frustrated, in full erection, but he finds the elegance and charisma of a racy gentleman. In spite of his hair and his casual and soggy clothes, it's unfair how he looks impressive. His jacket that he had lent me washed up on the floor when he came at me like a prey. Neither of us cares; I enjoy my mini revenge.

Do I hold a grudge? In this case, and with him, definitely!

Admittedly, I softened pitifully at his contact, and the pheromones turned off my neurons. Nevertheless, he's going to paddle hard! Especially since this place refreshes my memory about everything we did there and how it ended.

My self-esteem just found a more pleasurable way to give this control freak a run for his money.

You just have to stand your ground when he eats you up like that with his eyes. It's going to be hot…

"Good," he whispers, for him or me.

He doesn't say anything else, and neither do I. I stumble, I am hot, but I hold my head high in Super Girl mode! Attractive and determined, as my friends from the rooming house would say.

Once inside the penthouse, I take off my pumps. Absolutely everything around me takes me back to the not-so-distant past, to our passionate exchange of fluids, and to what I should no longer let him get to me for. His flip-flop was too painful, and his comeback moved me a little more than it should.

Is this a last dance like in the Kyo song? Before I fade away completely? I'm afraid so, let's face it. It's up to me to make a mark on his mind. Will it be my revenge, or am I fooling myself?

I don't know anymore…

"A drink?" Tiger offers me one.

"Champagne."

"Any brand preference?"

I imagine he has magnums in ultra-limited series of the world's top five. I don't care. As long as it's not bad, I don't care what name is on it.

"I don't know anything about bubbles," I admit spontaneously. "As long as they are good."

My frankness amuses him.

"Good… I'll see about that. Make yourself comfortable."

"I already am," I reply.

His irises dart at me. I reach behind my back to undo my zipper. He eats me with his eyes, walking backward until he disappears from my sight. My dress opens from behind, but I don't dare to go through with my challenge yet. I wonder about my motives. Why does this man who put me in all my states and that I had convinced myself to avoid absorb me again in his matrix?

What do I want?

"What do you want to start with?" Tiger asks me, back in his living room.

A bottle in one hand, a white robe in the other, and a towel around his neck. Not sure of myself, I blink without answering.

"Should I open the Veuve Clicquot first, or should I let you dry off?"

I pull myself together, try to play it sensual and mistress of the arena. I repeat, stripping off one shoulder, "To dry myself? Nah, I like to be wet."

He raises an eyebrow, acknowledges the shock, and moistens his lips. I can see his taste for challenge awakening at the predatory gleam in his eyes. The game begins… He drops the robe, puts the champagne on a console, and grabs a remote control. Music starts playing, classical music. I think it's "Flower Duet," one of the few pieces of this style that I know a little bit about.

"I like to get wet too…" Tiger titillates me.

The clean notes rise, intertwining with his words, sources of shivering. My cheeks heat up.

"We're talking about rain, right?"

"What do you think?" he whispers to me.

He sees me faint, and he seems to love it. I have to get my act together. I start to undress again and play the ingenue while mincing, "Let's say yes."

Tiger, incendiary and absolutely not fooled, presses another button from the remote, making a muffled light appear outside. He throws his towel and unhurriedly unzips his fly with a half-smile.

"So much better; let's get wet together, little bud," he concedes, pointing his chin to his terrace.

What?

Oh, shit, he starts his stripping and definitely pulls the rug out from under me. Very quickly, we find ourselves on equal footing in our underwear. Tiger takes advantage of this turnaround to get the bottle of champagne and start opening it. The lyrical singers' voices and the "Flower Duet" melody make the picture come alive before my eyes, more fascinating than I would like to admit. Tiger, in anthracite boxer shorts, muscles, tattoos, and erection displayed without an ounce of modesty, pops the cork of the magnum. He reserves a mocking mimicry for me, sexy as hell when he brandishes the sparkling bubbles at me.

"You bring that outside?" he tells me. "I'll get us some cups."

Damn, he's getting his power on you again. React!

My hormones go into overdrive despite myself; I'm almost ready to skip my resentments. Tiger makes me snap again. For seconds, I try to regain control by noting the indecent way he wraps his eyes around me.

Yes, he wants me. So, my body will be my instrument of revenge!

I move forward and grab the champagne. Our fingers brush against each other, which dilates his pupils more. I am close, very close to his hands, his sculpted abs, and his pecs.

"No need for a cup," I gasp before tilting my head and swallowing a long sip from the neck.

I unhook my bra and turn on my heels, heading outside his apartment with my drink.

Take this, Mr. Sex! The boot is on the other foot. I take back control.

47

Océane

I feel Tiger's lust permeating my pores as I walk outside. Sydney's skyscrapers in the rain and night lights welcome me. There is something unique at this precise moment. An aquatic, poetic, magical atmosphere. Classical music is in the background. A breathtaking view from the top of the TS Naval tower. Space, deckchairs and other facilities, greenery, and finally, the suffocating heat of the last days softened…

Tiger joins me. He is just…

"You're soaked again," he flirts.

He manages to make me feel like we're talking about something else, not rain. I stroke the bottleneck with the tip of my index finger.

"So do you."

Me, I wear only my tanga and my bra open in my back. He's still in his boxer shorts, his hair plastered by the rain whose drops are dripping on his body. I drink again, perhaps to draw from this excellent champagne the guts to continue my little game. Then I eject my bra. The celestial shower pours on me, sticks my mane on my shoulders, beads on my pink and hardened nipples, goes down my curves, and gets lost in my folds.

And Tiger, on the other hand, doesn't miss a beat. Silent, too silent.

I swallow a glassful of bubbly alcohol. My head spins slightly. Damn, I'll end up drunk if I'm not careful. I haven't eaten anything. Or maybe it's what's happening now that makes me drunk. The transgression, the scrambled codes, and this moneyed stallion disarmed in front of my nudity.

I give the bottle back to Tiger. Without taking his eyes off me, his tongue slides over the neck. As if only my taste could intoxicate him. He stares at my lips; I moisten them. Yes, he wants to kiss me, but I run away to a deckchair. Progressively, I become aware of my erotic power over him. His look makes me feverish, audacious, and crazy with desire. I introduce my thumbs between my skin and my small panties and roll this one sensually downwards. I bend over and get rid of them, Tiger's irises captured by mine.

My breath jerks, his blocks. There is something magnetic and violent in his pupils that devastates me inside. Never has a man desired me like this. No one has. The reciprocal is true and frightening: this lightning attraction that he inspires in me is unique, and I am afraid that after him, I will be even more damaged, weakened and—

Carpe diem, Océane. Just enjoy this moment.

I swallow, and he watches me. The storm is starting to calm down a little. Unlike what is growling inside me, inside us. What was my improvised plan again?

Ah, yes. Make Tiger wait. To give him a memorable boner to match the disillusionment he caused when he dumped me.

I step over the lounger in my birthday suit and sit down, half-seated. The drops of water cover my exposed skin. Fortunately, the summer weather allows me to enjoy this sensory madness without shivering from the cold. Just perfect, perfect for what I am about to dare.

I deliberately make Tiger hot by sucking my index finger. Obnoxiously, he grabs a chair and sits across from me, like a spectator admiring a private show without being allowed to participate.

I nibble my finger, give a naughty smile, and taunt him, "Is everything okay, Mr. Sexton?"

"Couldn't be better," he replies, his voice hoarse. "Please, continue, Miss Rousseau."

His attention crystallizes on me; he exudes a raw desire. Even if he holds back from jumping on me. Even if he still manages to behave like a gentleman despite the circumstances… I guess what he is dying to do to me, and my gestures blossom where his eyes burn me. Doing what he probably has in mind, my fingers venture suavely on my wet skin and under his eyes. It's hardly raining anymore; just a soft drizzle is falling now. Provocatively, I ask softly, "Did you miss it, Tiger? Do you miss it?"

I see his muscles tighten and his eyes darken. My slow caresses snake up my neck, down and play with the curve of my breasts. The tips rise, and Tiger's tormented lust electrifies me from second to second and guides me. The more I try to titillate him, the more I become languid and succumb to this flow of lava between us. I start to pant while grinding my nipples. Tiger stifles a guttural sound, his crotch bulging under his boxers.

"What did you say again?" I continue between moans. "That we had fun? Do you have fun now, knowing that I am free and out of your reach?"

With a simper, my palms embrace my heavy breast. I press them together. Captivated, Tiger grasps the bulge that betrays his condition.

"I do not need you to take pleasure," I support lasciviously while massaging my breasts.

"I know," he reacts, with a low intonation, sexy like hell.

One of my hands slides on my belly, my lower abdomen. My thighs spread, and Tiger inhales sharply.

"I can do whatever I want with whomever I want… Harry, another… another or on my own… Without you. And you have no control over that."

I brush my pubic bone, and he exhales and pokes at his wet hair. My fingers reach into my folds, and he stares at them. His breathing goes completely off the rails. I intensify my arches and the erotic noises that I make as I begin to masturbate. The pad of my index finger titillates my bud, then disappears into my warm wetness. I whimper, squirming, my gaze riveted to Tiger's. I assert, starting a delicate back and forth inside me, "I do not belong to you, Mr. Sexton. Do you hear me? You don't own me."

His jaws tighten, my thighs, ditto, for a moment, to tame the bliss that swells in my groin. I open them again to be sure to torture him with this sight of the forbidden fruit. Let him watch me getting wet, pulsating. My other hand kneads my breasts, and my half-open lips sigh. Greedy, I add a finger, then another, and start to lose my mind in front of this observer oozing testosterone.

The thunder rumbles, and lightning streaks the black sky. The elements are once again as wild as my senses. I accelerate, and a curse escapes Tiger. It gets me high and makes me more uninhibited. My touching gives me a tenfold pleasure when I see the effect it has on him. I see how respecting the distance I impose puts him in torture. I love this wild gleam in his eyes which sublimates his frustration of supreme male. And I moan, "Damn, it's too good."

He swears again in his native language. His pupils electrify me, and his virility stirs up the fire inside me. I go faster, shameless, as eager for pleasure as for revenge. I feel like a woman, beautiful, desired, and… powerful!

Tiger stiffens, while I become more flexible, more feline, and hungry. My intimate caresses and his gaze carry me away. My eyelids flutter. I believe that the storm is also reviving. I feel big drops crashing on my body. My head falls backward, and I arch my back, sensing the orgasm. As if the rain and Tiger's magnetic eyes on me made me touch the peaks.

Faster, harder, more indecent, eyes closed, I go back and forth inside myself. Even with my eyes closed, I feel his presence. And suddenly, under the rain, which starts again with pouring, I implode while panting.

I hear Tiger's "fuck!" which reinforces my well-being and gives a special flavor to my victory. Fucking orgasm!

And I got him!

TIGER

Under the icy jets of my shower, I wonder what is worse. Knowing that Océane is in the other bathroom, naked, alone, looking gorgeous? Or not being able to erase that damn watery orgasm she enjoyed solo on the terrace?

I thought I could take it with amusement. I'm used to edging as long as I lead the way myself. This was…

Holy crap!

The game doesn't amuse me that much anymore; she finished me off. She stood up, winked at me, and said insolently, "Don't move; I'll wash and dry myself now. Don't worry; I know the place."

I didn't retort; I have no desire to talk anymore. I rather want to—

Arf!

When my cock is back to normal size, I turn off the taps. I get out and rub myself with a towel, trying to anticipate what's next. Will she stay after this, or will she want to go back to her hotel?

And me, how long can I take it?

I go to my dressing room to get dressed and take a white shirt with me for Océane. Her clothes are unusable for the moment. The thought reminds me of that bare gorgeous body bathing in the rain. Fuck, I won't forget that anytime soon!

"I'm starving," my guest's voice greets me as soon as I arrive in the living room.

She looks even younger, wrapped up in a bathrobe, her hair loose and instantly dried. No more make-up, pink cheekbones, eyes set with mischief. She offers me an irresistible mixture of candor and voluptuousness. And the extension of my virility awakens stupidly, escaping my control once more. I prefer to branch off towards the open kitchen. Don't get too close, or my little phlegm will go up in smoke.

"What do you want to eat?" I ask. "I'll have it delivered unless there's something in the fridge that suits you. Anaïs is in charge of restocking it."

"As long as it's not Vegemite-based, it should be fine," she jokes.

I suppress a smile. So her delicate Frenchie palate is having trouble with our national spread. I still don't know the exact contents of the fridge and cupboards; my assistant orders according to my tastes. Océane comes in just as I'm checking what's in the various ready-made meals delivered.

"Hum…" she hesitates, stopping at my side.

As if unconscious of how she makes me suffer, she puts the index on her lips and frowns at the food. This same index finger was on her barely a blink of an eye ago.

Don't crack.

After inspecting my supplies, I clear my throat and offer, "Another local thing: kangaroo steak? Have you ever tried it?"

Her beautiful eyes deviate from me, stunned.

"Kangaroo steak? Oh, no, they're so cute!"

"Calves too, but that doesn't stop you from making *blanquettes* out of them."

She sticks her tongue out at me. My lower stomach goes wild.

Don't fucking flinch, Tiger; stay on the food.

"Well, I'll let you choose," I say, shifting.

Or I might just devour her on the kitchen counter. She reads the labels put on by the starred chef who has concocted the dishes and opts for the fresh tagliatelle with truffle duo. I go to the cellar to find a wine to match. Back in the kitchen, I pause to discover Océane at ease. She has put the dish to warm up and is rummaging around to find something to set the table.

What the hell am I doing? We are far from the uncomplicated fuck.

A few minutes later, we sit side by side on the stools in front of our plates. I take down my glass of wine, and she sips hers, then starts to gulp down her pasta while muttering a "hummm" of ecstasy. Is she doing it on purpose? It's getting harder and harder. I'm getting harder and harder.

"A delight," says Océane, turning to me.

She swallows and licks the corners of her mouth. A trace of sauce on the left corner hypnotizes me.

Don't touch her, don't touch her… Damn the honor code!

I grab her and take hold of her truffle-flavored mouth. Her cry of surprise makes my taste buds go wild, disconnects my brain, and strengthens my erection.

"Push me away, Océane. If you don't do it in two seconds, I swear to fuck you."

48

TIGER

The dilation of the pupils of Océane is accompanied by this small, shameless, and satisfied air.

"Counterproposal: I give you two seconds to say sorry again," she whispers.

"It's not a game anymore. I am serious."

"Me too," she insists while rejecting me gently.

She gets off the stool, beautiful, challenging in her immaculate bathrobe.

"Apologize, Tiger, and promise never to treat me like a nobody again."

Our eyes lock together and probe each other. No, she doesn't play anymore either; she shows me how much I hurt her. And with her past, I realize it better today.

I dig my fingers into my hair. A searing memory in my head punctuates her words. My fist clenches involuntarily. The perpetual warning flashes in my overpopulated head. I step back, away from Océane. Suddenly drawn back years to the evening of the discovery of the remains of the Garden.

My own voice resounds in my memory.

"Hey? Look at me, Eve… Look at me! There you go. You're going to come with me. You're going to come with me. Right now! OKAY?"

"With you? Forever? You swear to me?"

Another one has already extorted promises from me in a different context.

A moment of hesitation passes between Océane and me. I see her grow cold and realize too late that my silence has plunged her into interpretations.

"I understood," she concludes. "Only sex, you wanted your fix, and that's it."

I don't know what to say. In theory, yes, I was thinking of nothing else. To our interlocking bodies, our mixed fluids. This sensational fuck with her as our only distraction, our only refuge. Damn, I've changed my schedule just for this!

"I'm going home," declaims the object of this mess in my head.

"What? No, your clothes are unusable, and I want you to stay."

"Screw my clothes; I'll take an Uber in a bathrobe. Let's limit the damage; I think even a girl like me is better than that."

Shit!

"Wait, Océane. A girl like you?"

Since she's not developing, I insist, "Don't put yourself down like that. It's my fault… I'm sorry if that's the impression you got when I ended—"

"Ended what, Tiger? Our sex, to forget Sophia's 'dirty little secrets?' I'm the sex toy that makes you feel good about yourself; that's how I feel right now. I mustn't aspire to anything else, to something that doesn't pay!"

It's getting worse.

"What did you have planned?" she says accusingly. "Let me guess: to show up one night when you were bored to fuck me one last time before forgetting about me?"

She throws her speech at me while getting out of my way to run away. My mind gets confused between what I wanted before and what I want now. There were a lot of things filling up my life: business, my inheritance, the burden of responsibility, my wife, and the hunt.

And this blonde girl showed up, vulnerable behind her jovial and cheeky side. She is there, attractive, angry in the middle of this mess of duties, appearance, and control to which I am accustomed. With her, a new goal breaks down the previous ones. I shouldn't. But I also can't stand the fact that she's slipping away or that someone else has what she's granted me. I can't have—

Argh!

"That's not true," I defend myself, running out of arguments.

"Don't bother. I'm out of here."

"I'm telling you, you're fucking wrong!"

My rising tone slows her down. My self-control is breaking down. Her armor crumbles too.

"I apologized, Océane. I can say it a million times if you want. You have my word, I—"

"Forget it, Tiger," she sighs. "See, even with Sophia, you only give what you want to give: money. And you take a lot more. You don't have to promise me anything; I don't even have to be there. Again."

She rushes to get her things and rushes to leave without bothering to put them on. I barely hold her back at the entrance.

"Stop," she complains softly.

"No, tell me what you want. What you really want. Is it just a promise to treat you better in the future?"

Her back sticks to the wall, and I to her.

"We have no future; you know that. And I don't want anything anymore."

I untie the string of her robe, my mouth a millimeter from hers. I breathe her in.

"Everyone wants something, Océane. I've done a poor job of giving it to you, that's all."

"Not at all," she challenges me as I lazily spread the flaps of the terry cloth. "Don't do that, don't touch me."

I kneel down, brushing her skin up and down only with my breath. Millimeter by millimeter, I haggle, "How about I give you what you want now? You only have to tell me. What do you want, Océane? Why did you comewith me?"

My lips come close to her lower abdomen, but I don't touch her. Not against her will, although her eyes tell me that her body is not on the same tune as her words.

"Tiger…"

"Say it."

"Say what?"

"Tell me you don't want me anymore, and I'll stop everything."

"No…"

"No?"

"Don't… don't stop," she whispers.

Fuck!

I place a kiss under her navel, and she shudders. A second one below. A third, lower.

"I..." A fourth kiss trails along the edge of her pubic bone. "...am..." My lips go to her pube. "... sorry..." My breath goes through her slit. "So sorry, my sweet, and I..." My hands are firmly planted on her hips. "... I swear I'll never..." My eyes search hers. "...hurt you so much again."

I tilt my head and lick the crease at the junction of her velvety thigh.

"You have my..."

With the tip of my tongue, I go to meet her bud.

"... you have my word of honor, Océane."

Something totters in her beautiful eyes. Impossible to keep my attention on her eyes for long. Her petals harpoon me, and I go back to them, enticed. I lift her leg, put it on my shoulder, and hold it with one hand, grabbing one of her buttocks. My nose slides down the center of her, and my mouth wanders there.

"It's you who takes what you want to take now," I say to her.

"Damn," she whimpers when I tease the inside of her corolla.

"Are we agreed?"

I hear only her neck slamming against the wall and the long breath she takes.

"I am the object. Use me, Océane."

My plea is lost in her, my tongue too. Her open bathrobe forms a white curtain that hangs on either side. She does not stop me, no more obstacle. She trembles; she wets. I eat her, suck her, lap her, cajole her. Suavely, for a long time, I delight in her sighs.

"Tiger..."

"Can you feel how sorry I am?"

I reach deep inside her, push her into her depths. Meticulously. Her flavor spills out and whets my appetite. My fingers add to this languorous tango; her pelvis moves lasciviously, joining me, giving rhythm to my assaults.

"Fuck! Oh, fuck... Oh, fuck... Oh, fuck..." chants Océane in a weak, heady tone.

She excites me. My pleasure takes an unexplored dimension and propels me to the edge of madness. My mouth worships her wet sex. Mine stiffens, claims her. Her intimate lips palpitate against my hungry lips, and my tongue is active in her delicate flesh. She whimpers, "I'm going to… Oh, boy!"

I smile. Normally, I would have slowed down the tempo. To give her the same ordeal she's giving me. But I'm about to break down. I spit out, "Sorry, my sweet," I accelerate, apply myself, and panic her.

And she sprays me with her trance while shouting my name.

A queen. My queen.

I straighten up by supporting her. She looks stoned, like the lilies in the video…

"Do you want something else, pretty bud?"

"You, I want you," she whispers.

Hell, yes!

I drag her on top of me and carry her to the couch. I sit down with her still wrapped around me and kiss her fiercely. Her arms cross over my neck, and her fingers end up in my hair. This kiss is as sulfurous as a volcano in eruption. Lava fusion on my skin, electricity in my nerve endings. I lose it and pass my hands between us to unzip my pants. Océane helps me. Feverish, with an impatience of desperation, our bodies intertwine one in the other. I growl in insanity, block her kidneys, with my erection stuck in her. Thighs against thighs, her voluptuous bust crushed against my chest, our glances attract each other.

She disconcerts me mentally. She undulates on me, staring at me, and tries to get up.

"No… Take your time, sweetness. Fuck me slowly," I tell her.

I clutch her buttocks and raise her without haste. Little by little, our dilated pupils riveted on each other, I bring her down. She exhales when she reaches my guard again. We don't rush anymore; she slows down and absorbs me in her. Then thousandth by thousandth, she goes back up. I knead her hips, do not leave her eyes. She inhales, and I do too. Her return on me empties my lungs.

"Like this?" she asks me.

We inhale, then exhale together.

"You are perfect," I answer her. "Masterful."

She twists and embraces me in the hollow of her. Her walls enclose me. She slides again upwards. I feel her breasts swinging supplely, her mane caressing me. She returns, and I float. I want her mouth, but to deprive me of it to better contemplate her confers me another pleasure. As if we entered into osmosis.

Nothing exists anymore.

No more war. No more shackles. No more armor. No more need for filters here, now, with her.

I levitate, I savor each go, each return, each carnal dance with her inside that closes on my cock. Until to see trouble, to see her, in a kaleidoscope, superb fragments of an amazon who rides me in slow motion. Her orgasm precedes a heartbeat of mine. A fucking tsunami smashes me into a roll where I phenomenally come.

The first flood of endorphins… I struggle to keep my eyelids open.

Second flood… Océane tilts her head back while inhaling deeply, her chest offered.

Third flood… My fingers are embedded in her flesh, grabbing her with all my strength.

Fourth, her pleasure sprays me… The blackout! Powerful. Fatal. Devastating. Transcendent.

Part V

Some secrets more than others are made to remain buried, locked up, and barricaded forever.

Nobody must discover them.

Especially not her…

49

OCÉANE

I know that Tiger carried me to his bed. I know that he finally unburdened me completely of the robe. I know I mumbled about ruining his couch, and he kneaded my ass harder and told me I deserved he gets mad too. And he covered me with kisses. He nibbled me and kissed me, piece of skin after piece of skin; I was already at the peak of liquefaction.

I don't know how he got erect after more foreplay. But I do know that this time, he was the one who put me on all fours in the middle of his king-size. And he fucked me. Uncompromising.

With a passion, a ferocity to make everything swing around us. I still see myself grabbing the sheets and biting my lip to keep from screaming. I still feel the print of his hands that kneaded my posterior while savagely laminating me. I could almost still hear the sound of our bodies colliding. Feverish, caught up in a fiery madness.

I imploded with pleasure. He grunted with pleasure. Then he whispered to me, in a rocky voice, "You ruined my bed too; you really can't help it, naughty."

Between laughing, high, and tiredness, I collapsed into Morpheus's arms—and Tiger's—very soon after.

I stretch and grope for his hard, bewitching limbs. One of the four, or the fifth, maybe? Damn, that's it! He has made me as insatiable as he is.

"Tiger?"

No one. I roll to the side. It's four in the morning. The light of dawn floods the room with a muted hue through the bay window that also overlooks part of the spacious terrace from which a splendid view of Sydney by night stretches endlessly. Damn, I had forgotten how much this man stinks of money! In addition to sex.

I try not to let that old feeling of abandonment come over me again. He promised, he begged…

As I walk toward the room's threshold, I wrap myself in the oversized comforter that spreads out like a train. I leave in search of the tiger which dominates this ivory tower. There's an occasion to notice once more all the space which he has.

Don't we feel more alone with so many rooms and square meters? I advance in the semi-darkness. I end up discovering him from behind. Dressed. Well, his post-fucking hair is still disheveled, and his shirt seems completely unbuttoned.

"The line is secure. Walk me through it," I hear.

He's still there, working. He's definitely addicted to this, too: work. I'm about to turn back so as not to disturb him when something teases my curiosity.

"We're going to pick up the package… An unofficial source has confirmed the date and time of the transfer. Everything is done."

A transfer? It's about the prisoners, isn't it?

"Good," rejoices Tiger. "My lawyers are officially handling the Byrne case."

That name… the famous asterisk in my contract.

"For the other *packages*, do what you have to do. They have to spill the beans, no matter what."

My mind freezes, only to race again trying to unravel what I've just heard. Is it just me, or is this exchange turning into a mob baron discussion?

"Copy that, sir. Given the specimens, it'll be dirty, but we'll get them talking."

I shudder, a second unpleasant feeling rising in my gut. Is Tiger involved in some kind of dirty business?

"Perfect," he agrees. "Omega must own the paintings; he was an art lover and thought he was a fucking aristocrat. I want to know what he was projecting through Mike Woods too."

Wait, the guy from Sophia's restaurant? What's going on there?

"You'll find out; I'll call you as soon as we get it out of him," promises his caller.

"No, Terrence. I want to see it live; I want to see him suffer, don't skimp on the means."

It's becoming clear, I'm fucking a gangster.

"Count on us, sir. I'll take care of it personally. The boys will take care of the other one. They're gonna get it."

Oh, no! Go away, Océane!

But I remain petrified, between unhealthy curiosity and shock. Wanting to spy on what comes next.

"Any preferences on how to grill them?"

My blood runs cold. Tiger sneers.

"You have the file," he replies. "They have to taste it. Let it be long, relentless. Go all out; you have free rein. I want blood, sweat, tears until their last breath."

"Roger that. See you live, sir."

"Okay."

I can't move. I think I'm shaking. My mouth goes dry. My heart is pounding in my chest. My hands become clammy. Unfortunately, this state prevents me from reacting in time. Tiger turns around and sees my stagnant figure behind him.

"Fuck!" he says. "You're awake. How long have you been here?"

Long enough to think I was at Pablo Escobar's house.

"Who the fuck are you?" I revolt immediately. "What was that? Henchmen, the kind who do your dirty work for you?"

Mute, he plunges his fingers into his face, jaws clenched.

"Damn, I should have known that so much money and power at such a young age, it's obviously suspicious. Even assuming you had a big inheritance. What are you into?"

He's as stiff as I was a moment ago. Under tension.

"Answer me this, Tiger. I… feel like what little I thought I knew about you has just been shattered."

Nothing. Silence. I go into some kind of sudden hysteria and scream, "ANSWER ME!"

"Okay. I… Calm down."

Calm down? Hell, I don't even know if I'm safe now!

What if he decides I should disappear because I know too much? I can't help it; lots of creepy flashes are flooding my mind in turmoil. The news: this au pair girl killed in London by a French couple in 2018… Then, the famous Kelly, whose girlfriend holds the Sextons responsible for his "disappearance…" There are also the two unknown names marked in my contract and shrouded in mystery. And what's the deal with Mike Woods, Sophia's restaurant manager? Is he going to be in trouble soon? These piles add up to Tiger's coldness and his interlocutor. The angle I was standing at didn't allow me to see him or be seen, but he had all the makings of a kind of hitman, rigid, detached, and efficient. Everything is coming together in my head.

Tiger approaches, and I have a visceral startle. I start to move back to avoid him.

"Océane…"

"Don't touch me!"

He stops dead in his tracks and runs his palms over his face. Then he stares at me. Dark. Extremely serious.

"Fine. Then listen. This conversation was strictly confidential."

"Are you reminding me that I signed a damn deal to keep my mouth shut?"

"Maybe," he assumes calmly. "And also blaming you for spying on a very private meeting."

I swallow. I don't feel well; my stomach is in knots.

"Maybe," I admit. "But the point is, I heard and… we're not going to pretend it didn't happen."

His jaws tighten. Hell, what have I gotten myself into?

"Sit down," Tiger orders me.

"What?"

"Come and sit down. This will take a long time, and you may need it to absorb what I'm going to say."

Oh, my God! My legs are wobbly. I walk at a snail's pace on weed and let myself fall heavily on the arm of one of the living room sofas.

"Go ahead," I encourage him to drop his bomb.

Silence, reflection, silence. He plants his irises in mine.

"A few years ago—before we were married—I pulled Sophia out of a cult. A sexual sect called The Garden."

Lights out in my skull. I blink, widen my eyes, and start again. Suddenly, all the lights in my neurons start to flash at the same time, even those I didn't know existed until now.

"I… Okay," I stammer.

"The cult was run by two men, twin brothers who called themselves Alpha and Omega. The beginning and the end. The genesis and the apocalypse."

I am cold, cold from nowhere, so cold that I shiver from the inside. I can't do anything anymore, nor think, nor manage the violent palpitations that devastate my chest. Stunned, all ears, I regulate my breathing as best I can.

"Sophia's family died in a collective suicide within this obscure cult. She could have stayed there too."

The fear grows and strangles me with emotions. *"Particular childhood and adolescence,"* Tiger had once vaguely mentioned. I remember it. My breath stops, and my chest compresses.

God, how horrible!

"That's… that's why she was seeing shrinks and taking pills," I deduce in a trembling voice. "That sort of incantation she was reciting in a strange language the day she mixed her pills with alcohol is from there?"

"Yes," confirms her husband. "The sect had developed its own language to accentuate the feeling of belonging to their community and isolate its people from the rest of the population."

Damn! A lot of things are going on in my head. The atypical lifestyle in the Sexton couple, the sexual liberties they take. Was it for her sake that Tiger complied in the beginning, or did he already prefer this non-exclusivity? Was he happy not to be tied down, not to lose his freedom completely? He saved her and kept her while banging other partners with her consent. If Sophia was too mentally damaged to live within the norms of our society, maybe that suited her too?

A story outside of social conventions.

Then another question comes to mind: did Sophia awaken the chivalrous instinct of the rich kid who was looking for a meaning to his own existence? In any case, their sexual needs probably matched. For the first time, I think I finally see the husband in Tiger. A husband seething with a dull anger, pernicious in his darkened irises, ready to avenge his wife?

My heart swells, but I don't know what. Not to dwell on it, I focus on the story. I ask, "How did Sophia escape the massacre? Did you get her out of their clutches in time?"

"Not really… She was swimming alone in a river near the farm that housed the Garden's disciples. She told me later. This little transgression saved her life. When she joined the group, they were all dead. Well, almost, some members were missing."

"So, there are survivors?"

Tiger nods, but that doesn't diminish the monstrosity that it must have been.

"Sophia… Somehow, she was lucky in her misfortune," I say again in a small voice. "Well, that's easy to say. I imagine that after having been conditioned during her whole existence to serve a Master, to exist only through him and his community, she was nothing anymore, just empty, disoriented, alone, and broken into a thousand pieces. Without him, and out of this kind of thick cocoon, she no longer existed. Am I way off base?"

Tiger nods after a few long seconds.

"This is indeed a bit like that. No more reference points, too many fears. Disconnected from everything, including who she was."

Terrible. My heart tightens.

"Is this the context in which you met? When did you meet? How did you meet?"

"Before the mass suicide. By chance… I ventured too far while horseback riding at the river where she was going on a getaway from their farm. She… was surprised to meet an 'outsider.' I went back the next few days, and we… started dating on the sly. Anyway, I learned a few things about how they work. And I had planned to save everyone, at least the kids and teens. It wasn't their choice; it was the adults'… But it took time and a way to convince them."

I press the flaps of the voluminous comforter. My bare shoulders get goosebumps as I realize that kids probably died with their parents in this quagmire.

Oh God, not the kids.

"The ones… the ones who," I stammer. "The ones who got away beside Sophia. Tell me they were the little ones."

Tiger pinches the bridge of his nose and shakes his head. A wave of horror washes over me.

"No, the survivors are mostly the worst people who had founded or joined this cult. They got away with it because they had other motives."

I have palpitations.

"What kind of motives?" I almost squeak.

"Various perversions, manipulations on minors, teenagers, and other ritual sessions. I got some videos they kept… I'll show them to you if you—"

"No!" I panic, disgusted. "I don't want to watch such abominations."

He nods slowly with the air of someone who seems to be haunted by the images. Shivers run down my spine.

"A handful of them also engaged in sadistic practices," Tiger continues. "They called it deserved punishment for this and that. The guru, Alpha, thought he had pseudo-divine power over his followers, and he delegated the punishment part to his twin and his twin's right-hand man. One tortured, bruised. The other, voyeur and manipulator, decided who deserved these treatments and took pleasure in attending them."

I place a hand over my mouth, feeling sick. I don't know what prevails over me anymore: my nausea, the pain of compassion for the victims, or the terror that seizes me simultaneously? How can one find oneself under the control of such enlightened and twisted people? How does one end up being conditioned to the point of no return? To the point of dragging one's own children into it?

Poor Sophia. No wonder she has a hard time keeping it together after being raised there.

50

OCÉANE

The atmosphere in the penthouse is getting heavier. Dismayed, I try to summarize everything I've just learned in quick succession.

"So the leaders of this cult have been mentally and physically defiling the followers and their children for years and then inciting them to kill themselves?"

"Yes. The victims believed in this 'Final Flight' bullshit. For them, it was just a sweet step to a better world, the final and highest step in their spiritual quest."

"It's crazy to buy into something like that!"

Crazy and terrible. To come to this point, they could not even think and reason for themselves anymore. They had lost touch with reality. I try to understand by recapitulating, "And then. These gurus… If I understand correctly, Alpha, Omega, and their accomplices ran away?"

"Omega, yes," confirmed Tiger. "Alpha, the one posthumously identified by the Australian authorities as the sole leader, ingested potassium cyanide with his followers. His sick mind adhered to the mystical preaching that he fed to 'the people of the Garden.' He left with them. Omega, on the other hand, had a clear head. Intelligent and a fine puppeteer, he stood back, simulated, and pulled the strings to disappear with what interested him after the death of the members. In particular, with his favorite sidekick, a one-eyed man who was eager for the suffering of others. He was the Executioner of the sect, the Angel of Punishment."

"Damn it!"

"You said it."

Tiger starts pacing around again, like a wild beast champing at the bit. He retreats into a heavy silence. Shaken, I have difficulty digesting all this information to repress the scenarios that my brain tries to imagine. Tiger reopens his computer, types in codes, and selects a folder. The icons indicate numbered video files, endless.

Oh, fuck, there are so many!

Tense, I wonder about their content. Tiger turns around and nervously buries another hand in his hair, looking at me.

"Going back to what you heard earlier…" he begins. "I hired hands-on men when I was about 18 years old to track them down," he tells me after hesitation. "They're over-trained mercenaries, warriors of the dark side who carry out extractions, settlings of scores. They recover kidnapped people, stolen valuables, etc. You know what I mean?"

Yes, I do… Well, I think I do…

Let me summarize. So, Tiger has a personal vendetta against criminals on the run and has been doing so for years. Unbeknownst to the police and the world, he's been tracking these psychopaths underwater to make them pay for their crimes.

Damn! This reveals a frightening aspect of his personality: he is the type to take justice into his own hands, to take revenge. Without mercy.

I shudder. Because in his place, I don't know if I would have wanted these monsters to suffer in their turn. Would I have wanted them to die, or would I have just hoped that the police would catch them one day?

It's confusing in my head. And I'm not in his shoes.

There are no instructions provided after trauma; I know that for sure. We don't react in a standard way to the unbearable. I can imagine that… Some people go to the law and try to rebuild their lives with resilience. And a handful of people do not find respite until they have taken revenge and they have returned the pain and deeply hurt the guilty parties.

I know this personally because I have been on the wrong side, the guilty side, the unforgivable monsters. At least, I embody that in the eyes of a mother who wanted—and probably still wants—to destroy me out of revenge. Christine, Lucas's mother, has the same hateful determination towards me that Tiger has. She hurt me, and she dragged me through the mud. She would put me in a wheelchair if she could. Or worse. It often made me anxious in Paris, getting stuck in front of crosswalks, wondering if she wouldn't be able to run me over with her car one of those days…

So, here, facing someone who wants to punish people responsible for atrocities on children and adults, my first reflex is to think that revenge is also destructive. Double-edged. The more Christine lashed out at me, the crueler she became herself, inhuman.

How do I submit my point of view to Tiger? We don't have the same experiences…

I go ahead anyway, trying to qualify because of my own experience:

"Tiger… If you go through with it, this mission may leave you with a stigma. Of course, I'm not defending this garbage. The facts are gruesome and indelible. Just thinking that there were children there gives me goosebumps… But returning the favor will weigh on your conscience; it will eat away at you. You'll have fallen into the atrocity, too, you understand?"

His irises stop on me, cold, with no quarter.

"Are you trying to compare what happened to you in France with the abominations these degenerates are guilty of? Are you trying to compare the after-effects on your ex with the number of innocent victims that the Executioner and Omega have left behind? Tell me I'm fucking wrong!"

Our visual penetration makes me uncomfortable. Tiger darkens. With a gloomy expression, he rubs his budding beard. I let go, got up, and moved, eager to take a step back. I walk towards the room. My legs lack stability, and my heartbeat is strange.

In fact, I don't really know this man. Until tonight, I didn't know he could go so far. Without any qualms.

So, he can destroy someone out of revenge. Even if he has good reason to hate these sick people, it's no small thing to pay a mercenary commando to slaughter them in turn. Why not just hand them over to the police?

No. I don't know; I don't know anymore. I'm confused…

"Océane?"

I stop, turn around, and we study each other again. Seeing this implacable part in him stirs me up inside; I can't help it. His forehead wrinkles; he seems so solemn, so… far from the one I laughed and vibrated with.

"Everything is planned, carefully thought out," he says. "I'm not asking you to approve or not."

"No, I know…"

"It's not even supposed to concern you," he says. "It's about Sophia, the hell she's been through, and my duty to fix it for her and for all those people, all those kids. I've been dreaming of catching these bastards for a long time. I will not let my wealth tax and other donations go to support them in the prison system. They don't deserve to take it easy, even behind bars, not these people! Believe me on that too. As for the possible weight on my conscience afterward, I'll take it. I'll even sleep better."

Shit… he won't let go.

Even though I'm stunned by it, a part of me is also hurt and offended by my being left out. *It's not even supposed to concern you. It's about Sophia…* These sentences resonate painfully within me. As if my opinion doesn't matter in important things.

"Okay," I say in a whisper. "After all, I'm only here for fun and for a limited time. I shouldn't have eavesdropped."

The hardness of his features and the steel blue of his eyes support my words. An unbearable calm envelops the room and weighs on my shoulders.

"We agree," Tiger finally says. "I count on your discretion."

"Who do you think I am? Confidentiality agreement or not, I won't reveal your private life to anyone. Even less so with such an awful background story."

He takes a few steps in my direction. I don't retreat anymore. He takes a hand out of his pocket, brushes my hair, tucks a strand behind my ear, and argues, "I am aware of the seriousness of what I am undertaking, but as the saying goes: desperate situations call for drastic remedies. This evil can only be fought with an evil equal to what they have inflicted. You have to see what they have done," he says. "For you to understand me, you must know what they are guilty of, what they are capable of doing."

I let out a sigh and retraced my steps. Because I probably need to justify his choices in my head. Whether they suit me or not. And it moves me that he insists on sharing that weight with me now. Sure, he wouldn't have intended to if I hadn't overheard his conference call, but that's more secrets shared between us.

My desire to be accommodating, to be there for him, is stronger, despite my discomfort. I don't know. Nevertheless, I sit down in the place he occupied during his conversation. Tiger chooses a video on his PC and launches the media player.

"Look at this," he whispers.

A large white tent appears on the screen.

Dozens of children are standing there, dressed in identical tunics.

An uneasiness punches me in the gut. It's no longer a simple story; I see them, these little ones who were never able to grow up. My breath is racing.

They are obediently lined up, haggard, of different ages, and it is impossible to determine which are boys or girls. Their little faces, framed by long hair, wear a similar expression. Is it resignation? Is it fear?

No, they are empty…

I do not perceive this malice, this candid joy proper to the ordinary children. These are almost ethereal.

My teary eyes look up at Tiger, and I whisper as if they could hear me, "They are so quiet, so skinny."

"They're starving, drugged," he says.

A tear escapes down my cheek.

"But why?"

"Because at every stage, the cult gurus had a method of subduing the disciples, making them obedient. For the children, it was essentially with lack. The lack of food, the lack of love, affection, and contact with their parents. They said that this allowed the 'Children of the Serpent' to feel connected to each other and to recognize that they are all the offspring of Alpha."

"This is so twisted," I mutter angrily.

Anger adds to my grief. Even though I've only watched a few seconds of the movie. My attention returns to the screen when I hear that thing… The incantation Sophia gibbered when she was smashed.

All in chorus, the kids recite in an unknown language a kind of poem.

My hair stands on end; I feel a cold shiver shoot down my back. Then they continue in English, *"I am a Flower of the Male who blooms for The Garden.*

I am a Child of the Serpent who fights for The Garden.

I obey the Guides.

I respect the Dogmas.

I swear to stay away from the 'other,' that 'impure seed' that grows outside.

For I am special. I am pure in my faith.

I serve with happiness and dedication the Chosen of our temple.

I wait passionately for the day of Ascension, the day of our final Flight.

I live only for that.

I bloom, I invest myself, I give myself for this ultimate Privilege.

For my own, my true Family, for Alpha and Omega.

At every moment. Away from the impure seeds."

My breath catches in my chest. I look at Tiger; his jaws clenched, his eyes dark. How many times has he scrutinized these horrors, vowing to bring justice his way? Has he broken down and sometimes cried as he looks at them, knowing it's too late, that these haggard little angels no longer exist, can no longer be saved?

He doesn't talk about it. He leans in beside me and turns on a second video.

This time, they're bigger. Pre-teens? Teenagers? Difficult to say. The shapeless tunic has now become a kind of sari on the girls… You can distinguish their more or less budding breasts. The boys now wear pants. All are in white, and all still have long hair and this primitive air, a je-ne-sais-quoi of another time. It's strange, oppressive. I don't know what to expect.

Soon, there is movement. Someone passes among them, an adult.

"He is the official guru, the genesis, Alpha," Tiger's altered voice informs me.

I nod, caught, staring at the stranger. It's silly to say, but he doesn't look like a monster. That's even the trap: he has all the qualities of a seemingly benevolent man. A charismatic, seductive dark-haired man. A look that subjugates. A guy that one would easily want to listen to, follow, and idolize in certain circumstances…

The so-called Alpha stops in front of one of them and caresses his cheek with a "paternalistic" smile. Knowing who he is and what he has accomplished in this community, this contact makes me even more uncomfortable.

"What is he doing?" I am anxious when Alpha's hand brushes against the boy's mouth, lingering there.

"Wait and see," Tiger replies.

The guru mumbles something unintelligible to the teenager, prompting him to let him hold his lower lip. He lowers it, and my blood runs cold. Shit, there's a word in there! A tattoo?

"It's his 'Garden Baptismal Name,'" Tiger explains. "Everyone got one when they were 13. Engraved on the inside of his lower lip by the Executioner."

"The one-eyed sadist?" I ask, gathering data in my question-filled head.

"Yes."

"Does Sophia have one too?"

He nods, our eyes drifting apart.

"They had plenty of such rituals, all ending in branding and/or a sexual orgy."

"No. I... I don't want to; I can't see this," I plead with him, straightening up.

It's too much. Too harsh. Too sordid. And so awful to be a helpless spectator. Tiger doesn't insist. He turns off his computer, and then his arms wrap around me; his body sticks against my back.

"Omega and the Executioner continued in France, with new methods but always the same perversity," he confides close to my ear. "Young French boys found themselves trapped in an opaque club, which they called La Confrérie. These bastards have flown under the radar in Australia and Europe for too long, taking human lives and trampling on others. Those who survive among their victims are left with the after-effects of their trauma, including Sophia. Who is fighting for these victims, for these kids who were cut down in their childhood? Who is doing everything to make these sons of bitches pay?"

You... I say to myself softly. You, you've been fighting without wavering for years. For them. For your wife.

I don't have to judge that. What right do I have to judge it? I absorb this plea without objecting, overwhelmed by it all. I don't dare suggest to him to give up anymore. Emotions crisscross my insides, from empathy to pain, anger against fate, against these monsters. I feel bad; I swivel against Tiger. His eyes never leave me.

Damn, he's beautiful! With that deep thing in his eyes fixed on me. The quintessence of the male.

I crack up…

"Thank you for… sharing these archives and confidences with me, Tiger," I say. "I know that overhearing your conversation forced your hand. You probably wouldn't have told me otherwise. But thank you. You care about this, and I respect that… I… I promise not to betray your trust."

"Thanks to you," he whispers to me after a while. "I want you to know that I don't think I'm above the law; this is just a necessary fight, an exceptional situation."

He stops, expecting me to challenge him. I moisten my lips and remain silent.

"I don't usually discuss these kinds of issues," Tiger says. "Not with someone who isn't specifically assigned to me to do the work that goes with it."

"Does Sophia know?"

"No, she doesn't. The hunt has been going on for years. I didn't want to upset her for no reason, especially since her therapy had been on a roller coaster ride. There was a lot of doubt and a lot of relapses. And I found out that the reason she's been floundering again recently is because a combination of random circumstances has caused Omega to have access to Sophia again."

Dumbstruck, I swallow and ask, "What do you mean?"

"An employee of Sexton's, Mike Woods, has established obtuse relationships via the darknet with other admirers of the Garden. And obviously, Omega was monitoring these kinds of forums to feed his ego. He must have made the connection, contacted Woods, and tasked him with… remotely manipulating Sophia. Get her to fall under the influence again."

"Oh, damn it! How… how long have you known?"

"A few days. I felt like something was wrong, that Sophia was regressing in some weird way. We neutralized the threat."

He doesn't elaborate on the how. I'm not sure I want to know, so Tiger continues.

"Now that I hold all the cards, I don't want to lose control so close to the goal."

I breathe a troubled yes, before adding, "I understand… So, Mike Woods knew about Sophia when he got hired as manager?"

"No, no one knew; I had erased all traces of Sophia from the evidence collected on The Garden years ago. And my team hadn't found anything suspicious about this guy in their research on him before he was hired. Obviously, he got hooked on these perverts long after, and Omega, on the other hand, is twisted and smart enough to have spotted a major windfall when he knew where Woods was working."

"Damn it! And that led him to Sophia, a damaged survivor. To think I met this Mike Woods at Sexton's. Twice."

I shudder to think of his rigid posture and the look in his eyes that put me on edge. Looking back, I realize there was something indefinable, something fishy about this guy. How can anyone idolize monsters who have killed so many people and then go on the internet and get excited about it? It's beyond me, and it scares the hell out of me!

Tiger leans in; I am emotionally tangled, lost in his eyes. Beyond this earthquake, I feel more depth, more intensity in what we experience together. He and I share more than sex now. I think I like it.

Am I fooling myself?

"What are we doing?" he asks me without going any further. "Do you want to run away now?"

"No."

Tiger is still staring at me. Making me feel like I'm no longer just a "special friend" of their couple, an ordinary sexual partner. Unless I take my illusions too seriously. I lose myself in him. But he doesn't talk anymore; he watches me. And when he captures my lips, I soften under his caresses, under this possessive, imperious kiss.

Did we seal a tacit agreement?

The comforter falls, and his fingers run over my skin, already marked by his ardor. He may not have wanted it that way at first, but I have penetrated further into his secret garden. Despite him, despite Sophia, despite me…

51

TIGER

When Océane falls back to sleep, my insomnia persists. I'm under pressure, too focused on the final goal, and too immersed in this girl to lie peacefully.

I leave the bed and the room. I get ready and scribble a note for my blondie. I get the necessary things and go out.

The airport, the jet.

It's still early when I fasten my belt for the takeoff. The interval is finished; it's time to go back on the stage and preserve the appearance. Let them see us together, Sophia and me, unsuspecting, with our guests, officially returning to Australia. While the four of us enjoy a few days of relaxation with the Hoods, Operation Ares will be launched in France.

Nervous, I fiddle with my cell phone and end up sending a text message to Sophia. My wife thinks I am still in Europe, working, as I often do.

Thinking back about Océane makes me want to text her too.

Don't run away, sweetness.

I still want to do a lot of things to you…

I look for the peach emoji to complete my sentence, remembering her little provocations from earlier. My lips curve. She is surely sleeping, sensual and exhausted.

In the middle of the flight, my eyelids also get tired. In a transitory state, between sleep and my cogitations, the Sophia of before haunts my mind. I relive that cursed day in the Australian outback:

"The Guide was to take us all on our ultimate journey. Why did they leave without me? Didn't they want me anymore? Did they leave me behind?"

"No. Now you're free, you understand? You were pushing away the 'others.' I am an 'other' too, but I will be there for you."

She gets lost in my eyes.

"Free? It is in the Celestial Garden that I will be free. With Alpha, Omega, Byrne, Annie: my Family. Away from the unclean seeds."

"Jesus, wake up! It's over! Do you hear me? It's over! And it's going to be crawling with cops any minute."

I hug her arms, trying to swallow my own emotional mess. This feeling of failure. I search her crazed irises. Her confusion stretches on forever. I internalize and try to think of an emergency solution.

"Come on, come."

"To go where?" she asks me.

Good question…

"Home," I affirm mechanically.

She doesn't want my help; she repeats low incantations. Still hoping to be granted.

"I missed the Flight because I didn't deserve it? I disobeyed by going swimming without permission," she deduced with pain. "I didn't meet the standards of my faith."

Her gaze drops from mine and stops again on the horrific images that will be engraved forever in her head. Mine too. No matter what we do, they will stick.

"You were lucky to have escaped," I maintain. "Your solitary bath saved you."

She stares at me, weak, incredulous.

"No, not saved. They are all gone; they are the ones who are saved."

"They are not saved, damn it, they are dead! And I'm here, me," I say to get her attention again.

"You?" she says. "You come from the 'others.' It's here, my home."

"I won't let you go. I'll help you, okay?"

She is cold, the kind of cold that has nothing to do with the weather. Though her hair is wet, her frail body is shivering from the abomination she is experiencing live. And the terror of this life outside, the total unknown for her.

"Hey? Look at me, Eve… Look at me! There."

Her eyes stop on me, empty.

"You will come with me. Right now! OKAY?"

"With you? Forever?"

I can't promise something like that. She is lost, disoriented, and terrorized by what comes next. By the outside world and those she calls "impure seeds." I *have no idea what to do with her, but I know what I don't want.*

That's why I'm offering a helping hand to her.

"Swear it first," she persists. "You won't leave me?"

"I will be there for you."

"You will never leave me? Promise?"

It's getting urgent. To save time and get out of the way before it's too late, I agree to give her a token of good faith. I whisper to her, "I promise."

"And if you don't keep your promise?" she still stubbornly insists, unable to move.

"I will keep it. Trust me."

"I don't know…"

"I said I promise."

Our irises do not leave each other anymore. Her fingers end up desperately clutching mine. I can't measure her level of pain, of disappointment. The emotional earthquake that overwhelms her is different from my feelings.

If only I had arrived in time… If only I could have prevented this disaster… If only she hadn't…

"We have to leave. Come with me, please."

"Okay. Because you promised…"

Fuck! I flick my hair and stare at the clouds. Two days later, this massacre was on the radio, on TV, everywhere.

"A cult worse than The Family was again on our land."

"Why didn't Australia know about it in time?"

"Who could have done what to prevent this?"

"What would be the legal consequences if someone could still be held responsible?"

The interrogations have been flying, have made the front pages, and have been in the headlines. But there were as many gray areas as there were answers.

The arrival of the police force on the grounds of the Garden. The discovery of the bodies, an entire community decimated… Victims were counted, sometimes posthumously linked to people long gone. Some were linked to a past they had left far behind, to a family that had no news of them. Others—younger, too young— were identified by parentage with DNA.

And I took in Eve Hamilton, who became Sophia Sexton, my wife with a past that I reconfigured. My protege, because I feared that the untraceable survivors at the time would one day return to take her with them. She was too malleable, had a fragile mind; they could have remote-controlled her, made her do anything…

And rightly so, when I see what almost happened recently if we hadn't unmasked Mike Woods in time.

There seems to be no end to it, damn it!

OCÉANE

I drink my smoothie on the terrace, my head in the clouds. A strange feeling of well-being comes over me as I reread the note Tiger left me on the bedside table. Distinguished, masculine writing. And thinly veiled naughty hints.

My bud,
I still have your taste in my mouth. Your smell still permeates my pores.
Unfortunately, I have to go back to France to join Sophia and some friends. We will be in Sydney in seventy-two hours. And I will be inside you in seventy-two hours and a few minutes. I'll text you with directions when the time is right.
The penthouse is yours to do with as you please.
Kisses… all the way down… Can you locate the place?
TS

Aroused, I pick through the various assortments of my generous brunch delivered by Anaïs as efficiently as discreetly. I am alone in the ivory tower, and I still don't realize what turn our "relationship" has taken. My unfortunate discovery, the confidences, the videos, the details about Sophia's past…

Shit! Thinking about Sophia makes me fall off my little cloud the next moment. Her and her precious rule about compersion.

"It's a kind of pleasure you get from sharing your partner without feeling jealousy, a pillar in free couples. Compersion and trust. As long as the boundaries are respected, everything is fine." "Do you promise to slip out of Ty's life….?" she had specified to me.

It seems compromised to me now. Am I betraying her by seeing her husband behind her back when I no longer "work" for them? Tonight, the lines became blurred for me. At times, I felt as if Tiger was looking at me, touching me as if the planet Earth had been depopulated of any other female presence. Our meltdown in bed had a breathtaking flavor.

As a result, his latest text with a fruity emoji with sexual overtones makes me giggle like a middle school girl. Yet I shouldn't. Not with an experienced man with overwhelming responsibilities and a complicated personal life…

Tiger is too different from the guys I've known or could date. And I can't help but wonder who I am to him now after these revelations?

At best, a sex friend, a rank above the simple sexual partner he is used to. At worst, I'm just another booty call that still gives him a hard-on and that he'll easily replace as soon as he gets tired of it.

Damn! The exaltation ends in a mere three seconds.

I'm not hungry anymore. Guilt about Sophia and uncertainty about my unlikely duet with Tiger demolish my mood.

A duet with Tiger? What the fuck am I saying?

I run to the shower, suddenly eager to wash away every trace of this night. As much as possible. After all my attempts to turn my back on him, a monstrous shudder comes over me for having given him so much more this time. And that I loved that he gave himself away so much.

You're screwed, Océane!

52

Seventy-two hours later. Velvet & Diamonds, Sydney

The days and nights of waiting, the efforts to put my blanket, my alibi, in place in case of trouble have mentally exhausted me. We are at the end of the meter. The machine is launched…

I play the decompression game with Steen and Lilac Hood. Sophia chose the place: the Velvet. I would have preferred another club. This one now carries the memorable fragrance of a woman who squats in my mind during the lulls.

It went off the rails again at the penthouse last time. In a different way. Océane found out too much…

But I fucking miss her. Unfortunately, I have to keep a low profile. For the time being, there's no room for arguments between my wife and me. I'm already in the news on the continent with my press release about the aborted Carter Industries takeover. My predictions are in line with the real-time consequences of the stunt with Shanna; everything is working out perfectly on that front. The next step is to go after this company and say goodbye to Carter…

It's much less simple for the military precision extraction that targeted the Australian detainee transport van in France this morning, local time. Operation Ares has been launched, and it's silly, but I can only talk about it with Océane.

Damn it, what is this need?

"We'll leave you guys to it," declaims Lilac Hood. "I am going to wiggle with Sophia."

Steen, her husband, raises his glass and says something to him in sign language. We tend to forget her disability; Lilac blends in so easily with the hearing crowd.

"See you later, Ty!" Sophia says to me, delighted to have a dance floor friend.

I answer with a wink. Hood takes the opportunity to start a discussion about the criminal organization of sexual deviants dismantled in France: *La Confrérie*. Of course, this spreads like wildfire; everyone is talking about it. Given my friend's profession, his films documented to the last detail and knowing the weight he has in the media sphere, I suspect he must have his network. Reliable sources that divulge crucial information to him.

But how much does he know? I mean, more than the public. I see how the lands lie, but I don't give away the bottom of my thoughts. The volume of the music forces us to tilt our heads towards each other to cover the sound system of the nightclub.

"I heard that they have linked this *Confrérie* to the attacks such as the one on the French-starred chef, Angèle Moisson," Steen tells me.

"Indeed, yes… Sophia and I have often eaten in her restaurant. How come she was targeted?"

"I wondered that myself, too," Steen replies. "The responsible person, according to the forensics in France, is an Australian. His pseudonym in this club was One-Eye. The seal used for the markings would come from his personal collection and would obviously bear his fingerprints. As well as the knife used for the mutilations."

One-Eye, aka the Executioner. I am not surprised.

This animal couldn't help but indulge in his favorite vices in France, as he did in the Garden. A dark pleasure pulses through me, knowing that my team is taking care of his disfigured face. An eye for an eye, sadism for sadism. This time, this idiot will laugh a lot less… I smile inwardly and drink a glass of scotch.

"I hope he'll soon be crushed by the justice system," I pretend to be moderately pleased before diverting the conversation to neutral ground.

Hood stares at his wife. She wiggles, shakes her red mane, laughs, and sings with Sophia.

As for me, I miss her. Océane didn't answer my previous message, nor the one from the beginning of the evening where I told her the place and the time of our arrival. I only fantasize about this: that she will give me a signal on my phone.

But nothing. I straighten up and hold up my phone.

"An urgent phone call; I'll be back," I say.

"Don't worry. I have some things to go over by e-mail with my assistant in the meantime. And I keep an eye on our wives," he jokes.

"Great."

Outside, I call Océane. One ring, two… three…

"Hello?"

Her sweet tone rings out, and I exhale.

"Are you ghosting me, my bud?"

"No… Well, I don't know," she hesitates. "How are you?"

"In need of you, I can't focus," I confess.

She is too quiet. Something is different.

"At the same time, in the middle of a nightclub, it's hard to concentrate on anything else than on some sexy silhouettes wriggling around just to get your attention, isn't it?" she finally replies.

"There is none. It's completely dull and empty in there. You're not there."

"You're a smooth talker," she says.

"No, just hungry for you. I want to see you."

"Tiger… I don't feel comfortable sneaking up on you; there's Sophia."

Think…

"She won't know. I would have acted transparently if the current situation wasn't special, as you know," I plead. "We'll wait for this to settle down in the next forty-eight hours or so, and I'll get you back to the house. I'll talk to Sophia."

"I'm not sure," she says doubtfully.

Shit!

I press down on my eyelids.

"You know what the worst part is?" whispers Océane. "You're making me a very bad girl… I'm turning into a total bad girl who stares at your sexy butt in those jeans instead of getting the hell out."

I freeze. I turn around.

"Where are you?" I ask.

Filled with hope, all my senses go on alert. I search the surroundings.

"I shouldn't, we shouldn't anymore," she says to me with an almost sad voice.

"I want to see you; I need to see you."

"Tiger…"

I feel the flaws in that one word she says. My name wrapped in a "my brain tells me to stop." Mine too, but I can't fucking obey it!

"Maybe if I added the magic word? I can't help but negotiate, even though my reason tries to tell me otherwise. "Please, Océane… Please."

I follow the rhythm of her agitated breathing as if suspended in nothingness, waiting for her to reach out to me.

"I'm hesitant to get out of my Uber," I think Océane confesses, despite herself.

"What vehicle? Just tell me where you are."

"The green Ford, on the corner."

I let out a sigh. It doesn't mean she'll get out of the car, but stupidly I take it as a gift. Yes, it's silly, yet I examine the scene. A window drops, and Océane's blonde hair materializes, framing her face sparkling with mischief. Our eyes catch each other…

"Come, just to… chat," I say, negotiating. "You won't even have to enter the nightclub."

She still hesitates. I step aside so as not to upset her further.

"Do you really want to talk, Tiger?"

"I won't do anything you don't want."

Time drags on, and her silence stresses me. She is going to refuse. After an eternity, the door opens, and she gets out.

Goddamn it, yes!

My eyes caress her from afar. Linger on her naked legs exposed by the small silky skirt, which twirls when she starts to walk. And go up finally to be planted in her eyes. I cross the mini distance which separates us and extend my hand to her.

Our fingers intertwine, and I am instantly electrified. This impalpable thing she unleashes in me doesn't diminish; it continues to swell. Pheromones gush, and neurons extinguish. Stupid? Yes, but I'm getting a hard-on. Not since my bachelor party have I been so relaxed, casual, and eager. I check the entrance of the club and pull her running. At first surprised, Océane ends up laughing while following me. I have become almost a kid again. No, a teenager on hormones, ready to do anything to get a hit from this chick.

"You're not going to make me run a half-marathon in heels," she grumbles, laughing.

We arrive very quickly in the private parking lot of the Velvet, where two of my cars are parked. One was lent to my guests, and Sophia and I took one to go out. I unlock the black Maserati and throw the keys to Océane.

"Climb in."

"What? You're letting me drive?"

"You have your license, right?"

"Yes, but… Damn, I've never driven a car like this."

I switch to the passenger's side and conclude, "All the more reason to do so. I'm tired of always having to control everything; let's be crazy for once! Come on, get in; I'll guide you."

Stunned, she seems not to believe it for several seconds.

"You've gone crazy!"

"Maybe."

Océane settles down, excited by this perspective, sublime with her pink cheeks. Her green eyes are riveted on me, set with emotions that jostle each other. Mine devour her. I spout out driving instructions to her. Her irises shine, and her teeth bite her lip. She gives in and makes the engine's horses roar.

"Yes! Let's get out of here, sublime pilot!"

"Woohoo!" says Océane in a rush of adrenaline.

In the beginning, she is extremely cautious. Fearful. The drive unfolds as if she were in a driving school car, trying not to disappoint the instructor. I do not intervene, and I let go of control. Gradually, the intoxication of speed takes hold of her.

"Oh, boy!" she gets excited, red with pleasure. "I feel like I'm just floating on the asphalt; it is insane!"

I burst into laughter.

"You see that you need a car. You like it."

"No, I didn't say that," she protests, nevertheless exhilarated by the effects of my machine.

"Yes, you did."

"Absolutely not!"

"I'm not listening to you anymore!" I answer by pushing play on the music, which was mute. Tonight, I'm letting go of the reins.

The remix of "Habits" by Tove Lo invades the car. Océane gives me a mischievous look.

"Cool, I like being your boss."

I laugh with her before adding nonchalantly:

"So, beautiful boss, just for the record: the order has already been placed at the dealership."

Her eyes are still on me, wide.

"Tell me this is a joke."

"Watch the road, sweetheart… I might hurt my cock a lot if we have an accident now."

Her attention is lost on my crotch, and she turns peony red. Her pupils, already dilated by the adrenalin, worsen my state.

"You're not serious?"

"I'm dead serious about both. You can change your Bugatti's brand, range, and color if you want. I haven't set a limit. And as for my erection, I'll only touch you if you want me to."

"Damn it, Tiger!"

"The road!"

I'm laughing because my timing is perfect for announcing my gift purchase. Océane forces herself not to give in to her instinct: to challenge me. She presses the gas pedal and slaloms between the vehicles to the sound of *"oh-oh, oh-oh… Stay high all the time…"*

I don't know where she's taking me, and I don't care. I don't think she even knows. Between driving a car and knowing that she now owns the model of her choice, I think I've got her all shaken up. We leave the city; I don't care how far we drive or how long it takes Sophia to realize I'm not coming back.

Total letting go! It's my decompression chamber. And it's great to see Océane in this state of euphoria. She brakes suddenly. Out of breath, beautiful.

"You bought me a fucking luxury car when I had declined your offer?"

I start to open the door to get out.

"Is this the conversation you want to have now? Didn't it excite you to have had so much technological and mechanical power in your little hands?"

She gets out in turn and takes another look at the stiffened member in my jeans, bugging in the middle of her protests.

"I... I don't want your—"

"My what? My cock? Say it! Tell me that your body doesn't react like mine down there."

I point to her little skirt with my chin, challenging her.

"You're horny, I can tell."

"No, not at all."

"Pretty liar. Your eyes tell me otherwise."

"Do they?"

"Yes, they do."

She is silent, and I smile.

"If you're so sure, come and check it out," she suddenly braves me.

Her change of heart destabilizes me.

"You allow me to..."

"Obviously, you don't care about my agreement, do you?"

I frown and say, "It's not the same. If I want to give you gifts, I can be stubborn, but your body is strictly yours, and I will never go beyond your consent."

Her defiant face softens. She approaches, and a more playful glow lights up in her green marbles.

"In reality, you didn't just want to talk, did you?" she accuses me, a half-smile on her lips.

"Yes... Okay, no."

"You are a hopeless case," she teases me. "I almost feel sorry for you."

"No kidding?"

The best part is that she lets me get her. She's still trying to push me.

"What about talking about that car I don't want? What's more important? To give it to me or to be allowed to touch me?"

"Option two, without hesitation," I murmur against her mouth.

"Perfect. You see, we understand each other, Mr. Sexton. I decide what I need or don't need."

"And what do you need right now?"

Instead of answering me, she brushes my chest. I try not to break before she gives me the green light. When she kisses me, my self-control is hanging by a thread. Her fingers slide in my hair, on my neck. The kiss makes me dizzy as it deepens. Damn, I want her!

I move Océane towards the side of the car and tilt her bust there. Without resistance. I believe besides that; she likes to feel me crazy about her body. In a record time, I fold down her skirt, shift her underwear without bothering to remove it, and I embed myself in her from behind.

"Oh, yes!" she pulsates under my fierce blows.

"Fuck, you are soaked!"

"Are you sure?" this little calamity persists. "Check again."

We move towards the hood, and I flatten the top of her anatomy against the flat surface of the car with my palm and raise her rump to meet my cock to dig her harder. Frantic and vigorous, I pound her. She pants and moans.

"We are less the smart one, my sweet? You want more?"

"Yes, more! You make… Fuck, you…"

The rest dissolves in a gibberish of sighs and exclamations. I shake her with wide and brutal penetrations, clinging to her buttocks that I knead. My thighs hit the back of hers. Océane's gasping complaints intermingle with my lustful comments describing precisely what a pleasure it is to be inside her.

The apotheosis ravages us. Humid, sensual as always with her. Dazzling!

53

Océane

I am exhausted. My cheek stuck to the car's body, Tiger still wedged in me in my back, in the middle of nature; the voluptuousness assails me from all sides. It is like the end of a hectic carnal marathon, and the pleasure surges with unheard-of violence.

"Can you stand?" asks Tiger's virile voice, a little out of breath.

"I have no legs left."

He laughs, withdraws… My skirt is still folded on my waist, and my lover puts back my lingerie, which he had just shifted, in place. He can take it off; we've ruined it. Instead, I feel his lips and fingers cuddling my buttocks through the light cotton bordered with lace. The warm evening air on the soaked fabric and our fluids—no, the dew, as Tiger calls it—run along my inner thighs.

"Don't move," he says.

He seems to have returned to the car but returns quickly. I think he kneels down, gently removes my panties, and wipes me with tissues. When I finally stand up, I am dried and naked under my skirt—surely all crumpled—that he replaces. He stares at me without saying a word. We remain like that for I do not know how much time, face to face.

My God, I sink. This guy is an incitement to stupidity.

I am aware that I have once again crossed the line with him. Like an alcoholic who convinces herself, she's on her last drink but can't let go of the bottle. And Tiger is one hundred degrees of alcohol, the paroxysm of drunkenness that consumes everything in its path. His heady perfume, the features of his face with that, and his magnetic gaze move me more than I should.

I've tried to tear myself away from it all and keep returning to it.

"Are you all right?" he asks me, running his fingers through my disheveled hair.

What can I say? I prefer to evade, "We should go back, and I should go back to the hotel. Your wife will be looking for you."

"I know."

What are we doing, Tiger?

I can't say it out loud. Nevertheless, the question keeps looping in my head. Yes, he is in an open relationship, and they both have the right to go elsewhere. However, even if we can't really talk about a classic extramarital affair since it is consensual between them, would Sophia approve of the effect her man is having on me now? The things I only share with him.

And him… Why the fuck won't he let me try to forget about him? It doesn't help that he's coming back and proving that he knows how to weaken me.

"You didn't tell me if you were okay," Tiger grumbles.

"I… Yes, I'm good," I answer under the intensity of his visual examination.

He plays with a strand of my hair, then cups my face. I whisper, "And you? How are you doing?"

Mute for a long time, he finally sighs.

"It's complicated," he replies.

"And what else?"

He seems to be introspective or searching for what he can or wants to tell me. I am overwhelmed, hanging on his words, waiting for I don't know what. It's silly, but I feel hyper-sensitive all of a sudden.

Vulnerable.

"In the end, it's only with you that I can talk about what I did in France," he confesses.

It's not what I expected. In fact… What did I expect?

I nod, shoving my hands into his back pockets. Our bodies move closer together again.

"I kind of cornered you on this, but I'm… honored to be in the know, Tiger. I… I assume that in your position, you often have to make tough decisions and deal with the consequences alone."

"I do."

A crucial point suddenly flashes: he may never have had a confidant. He's alone at the top, steering a huge ship at age 29 and facing responsibilities and choices that impact more than just him. He is a man of power, ultimately as lonely as his wife, but in a completely different way.

"Heavy is the head that wears the crown, as they say," I comment.

He nods and smiles at me.

"No, I'm not a fucking fairy tale prince. I wasn't for Sophia or anyone else. But I've been taught chivalrous values from another time… Like 'know how to be merciless with the enemy who deserves it,'" he seems to paraphrase.

"Is that your father you're quoting? Did he raise you that way, with some kind of code of honor?"

"He wanted me to know how to take responsibility in any situation. Never back down. To act when necessary."

"He… He was probably the kind of man you respected and feared. You look like him."

A kind of veil darkens his eyes. His jaws seal hard. He closes himself again in silence. Touched to know that in him nevertheless hides the boy who wants to make his father proud, I inquire, "And did your men manage to… execute your orders? Did you get those monsters?"

"It's in progress… I needed to relieve the pressure. By tomorrow, they'll be done."

I nod without batting an eyelid. They're going to torture them; I know that. I shudder to think that they will probably eliminate them afterward. There was such a coldness when Tiger gave his instructions.

How do we feel after that?

I searched the web and read some old articles on the subject. Chilling facts, a police investigation that has been stalled for ages. No doubt, a feeling of injustice is rooted in dozens of people linked to the many victims. But, of course, the Sextons are not mentioned anywhere; Tiger has indeed erased the traces of his wife's past. And he decided to fight for her, as a determined dark knight, for ruthless revenge.

And he succeeded there too.

However, he doesn't seem happy or proud of himself. Just gloomy, like a war general after the execution of the enemies he targeted. I don't know what to make of it.

"I… I understand that you needed to decompress," I say. "Does… Sophia finally know that you've… avenged her family? It won't bring them back, but maybe it will appease her a little?"

"No. I haven't told her anything yet. I'm waiting for the latest information my team needs to get from Omega to find out what happened to some of the missing members. Like Annie, Sophia's older sister."

Stunned, I blink. The veil lifts for me on the other mysterious name.

"Oh… so she wasn't in the mass suicide either?"

"No, she wasn't. Neither was Byrne, their brother."

Tiger releases me, steps back, and tilts his head back to stare at the dark sky. I struggle with my questions. Realizing that Sophia survives by wondering what happened to some of her family. No, in fact, she acts as if she were dreaming of their arrival one day. Otherwise, she wouldn't have strangely put their names in my contract, as if her family was incomplete and they would come back to her one day to form a whole with her and her husband.

Holy crap, that's it! Her old life, this cult, she still carries them with her. And maybe the guru who used Mike Woods from a distance has managed to reactivate all of that!

"Do you know anything about Sophia's brother?" I ask, remembering the conversation I overheard at the penthouse.

"He's alive. He was in Paris the whole time," says Tiger.

Boy, that's crazy! Finally, some good news.

"Sophia will be overjoyed to hear it," I remark.

"Probably. I have doubts. I do not know yet in which psychic state he is. Sophia is quite fragile, despite notable progress and the facade that we built over the years. I must negotiate this turn well, not to precipitate or bias the effects of their reunion."

"I see."

Shattering scoop: Tiger Sexton is not insensitive. His analysis of the situation seems even more subtle to me; he takes his wife's emotions into account and protects her repeatedly. Even if Sophia suffers from the platonic aspect that frustrates her with him, how many men would do what he has set up for her? How many would come to such deployments of means, of skills? How many would devote so much time and determination so that, finally, those who hurt her would be punished?

I come back to curl up against Tiger, and he embraces me. Irrevocably, our mouths come together for a kiss that turns me upside down. I am not sure of anything anymore. Tiger goes to open the passenger side door for me this time.

"We have to go," he whispers.

"Yes…"

"Should I drop you off at your hotel?"

"No, meet Sophia at the club; you can leave me there. I'll take an Uber."

I need to be alone to think seriously. My feelings are not clear at all; the more it goes on, the more confused I get. I run too much risk of getting attached to the wrong guy. Already taken by a woman I like as much as I feel compassion for her. Yet, in spite of all this, I'm freaking out wondering when this married man will kick me out for good.

Shouldn't I do it before him? To suffer less? And not make his wife suffer unnecessarily?

Our glances are locked on each other; his on me is enigmatic.

"Go and find Sophia," I say to him, vainly trying to preserve myself from this pain that grows in my gut.

I shut myself down like an oyster, like a survival reflex in front of a future pain that I can neither avoid nor take.

TIGER

Océane is not wrong; it was risky, impulsive, and visceral too. I wanted to be with her, nowhere else, and with nobody else. And boy, does it make our lives difficult! Hers above all.

"Okay, I'll call my driver, he'll come with another car. He'll take over from the club and drive you wherever you want."

"No, that's fine," she refuses. "Thank you."

She puts distance between us. Probably so as not to take up any more of my time because of Sophia. Or because she's starting to see the three of us in a more serious light and would rather step back? Stop everything?

In that case, make it easy for her. Let her walk away. For her sake…

I know that, but a kind of uneasiness is spreading inside me. Maybe it's because she's the only one I've ever shared things with in my life. Normally, I act, plan, move forward, and remain the only one in charge.

Because some secrets stay that way for good reasons…

So yes, we messed up; I messed up. I cast a sideways glance at Océane. She's been getting unwanted confessions out of me, and this sloppiness is working on me too. This is fucking insane! And it's completely irresponsible of me. I've broken the golden rule of keeping absolute control over everything, including the fuck partners in my relationship.

Now, how many limits have I crossed with this woman?

I mustn't let this exit blow up in my face. It makes the return trip much less fun. My reason comes back, pointing out the need to take the reins immediately.

I turn the alternatives over and over in my head while riding. Our arrival cuts short the dilemma: Sophia camps right where I was in the almost deserted underground parking lot. She has been standing in the middle of the cars, in this place, since I don't know when. And at a rough guess after several drinks, but clearly less cheerful than at the beginning of the evening. Her eyes are rounded by discovering Océane.

Here we are. Every action has a consequence. It's going to blow up.

54

OCÉANE

Shit, Sophia is here!

This was precisely what I wanted to avoid tonight, in my current state of confusion. Don't cause any more damage; it's screwed. Tiger parks himself, jaws sealed. As for me, panic overcomes me.

"Breathe," he tells me in the car. "Let me handle it."

He opens the door and gets out. I imitate him, less sure of myself than he is.

"Explain things to me, Ty?" attacks his wife directly.

I notice her mascara that has run, her puffy eyes, and the strong smell of alcohol. She is in a pitiful state. Yet, I'm the one who feels like crap because I'm partly to blame for this disaster. I think… I think I'm starting to get addicted to her guy, like her. It's a billion times uglier to admit it to myself! Disturbing, tetanizing, and hard to deal with. So what about Sophia? We need to stop this emotional carnage.

"Tiger, I…" I begin, not knowing how to do this smoothly.

"Okay, I'll explain, Sophia," he cut me off. "I contacted Océane again. We went for a ride."

Self-confidence at all costs. He draws up a censored summary without blinking. I am far from matching his legendary phlegm. Uneasy, I look at Sophia, cursing myself for having cracked after the official end of my commitment to them.

"A ride?" repeats the interested party. "Is that a politically correct way to admit you fucked her, Ty?"

"Sophia, listen——"

"You shut up, Océane! I'm talking to my husband," she says, cutting me off. "To you, Ty. Just look at her. You stink of sex! How long has this been going on? How many 'drives' have you done with her after you supposedly fired her?"

Tiger purses his lips without retorting. I'm at the height of embarrassment. In the conventional scheme of things, I am the "other woman," the "mistress" caught in the act with the adulterous husband. If there had ever been a conventional aspect between the three of us. But everything is much more blurred and atypical. Their couple is. In their contact with them, I went off the marked path, off the straight and narrow that I was trying to regain after Lucas.

And you loved it, didn't you?

My conscience scourges me, too late. No, it's just more vehement at this second. I ventured too far, too intensely, until I got stuck. Their relationship, this in-between, is an abyss that sucked me in. Bottomless; impossible to get out of it without pain.

"How many!?" shouts Sophia. "Of course, he won't say anything, that's the thing! Very well, then you answer me," she roars while turning to me.

Help me! The walls of the vice tighten, crush me. My eyes in those of Sophia, the vertiginous well closes. I don't want to hurt her; I never wanted to. But I did it, damn it, yes, I did it. The famous compersion no longer holds.

"I…" I say, trying to put as much sincerity into it as I can. "I was angry with Tiger because of the way he kicked me out of the house overnight. I… I didn't understand why he—"

"And that's when circumstances led you to think I was a poor drunk on drugs," she interrupts. "Did you forgive him and take your clothes off to comfort him?"

"No, Sophia. I know that what you went through is not insignificant. I want to comfort you most of all. With Tiger, it's not that, it's…"

I glance at him and see how he is tensing up. The blunder! I'm talking about the things he told me about Sophia's past! Things I'm not supposed to know. His wife ticks. Of course, she does. And I'm suffocating. Inevitably.

After betraying her, I betray him. Total crash!

"I can't believe it, she knows?" says Sophia indignantly, without me being able to catch up. "Not only do you still want to fuck her, but you open up to her?"

"Enough!" says Tiger. "We'll talk about it in private."

"No, let's discuss it now!" insists Sophia. "The three of us are involved, right? What did you say to her, Ty? Uh-huh, you stay!" she shouts at me as I take a few steps backward and reach for my phone.

Certain that my presence would make things worse, I would have preferred to leave them alone. To escape from the abyss. Too late! From now on, the three of us are sinking, trapped by our choices, in this "trouple" on the verge of disintegrating. What part of the responsibility to attribute to whom? What's the point? In any case, believing it would happen without a hitch was utopian. Seeing Tiger again didn't help.

He and I have…

We moved her out of the way. I turned down Sophia's advances and even walked out of her life. While Tiger continued to neglect her carnally as well. She was the only one who lost out.

Are you sure? Sure about the real loser?

"What did you tell her, Ty?"

Tiger grits his teeth and shoves his hands in his pockets. She pivots to probe me. Cautious, I shrivel up. What do I do, damn it? My anxious gaze oscillates between them.

"What did he talk to you about, Océane? About The Garden?"

"Stop, Sophia," her husband summons her. "We're in a public place; someone could hear us or film us at any moment."

"I don't care!" rebels the interested party. "Why would I keep silent if you make confidences on the pillow?"

He tries to approach her, but she dodges him. The tension rises a notch.

"Is that it, huh? Answer me, Océane!"

"I… Yes," I stammer.

"Great!" exclaims Sophia with irony, without any joy. "Everything? He told you everything?"

"You leave me no choice," says Tiger.

He loses his calm and rushes on her to seize her. Sophia struggles, ducks, and starts giggling strangely.

"Are you nervous, Ty?" she notes.

He bounces towards her and catches her this time. Everything goes so quickly. Sophia, more sarcastic, mocks him while he tries to lead her toward his Maserati.

"That is enough!" he thunders.

"She doesn't know," persiflage Sophia. "You are nervous because she doesn't know."

"What? I don't know what?"

"We're going home, damn it! And you shut up!" her husband snaps.

Intriguing… Why does he seem to want to stop her from continuing? Only because a witness or a camera could spy on us, or for me? A bad feeling knots my stomach. Tiger manages to confine his laughing wife in the car, in the seat I occupied not so long ago.

"He didn't tell you about the Flower Queen—"

"Shut up, for God's sake!" he gets angry.

I'm standing still. I've never seen this control freak with such a troubled, threatening eye.

"I'm not the only one to have experienced this past so shameful for the gentleman," spits Sophia to me, satisfied to strike a slap that Tiger cannot counter. "Yes, his dearest mother is also in the batch, my beautiful."

"SOPHIA!" he shouts while hurriedly getting back to the driver's side.

What the hell is this?

"What?"

"Courtney Sexton had joined The Garden," boasts his wife. "With his beautiful 12-year-old son. He grew up there!"

OH, FUCK!

My jaw drops, and surreal palpitations stir my insides. Incredulous, I stare at Tiger in order to draw his blue eyes into a denial. It doesn't come. No, he pierces me with his silence.

"Wait, that's not all," Sophia elaborates. "The Flower Queen was in high school with Alpha and Omega."

"Sophia," Tiger threatens, teeth clenched, his unfathomable irises focused on me.

"No, let's say it, Ty. She's our confidante now, right? So, she deserves to know everything. Like, for instance, that you're not Nick Sexton's biological son, but Alpha's. The Garden is a family; we enter by blood."

I think my pulse is stopping. Tiger closes his eyelids. I see his Adam's apple rise and fall, his breath coming out of his chest. It can't get any worse; I'm suffocating, buried alive in their real secret garden.

"No…" I whisper. "Tiger, say something."

He doesn't answer me. He is as if engulfed in a black veil that unfolds, wraps him up, and makes him suddenly unrecognizable to me, different, unfamiliar. His reopened eyes remain frozen in front of him; they don't blink, and nothing in him moves anymore.

Why am I shaking like this?

"Oops, that already makes too much for you, my darling?" mocks Sophia. "I don't have to add that we are half-brothers and that we all fucked together under the eye of Omega, who loved to watch it? But how many secrets did you really tell her, Ty? Just one?"

"Tiger? Tiger, look at me!" I start to panic.

"He won't," Sophia comments sarcastically. "He won't because now you'll read his true nature. You have been a substitute, Lily. A palimpsest of what Annie, I, and many other girls have been to him."

Lys.

A delayed translation emerges in my saturated head.

Lys. Lily in English.

It wasn't for Lilia, my middle name, or a whim to annoy me. It had another meaning all along. Just like little bud… Were these cult vocabularies?

Fuck, I'm going to fall apart.

"Ah, finally!" gloats Sophia, pleased with my pallor. "Do you understand everything now? False little Lily of passage, not marked nor initiated. You were only a poor copy because of the power that he had there; he will never find it in this life. Even if he does everything to erase this part of his life from the face of the earth, he has it in him… You fucked the impostor, Océane. I'm married to the real one, bound to me forever. By blood, by sperm, and by—"

The end is lost in the squeal of tires and the roar of the engine. Taking off like a rocket, Tiger comes out of his frozen state. He takes his wife with him under my stunned look.

Shocked, speechless, with a dry throat, I see the vehicle leave, abandoning me in the heart of the nothingness of the basement.

Damn, it's his past too!

The tattoo on Tiger's groin… Its design resembles the lily

symbol of royalty, nobility, and knights of another era. It was right in front of me.

He has a distinctive mark, and I missed it! But what an idiot!

55

TIGER

Damn it! I can't loosen my fingers gripping the wheel. I rush on the asphalt, imprinting the fury in my veins on it.

"Did you see her pretty shocked face? She thought you were a saint. An almost 'normal' guy stuck with a chick with a muddy past."

"SHUT UP, EVE!"

Her mouth rounds with her eyes. The silence falls again. Her eyelids close furtively before focusing on my profile when I force myself to concentrate on the road.

"It's been a long time since you called me that," she minces in the language of the Garden, soothed. "My Lily name, I am your Garden Flower forever, Ares."

"Stop it!" I command in an unnaturally low, almost whispering voice. "Take that shit back. Don't. Say. That. Fucking. Name. Again!"

"Yet you are Ares, a Chosen One of the Garden, the invincible among the Children of the Serpent, the favorite of our Guides, the son of Alpha and the Queen of the—"

"I swear that if you say another word, I will…"

The rest of my threat floats in the unbreathable atmosphere. My breathing quickens, my pulse races and my knuckles turn white around the wheel.

"Forever Ares and Eve. It's in us, and it's just us."

Damn it, shut up! Make her shut up, damn it!

"These are your sisters, Ares," she recites in the language of the Garden. "You are also their Prince; they are all yours…"

This disturbing passage awakens the incessant incitements with which I was showered there. Yes, I denied, resisted, and tried to cling to the landmarks of my first eleven years. The ones where

I thought I knew my real father. The ones where morals and other values had been instilled in me. The ones where incest was wrong. The ones where my mother didn't offer herself to other men and didn't let bad guys push me to fuck lots of young girls as lost as me…

And LSD, with its psychedelic lights to keep us in a pseudo-mystical dimension. They broke my preteen mind. At that pivotal moment when I was supposed to be building myself, discovering myself, and growing up after Nick Sexton's death. They blurred my certainties, erased them, to supposedly make me reborn.

And they renamed me according to their rites…

"We are Eve and Ares," Sophia continues in a language that reverberates like the echoes of an unbearable truth.

Shut up! But I do not know anymore to whom I ask to shut up. Sophia or my head?

"They are not my sisters!"

"Yes, they are, Ares. And you felt it deep inside you… What you just did with Annie and Eve fully expresses this filial love, this blood attraction. You have loved them in the most carnal way possible. You are one of us, Ares, Child of the Serpent. 'Tiger' was only a dead illusion with your false father, an invention of your mother to save this marriage which does not exist anymore by hiding her adventure."

"Noooo!"

"Everyone knows it here, Ares. And we were all waiting for you, all the Lilies were waiting for their brother, lost among the impure seeds… Your mother is repenting today, and she is devoted…"

"NO! I want to go home; Mom is wrong. She is lying! I am Tiger Sexton, son of Nick and Courtney Sexton."

"Illusions… This is your home. You are in your true family. Tell him, my Queen."

"It's true, my darling; The Garden is our home. You have been named after someone else, but Alpha is your progenitor."

AAAAAAARGH!

It won't lock anymore. No more filter. The indelible memory of the joy that shone in the Executioner's able-bodied eye twists my synapses.

Stuck, tied up, clueless, forced to listen to them. Again and again.

The motherfucker loved to feel me cracking up. Alpha and

Omega's repetitive speech, corroborated by my own mother, was reaching me where sadistic burns, belt beatings, bags over my head, and various corporal punishments had failed to weaken me. That crazy One-Eyed Man finally saw that some form of pain could pierce me; he measured the impact and force of the words in my head.

"It's up to you to make it happen, to make it happen again—"

"SHUT UP, SOPHIA!"

The locks jump from everywhere. Everything fuses and overwhelms me. The barrier between the past and the present breaks. I relive, without wanting it, things buried under layers and layers of censorship. For an eternity, I thought that by destroying the evidence—material and human—I would eventually erase my stigma as a cult child and teenager.

But fuck, I still get a hard-on looking at some of the images of other members! Always out of control, obsessed with what I did there myself over time…

Ares…

I lose control over my brain for the second time in my life! The memories become irrepressible. My speed increases, increases, roars and goes wild. In the vain hope of regaining my self-confidence and composure, of covering the rest, of erasing the ghost of my mother. Unfortunately, this one, in Queen of Flowers, continues to smile at me, languid in the arms of Alpha. And this crank man denudes her under the vicious glance of his voyeur twin: Omega. I want to vomit.

I shake my head and press my eyelids to annihilate this vision. When I open them again, I discover the biker coming from nowhere too late and turn abruptly to avoid him.

The car drifts; it is impossible to slow down or stop it. Sophia's terrified screams fill the car. Definitive loss of control. A frightful crash! Ares, Ares, Ares, Ares.

Lights out.

OCÉANE

Exhausted, I turn on the TV when I get home. To fill the unbearable silence. To escape the insomnia. To take the masterful slap I took. How long did it take? I wandered, phoned Louane. And ended up in a bottle of vodka with a bar and the whole gang.

No, in a bar with a bottle and…

Okay, maybe I'm a little bit drunk. But unfortunately, still not enough. The sudden urge to vomit makes me feel even more miserable. I run to the bathroom and fall to my knees. Minutes later, I rinse my mouth and splash cold water on my face. I come back to the room, holding my stomach.

Nice idea to have accepted the glass Louane handed me when she saw me arrive, white as a sheet. Yeah, it was really a genius idea to throw myself on alcohol to destroy my brain. It didn't work. I collapse on the bed. The scene in the parking lot assails my muddy mind. Endlessly, still shocking and violent. How could I have—

"News flash: Ship owner and businessman Tiger Sexton and his wife Sophia have just had a terrible accident."

My heart is racing. I sit up too quickly, not feeling well, but sobering up fast. I grab the remote and turn up the volume.

"They were driving one of the billionaire's cars—a Maserati— and had apparently just come from a night out with friends, film producer Steen Hood and Hood's wife.

We don't have any more details at this time. We'll keep you updated as data is distilled down from TS Naval's communications department."

Oh, my God!

I leap out of my bed, frozen, shivering. I grab my phone and call Tiger's.

"Sexton. I am unavailable; please leave me a message or contact Anaïs."

Shit!

I try again and get her answering machine. Feverishly, I try Sophia's. Messaging, idem. An unprecedented panic fear shakes me. Anaïs, the personal assistant… Do I have her number? Fuck, I'm shaking too much. I find her; I don't breathe while listening to the ringing. After an eternity, she picks up. My lungs are saturated with air.

"Anaïs, it's Océane. Are they well?" I ask without preamble. "I'm not able to get them on the phone."

"Good evening, Miss Rousseau. I can't—"

"No!" I cry out on the verge of hysteria. "Don't give me the kind of line you give to the wriggling press. I want to know where they are. Tell me they're okay!"

"Miss, I'm not allowed to disclose the medical or private details of—"

"Are you fucking doing this on purpose? What would he think, Tiger? Put him on!"

"I can't do that; I'm sorry."

She apologizes and hangs up on me. I can't believe it! The crash site images seen from a helicopter are playing over and over on the TV screen. Terrifying. The Maserati is crushed, almost like a concertina, against the guardrail of the highway. One cannot come out unscathed from such a horror scene.

Are they...

A sob rips through my chest. I quickly gather my things and leave the hotel room in a hurry. Outside, I hail a cab and indicate to him the address of the Sexton's Sydney residence. Peter will talk to me; he will have no choice. I will not stop!

"Uh... I am afraid that the perimeter is cordoned off around this area, miss. Every journalist in the country, for that matter, probably the police as backup, and Tiger Sexton's security detail are standing at the ready."

Of course, the macabre hunt for a scoop!

"Oh well, let's go anyway. Get me as close as you can."

"It's up to you," says the driver.

I remember I registered their home number when I took over my job with them. Crossing my fingers so that I don't get filtered out by massive calls from curious people, I press the green button.

A ring. Breathe, Océane. Two rings...

"Property of Mr. and Mrs. Sexton, good evening," Peter's stilted voice greets me. "Who am I speaking to?"

Boy, I've never been so happy to hear their butler. Perhaps only a few intimates have this private number of the Sexton house if he picked up in such a context.

"Peter, it's me, Océane. I'm on my way; I need to get through," I say, my voice quivering.

"Miss Océane?"

"Yes. Let me come in, please."

He pauses. I blow out another plea.

"Very well, miss. I'll inform the security team. Please call me back five minutes before you arrive to best manage your passage through the gates."

"Thank you!"

Tossed from one emotion to another, I counted the seconds, and I champed at the bit, I am anxious, and I sink into pessimism. That lasts for ages because while approaching the domain, a hallucinating traffic jam blocks us. Cameras, phones, photographers, and a human tide of strangers on the lookout, overexcited, hopping up and down. National and cable TV channels, and foreign reporters too.

It's insane! I realize even more that a catastrophe has occurred. According to the untimely comments of the cab driver, the situation is more or less the same in front of the TS Naval headquarters and two or three of the country's most highly rated private hospitals. Just in case the Sexton couple was admitted to one of them. Apparently, during the evacuation of the victims, the Tiger staff covered their tracks, and the population was unaware of the essentials. No one knows more…

The victims. This word hits me in the gut. Unimaginable just a few hours ago. He was kissing me, pressing himself against me, making me gush with pleasure. And Sophia…

My God, Sophia!

New tears come to my eyes. It's too brutal, unpredictable, insane. And this pain in my chest pulses too hard, though I don't understand how it can devastate me with such violence. I am scared to death. I make my way as best I can after leaving the cab. I call Peter back and tell him where I am.

Almost beside myself, I am "fished out" in the mass by guys with earphones and military faces in black fatigues. They seem to have my face in their skulls, considering the time they take to flush me out.

"Océane Rousseau?"

"Yes."

"Follow us," orders one of them.

The course is chaotic, I am jostled, and they are agitated. Microphones are set up, and they try to discover my identity. Why do I have the right to pass? Did they survive the accident? How are they doing? Why this radio silence?

Questions are flying, and flashes of light are blinding me. I am in a pitiful state. Finally the end of the journey, I am in the hallway. I fall into Peter's arms and cry without being able to explain this upheaval in me.

"Come, miss. You have to sit down," the butler decides.

I follow him, groggy.

Did they survive? This question, uttered outside, absorbs the crumbs of strength that it took me to reach the house. No energy left, just a cold sweat, a panicked heart, a tetanized mind.

"I failed again. I had promised Mr. Sexton Senior that I would look after his son," Peter murmurs, moved. "I saw Mr. Tiger born and raised until his father died… I swore. I swore, but madam was inconsolable… Then she started to change… And one evening, she left with the little one… I promised his father to look after them, but I failed, and now I could see that something was brewing again. I failed in my duty again, I—"

He probably realizes that grief and worry have loosened his tongue a little too much. He censors himself, reprimands himself, and does not reveal more. His interrupted words corroborate the bomb dropped in the parking lot.

I had only focused on the apparent evidence of Sophia's trauma. But Tiger?

With the grief, the emptiness, and the pain, her mom was fragile. Bad timing for a reunion with the evil twins Alpha and Omega. And perfect timing for them. They knew what string to pull to exploit her flaws. That's what manipulators like this do, right? Spot the naive, vulnerable, unhappy, etc., people. And rip them off. There, the back work was done for them; they knew her from before. Worse, one of them had already been her lover in her youth.

The image of the kid that Tiger was haunts me. That of a little boy who had just lost his "father," the man who had raised him. The image of the overpowering, invincible Tiger cracked in my head. Sophia was not well, but neither was he. I can't lose him like this on an avalanche of secrets revealed in a three-way fight. I can't lose Sophia without begging her to forgive me, either.

No, I can't.

"Have you heard anything, Peter? No one would give me any information."

"No, we are in total ignorance, miss. I only know the name of the clinic where the rescue team took them by helicopter. Since then, nothing more."

He flinches, apologizes, and leaves the room to retreat to who knows where. Alone in the living room, I curl up. When he returns, I'll get the address of the clinic and try to force them to let me access them.

I'll take my chances. Anything but this excruciating blur.

56

PETER

MISTS OF THE PAST...

PROPERTY OF THE SEXTONS

"Peter, I hear what you're saying. But I can't help Eve without Mr. Sexton. From what I understand, both of them have been in the grip of their minds for many years."

"I know, Dr. Murphy… He's also deeply broken, even if he won't admit it."

"He can't just play the savior with her and pretend he can handle it on his own. Try to convince him… He's a fighter, and they're still young. Both need therapy."

"I'll talk to him again."

A noise occurs. Followed by an awkward silence. Mr. Sexton has returned, by surprise.

"That's not necessary, Peter; I heard you plotting," he says.

"Sir, I—"

"No one is going to make me sit and babble about how I feel or should feel anymore. I've had enough for five fucking years! And I got out of that place on my own!"

"It's not what you think, sir. Dr. Murphy was referred to me by your treating physician, he is bound by confidentiality, and he has the expertise to—"

"Damn it, Peter! I'm fine. The reason I let you back into my employ when I got back here was not so that you could fiddle around behind my back. I just didn't have anyone reliable to turn to anymore to recover—"

"I know, Mr. Sexton. You can always rely on me. I promised your father on his deathbed to look after you and your—"

"Stop! We don't talk about her! Never, Peter!"

New silence. I shrivel. The therapist's throat clearing echoes.

"If I may say so, Mr. Sexton, your butler is right, he—"

"You don't belong here, you! I saved her; I saved Eve. It's up to me to fix her now."

"Even if you are damaged yourself?"

"I'm fine!"

"Okay… I understand your mistrust. It's quite normal after such a long experience and the social position of the Sextons. But you are an heir whose comeback after a mysterious and long absence from his mother doesn't go unnoticed… Moreover, you have taken in a broken girl who has just tried to commit suicide. She will try it again because of her psychological fragility. Your trusted doctor is a friend. He and your butler both felt that the situation was far too serious and complex for you, who is also a survivor, a victim. You must—"

"GET OUT! Get the fuck out of this house, Mr. Shrink! I was never a victim, and I'll manage without you! Get out of my house!"

PETER

NOWADAYS…

"Peter?" calls my colleague. "My God, you're crying. Have you heard from the clinic?"

"No, Mary. I was overwhelmed by the past, the guilt… I have to go. Please don't tell Miss Océane. I have to… I can't leave that kid alone again. I'd never forgive myself if he didn't pull through. Cover me while I slip away."

"Okay."

OCÉANE

About five minutes later, not seeing Peter come back, I go to look for him.

"He's gone to freshen up," Mary, the cook, tells me.

"Okay, thanks."

I wait, searching on the Internet for possible scoops on Tiger and Sophia. Still nothing new, but alarmist assumptions are in abundance. I think I'm going crazy; I'm pacing around. After a while, my pacing extends to the innumerable bathrooms of the house to find the one where the butler has locked himself in. I even enter the servants' quarters on the first floor for the first time. No trace of Peter. Nor in the right and left wings of the floor. I linger in Tiger's room, overcome with melancholy. I pull myself together and run away before I crack. Outside, we hear the bustle of the journalistic anthill behind the high walls and locked gate. Even if the reporters are kept at a distance, we know they are on the lookout. I prefer not to hang around too much and end up with stolen photos. They had already taken some when I entered without knowing me…

The huge outdoor green space is empty too. Still no Peter. I wander around the pool, my head full of memories with Sophia. I think of my first day here and of so many other things…

You are not their family; no one will tell you anything if you don't get your hands on their butler.

I continue my unsuccessful search. Is it possible that Tiger's most trusted employee ran out on me? To go where, to the hospital?

I urge the other servants to help me find him.

"Sorry, miss. Peter has left urgently," one of them finally confirms.

He really ran away like a thief!

"Where did he go?"

Is it at someone's request? If so, who? To keep me away, like Anaïs did? Damn, I'm psyching myself out!

I am met with silence when I try to get clarification. Was there any fresh news that prompted Peter's hasty departure on the sly? Do the others really not know, or are they afraid of losing their jobs if they talk without explicit permission?

I'm not going to stay barricaded in a house without its owners. But I don't know where to go or what to do. Confused and worried, I call Anaïs back, in vain. I snatch the cook's phone to dial Peter's personal number. He does not answer anymore, and neither does she. In this golden prison, I have only the always succinct news on the TV and the creepy extrapolations of the rags on the Web. They rant about the worst possible scenarios.

What if you don't even know where they are and if they are still… alive?

OCÉANE

ONE, TWO, THREE… SEVEN DAYS LATER. SYDNEY

Day seven. I am on the verge of insanity.

Filled with anxiety, I am still forced to follow the situation from afar, isolated, removed from the now-locked world of the Sextons. Sorting out the flashy fake scoops and the overly succinct official information. There was no announcement of death; that's already that…

In my new morose routine, the days follow each other and look the same. The front pages of the news, idem. However, for the umpteenth time, I lend my ear when the newspaper starts:

"We have just learned. The CEO of TS Naval, Tiger Sexton, was released from the St. Anne's Clinic early Friday morning. He and his wife were victims of a car accident…

Sophia Sexton is still in the intensive care unit of the private facility, with top specialists at her bedside. Tiger Sexton, on the other hand, returned to his CBD tower. He immediately returned to the controls to stop the buzz and speculation that his condition had generated in the Sydney Stock Exchange and the business world at large.

Indeed, Sexton has scheduled a press conference for…"

My God, is he okay?!

I freeze while the car radio of the Volkswagen van continues to play. We drive with Louane, her boyfriend, and Garrett. Garrett, as obsessed as I am with every bit of news about the Sextons, has changed the station, swapping the lively music we were listening to for the news.

I wasn't originally in the mood to go on a weekend trip with them. But Miss Louane didn't leave me any choice. Here I am on a road trip through the sublime and vast Australian expanses, unable to savor the miles of beach, greenery, and the joyful atmosphere of the group. Inside, I am distraught; my mind remains hostage to a world that is not mine, with a couple I don't know as well as I thought…

What about Sophia? Damn, why can't I move on?

"I knew it!" enthuses Garrett. "This guy is invincible; he always gets off."

"Stop fangirling and put some music back on!" moans Louane, sitting next to me.

Her boyfriend, as co-pilot, goes ahead of Garrett and obeys his darling with a smile. Me, I bug. And Sophia, how is she? Damn, I'm getting feverish in spite of myself while Louane starts singing to Rihanna again.

The Sextons and I have a lot on our minds.

Will he call me? What if he's got after-effects, amnesia, and has forgotten me? What if… Would I be too pathetic if I took the initiative to call him?

Maybe he's too busy straightening out his empire. Or maybe he's just decided to ignore me for good. Everything went to shit long before their accident.

"Fake little Lily passing through, not marked, not initiated."

And they are brother and sister!

Damn, this fact that I tried to repress as far away as possible resurfaces when I learn that one of them is off the hook. They are brother and sister… Now I feel bad again. Everything changed so suddenly.

"Hey, you look pale," Louane worries. "Are you getting motion sickness? Shall we stop for a while?"

"I… No. Well, yes. A little pee break, if you don't mind?"

"Okay!" agrees Garrett behind the wheel.

As soon as the van comes to a stop, I take off and try to deal with the turmoil inside me, out in the open. For seven endless days, I've focused on their condition, holding back the effects of the bomb that devastated me before their accident. I worried about them; that was all that mattered. That they were saved. Is Sophia's condition as critical as the media is assuming? Even with this new information, how do we know that Tiger isn't just pretending to be okay, despite possible serious injuries? I have considered so many alternatives. His death, both of their deaths… Or irreversible after-effects… I lost sleep over it.

And that had overshadowed my questions, my shock about this community and all the other shadows and horrors on the board.

They come out of a cult, and they are brother and sister.

Fuck, this unbearable truth is pounding in my head now. I light a cigarette and notice the tremor in my fingers. Tiger is alive and his wife—his sister—is surely in bad shape.

It's all over. There can be nothing left after this.

I don't belong here. I need to get drunk, to move on, to… Shit, my phone is ringing!

I read his feline name on my screen. When you think of the devil, well, the tiger… But I panic, hyperventilate, and hesitate to pick up. A part of me has been hoping so hard for this call for the last seven days. In spite of everything… The ringing is insistent, and the others look at me. I end up moving away from the group to answer.

"Yes?"

"Océane?"

An expletive in English, his voice hoarse, his breath, the bump-bump in my compressed chest…

"H… How are you?" he asks me.

How am I doing? Fuck, everything has fallen apart inside me, in my head, in my heart, under my feet. I breathe in and out before replying, "I don't know."

Trouble is setting in on both sides. It is too silent.

"I hear about you from the press, like everyone else," I murmur at last, as a faded anger bubbles up inside me. "After all, I didn't deserve to be kept informed, did I?"

"I'm… I'm sorry my staff followed my instructions to be discreet in case of a problem. I've had these arrangements in place long before I knew you. They just followed those old instructions to the letter."

"Knew, that's the word. I don't know you, Tiger. If your… if Sophia hadn't gone nuts, it would have been like this all along."

He shuts up. Our breaths intermingle.

"Shall we leave, miss?" says Garrett.

"Who was that?" Tiger is immediately interested.

I signal my carpoolers to give me a few more seconds. And I whisper into the phone, "None of your business. Just tell me how you're really doing and how Sophia is doing."

"She came out of the induced coma, her prognosis is no longer vital, but she is seriously injured. Me, I… I left against medical advice. I had too much stuff on my plate."

Of course! The world can't turn around without him, right?

"We have to meet," he says, his tone imploring.

"I'm busy this weekend," I reply, overwhelmed with incomprehensible feelings. "I'll let you know when I have the time and the wish… If I ever have them."

"Please… little bud."

I get chills because now I know what it refers to…

"I… I am not a bud, nor am I a Lily, Tiger. I can't be something I don't know anything about. Like Sophia said, I'm not like you."

"Fuck!" he snaps.

Even though his voice is too muffled, as if he's taken the phone away from his mouth to swear.

"This is exactly why you weren't supposed to learn this… So we could have a chance at something more 'normal,'" he says.

Except that every time you looked at me, wanted me, touched me, I was a Lily to you. And I didn't know that your wife is also your… holy shit!

"And what is normal to you, Tiger? There's nothing normal about your life."

He's silent for too long this time; I wonder if I should hang up. I try to remain dignified between my anger and my emotional confusion about the whole thing.

"We have to meet again," he insists. "I beg you. You can ask me whatever questions you want, and I'll answer them."

Really? Or is he just trying to lure you back into a perverse matrix?

"I don't know… I have to go," I say before hanging up.

In order for him not to have time to argue, to confuse my neurons and hormones. I need to see things clearly, to take control of myself.

I can't relax when I get back into the van. I'm not going to think about anything else all weekend! I know it, I feel it, and I regret this weakness.

57

TIGER

You disgust her. You frighten her. You have lost her…

I leave the empty operating room in which I had isolated myself to call Océane. I had come back to see Sophia, but not only that… Byrne was admitted there as soon as he arrived in Australia, according to the instructions I had given to my lawyers before the accident.

Byrne Hamilton was treated—obviously, there was police violence even if all the protagonists deny it, including himself—and he will then be hospitalized on the floor reserved for psychiatry. For as long as necessary. Dr. Murphy is on the case since he is a regular of "anomalies" in my entourage…

And in me…

I had to end my patient status. No need to be infantilized and force-fed with medication; I was always against that after The Garden. Before, as a child, it was already a pain in the ass to have to see a doctor too often. With everything I've been through since then, it's even worse. I don't like being put under a microscope. Whether it's in my head or on my body.

Here, it's only physical trauma, a few cracked ribs, and visible bruises that have worried the medical team, but luckily I don't have any internal bleeding, serious fractures, or brain damage. Well, at least in theory, since I don't feel anything!

But, damn, my memory is intact. Too much shit, too many emergencies to deal with to stay in a bed, surrounded by overzealous nurses and doctors.

In front of the door to Byrne's room, I pause. When I woke up in a hospital bed, my priorities included Océane. And she just blew me off.

Which is understandable. For me, it's just awfully late to be reasonable!

This whole thing has taken an unexpected direction; this unveiling needs to be explained to be straightened out. It's eating away at my mind that she sees me differently today. The door opens before I decide to enter. I find myself face to face with Byrne's gray eyes.

"Hi, I was looking for you," he says. "I was going to call you," he adds, holding up my business card with my business number on it.

Anaïs gave it to him when I was still stoned on morphine. Just like she managed other emergencies, like keeping the access locked to anyone outside my private sphere.

And she must have felt that Océane was part of the set to be kept away. When I might have preferred to have her with us... Ugh, I don't know anymore. I just know that I have to catch up on some shit. Others are no longer fixable. I reply, "Cool, I'm here for you."

We walk into his room together. Spacious with all the comforts. I look at him for a long time, prey to my last memories with him, in the Garden. We grew up together and went scuba diving together; I had certain privileges of that kind after I was knighted... We went through the orgies together, the bullshit prayers, the Children of the Serpent training too.

Disturbed, I close the door behind us and ask him, "How are you?"

"Bad... For some things I did in Paris, to Loup, a friend. And to Maureen, the woman I loved," murmurs Byrne. "But I think I'm also happy to be back, to know that you and Eve survived. I didn't know that until Loup's brother told me while I was in France."

"My guys told him to give you this information. You know I would have done anything to get you out of there."

"Get me out of there like you got out of the Garden one day?" he throws me resentfully. "I didn't know who you were anymore, Ares. I didn't even know if the Executioner hadn't found you and cut you up for betraying your Family."

I rummage through my hair, my jaws clenching. Damn, the eruption of this stinking past is not going to stop!

"I went and mobilized the necessary means to get my mother

and all the kids—including you—out of this mystical mess," I say.

No matter how much I justify myself, I've never stopped blaming myself for coming back too late. The memory of the piled-up corpses disturbs my breathing. My mother was there, lying with them, pressed against Alpha.

She killed herself with them.

That cult had consumed all of her. No more reason, no more ability to think for herself, no more grief over her widowhood. Only senseless and irrational obedience, an abnormal well-being with them, a total devotion. Even I didn't matter as much as those guru bastards. I tried to make her react, to rekindle her neurons regularly shot with LSD and stupid preaching. To get her to run away with me.

But nothing. She only dreamed of group fucks and the Final Flight.

If I knew how to resist and pulled myself together after sinking with her and all the others, my mother wouldn't fight. She let go. Her free will didn't exist anymore; she was relieved of everything and submitted to the will of a third party who thought for her and dictated how she should live.

Byrne stares at me, as dark as my thoughts. A memory takes root in my mind.

That of the day I threw out my hypothesis about their true progenitor at the Garden. Questioning a prayer I was forced to recite. It was at the very beginning… I still had the strength and the desire to rebel. I hear myself vehemently rebutting: "Nonsense, Alpha doesn't create anyone with the blessing of the Sacred Serpent! You have your real parents here! Look at Byrne, for example. He, Annie, and Eve are mixed. Their mother must be the only black person here. And I know my mom and my real dad! Courtney and Nick Sexton!"

So many certainties jostled for each of us, compartment moved, truncated, tangled afterward. I had my first forced "prayer of repentance." They locked me up with Omega and the Executioner, delivered to all the perverse ideas of torture that they had concocted to "bring me back on the right path."

My body has no memory of pain. On the other hand, my mind, which ended up failing… for a long time, will remember it forever…

I grit my teeth and breathe in to straighten out my saturated gray matter.

"You've let us down," Byrne tells me again.

"I didn't abandon you," I maintain. "You were my family; you still are."

"Don't you fucking use that word anymore!" he snaps. "People like us don't know anything about what family really is!"

He's not wrong… Everyone fucked almost everyone or attended the initiation rites of the youngest. Most did not know their real filiation. Incest, sacred bonds, taboos, and the prohibitions of real society did not exist on the farm. They worked hard to deconstruct, to reprogram the education I had received before, during the first eleven years of my life. Right, wrong, what I thought I knew. Not hesitating to drug myself without my knowledge, like all the followers of the sect. In order to be more receptive to "sensory and divine experiences."

At the age of 12, barely pubescent, I ended up getting laid on command. I became a soldier of the cause, a stud, an uncensored sex addict, and a lot of other shit. For too long. My mother never got the jolt of clarity I was hoping for, so hope died, and my brain became more and more malleable.

"I want to see Eve. Is she the only one left? Did you find Annie, or is she… dead with all the parents?"

I grit my teeth, thinking hard about the best way to announce what my men have learned after long hours of torture on the Executioner and Omega.

"There's only Eve left… Her name is Sophia today," I confirm. "I… I thought you knew about Annie. Wasn't she with you during your escape from the cult with the other part of the former leaders?"

I thought so for years. That everyone I didn't see among the dead was still under the thumb of the evil twin and his one-eyed sidekick. Under the radar and still as rotten as ever.

"No," denies Byrne. "We were split into small groups. In my convoy, there was just the Executioner and the twins Cain and Azura. I was convinced that we were the only survivors. Later on…"

Yeah, those two, we found their tracks. With their new French identities and the pseudonyms of Typhoon and Echidna in the filthy obtuse brotherhood where they failed. Byrne—who was Aaron in that other disgusting circle—stops talking for a moment. He rubs his swollen face in places and grimaces. Which brings up a question again that eats away at me.

Did he get into a fight before his arrest in France, or did they beat him up in his cell to get information out of him? I need to know for sure. Know how to cover myself just in case… and how to attack the cops involved if necessary. If there was police brutality, whether they got information about The Garden or not, my lawyers would destroy the cops involved and invalidate all the data collected.

"Later?" I insist, on edge to find out what happened next.

"Later, I ran into Omega again. And I understood that he was the mastermind behind running away. He had helped found a new organization in a castle of debauchery. I was still trapped in a life that had been decided for me."

"Yeah, *La Confrérie*. My teams identified the founders. The Executioner and Omega have obviously made friends in Europe who are just as perverse as they are."

"Exactly. They were now One-Eye and Shadow, more powerful than ever and well surrounded."

"That's over now. Each one of them gets exactly what they deserve, believe me."

"Mm, yeah…"

At least we agree on something, right? Byrne sits back down, too badly. We both look terrible, but I stand there, stiff with apprehension. I have to tell him. To Sophia, ditto, when she can take it.

"Byrne, Annie didn't make it. She was alive after the Flight; Omega took her with him when he escaped. She and the little girl she gave birth to at the Garden."

"No?"

He straightened up.

"They had kept them with him? Were they in France, too?"

"Yes, I got confirmation of that."

"And what… what happened to them?"

"They lived with him there, hidden in a mansion. Like human puppets to distract Omega. And from what my investigators learned, he and the Executioner killed them when Annie tried to leave with her child. The French police exhumed their bodies."

Byrne lets out a scream and slams his fist against the wall. Pain twists his features.

"Damn, they should have been bled like pigs, those two sons of bitches!" he rages. "One-Eye was trapped; he was done like a rat with the mutilations on the targets in Europe. We had him!"

I tick, but I don't interrupt Byrne. An almost mad glow shines in the depths of his eyes, fueled by too much trauma, horror, guilt, and rage endured throughout his life. It seems to have demolished parts of the light in him. Inevitably. Aren't we all pretty much there? Him, Sophia, me.

"I guess," I say to punctuate Byrne's words.

"That bastard knew he was in danger of going down; I'm sure he realized that sooner or later in the investigation in France, suspicions would converge on him and his record as the Garden Executioner with the barbaric acts and marks affixed to these people… Instead of freaking out about being cornered, it excited him and made him want to kill them one by one. This overkill galvanized him. And then everything went wrong."

My jaws clench. I'm afraid I've grasped the unspeakable.

"What a fucking mess!" my "brother-in-law" rages. "Loup, his girl, Maureen, and so many others have paid the price in Paris by their fault. The cyclops and the other heartless deserve the worst; the clink is too sweet an end for them."

"Don't worry about it," I say carefully.

"No, I just can't get over it, man. How can I accept that they're just sitting in cells still hard from the memories of the evil they distilled into so many people's lives?"

"I understand you…

I can't stand such a "humane" punishment for them, either. I hesitate before adding, "In fact… by now, they will never be able to hurt anyone again. You have my word, Byrne."

Our eyes lock together, charged with a common hatred. My cult brother reads the unspoken in me. It's over; the circle is complete, and these monsters will no longer exist. I have live proof of this, just as I have the videos of the atrocities we all suffered because of them.

"Are you sure?" he asks me darkly.

"You know me."

He falls back, ass over heels on his bed, exhausted, and mutters with a sort of relief, "Fuck. So, it's over."

I press my eyelids and clench my teeth. No need to discuss the details; he understood. And he digests the news, breathes, and rubs his hair. After long chaotic breaths, his nerves relax.

"That's it, Maureen, that's it," he repeats softly as for himself.

It is the woman whom he loved and lost in La Confrérie. A wound obviously remained open...

"We must inform Khà Gai," resumes Byrne.

"Who is that?"

"Marjorie Dumont, in Paris. For Loup, for her and others... she'll need to know that these fuckers are no longer a threat."

I make a mental note of this and nod silently. This lady's name came up in the file on Morgan Sinclair, aka Loup. She is also mentioned in the list of assisted witnesses of the French justice... So she is not an ordinary girl of *La Confrérie*. I will see; maybe I will contact her later.

That's all I'll say. Byrne and I stare at each other.

"Did you marry her?" he catches me off guard after a long moment. "Eve's name is now Sophia Sexton, so you're with her?"

"Yes, I am."

"Why?"

"What do you mean why?" I put myself on the defensive.

"Dude, you weren't interested in Eve any more than you were interested in any other Garden Lily. Don't give me some bullshit like you fell madly in love. You, you're not capable of feeling that kind of feeling."

Of course, in his eyes, I am still Ares. The invincible, the insensitive. The one who fucks around, who can be beaten to a pulp without flinching, and who returns the blows with an unstoppable fury that nothing can touch, especially not emotions. So I'm still that guy whose every trace of being in that cult I've erased, that guy who I've put a social filter on to readjust to the outside world.

To become again the "impure seed" that I was at the beginning, at my birth. A Sexton with a pedigree to preserve. And yet, no one can erase it all. Especially not this...

"I married her to better protect her, Byrne. And maybe I protected myself, too, I admit. At least, I was convinced of it at the time. We were not like other people, like normal people. I was torn between two worlds, two realities. Eve was even more lost than I was, frozen in a mirage. After the basics received in The Garden, restarting her life from scratch was insurmountable for her. I felt capable of overcoming everything, and I had to teach her the norms of real society to offer her an official, stable and sheltered existence. But also citizenship, a birth certificate…"

Everything that the children born in the sect were deprived of and never knew. Their parents, under the influence, made offerings of them to the guides; they were the "property" of Alpha and Omega. They belonged to the Garden as Lilies or Children of the Serpent, devoted, obedient, marked, and appeared nowhere else. An army of little puppets turned into ghosts like their progenitors. Without legal existence with the civil services. Unlike me.

Officially, I was still perceived, known, and recognized as "Tiger Sexton."

"I see," says Byrne. "Now she really exists."

He and I both know the value of that simple verb.

"Yes… After The Garden, your journey in France, you also need to take ownership of your life. To choose under which identity you want to exist fully. I promise to help you; I am here for you, I promise."

"Help me how? Are you going to marry me too?"

Against all odds, we both end up laughing.

"Don't take it personally," I reply, "but I decline your offer. Dicks have never been my thing."

He laughs his ass off.

"Oh, yeah, I remember that! All those lilies moaning in your arms in the ritual tent. That degenerate Omega had a hard-on."

I know, damn it. I know…

58

Océane

Idle and alone again in my hotel room at the beginning of this week, I give the key to my room to the receptionist and answer politely to her, "Have a good day, miss!"

Good, it won't be. I'm too lost for that.

Nevertheless, I start my resume distribution tour again. Even though the indecent amount of money wired to my account by the Sextons keeps me out of trouble. And even if I could spend the rest of my stay idling, lounging on the beaches, traveling around Australia, and going to bars and nightclubs, I need some kind of balance.

Keeping my mind busy and working has become imperative.

"The devil makes work for idle hands," as my mother used to say. So, I doubled my motivation in the search for a new job. Not to succumb to the ultimate vice again:

Tiger Sexton.

I don't want to call him back. I panic at the thought of seeing him again because I don't know what stupid reaction I might have in his presence. I'm afraid that this damn chemistry between us will get me into trouble again. Literally and figuratively.

And then there's Sophia. There has always been Sophia. There will always be Sophia.

I don't have to get caught up in complications to spice up my life anymore. Simplicity suits me just fine. Doesn't it?

Half-determined, I continue with my spontaneous job applications, crossing my fingers when someone kindly tells me that I might be contacted again. In the afternoon, I hang out again without any desire to go back to the hotel. Tiger might show up…

Without really knowing what I was doing, I ended up in front of the Velvet & Diamonds with the owner's card between my fingers. This one had offered me a job, right? In the worst case, if I don't find anything else, I could…

Hell, no!

It would be a sure way to see the Sextons again, wouldn't it? Although by the time they're willing and able to set foot there again after Sophia's recovery, I'll probably have left this country. It's worth a try…

I enter the club, not completely sure what I want.

TIGER

I just left a business meeting, the last one I had to rush through to prove that I had effectively taken over the reins. Uncle James was too fond of trying to control my board of directors in my absence.

There was a reason he was ousted. The man is incompetent, power-hungry, and narrow-minded. Of course, once again, he was disgusted to see me come back as right before my majority. This son that his brother wanted as the sole heir to the Sexton estate. Even though I won and got it all back, the grudge is strong. I can never respect that scum!

Clear your head, clear your head. Take a breath.

I hit the brakes in front of TS Naval. I don't want to go home. The penthouse is Océane. Sydney's property too. I feel her everywhere. Although I also feel guilt, given Sophia's condition, I can't get this blonde girl out of my head. I hesitate for a moment, then pick up my phone again. It rings, but she seems not to want to answer it.

Pick it up. Damn it, pick up…

"Tiger, I told you to give me time to—" she starts in a weary voice.

"To digest? To hate me even more? To be disgusted with me? To run away from me?"

"Even if I do all that, I have the right to do it after what happened, don't I?"

"I'm not arguing with you, Océane. I just want you to give me a few minutes. Do we deserve this?"

"*We?*" she repeats, incredulous.

"Yes, *we*, you and me."

Her silence disarms me. I would almost prefer her to jump down my throat to insult me.

"There is no you and me. You and Sophia are inseparable. Even for me. And she… she was right; our paths must part. You don't have to answer to me, but to her."

I take that truth hard.

"All right."

I'm the one who hangs up. I have never felt so alone. My head is spinning, and the dizziness I have had since I left the clinic is returning. Stronger. With hot flashes. Either this conversation is shaking me in an unusual way, or something is medically wrong. I can't fall apart now, yet my vision is blurred, weakening…

Océane

Ten days later. Sydney

It's over. Everything is over.

No more Tiger, no more Sophia. At least, not for me. But it hurts like hell; it's worse than a "traditional" breakup. It's painfully unique and suffocating because these two meant so much to me. Intensely and in a different way, they each filled a gap in me. Perhaps I did the same for them?

Right, fool yourself, girl. That's how the pathos starts.

Too hard to keep moving forward without looking back. Again, because my choices were a flop. So I cling to that umpteenth self-motivation mantra: yes, it's over; it's all over.

I took the job I was offered at Velvet & Diamonds, waitressing in the restaurant area. Working nights has a positive side: I'm so exhausted in the morning that I sleep like a log all day. And in the evening, it's back to work, without respite, to think as little as possible.

I'm going to make it, overcome this obstacle.

I doubt it while adjusting my uniform, white shirt, little black skirt, and matching pumps. Sexy, but not so practical when you walk all evening between the kitchens and the dining room. I return to the room to take care of the customers that the hostess has installed at one of the tables assigned to me. As I approach the man whose back and neck I can only see, I have a strange feeling. A woman I don't know is sitting in front of him… Then, this instinctive feeling is confirmed when I stop at their level.

Oh. Shit!

"G… good evening, mam… sir. Welcome to Velvet; I'm Océane," I say as I tangle my fingers on the two restaurant cards I'm holding.

My gaze is suddenly locked on Tiger's, without any mental preparation, completely caught off guard. The lady answers me. But he doesn't move one iota; his magnetic eyes stare at me without an ounce of surprise.

He knew I was working there. He came on purpose.

"I'll… let you look at the menu. Would you like something to drink while you wait?"

"Shanna, can you take a smoke break outside, please?" commands Tiger calmly without turning his eyes away. "And take your time."

Intrigued, the other one stares at us in turn. She smiles and stands up.

"Good idea! I had indeed suddenly wanted to smoke," she teases him. "By the way, nice to meet you, Océane," she says to me.

She grabs her bag and her car keys, in all likelihood, and leaves, leaving me speechless.

"Sit down," Tiger calmly tells me.

I glance anxiously to the left and right. I notice with amazement that the place is unusually empty. As if it… had been privatized at the last minute so that there would be no witnesses to this moment.

"What are you doing here?"

"I came to eat," he ironically says. "And perhaps to discuss if you allow me."

I freeze, inwardly devastated.

"We… we have nothing more to talk about. It's over, Tiger."

"I don't think so. If you'd rather, I'll do the Q&A on my own. Then I'll leave."

I swallow and shake my head.

"You just want to talk? I doubt it. It's funny; once again, I have this feeling of *déjà vu*. We're in a vicious circle."

"I'm serious."

"You always are, Tiger. A twisted, serious dictator."

He takes it in, bites his lip, and then suddenly, with his index finger and thumb, he lowers it. That lip. A thick, black line is etched into it. I blink.

The tattoo in the mouth. The marking they administered in the sect at puberty. My heart misses a beat as if a part of me still wishes he would swear to me that Sophia had made it all up, that she was out of her mind, ranting because of jealousy.

But no, it's really there. Surely under this line, a name was erased. A part of his past was killed forever. A shiver runs down my spine.

"It was written by Ares," he confesses. "Listen, we won't have sufficient time tonight to tell you everything I want and need to explain."

"Ares…" I repeat, dumbstruck, moved.

He tenses up when he hears it.

"That makes me the biggest impostor. When one lifts the veil, that one unlocks all; I am nobody. And sometimes I get lost in this icy void made of scratches and ghosts."

His frankness is striking in delivering this brutal confession.

"I have respect for you, Océane, as I have for few people," he argues. "That is why I want to have this conversation with you. In a neutral place."

I moisten my lips because his attention deviates there. As if to tell me that this choice of place is wiser for both of us. Anywhere else would have been a mistake. This thing between us electrifies the air too easily and gives me goosebumps under his blue eyes.

"Please, sit down," he repeats.

"Okay."

Instead of serving, I settle down like a customer of this fancy restaurant. Well, a lost customer. Tiger is waiting to order from a second waiter who is sent to us. Scotch for him…

I'm going to need some hard liquor too?

"Vodka," I say, my voice weakened.

The seconds pass, locking me in his eyes. We don't brush against each other; nevertheless, my hair stands on end, and my breath becomes disorganized. Everything jostles in me: the interrogations, the reproaches, the uncertainties. And this stupid need pushes me to adore the way he has to contemplate me as the world's eighth wonder.

I throw myself on my glass as soon as it is filled and keep the bottle to give me composure. I take a breath and ask him, "How long were you in that cult, Tiger?"

"Five years. I had just turned 12 when my mother sought refuge from her grief over the death of my… father. Of Nick Sexton. And I was 17 when I came to my senses. At least I had an ersatz free will that woke up one day, so I tried to repair the damage."

I absorb his words. His entire adolescence was spent in a freedom-deprived, brainwashed, deviant environment. Probably a lot of his first times too. First kisses, first emotions…

No, he's not an ordinary man. Neither is his wife.

"How long did Sophia spend there?"

"She doesn't have an exact date of birth. About eighteen years, I would say… She was born there and only left The Garden when it was over, as I told you before. I forced her to follow me; she was in shock and lost… More than me."

"Did you love her? I mean, were you already a couple in the… Garden?"

"No. There was no such thing as a couple; everyone had multiple partners. And sometimes, the guides would make and break relationships to better manipulate the whole group."

"Their notion of brotherhood was very shady, too, from what I understand. So, what's your marriage all about, Tiger? Is that your sister?"

"I was led to believe that for a while. I doubted it; I knew where I was coming from… Afterward, my brain was so screwed up that I believed it. I felt like yet another son of Alpha, as they put it in the skull of every child in the cult. Later… Peter managed to steal for me and provide me with the DNA of my uncle, James Sexton. Peter worked for him when my mother left with me… Anyway, I wanted to know for sure when I started my therapy when I was 19."

"And?"

"It didn't work out. Sophia is… She's really my half-sister, DNA test to prove it."

"Damn!"

He studies my reaction, himself pale and stiff but still filled with a destabilizing charisma.

"There's nothing carnal between her and me since. But I'm still learning to see myself as a Sexton. Not a Hamilton. Because I realized from Peter that Nick Sexton, my… father on my papers, knew the truth. Especially because of my congenital analgesia, he had put me through a battery of tests when I was a kid. He had discovered, among other things, the adulterous relationship of my mother. I had been conceived with another. This implied that my… mother would intermittently see Alpha, her childhood boyfriend when her relationship was shaky. I was too little and imagined that everything was perfect in their marriage. It was far from it, but Nick knew that."

"And what did he do?"

"He thought he had a hand in it, working hard to get the family business back on its feet. Feeling that he was too often absent, the pain of the deception was diluted in his remorse… His wife ended the affair, at least, I think. And Nick loved me. This man really loved me as if I were his. So much so that he made Peter swear to always take care of us and keep this secret. In his eyes, I was and should remain a Sexton, his son. Because he was crazy about his wife, he ended up covering up this story… I never had to doubt his fatherly love."

Tiger downs his glass and refills his second one. I fiddle with mine, with a lump in my throat.

"He must have been a wonderful man."

"A role model for me. Especially after… when I had to hold on to something to keep from falling apart. As bad as I felt about myself, I had to honor his memory and clear his name of all that tainted it. I had to live up to her expectations of me, to be better than… my mother."

"So, did Sophia fit into this same context? Was she just a dirty secret that became a duty? A way to ease your conscience? For not being able to save your mother and everyone else?"

He remains silent for a long time. His head nods slowly.

"When I married Sophia, I was too young; I had too many horrors in my head, especially the guilt of not having been able to do anything for my mother," he admits. "Sophia only knew me; she clung to me. She was terrified and lost."

I can imagine…

"She was my responsibility," says Tiger. "For my part, I was trying to find my place in the life I was supposed to have under normal conditions if it hadn't been for that clean break, those years stolen by the cult. Well, at first, before I was fixed on that. I was obsessed with getting my inheritance back. Not for greed but for Nick Sexton, the only real father I had. After I knew, I wanted even more to be the son he deserved to have."

Because this man has passed on to you his nobility of spirit. No, Tiger Sexton is not an impostor; he is the indelible trace left here on earth by this Nick Sexton.

This is sometimes worth more than the genes we did not choose or the blood that runs in our veins. Without daring to express my opinion, I know that I would have liked to meet his father, to tell him that everything positive about Tiger comes from him…

My eyes are wet. Tiger stares at them, unsure of what to do, helpless and so… broken actually. Even though he has sealed everything up and built up an ironclad armor. His wounds, his sufferings are there, certainly complex, deep, but so well hidden that it has made him unapproachable…

"How did you do it?" I say after having drunk a sip of vodka.

"I worked hard. I learned in a hurry everything I needed to know to take over the reins that were rightfully mine—according to my father's wishes—at the head of his company."

"It must not have been easy."

He agrees bitterly.

"In addition to my conscience which told me that I was not legitimate, my guilt and other direct consequences related to the cult… I also had to juggle with Uncle James. He opposed my taking power under the pretext that I had to be of age, have studied and obtained the necessary university degrees, etc. I was afraid he would find out that I was not his brother's biological child. I had an irrational fear of failure, and especially of disappointing my father."

For a moment, he struggles to speak. I see the turmoil in his eyes, all the things that tug at him… Even years later. And that chill has probably never gone away. I inquire, my chest tight, "He never knew?"

"No… In itself, this would not be a problem in the estate since my father made all the arrangements. But there was another obstacle at the time: an archaic clause imposed in the Sexton line. To take over, I had to have a stable life and be married."

"Damn! Psychologically, you were in no condition to… I mean, I guess your relationship with women was completely distorted."

"Maybe it still is a little bit today… Until you…"

My heart leaps. I don't know what to say to that. Tiger seems almost freaked out that he said it. He hurriedly went on, "His brother had gotten the respect and admiration that James lacked. My father surpassed him in everything. So James took his resentment out on me, Nick's extension of him. If only he had known…"

"He would probably have humiliated you in the public square by spilling the beans; in the end, your father's name and memory would be tarnished," I understand.

That is the stakes. A noble battle on the one hand, against resentment and greed on the other.

"Thus, James, seeking to discredit me in order to disinherit me, stepped into another breach that I did not expect: he tried, as a last resort, to make me look like an unbalanced person, unable to manage because of my past. That's when I understood."

"Understood what?"

"That he knew about The Garden. He was the only one who knew the truth about my mother and my disappearance. Or rather, our so-called retreat from the society life, the official version."

I watch him take another sip. His face darkens, and he rivets his blue marbles to my questioning and distressed gaze.

"I… I'm not sure I understand everything, Tiger."

He pinches the bridge of his nose, then says, "When I was enrolled with my mother, I thought at first that no one would come to our rescue because no one knew where we were. We had left civilization on the sly… I tried several times to run away to warn someone. Peter or my uncle, what was left of my references. In fact, I could never get very far for years. I was caught, punished…"

The Executioner. I have goosebumps and so much bitterness.

"No savior showed up," Tiger continues. "I realized after my successful escape when I was 17 that James Sexton had let my mother be taken in by Alpha without lifting a finger or trying to pull her up. He watched her go downhill… It suited him to have us vanish into thin air. His greed came before his humanity, before his nephew who was a burden to his ambitions."

"Oh, my God!"

"That asshole, even though he never knew I wasn't his brother's biological son, didn't look for us and didn't count on us coming back. Peter found out—unfortunately, too late—that they had made a deal. James gave my mother cash to get her shares back and to expropriate us. This money and the Frida Kahlo paintings that my father had given to his wife while he was alive ended up in the hands of Omega in France. The 'Queen of Flowers' had donated them to the Garden."

Tiger stands up, suddenly unable to sit still. He paces back and forth. I stay glued to my chair, deeply shaken. He seems to have a visceral grudge against his mother too.

Between her and his bastard uncle, I realize how much fate was against him. And this cult and everything that happened in it nailed it.

And I see a stoic fighter still standing strong after all that.

59

TIGER

I pace around the restaurant, riddled with memories. I try to close the doors, but there are no more locks. Not with her. I can't close myself, can't stop her from seeing deeper into me. The look in Océane's eyes, her very real emotions reach into my guts.

That famous cursed evening, damn it, I can't stop the mental images either.

In the Australian outback. Eleven years ago… Under the main tent, the huge symbol is drawn with chalk on the ground. The emblem of the Garden, this fucking reptile! Offerings, wreaths of greenery, and flower petals line the path to the circle. Cups have fallen; they litter here and there in a scent of apocalypse…

I'm groggy; it can't be real. They? Are they all… No, not her, not her, not her, not…

My breathing stops. My retina refuses to print what I am facing. Even the children are inanimate in a frozen silence.

Am I too late?

Far ahead, it looks like Alpha, self-appointed "supreme guide." Fuck, he, too… and other members… are lying there.

My heart lurches. Where is she?!

"Mom?" I can't pronounce this word for so long… Where are you, Mom?

I arrive after the massacre. The fear freezes my bones. Guilt too. I should have done more to get them out of there. I should have come earlier, even if I didn't have a plan…

Their final damn flight! The meager hope that was making its way into my shocked mind was fading with each heartbeat.

Did she stop in time?

Yes, it's still possible. I hope you made the right decision… For once…

I start looking again, dazed, unable to count properly. I can't trust the result: are there any missing? I think they are not all there. Who is missing? What are the reasons? Where are the ones I can't see?

Horrified to have to check the faces to be sure, I suffocate. The sight of the kids frozen in the fetal position gives me goosebumps. It's drumming in my chest. My sweaty hands lift up hair in an attempt to identify it; I pray all I can that she is somewhere else. If there is a God who listens to me, please let her be far from here, safe and sound.

Come back to her, less stupid!

Ridiculous prayer, but I cling to what I can in front of this hell. The heaps of body envelopes. No more life. Bluish lips, cold skin, pallid complexions. I fall on my knees near a body, and I hyperventilate.

I recognize her.

My mother, their Queen… Fuck, you drank it too. I shake her, then hug her with all my might.

Why? Why? Why didn't you understand that you were getting stuck?

"Noooo! Not without me! Noooo!" shouts a female voice.

Cracking the morbid calm of the place and bringing me out of my state.

React, Tiger. React. You have to react.

I can't let go of the lifeless body I'm still hugging. But the hysteria of the chick behind me forces me to turn back to her.

Get them out, get them out… That's what I was planning.

"Are they all gone?" she asks me, sobbing.

She, too, is looking for eyes but can't fix them on anyone. Looking horror in the face is unbearable for most normal humans. Me, I'm already screwed up at the core. It must be worse for her, I imagine.

"I am Eve, a devoted Lily of the Garden. They can't go without me, not without me," she repeats.

I get up, stunned. My body and brain try to get back on track as best they can. Not that I have the strength, but the one in front of me is a thousand times more stunned to see her reality breaking up.

Eve, a devoted Lily of the Garden, I remember her. It is necessary to get her out of there. And her companions, if there are any left…

"Hey," I whisper. "Are there any other survivors?"

Shocked, she doesn't react. She seems unreal to me, just like the rest. It is senseless, unspeakable. Outside, the world continues to run "normally" in the rest of the country, while a bunch of people have just died together in this shitty place isolated from everything!

"To the Celestial Garden… not without me, not without me," mumbles Eve.

"Hey," I say again when my vocal cords manage to make a new sound. "Is it just you?"

"All of them are gone… All of them except me. It was all together. All together."

All right. I try to do the math again, according to the data I had collected before… I look again at the lifeless body I was holding a few seconds ago. I clench my fists, directing my attention to the girl.

"So, you were lucky. Where were you?"

"In the Celestial Garden, not without me, not without me…"

"Look at me," I say, trying to get her out of her monologue.

You're fucking alive! All these lost souls can't say the same anymore. Neither can my… mother…

Eve's eyes have a crazy gleam in them, all lights out in her, just that glimmer of unwavering belief. We are both shocked, but not for the same reason. I ran here to save as many as I could; she wanted to "fly away" with her people.

In the end, we both failed.

"Not without me, not without me, not without me," she keeps on repeating. I shake her. She recites a prayer in "the language of the Garden."

I try to explain the situation to her in a rational way. Unfortunately, reason is banned from this place. How can I blame her?

"We don't have much time," I tell her. "You have to get out of here; come with me. Help me carry her."

I walk back to the cold, softened body on a carpet of petals. And I have the impression of speaking in the void. Deep down, I don't know what the hell I'm doing anymore. But I'm not going to put down roots here. Too many deaths, too many questions, too many suffocating negative waves.

And I have to get her out of here.

Peter is waiting for me far away in one of Dad's Bentleys. To support me. Even though we're too late. Way too late. I have to shake myself!

"Eve! Come with me," I say, coming back to squeeze the shoulders of the only survivor present. "The police will surely come; there is only you to save."

"No, 'the others' won't save me," she whispers to me. "I respect the Dogma. I distance myself from the 'other,' from the 'impure seed' that grows outside," she begins to recite fervently. "You have become someone else, Ares; go away!"

"Nobody wants to hurt you, and neither do I. I want to help you. And the police must do their job, even if they show up too late."

"No... The Children of the Serpent will not let them desecrate our land," she persists in a whisper.

"There's no one left with you, Eve. Let me help you; I couldn't do it with..."

My voice chokes for a moment.

"No one will 'protect' this shitty place anymore!"

"Blasphemy! You are impure! I have faith. The Snake protects its young... The Guide was supposed to take us all on our ultimate journey. But they didn't want me anymore. They left me behind. Why did they leave without me?"

"Damn it! Now you're free, you understand?" I say. *"I'll be there for you."*

60

Océane

Tiger seems to be elsewhere. Tormented. Tortured by the darkness inside him. As if he was silently screaming, bleeding from the inside. His breathing is anarchic, saturated. He keeps walking, clutching his hair.

"Tiger? Is this too much for you? Let's stop shaking things up if you—"

"No! I…"

He stares at me, almost lost.

"Where was I?" his cracked voice asks me.

"You were talking about James Sexton."

"Yeah… Long story short, I had to shut him up and live up to his standards in every way."

Anyway, he was under too much pressure after going through hell. Especially at the age he was when he ran away from this community. Plus, there was the finale, the death of so many people he had been around.

And instead of supporting him, his bastard uncle was willing to push him further down for his inheritance!

"That man is disgusting!" I say, outraged.

Tiger gives me a half smile. As if to prove to me that it doesn't bother him anymore, that he has transcended it.

"Millions and other valuable assets were at stake. It's never clean in these circumstances," he philosophizes.

No, money is not supposed to be more important than the values, the moral sense, the blood ties between two brothers. Because it was his brother's son, for God's sake!

"How did you do it?"

"I've tried to keep my mind strong. It helps to be innately insensitive," he says sarcastically. "My congenital analgesia may have helped... No pain, just hate and determination. I became self-taught; I learned on the job to assimilate the essentials at a crazy speed, almost to the point of overwork. I had to convince the important people in the company. I worked like crazy. Then, some of my father's faithful collaborators were still there to support me if needed. An internal chess game. After I came of age, I got rid of James, who was squandering everything with his mismanagement... He had sold off part of our assets to Carter Industries, among others."

So, this dislike of Harry Carter also stems from that. His family took advantage of the Sextons' bad situation.

"Of course, I had to get everything back from the Carters later on."

Which must not have been easy either... And I thought, when I met the Sexton couple, that Tiger had probably taken it easy in the best private schools and the most prestigious universities. That everything had been easy for the rich heir that he is. I was so wrong.

Unable to speak, I take another sip.

"And... Peter has always been there as a bridge between what I could have been and what I have become by force of circumstance," Tiger continues. "He spontaneously put himself at my service. He had a lot of respect and admiration for my father. I also had Bindi and Anat at the stud. They were my reference points, a kind of lighthouse that kept me on course..."

"Thankfully... Because you were sailing on rough waters, and you also had to be a rock for Sophia."

A chain of duties and responsibilities. Of goals to achieve and rigor to make up for the time "lost" in the cult. Fuck, I understand better. This mania for control, this need to master everything. He had no choice.

There was no room for lightness or even... love? I mean, maybe Sophia and him loved each other in all that chaos? Disturbed by so much upheaval...

A twinge of guilt prevents me from asking. Their bond may have been unhealthy and painful, but it withstood everything, especially the worst.

"Sophia?" understands Tiger without my saying so. "I was sure I had to protect her; we needed each other, I think… You people can only imagine… We keep real traces in us. Of all the perversions, of the orgies, of the no-limit fucking, of the deaths… Fuck, yes, of all those deaths! I told myself that no one could understand me and accompany me better than her in our fight to reclaim our lives. And vice versa."

A stressful, haunting, necessary question continues to laminate me from the inside. Tiger has finally stopped walking. The demons of the past give way to his doubts. All his attention is focused on me. He has laid himself bare, yet he is still disarming. It's even worse; my heart shudders with fear when I finally dare to ask, "How do you feel about her, Tiger? What feelings do you have for Sophia today?"

TIGER

My feelings…

I'm not even sure I know exactly how to identify them, how to define them. And yet, I have wasted time in therapy, in my sensory deprivation chamber, in women, too many women… Unable to find the right words, I remain mute in front of the only one to whom I have just poured out all this.

Océane's sad look reaches me more than any other has done before. She takes another drink, then stares at the bottom of her glass. I sit back down. I think she's dodging me. My hand reaches out to hers and grabs her over the table. When she looks up, I see that her eyelashes are beading with tears.

"I… I understand," she says, pulling her fingers away. "What you and Sophia have been through together is special, unique… You have lived in two worlds and experienced two realities together. Even if now, you know that there was incest… you didn't separate. That, I confess, is beyond me. I'm not up to it… But I sincerely hope that she will recover quickly and well. I… I have to go back to work."

Damn it! A nameless terror starts to growl inside me. I've said too much. And in light of morals and social norms that have never been erased for Océane, I know what a man like me looks like.

Too debauched, too perverted, too different, too broken.

I know it, but damn it, everything in me refuses to let her escape. Escape me.

"I…" she starts. "I thank you for coming to explain all this to me. I have to go."

Océane gets up. I reel off without thinking, "Wait!"

"Tiger, don't make this any more complicated."

"Does seeing red when someone else tries to get from a woman what I would like to be the only one to have to correspond to a feeling? Does thinking about her, even at serious, unlikely times, mean anything? Does realizing that I miss her to the point of suffocation, that she haunts me more than any ghost of the underworld I've been through count?"

She holds her breath, I feel her on the verge of tears, and my anguish fizzles out! Frenzied, I add, "And love to make her laugh, make her blush, make her wet, make her come? Is that what we are talking about, my sweet?"

Does she see me distraught? In a loss of control?

"Tell me, tell me if what I just said sounds like feelings, Océane. I'm begging you."

"I… I guess so," she whispers.

"Then no, I don't feel that way about Sophia. I never felt that way about her, or I wouldn't have done this…"

She blinks as I slowly push a kraft envelope toward her.

"What is it?"

"That's for you to find out…"

She lifts the edge, her fingers trembling. My nerves intensify as she pulls out the documents and begins to read the first page.

Her beautiful eyes become round, almost catastrophic. They freeze on me.

"You… you…" she hesitates. "Damn it, is that…"

"The divorce papers, finally signed by Sophia."

"Oh, fuck!" she staggers.

She falls back on her chair, pale with shock.

"I… I don't understand."

I take a long breath.

"This is not the first time I have wished to end our marriage. When I felt that she could stand on her own two feet, there were unsuccessful attempts… Nothing was ever easy between us; she was having a hard time with my rejection after the DNA test. It created more confusion and triggered depression and relapse. I had several suicide blackmail attempts on her part. It was like we were stuck in an unhealthy box, and we had lost the key."

Océane probes me; I hold her gaze. Too many emotions are coming out to make her dizzy.

"Why now?" she whispers. "Why is she giving in this time? Is it… my fault?"

"No, the accident. We had a near-death experience together. I think it made her think as much as me about our choices, our mistakes, and all those chains we haven't really managed to break…"

"But precisely, she is also weakened by the accident," underlines Océane. "Is it the right time to leave her, given this fragility in her mind? What if she flinches again?"

This protective side that she adopts towards Sophia… Does she fucking understand that this also makes her unique in my eyes? In our relationship, any other woman in my bed would have just tried to use that to her advantage. And Océane is worried about Sophia.

"I think she's finally ready to let go… I'm not giving up on her; just clarifying the situation with clearer boundaries. But I will always be there for her, and she knows that."

Océane, livid, moistens her lips and fiddles with her shirt collar.

"Probably…" she hesitates. "But after the time I spent with Sophia… I saw how vulnerable she is, how much she has you under her skin whatever she does… You, you have closed this chapter in your way. Only I can't help but doubt, feel guilty, freak out for her."

"Sophia is in good hands with specialists. And her brother—not just hers…—has been found. I'll do what it takes… but I need you. I've been fighting alone for a long time, and I've never been afraid to move forward. Until this moment… I am terrified of the first step I will have to take without you if you reject me. Terrified of all the seconds, all the fucking days that will go by without you."

Océane's lips part and close, and her beautiful eyes fill with tears. Her fear, her fears, I read them in her eyes. I think I see something else too… I get lost in it…

"I don't want to go on without you; nothing will make sense without you," I say, my voice hoarse. "Because I hate the man I am, the one I was forced to be until I met you."

She doesn't make a single movement for a long time. Her bewildered eyes search me; her cheeks become wet. My breath goes in a spin as she starts to back away.

No! Fuck, no!

"Let me think about it, Tiger. That's… that's a lot to take in."

She practically runs away. I try to respect her will, her need to step back, to have space. Whatever it takes, and however long it takes, even though for the first time in my life, I really want to chase a woman. After this woman.

61

Océane

It's too much, way too much. Too heavy. Too complex. Too serious. Too much everything!

My confusion fizzles out. My guilt too. At the end of an excruciating night of insomnia, I'm in total freak-out mode after all this. Not being able to talk about it becomes unbearable because, personally, I can't manage anything anymore; I don't know what to do. In the morning, on a whim, I call Louane.

"My chick? Is everything okay?" worries the drowsy voice of my girlfriend picking up.

On the verge of implosion, I give her a rambling speech.

"Wait, breathe and start again. I don't understand anything," she replies.

I inhale while trying to put some order in my overheated head.

"Sorry to wake you up. I… I think I'm going to leave, my darling," I tell her again. "I'm going back to Paris. You've been so nice to me that I wanted to warn you and say thank you, not to leave like a thief."

"What?" says Louane, astonished. "So fast? What happened? You were here for a year and didn't even get halfway through."

"I… It's complicated. Way too complicated."

Shit, I'm staggering; my voice is cracking. A lump is forming in my throat. Unfortunately, I am unable to share with my friend what is happening to me. I ran away from a life that was going to hell at home to make a new start. And here I am, entangled in something even more chaotic.

Tiger got a divorce. Fuck, he's divorced, and my heart races every time I imagine what Sophia might do now!

This woman is more fragile than ever, possibly suicidal. And I'm disturbed by their incestuous past, and I couldn't bear to be the cause of a second life being shattered. Especially not after everything that happened in France.

I exhale, inhale again and hold on to this resolution.

"My cab will be here soon," I tell Louane. "I hope we'll stay in touch, chick. You've been a great friend."

I hang up the phone before bursting into tears during an interminable goodbye. Or for fear of saying more than I have to. I have to keep Tiger and Sophia's secrets. I owe them that much. And it hurts so much to have to give up, to listen to my reason for once. But there are not thirty-six thousand ways out.

Lucas weighs heavily on my conscience. And Sophia is added to it. Two collateral damages that haunt me and leave me with a bitter taste.

Things have gone too far off the rails; we can't build hypothetical happiness on the misfortune of others. I definitely feel incapable of doing so. I lock my bags, and I rush to the Sydney airport to take a one-way ticket to France. I kept checking the surroundings, panicking at the idea that someone would prevent me from boarding. Tiger, his henchmen, Louane. But nobody appears. Proof that nothing keeps me here anymore.

Once on the plane, before turning off my mobile, I email Myriam just to have a place to stay and not to sink alone in Paris…

And twenty-four hours later, I'm back home. In an environment that I hope is less oppressive and simpler. And since then, days go by…

"You look so sad. Can I do anything?" Myriam asks me on the tenth day.

I try to smile as I reach for my bag.

"You are already doing a lot, Myriam. Thank you for everything."

"You can't thank me forever, sweetie. It's my pleasure to have you here. You stay as long as you need to. Besides, my girls love you."

"It's mutual," I say with a lump in my throat.

It's a good thing these two kids are here to lighten the mood. In front of them, I always try to change. When I play with them, I can swallow my tears, try to repress my dark thoughts, my lack… But it remains hard. I don't know how I still manage to get up every morning.

"Are you going out?" Myriam asks me.

"Yes…"

I hesitate, then show my phone to confess, "Lucas answered me. Unless it is his mother who pretends to be him. We have an appointment. I need to talk to him; my guilt will never lighten if I can't explain myself to him and apologize."

Myriam blinks. She knows about all the evil that Christine, Lucas's mother, has distilled into my life here in France. To the point of making it a living hell.

"I'm not sure it's a good idea to go alone," she doubts. "This woman has an irrational hatred for you."

"I'm a big girl; I can handle myself, don't worry."

Myriam purses her lips and nods. She and I have had long discussions at night since my return. I have come to the conclusion that I am afraid to move forward because the past is weighing me down too much: I need to put things in order. I have to start learning to forgive myself if only a little. Regrets eat up my existence. Myriam knows it; she seems to respect my choice even if her fears towards Christine are justified. The years that have passed since the brutal beating of Lucas don't change anything. And then, Victor is now in the wild. On probation. That's why I preferred to live at a friend's house for a while instead of hiding in a hotel room. To be less isolated, to feel less exposed…

However, fear gets into my head as soon as I go out. Fear of reprisals, a mother's resentment, and an ex-convict who resents me for denouncing him.

But I take responsibility. I have to face my mistakes and their consequences. Whatever they are. Fix what I can.

On the bus, I ponder all this. I keep looking around, feeling like I'm walking in a void without a net. The vibrations of my phone make me flinch. A face from another life appears on the screen, a life I force myself to forget in vain. It's Louane. I pick up the phone while getting off at my stop.

"Hello, my chick," she says, with a cheerful intonation. "Are you well in your greyness? Because I miss you too much!"

"Girl, if you only knew how much I miss you too."

I miss everything about Australia, actually. Some people who live there in particular. An admission that I bridle with teary eyes again. Boy, I've become a real tearjerker!

"So, tell me," Louane continues. "You wouldn't have hidden from me something very important by any chance?"

I freeze in the middle of the sidewalk, frightened, and I whisper into the phone in a weak voice, "What do you mean?"

"Well, a fancy car has been hanging around for a few days in front of our apartment. Garrett attests that it's a Sexton car; he recognized the personalized plate."

I swallow. Oh, hell, no!

"Océane?" insists Louane. "You still there?"

"Yes… I'm listening."

"Another clue," she says, "I spotted a beautiful, ultra-sophisticated blonde who looks just like you in the press photos from old James Sexton's gala…"

Louane lets her words sink into my head in panic for several seconds.

It's fucked up, she knows. How many people have seen the same evidence and drawn their own conclusions?

Since I still can't utter a single rebuttal, my girlfriend ends her conclusion, "It's just crazy, but I'm obsessed with a question now. Could your sudden departure have anything to do with the sulfurous Sextons?"

Cornered, I close my eyelids. No story comes to me. My heart is beating too fast. I finally admit tacitly, "I'm sorry, Louane. I… I signed a confidentiality agreement… I… It's not to keep you out; I just can't…"

"Oh, my God!" she cries on the other end of the line.

Silent, I shudder as I await her verdict.

"Great!" exclaims Louane again. "I understand now… Well, I think I do."

"But you…"

"Don't worry. I don't blame you. And I promise to keep my mouth shut."

My friend raves for a while, making assumptions that I don't really confirm. But I don't deny it either. Anyway, my relationship with the Sextons is becoming an open secret in Australia. How long before my identity is discovered and exposed?

What will Tiger do?

This thought hits me in the heart, long after my conversation with Louane. I feel even more confused when I ring the bell at Lucas's house, with a lump in my stomach.

It's his mother who opens the door. I have to assimilate too many emotions at once. The discovery of Louane and the fact of finding myself in front of one of the people—perhaps the one— who hates me the most in the world.

"Hello, Christine," I say, my hands sweaty and my stress level high.

"Is it Océane?" I hear from inside the house.

Lucas's voice. It stirs me instantly, carrying painful and bittersweet memories but also a tenderness that I was prevented from expressing after the tragedy.

His mother glares at me, then shifts to let me in. Her animosity toward me hasn't disappeared; it's just less explosive than before. At least, I think so...

"Yes, it's her," says Christine, still watching me.

Uncomfortable, I don't dare to go any further. Waiting for a sign, a *je-ne-sais-quoi* from her that doesn't come. She simply leads me to her son, immobilized in a medical bed.

I finally discover the boy of my 16 years, the one of my first kiss, of my first time. He is now so frail, so damaged. Tears come to my eyes. But Lucas smiles at me.

"You're still as cute as ever," he says. "And much more tanned than me."

Between laughing and crying, I rush towards him to give him a hug.

"You're still just as much of a smooth talker and handsome," I reply.

"I know; I think my home nurse has a serious crush on me."

And suddenly, in spite of the frame, of his state, of the tension between his mother and me, I find my Lucas. He laughs; I don't perceive the slightest reproach in his misty eyes. Just emotion. I nod, also moved.

"In truth, my mother doesn't hate you anymore," he whispers to me as my ear is close. "She's just too stubborn to admit it to you. I know you, Océane. I know you had nothing to do with it. That bastard Victor and his gang are the only ones responsible. The only thing that sticks in my throat is that he was released."

Without expecting it, I hear Christine say in the doorway, "Océane, I... It took me a while. Our lawyer, the investigators, and... other people got me to bury my resentments. We all have to move on now. Your testimony carried weight. I... I thank you for that... And for everything else..."

Shocked, I turn to look at her. I was wrong; it is not animosity that she shows towards me. It is suffering, the distress of a mother who has seen her only son's life changed forever. Permeable to this shared pain, I am nevertheless not sure I understand this "everything else," but I am no less touched by it. A heavy, dark, and terrible chapter of my life is finally coming to an end. This is so much more valuable. I nod, squeeze Lucas's cold fingers as I reply,

"Thank you for telling me that, Christine. Anyway, I swear to you that all my life, I will still blame myself. If I could go back and avoid—"

"Don't torture yourself with this anymore, Océane. I mean it," Lucas interrupts me.

I start crying again. I have a strange and ambivalent feeling of relief and sorrow.

I have to turn the page now. Will I be able to?

62

Océane

Twenty-two months later. Bayonne, France

It's raining cats and dogs.

The sound of "Duet of flowers." Me under the rain, lying naked on the deckchair. Tiger soaked, in boxer shorts, devouring me with his eyes…

I shake my head but remain static in front of the window, watching the drops fall. I still don't know where I stand. I just try to make sense of my wanderings. Not to spend my life wallowing and to get up and run away. Like almost two years ago.

Although Lucas and his mother forgave me, a boy ended up severely disabled because of me. I could not foresee and avoid what happened to Lucas. But with Sophia, I could make better decisions. Even if I had to suffer for it. And I did.

I'm still trying to convince myself that I was right to leave. Only with Louane did I keep in touch. That long-distance friendship survives pretty well. I needed some distance. A lot of distance. Leaving Australia early and coming home was not easy. It still isn't today. The emptiness, the lack, is too suffocating…

And then I see Tiger everywhere, literally. In the press, on the Web, in my head, in my dreams, he is everywhere. Okay, seeing him on the cover of magazines with a face to ignite the panties doesn't help me. In spite of him—because I know how much he hates being talked about for something other than his work—he has become the most fascinating divorcee in the celebrity world.

Divorced… A little word that ravages my thoughts makes my meager certainties sway.

Tiger is too sexy. Too powerful. Too mysterious. Too magnetic not to arouse voyeurism. Strangely, I was spared. Did he have anything to do with it? No paparazzi after me, no proven statements about me. I remained a "friend" seen a few times with Sophia. But everyone wants to know if he's really alone. We're still trying to figure out who he disappears with when he's not seen in public. Who he eats with. Who he fucks with.

By "we" I don't just mean the media, the Web, or the public. I'm dying to know it, too, even if it's also the biggest fear in my heart. Because this scoop would be the proof that he has turned the page too. And it would prove to me that if he didn't insist, didn't chase me, it's because my decision was the only way out.

For Sophia…

And having seen nothing negative about her, especially no announcement of death, I tell myself that she may be fine. Or at least that means she didn't take one too many pills…

"We all have to move on," Lucas's mom said. So all's well that ends well?

"What are you thinking?" my colleague Gaëlle interrupts me in my thoughts.

That even the rainy days were more beautiful, more euphoric in Sydney…

"Nothing… I think I just like the rain," I say.

"You're weird!" she teases, laughing. "At the same time, with your name, you can only like water…"

"Girls, it's starting!" the deputy mayor calls out to us before I reply that she's talking nonsense.

Gaëlle and I hurry, laughing, towards the meeting room. We are the two students who work part-time in the department dedicated to education and youth. A small job that looks better on my résumé because I've gone back to law school. I can achieve this dream and work one day to straighten out the minors who are drifting away. To help children, like some wonderful people have done for me. So that there would be fewer guys like Victor and his buddies, fewer kids with broke lives like Lucas… And maybe make my mom proud from up there.

I would have succeeded in at least that.

"Oh, gosh, sex bomb in sight," Gaëlle swears softly as soon as we push the door. "Look at this handsome guy!"

Thank God she whispered it because my heartbeat, which suddenly accelerates, might make a monstrous noise. That's all I can hear now; the sound of my panicked pulse. I swallow my saliva, stunned. Gaëlle pulls me by the hand to sit down.

These eyes…

Tiger's intense eyes immediately stop on me. They take me hostage. My body is completely covered with goosebumps, and my brain gives up. Sudden death of my neurons.

He… Is that him? What is he doing here?

"Lol, did you bug or what?" laughs Gaëlle while leaning on my ear.

I realize that I have indeed moved forward in automatic mode. Sitting with the rest of the municipal team, I feel like I don't have any control over my body or over my mind.

Tiger Sexton is in the room. I can't fucking process this slap!

"Well, says the mayor. Good morning, everyone. I've called you to this special meeting to announce, on the one hand, the much-anticipated end of the fundraising."

What?

"By the way, I would like to warmly thank the two young women who have actively invested themselves at our side for this fundraiser. I name Gaëlle Legay and Océane Rousseau."

His gaze never leaves me. Not for a fraction of a second. And what is terrible is that I blush, fearing that I am suddenly like an open book. Gaëlle at my side goes from being a tease to a friend intrigued by this sensational ride.

"You're redder than my buttocks after a sunburn," she whispers to me. "Who's that guy? He's staring at you like you're the only one here."

The others applaud; all look at us, Gaëlle and me. If she gives away the change, I don't. I tremble. The incomprehension, the shock, and a lot of unspeakable emotions shake me.

"He's famous, isn't he?" my friend whispers again. "His hottie face looks familiar."

"In addition," adds the mayor, "these two pieces of information are related; our very generous donor wanted to meet the team. So let me introduce Mr. Tiger Sexton, an Australian businessman. As you know, we launched this fundraising campaign to finance an ambitious project undertaken by young people from our difficult neighborhoods and Mr. Sexton—"

"Ah, yes, the Australian tiger! I can't fucking believe it! Hey?" she insists in front of my silence during the speech. "It's indecent how he stares at you."

"It's… No, I…"

I'm floundering. Tiger, whose name is mentioned for the second time, runs his hand through his hair and finally gives Mrs. Caloni, the mayor, a look. I try to pull myself together. It's no use; the sound of his voice rises. That crisp English accent, in impeccable French, and her husky range envelop us. His charisma does the rest.

"Thank you, Ms. Caloni," he says. "Good morning, ladies and gentlemen. Thank you for your welcome. I am delighted to participate in such a project; it has been a while since I was looking…"

His irises lock on me again. What the hell is he doing? Damn, it's hot in this damn room! I… I need to get some fresh air.

"I was looking for a…" Tiger continues, putting me through the wringer. "A worthy cause…"

I get up and rush out. My chair falls. The general attention, the "are you okay?" and other reactions don't stop me from rushing to the door. I don't feel well; what's with the fucking tachycardia?

Outside, I take a deep breath of air. And I'm soaked in less than two seconds. Damn, I forgot it was raining!

"You certainly do like to get wet," his voice sounds behind me.

I turn around and throw a worried look at the windows. Gaëlle is glued to the window, and she is not the only one…

"Me too, in fact," continues Tiger. "With you."

I swallow; the emotions clash in the hollow of me, vivid, crazy. I need to know.

"Why are you here?"

"For your fundraiser…"

Of course…

"The only sign that my staff found about you on the Web was a photo on the Bayonne City Hall website."

Alongside several other young people. My full name wasn't even mentioned in the article he was talking about. There were just the first names of each one. That was enough for him. Well, knowing him, I doubt very much that he ever lost track of me.

"I see," I say in a breath.

"Are you going to run away from me again and hide further away?"

My whole body tenses up; my breathing becomes disturbed. I try to justify myself, "I wasn't hiding... I just avoided the risky areas: Sydney—no, all of Australia—and the Paris area, too, because of Victor. I chose a new place for a new start."

"The farthest away from me as possible," he concludes.

He gets closer; we are too close.

"And I told you, Océane. I told you that my life without you terrified me."

"I... I had to leave."

"Without warning me? While I was waiting for you to 'think?'" he starts to raise his voice. "Do you know how many times I had to stop myself from jumping into the jet? How many times you... I almost gave in? It cost me to give you your space; I tried to respect your decision and give you time to... to think. And you, damn it, you ran away!"

He doesn't hide his fury anymore. His gestures are nervous, and his look is intense. No, desperately intense. This detail upsets me.

He missed me. He freaked out that he lost me.

"I didn't... I'm sorry, Tiger."

His hands come to hold my shoulders, his eyes searching inside me. And the rain, the witnesses of this scene, everything ceases to exist at this touch. I am caught by him, caught by what he expresses to me by all his pores. Devastated by this lack of him that nothing has filled.

"Am I so monstrous, my sweet?" he almost implores me. "My secrets, my past, the man that I am so repulsive that you could not bear the idea of seeing me again?"

I'm cracking up. Is that what he thought?

Repulsive? No. That's not exactly how I feel. Rather, the right adjectives would be deeply disturbing. Discovering the reality of the convoluted, devious, twisted bond between Sophia and him doesn't leave me unscathed. No question about it. But most of all, recognizing that my attraction and feelings for Tiger have not, in spite of everything, faded away is also working on me.

It has withstood the revelations, the distance, my reason…

Surely, their past is not insignificant, nor is their stigma. Far from it! He and Sophia were victims and guilty of the perversions which immoral adults dragged them into when they were kids. Scarred forever by it all. Nevertheless, the man I know is not only this sordid part of his life. He's more than that to me because he came out of it more combative, stronger, and more determined in the face of his responsibilities. And I still find him fucking attractive, charismatic, and impressive.

So I can only contradict him with a sigh, "No… I don't feel revulsion, Tiger. You've turned me upside down, it's true. And it would have been too hard to say goodbye to your face. I didn't want to be responsible for Sophia relapsing, but I also knew that if… if I saw you again, I would be the one relapsing for you."

"Maybe I asked too much of you. For a normal person, I know what we look like. That's why, selfishly, I wished at the beginning of your contract that you were a girl capable of the things your ex's mother accused you of. So I could hold on to the idea that you weren't smooth either, that we weren't tainting your purity. I was trying to clear my name somehow. Then I realized that you were innocent, but I… Damn, you were already way too deep in me!"

Damn it! So late, I'm starting to decipher the reaction he had at stud after our first time… I blamed him for suddenly putting distance between us when he was mostly tortured by his conscience.

"I made my own choices, Tiger. You're not at fault for them."

"Maybe…" he hesitates. "But I have only one word, Océane. I swore I wouldn't abandon Sophia; I told you she was in excellent hands, and I made sure of that. You could have trusted me with that, just as I trusted you when you asked me for time to sort things out."

We stare at each other under the downpour in the silence that follows. Raindrops bead on her lashes. It may not be pain, but what I read in him is so similar to the emptiness, the pain that has pierced me since my return to France.

"I'm sorry, Tiger. I think… I was afraid of this passion, of this fucking alchemy as you used to say it," I say again, with a fragile intonation. "Everything was forcing me to cross you off for good, but I couldn't. I was afraid of where it was taking us, against all odds."

His palms gently migrate to my face, and his lips are just a touch away from mine.

"Believe me; I've tried to let you walk away too. The relentless truth is that you are all I want in the world. I do and always will make sure you have nothing to fear."

I shudder at that statement.

"I am ready to fight for you, for us. I am ready to face everything to be with you, to take care of you. Don't you still understand that?"

Suddenly, a question intrudes among the chaotic feelings I am struggling to control. Like the beginning of a suspicion, I remember his other commitments when we were sleeping together, *"if you need a powerful ally in France..."* But yes!

"Tiger, did you... intervene in any way when I returned to Paris?"

His eyelids crinkle, and he waits for me to elaborate.

"When you say you'll make sure I'm safe, it's not just about Sophia, is it?"

He doesn't deny it. Suddenly, the truth hits me hard!

"What exactly did you do about Victor and Lucas?"

His eyes become flustered; he seems to be thinking, searching for words so that he doesn't probably put me on the spot.

"I made sure that the one called Victor went back to prison for a longer stay before he got to you. This little prick was serious; he was planning to get revenge."

"Shit. When?"

"About the time I realized you were back home. I had him watched... He got a gun off the black market... The good news is he's not about to break another life."

The backlash saws me and stops my breathing. I was unconscious, so Victor would have... Oh, fuck!

"And... what about Lucas? His mother gave me a rather mysterious thank you. At the time, I didn't understand it, but..."

"But?" says Tiger, probing me.

"You intervened without my knowledge, too, didn't you? She didn't forgive me so easily and miraculously."

He hesitates and finally opines calmly.

"I had to make this boy's life more comfortable and to relieve his mother as much as possible. I... also had a conversation with her about you. Don't blame me; I needed to secure Paris for you. If it was your choice to stay in France, then I didn't want anything or anyone to spoil this new beginning. I… You weren't supposed to ever know what I did behind the scenes."

Dazed and stunned, I don't utter a sound for the next few seconds. He looked out for me. In every way possible, without ever coming directly to disturb me. Without forcing my hand to come back to him. No one has ever done so much to ensure my well-being.

"Are you angry?" asks Tiger, confused by my silence.

"No, I'm… Fuck, I'm…"

I'm losing it. Tense, he tries to understand why I'm in this state. I explain to him, my voice hoarse, "You were there for me, even when I left you in the lurch."

"It's not a big deal. You deserve to be happy and safe."

"Damn it…"

With his thumb, he wipes a furrow on my face: a mixture of rain and tears. Our mouths come together, brush against each other, and our breaths intermingle.

"Do you still prefer to stay here? Come with me," he begs.

"Tiger, I…"

"Come back to Australia. It's been almost two years, Océane, an eternity, and every day has been agony. You'll see for yourself that Sophia is fine, and you don't have to feel this loyalty conflict anymore. Because this thing between you and me isn't dying, it's getting stronger with every breath I take. It makes me care about you wherever you are. But yes, it would be even better if you came back with me."

This time my lips part. My body presses against his. I want to fight, only I feel lonely, lost, and too bad without him. Seeing him again, knowing how much he is capable of for me, weakens me in spite of everything.

"I don't know, Tiger."

"I'm begging you. I… I can't get over you. Let's break our chains. We can do it together: you and me."

Breaking our chains… That's exactly what it is. But it seems easier to say than to do.

"If ever… if ever there is the slightest risk that Sophia will suffer, I can't live like this," I tell him. "I won't hurt anyone else, even unintentionally."

"The one who suffers is me. I don't know how to fucking explain it to you, but when it comes to you, I'm not insensitive, Océane. You've been killing me slowly for too long now. I can't take it anymore. Come back, please."

I try to cogitate and get lost in his beautiful, tormented eyes. My reason is agonizing. He probes me, gives himself up, and shakes me up. Then, suddenly, his kiss catches me off guard, makes me dizzy, and makes my legs wobble. Tiger expresses to me more than a violent desire. Inextinguishable, it is a true storm of feelings that sticks one to the other. Crazy, tortured by this separation too brutal, too long, braving the elements around us.

Should I give in? Should I take this risk?

63

TIGER

SIX DAYS LATER. SYDNEY

**"The tiger is no longer on the market; he has found his tigress…
in France!"**

This headline makes me smile again as I think about it. I'm
less amused by my blondie's fears when she finds out. She doesn't
have the peace of mind of Sophia, and I can understand that. A
stolen photo of poor quality of my reunion with Océane in Bayonne
circulated very quickly. Widely relayed to my home… Our home.
Because I don't intend to let her evaporate in nature anymore. Even
less when I see her strutting around in fine lingerie and a tiny white
dress, sexy enough to make me go crazy.

I know that nothing is won. This torrid alchemy exceeds us
and pushes us inexorably toward each other. However, she still has
doubts. She can still leave at any moment and destroy my deserted
existence again.

So, right now, I savor the moment. I fill this gaping hole that
she left in me when she disappeared from my life. Océane, proud
to have tied my wrists to the bars of the bed, overhangs me. With
a delicious smile on her lips, she plays with her loose blond mane,
on which sits a nurse's disguise headdress. She has everything of a
living, burning fantasy. Her mini dress reveals her bare legs, goes up,
molding her bust, and finishes in a cleavage to burn my neurons.
When she turns and bends over, her sublime rear end reinforces
my erection. The cut of her lingerie underneath is indented on her
buttocks, giving me only one desire, to plant my teeth there to nibble
it.

"So, you've been in pain for almost two years, Sweet Pea? Is it really true?"

With a burning gleam in her glance, she looks at my nudity. That of a man who doesn't hide anything from her anymore. Naked in the bed, the shackled wrists. I tied myself on one side and let "nurse" Océane block the other, curious to see what she intends to do with these thirty minutes of power. Sorry I meant auscultation.

I smile in my turn because I have a very precise idea of what I will do with my next thirty minutes…

"Yep… Very bad. I can show you where if you untie me."

"Nah, you're a too boisterous patient. I'll figure it out on my own."

Her visual, mischievous scrutiny of my body makes me hot as hell.

"Not sure… I promise I'll be obedient."

"Of course… Why the cheeky smile? Still feeling super powerful, Sweet Pea?" she challenges me.

"Come here… Take a closer look at me."

"Hush. It is not you who gives the orders," she rebels.

She climbs into the bed and straddles me. For lack of my fingers, my eyes slide on her. From the tip of her pumps that she keeps on her feet to her thighs, her pelvis, her lower abdomen so close to mine…

"I come because I want to, and I will do what I want with you," she warns me. "And prove that you are not hurt anywhere."

"Except maybe there?" I say to her by directing my glance toward my erection.

She brushes it, and I sigh. She starts again, pretending to be innocent.

"How am I going to fix this?"

She bends over; her belly grazes my cock lasciviously, and her mouth descends on my pecs.

"My diagnosis: you're not in pain. You are just frustrated, very frustrated, Sweet Pea."

She caresses me, I moan and her tongue, damn it! She plays with my tense cock, and inflames my epidermis. My disease is to like too much to feel her skin, to feel her smell, to feel her all. And I begin to break down slowly. My fists clench, and I make a guttural protest.

Don't heal me; make me more addicted!

"Shhh," Océane is still telling me. "Or I promise not to put an end to this very… interesting state."

"You're the most sadistic of all nurses."

"And you're not just another patient, Mr. Insensitive."

She pinches me with all her strength, but it is a waste of effort. Then her mouth rests on me to bite me. My excitement grows. No pain, indeed, but I take my foot when she starts sucking on my neck, bites me, and goes up.

The kiss I long for finally arrives. I can't block her from devouring me, so she takes advantage. Having fun running away and coming back to nibble my lips. She stretches my bottom lip and slides her nails across my face.

"I'm going to give you a shock treatment. You are at my mercy," she whispers to me.

"Okay, my tigress. I am at your mercy," I admit, my voice too hoarse of fervor.

This surrender earns me a kiss. Breathtaking, electrifying, calcining, but too short.

Fuck! Come back…

No, she wriggles on me. She knows that I am burning, that she is killing me slowly. Her mouth goes back to torture me more and more in the south. She alone knows how to make me hurt in her way. My groin contracts, my hardened cock throbs, and I clench my fists tighter as I pull at the bonds.

I want your mouth, Océane. I want your lips…

"I'll take your pulse," she decrees, naughty.

She licks the contours of my cock, subjugates me, and I go crazy. I move to indicate my impatience to her. She teases me and goes up without touching my cock. Her hair caresses me, and her nose sniffs me. She kisses me again. At length. We lose our breath, get carried away, and it goes off the rails. Our tongues come alive, and my temperature rises to a crescendo. This fever, she is the only one responsible. At the climax, I can't bear to desire her so fiercely. I growl against her mouth, "How does that thing under your dress come off?"

"In the crotch," whispers Océane… "Too bad you have no control; you can't undress me."

She smiles and offers me her lips to seize mine better. Her wet slit leans against me while she stirs suavely.

Resist. Resist. Resist.

I can't fucking do it anymore! Quick, methodical, I take advantage of our next kiss to undo the knot that held the wrist I tied myself. She didn't suspect it, but this trick is my plan B to never be totally immobilized.

Impossible to completely lose control of my environment. Océane realizes this when my suddenly free hand slips between us and pulls on the snap closures of her bodysuit.

"Cheater," she accuses me while I touch her revealed pubis.

"Are you going to punish me?"

Instead of answering me, she undulates on me, puts her palms on my chest, and pushes me onto my back.

"So this is the punishment you are looking for? Is this your remedy?"

She lifts her hips and rubs her murderous wetness against my dick.

"Yes…"

"What therapeutic torture are you hoping for, Tiger? This?" she meows as she slowly impales herself on me.

"Argh, fuck, yes!"

She takes me up to the guard and sits there, sublime, rebellious. Her arms tighten, and her hands fall on my chest. Her intimacy embraces me. She dances slowly, tears me a sigh.

"You know that I'm not going to authorize you to cum, huh?" she challenges me, bewitching.

"Argh, you kill me!"

"You are my VIP patient; it is only the beginning. First treatment: you are going to make me cum. Just me, not you."

"Whatever you want."

She bends down, sticks her breasts, and grabs my mouth. My free hand goes back to grope in the sheets, searching for what I let go of to detach myself. Océane withdraws, then wraps me again in her. Her cocoon of softness slides again and again on my erection. Her bust straightens, her eyelids close, and her head tilts back. She rides me faster and faster, and her wet walls intoxicate me. I don't contain myself anymore; it comes out, "Marry me."

She stops suddenly, out of breath. Her eyes open and focus on me.

"What did you…"

I repeat, "Marry me."

I hold out my closed fist; my fingers unfold before her. Breathing unevenly, I rephrase, "Océane, Lilia Rousseau, I would like to be officially at your mercy. To be the only one to see you like this, breathtakingly beautiful, the only one to benefit from your special care, and the only one to offer you orgasms. Will you marry me?"

For endless seconds, I watch for her reaction. My cock pulses inside her, my heart pounds too hard, and my whole being hangs in suspense, clinging to her lips.

"Océane?"

"Yes."

"You…"

"YES! Yes, I fucking want it!"

She bends down; our fusion becomes total, passionate. She cries, and she laughs. Our kiss has the salty taste of her tears, and my desire for her can no longer be suppressed. I undo the second tie around my wrist to release myself completely. Prompt, craving, I rock her on the bed and penetrate her brutally. Her legs wrap around my back.

"Now I'm free to get laid with the future Mrs. Océane Sexton."

I don't leave her time to object; I just swallow her sighs by accelerating. She whines, arches her back, offers herself, and implodes in a masterly way. All in liquid.

Damn, I surrender.

OCÉANE

How many times have I floated? I lost track of time. Tiger and I are drenched in fluids, gasping for breath, and collapsed in the sheets. During this respite, the aftershocks of my pleasure still thrill me.

"We're an hour late," Tiger tells me as he rolls to the side to grab his phone.

I let out a mixture of a sigh and a lazy moan.

"Nahhh, I don't have the strength to get up anymore, Tiger."

He laughs and comes back to pinch my buttock.

"Sophia is waiting for us; we already pushed back," he reminds me. "But I can cancel if you don't feel like going anymore."

"No…"

I straighten up. My messed-up body is full of endorphins. Tiger devours me with his gaze again; then his eyes trail over the diamond on my ring finger.

"I'm going to get ready."

"Are you sure?"

"Yes."

I get out of bed; Tiger starts texting. Probably to apologize for our tardiness. I head into the shower and let the warm stream trickle over me. With my eyes closed, I try to regain my senses.

I am engaged. Crazy in love. And we're going to my guy's ex-wife's house for dinner.

Even though Tiger and I have talked about it a lot, even though I am partly the instigator of this upcoming reunion with Sophia, with whom I need to clear the air, a sneaky nervousness swells in my gut. I've been living cooped up with my tiger in the penthouse for a few days now. Fucking, talking, eating, fucking again, sleeping, starting over, and enjoying our bubble. I'll have to face the outside of the bubble too, now, see Sophia again. It's time…

Tiger joins me underwater. His muscles curl against my back and the curve of my buttocks.

"It's going to be hard to get your nose out again," he whispers to me as his fingers get more and more aggressive. "Really hard…" he repeats.

I know what he means. I can mostly feel it. What the fuck is he running on? I let myself go against him.

"You're tense," he notes. "I'll take care of you. Let me be your private nurse now."

He grabs the shower gel and sprays me with it. And very quickly, his fingers skate on my skin. They knead me, massage me, and weigh up my breasts.

"We will be even more late if you… Oh, gosh…"

My nipples react, shivers arise, and his mouth moves around my neck. He takes his time. The washing turns into sensory torture under the jets. When he lifts me up and wedges my back in the corner, I feel liquefied, feverish. Tiger passes a hand between us and pushes his sex inside me.

"What the fuck is happening to me with you?" he complains, quivering with desire.

"I don't know… But I think the same thing is happening to me."

He kisses me and eroticizes every part of my body.

"I want you all the time; I want you much too much, Océane," he confesses to me against my mouth.

The next second, he possesses me slowly but with such vigor. Each blow makes me lose reason. His rigidity fills me, kills me. Taken of tremors, I cling to him.

"I love you," I confide to him at the edge of the enjoyment.

My voice is almost sobbing because what I feel, what he makes me feel, is just insane. Much too intense. He locks his gaze on mine; I read there the "me too" more violently. No need for words. He digs my pelvis and makes me fall into a bottomless pit. While I disintegrate in his arms, Tiger whispers in my ear, "At your mercy… Entirely and every second."

My God, I am falling.

64

OCÉANE

With a monstrous delay, we finally arrive at Sophia's house. A huge and sublime house with a more feminine look than the property she shared with Tiger. It looks much more like her, without any masculine touch that is visible from the outside. Inside, ditto, I guess. A profusion of flowers, shrubs with a rounded cut, walls with pastel colors…

This is indeed Sophia's home. Only hers.

So far, Tiger has been trying to relax me… And if all the apprehension of seeing his ex again had flown away in his arms, everything comes back to me like a boomerang.

"Are you okay?" he worries as I start to stress again when I get out of the car.

"Yes, I'm fine."

"You don't have to; we can leave."

"No, I want to see how she's doing, and I think she and I have some things to talk about. It won't work if we keep it blurry."

He looks at me through our sunglasses and nods.

"When in doubt, if you want to leave, we'll leave. Okay?"

"It will be fine," I say.

As much to reassure him as to reassure myself. And then, I cannot avoid it indefinitely; it is part of our life…

A big man with clear eyes opens the door to us. Obviously in a joyful mood, he immediately takes Tiger in his arms.

"Thanks for the gift; it's just what I needed, man."

"I'm glad," Tiger replies, patting him on the back.

They let each other go, and no one explains to me. Tiger puts his arm around my waist again, and I feel a bit awkward. The other looks at me, a little curious look on his face.

"Is it her?" he asks.

"Yes, it is."

Then, turning to me, Tiger adds, "Byr— Aaron, this is Océane. Sweetheart, this is Aaron."

The famous brother… of the two. I assume he has chosen to be permanently named Aaron. One of the things I learned from my intimate discussions with Tiger was that children born in the cult had no legal existence. They were not registered; names were given to them by Alpha during their first rite as Children of the Garden and then engraved on the inside of their lower lip in their thirteenth spring. And all of them were Hamilton, like Alpha and Omega…

Somehow, Tiger was lucky enough to regain his identity after his release, unlike the others. They were just sort of ghosts who had been robbed of their own lives, strangers to everything. Sophia, Byrne…

Finally, Aaron probes me with a smile.

"Nice to meet you," he greets me in French.

"Nice to meet you too, Aaron."

"I've heard a lot about you; I understand everything now," he comments with a mischievous look.

A question of circumstance blossoms in my head: good or bad? Before I can ask it, Tiger shoots back, a half-smile on his lips, "All of it? I don't think so."

The two of them seem to know so much about each other that their exchange of glances is not at all harmless. Then Byrne laughs and says, "Relax, man."

"I couldn't be more relaxed," says Tiger, whose fingers remain possessively on my waist. "By the way, where is Sophia?"

"Learning how to change a diaper," Aaron retorts.

My eyes widen. Did I miss something? My irises search for my man's, then return to the brother.

"What?" I say in a breath.

"Ooh, she's freaking out," Aaron laughs.

Shit, I must be white as a sheet! Tiger snaps and hastens to explain to me, "I invited a couple of Aaron's friends to spend a few days of vacation with him. I think we're talking about their son."

So that was the "gift" he was thanking him for?

"Oh… I see."

A small, satisfied smile graces Tiger's lips.

"What were you thinking?" he teases quietly, leaning into my ear.

"Nothing at all," I defend myself, even though it's obvious I was freaking out for a split second.

"Of course…"

Aaron laughs and invites us to head to the living room.

Yeah… You two have a weird sense of humor.

TIGER

Océane sticks her tongue out at me behind Aaron's back. I suppress a small laugh. I loved the look on her face when she thought we were telling her that Sophia had had a baby.

Marjorie, Aaron's French friend, joins us first. We met before when I was doing the follow-up to the Ares operation. Since I had a lot of time to kill for twenty-two months, and one night I went crazy and landed unexpectedly in Paris with a visceral need to go find Océane, I tried to make sense of this madness. To restrain myself and give another use to this trip…

Morgan and Marjorie were part of the collateral damage of the escape of Omega and the Executioner. So I decided to contact them. Naturally, the wounds of the past weave a bond between them and us. All survivors, each in their own way…

"Nice to meet you, Océane," Marjorie continues, giving her a kiss. "Don't worry; you're going to see the object of all the attention in—"

As she says this, a tiny man—all proud of himself—runs towards us with his little bodysuit open between his legs.

"Octave, come back, we did not finish!" calls his father, who comes back behind him, followed by Sophia, laughing.

Amused by the scene, we look at Marjorie intercepting the boy and covering him with kisses. Aaron teases Morgan about his parental authority. And Sophia discovers us.

"Oh, Ty, you're here!" she shouts.

She hesitates; I defuse her embarrassment, lean in, and kiss her on the cheek. Océane straightens up, and Sophia swivels towards her. For a moment, there is only that. This uneasiness. The two stare at each other, moved, embarrassed. I tense up. We have been through a long transitional phase to get to this point. I did everything I could to manage the aftermath. To make sure that Sophia was well taken care of therapeutically and emotionally. Aaron has settled in with her, Mary, and much of my staff.

And I'm learning to listen to her, to be there for her, without unhealthy ambiguity. So far, I think it's worked. But now I suddenly have an ounce of doubt.

It's Océane who walks up to Sophia. Shy and sincere, her eyes riveted to hers.

"Hi… You look good," she says. "Thank you for the invitation."

Sophia makes the following steps and falls into her arms.

"You're welcome," she answers. "I didn't realize how much I missed you."

"I missed you too."

I catch my breath. Damn, in fact, Océane wasn't the only one who was consumed by nerves!

The introductions start, and the conversations start again. Aaron serves drinks. When Océane wraps her fingers around her glass and sits down beside me, I notice a crucial detail: she has removed her solitaire. This thoughtfulness speaks volumes… She must have felt the timing was wrong to announce our engagement, and I agree with her. One thing at a time, as long as she is mine and doesn't run away again. I know that a lot of this will depend on Sophia. I'm anxious to know that I may lose Océane if she feels that she is a source of relapse for Sophia. She set this condition when she returned to Sydney with me. Our eyes meet. No, nothing is won one hundred percent.

Don't touch her too much or kiss her.

Okay, Sophia, now knows that we are together, but even if it is thanks to her that Océane entered my life, it is also thanks to Océane that all our locks have been broken. On a Garden. And on the secrets that were eating away at us, which we must now heal…

"He's so cute," compliments my Frenchie, following little

Octave with her eyes.

This one, bursting with energy, slips between Sophia's arms to join his dad, who intercepts him and raises him in the air to tickle him in the belly with noisy kisses. The kid laughs to the bursts and wriggles happily. Marjorie watches them tenderly.

Suddenly, a strange feeling comes over me.

My eyes turn to Aaron and Sophia's faces. The expression I see there fleetingly sends me back to a different feeling, but one that I grasp in my heart: they have never known this. The real and pure love of a parent. In the Garden, the weaning of affection began at birth with the babies; that's when the conditioning began, the hold…

But I received this love from a man from whom I don't carry any genes. A man that I dream of making proud because I am proud to carry his name and to increase its power day after day. His blood doesn't run in my veins, but his values are engraved in me despite all that could have erased them…

This thought brings me back to Océane. My blondie succeeds in stealing a kiss from Octave, who runs away at once, happy to have found how to untie his bodysuit by pulling on the snaps.

"I let go of the case," declares the dad to his girlfriend. "It's your turn, Jo."

Océane is ecstatic, and I take the opportunity to lean toward her ear.

"Can you see us doing the same?"

Her eyes lock onto mine, beaming and questioning.

"Do you want children?" she whispers to me.

"I want everything with you."

For a moment, we look into each other's eyes, measuring the significance of these words. It's true; I'm a complete novice when it comes to real relationships. I've been a slave to appearances for most of my life. Then this woman gave me electric shocks and took control of my heartbeat.

She nods gently.

"Yes… Maybe… But first, I'd like to finish my studies, register at the Sydney Bar, and…"

"And?"

"And come up with a more refined version of how you

proposed to me… one that can be told to… our future baby.”

Bringing it up spreads an infectious emotion through her. Océane winks at me in a mischievous way that is meant to be discreet. My laughter is much less discreet. I already have too many schemes in my head involving the conception of this kid. I try to behave myself, considering the place, the other guests, and Sophia.

“You’ll get a second one, gentleman’s version,” I promise her, putting on a serious face. “Easier to tell and a proof of my love… Even if the first one will remain my favorite.”

Océane turns pink. She knows how I feel about her, even if I say “I am at your mercy” more easily than “I love you.” But I learn it for her.

Going back to our censored version of my proposal, hiding the truth is nothing new for me. Only it’s never been for fun… I’ve often—no, always—felt like I was playing imposter roles, not fitting in anywhere.

Except with her. Except in her.

At one time, after the Lilies, I fell into various sexual wanderings. Excessive sessions with call-girls and Dominas in search of extreme punishments for all that haunts me on a daily basis, these deaths, these failures, these orgies. Maybe I wanted to reiterate what I suffered at the hands of the Executioner, those “punishments” that I still believe I deserve… Or was I in desperate search of self-medication to push the limits… Maybe unconsciously, to feel something, as Dr. Murphy assumed? I was looking for that “human” part in me, the part that would connect me to Nick Sexton and make me finally feel whole, normal, and worthy of him. I wished I could feel the pain in my flesh, if only once. And nothing worked.

I could have fallen into it again when Océane left me. But I realized one important thing: I didn’t need that anymore. All I crave is her.

With Océane, I live. Something real, where the intense replaces the unhealthy. Where I can plan to cultivate our own secrets with her. Incandescent, sublime, wet, torrid, precious secrets without shame, without guilt or shackles as I was used to, but jealously hidden in a box. She’s right; we’ll be careful with Sophia’s balance. But I will fiercely erect new locks behind which I am proud to be addicted to Océane. Only her.

No need to share it with anyone else right now. I want to live these moments behind closed doors with my future Mrs. Sexton. All mine and I at her mercy.

In our highly protected area, OUR private garden, I remain unarmed for her. And I measure my chance to experience this intense, unique, mind-blowing thing. So let's lock me up with her, be confined to her, and throw away the key!

Because I'm at her fucking mercy. Irredeemably.

AUTHOR'S NOTE

A note from Mr. Sexton:

*You've stepped into our privatet garden, discovered things… Thank you
for keeping that access locked.
We are counting on you to avoid possible leaks and revelations in the
excerpts, comments, and opinions.
You now know what is at stake…
Kisses.
TS*

THANK YOU FOR READING!

We sincerely hope you enjoyed reading this book as much as we enjoyed publishing it. If you did, we would appreciate a short review on Amazon or your favorite book website. Reviews are crucial for any authors, and even just a line or two can make a huge difference.

ACKNOWLEDGMENTS

Words. What fabulous little things, aren't they?

They have such power, such impact. As with Océane, we often tend to be more affected when they carry negative vibes and turn into bashing. The more gratuitous and violent it is, the more the intention of the person who uses it is to harm; the more these words hurt, the more they leave traces. But they also build our personality if we continue to move forward despite everything.

On the other hand, words also have this magic faculty to become a balm to the heart. To make you feel good, to fill the gaps, to chase away the boredom, or just to help you escape for a moment. And thus, to leave on a journey through the writings gives oneself shivers sometimes. That's what I'm passionate about! Creating or enjoying an emotional roller coaster through reading and writing almost endlessly.

Don't words allow us to open up to others, the world, and multiple imaginary worlds? They stretch the field of possibilities, so I like to play with them, to give life to characters, to make them vibrate, to stumble, to doubt, to suffer in order to better raise them later…

Because, in my humble opinion, our greatest freedom is that everyone is able to do what they want to do. To choose to knowingly hurt your fellow man with words or to support him. To seek to flay, denigrate, or to comfort with it. To spread more positive emotions, to try to sublimate an already complex daily life, if only with little things.

Yes, a simple word can be a weapon or contain so much kindness, dreams, gratitude, and affection.

So, in these last pages, I choose to use them to tell you how much I love you. And above all, THANK YOU!

Thank you from the bottom of my heart for being here, you, readers.

Thank you to my darling "Olygirls" (I didn't come up with the name, did I ;)). This novel, ours, is dedicated to you, with all my tenderness. I had so much fun writing and sharing this story with you to spice up our Friday nights on Facebook more than a year ago now. Tiger, Océane, and Sophia have given rhythm to our exchanges and brightened my weekends with you. Not to mention the fabulous illustrations of my beloved Myriam. I hope that the final result will have given you as much pleasure (I am stressing while waiting for your verdict, your "words"…). Thank you for the laughs, the smiles, the jokes, the comments, and each of your little attentions. Thank you for keeping my modest private group and my little pen alive. I am infinitely grateful to you.

Mary, Gaëlle, Nadège, Françoise Drély, Katell, Chris Doe, Nathalie, Soizic, Miel Pops, Rebelle, Sureyya, Jen Nie Mahé, Éloïse, Jocelyne, Akane, Cindy, Marie-José, Laetitia, Claire, Sarah and so many others. I apologize for not being able to list all the names or pseudonyms. I don't want to offend anyone; you have all taken up residence in my heart, rest assured.

Thank you to my faithful and lovely friends. My dear Myriam, Laure, Justine, Aurora, Virginie. You are present behind the scenes in the good and bad moments, always with the right word and the same sincerity. Even when I am a lone wolf in my cave, I know how lucky I am to know you :).

Thank you to my husband, family, and in-laws for distilling so much joy, love, and support into my life.

An emotional thought for my sister, who was going through a complicated time while writing this novel. I bled with you and will do it a thousand times over if I have to. Now we're going to heal all those nasty wounds in tandem. Because "what doesn't kill us…" And I can't tell you enough: I love you.

Thank you to the Crazy on Facebook (a ton of love), the reviewers, and Instagrammers (special mention to Madame Lecture and Pauline Bookaddict; you touched my heart). Thank you to each reader (from those who discover my writing to those who have been here for a while or longer). I hope to see you again…

And last but not least, a huge THANK YOU to Addictives for their warm welcome. Thanks to the authors—to Milyi—who spontaneously welcomed me (a lovely attention). A big thank you to Maud: it was a pleasure to work and discuss the characters with you. I also thank the whole team and hope that this adventure we are starting will be sensational!

See you soon, dear readers, to vibrate, to ride together through new characters and emotions, new lands, and new words. Passionately. Again and again.

LOVE,

Oly

Myrina Holmes Demons and Wonders
by *Anna Triss*

I'm Myrina Holmes, the top Tracker of Infernum, tasked with neutralizing supernatural creatures who disobey our laws.

In my world, demons have legions. Fourteen to be precise: seven dedicated to the cardinal virtues and seven ruled by the deadly sins.

As a marginal hybrid, I belong to neither camp, which suits me just fine. I love my job and my life on Earth when I'm not on a mission. Except, of course, when mysterious corpses literally fall from the sky to torture my brain and when my succubus half-sister starts hanging out with the most detestable Hybresang there is, Kelen Wills.

A supremely powerful sinner, commander-in-chief of an elite army, he doesn't embody one deadly sin. No, he possesses all seven-with a penchant for lust, anger, pride, and gluttony. But keep that detail to yourself...

Anyway, this guy has made it his mission to seduce me, probably because I'm the only woman who can resist his dubious charms.

This Hybresang can go to hell, because I have other midnight demons to deal with.

My Hipster Next Door
by *Mag Maury*

In Liverpool, the barbershop Hipster Maniac is an institution. Run by three bearded, tattooed friends, it is the place to listen to great rock, get a trim, and have a drink.

But for Line, it also spelled trouble. For starters, when she first got to the neighborhood, she rear-ended Jordan's car, who turned out to be one of the three barbers. Then she discovered that they were neighbors in business and residence! So no way can she escape this muscle-flaunting, smoldering man who is covered in tattoos and... completely insufferable!

He draws her near only to push her away. He toys with her shamelessly. But worst of all he hates Christmas whereas that is Line's very favorite time of year!

Beneath a backdrop of festive fairy lights, intoxicatingly passionate kisses, and blistering banter... It's on!

The Cocky Heir
by *Ana K. Anderson*

She is about to get married. But not to him.

Quinn MacFayden, an accomplished expat businessman in New York, is set to return to Scotland in extremis to protect the precious family legacy. His 91-year-old grandfather is about to marry a perfect stranger sixty-six years his junior... And that is out of the question! Quinn swears it. Over his dead body will Dawn Fleming ever be part of the family!

But Dawn is not a future bride like the others. She is nowhere near the gold digger he imagined and, above all, she knows just how to stand up to him. And so a game of cat and mouse begins between them. A war with no holds barred and where surrender has never been so tempting...

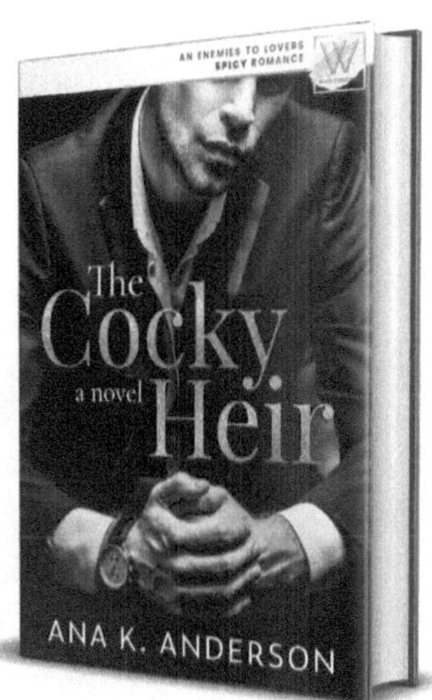

My Stepbrother: A Sexual Revelation
by *Sophie S. Pierucci*

Cassie is a highly intelligent young woman... Too much so for her own good!

And she is as daunting as she is intriguing. Carl, the son of his father's second wife, would hardly say otherwise!

Carl is the exact opposite of his steady father. He is a player and a slayer. Afraid of nothing and no one. Except for Cassie when she asks him to introduce her to the pleasures of the flesh.

And when the situation gets out of control, it is too late to turn back, and the two lovers find themselves ensnared in forbidden passion. Forbidden by everyone: society, their parents, their friends.

But how to resist the desire that consumes them?

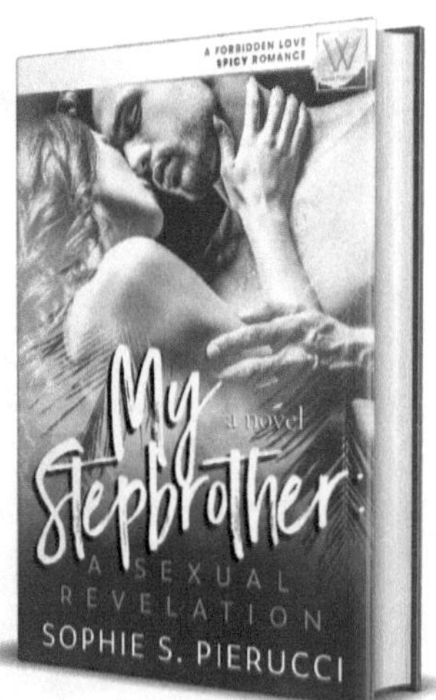

Roommate with my Boss
by *Erin Graham*

Boss, roommate, fake fiancé… real lover?

Étienne is cold, charismatic, and he never shies away from a challenge.

He masters everything down to the smallest detail… until a little accountant with an unlikely look and flowers in her hair inserts herself into his daily life.

She is whimsical, full of life, laughs at the rules and gets around them, talks all the time except about her past… and she drives him crazy. Yet, it's impossible to fire her.

She needs a job and a roof over her head; he needs a fake fiancée…

Is it a deal?

Your Power Over me
by *Missy Heart*

A family home heavy with secrets, a dangerously charismatic owner.

Will her arrival at Iron House be the end of her?

Ever since she was a teenager, Lovisa has known it: at Iron House, anything can happen, especially the worst.

However, when she is forced to return to the family home for her stepfather's funeral, her heart races: she is going to see him again, this "brother" who she never wanted and who yet turned her whole world upside down.

Now at the head of a drug cartel, authoritarian and brutal, Niklas is nothing like the teenager she knew nine years ago. At his side, Lovisa finds herself immersed in a harsh, ruthless—but fascinating—world.

Irremediably attracted to this man who wants her as much harm as good, will Lovisa manage to fight her unmentionable desires? Or will she give in to Niklas' magnetic darkness?

Touchdown
by *Sonia Birdy*

She's a runner, but the campus star quaterback runs faster than she does!

Rocky has had a chaotic life from which she concluded three fundamental things: life is a succession of problems to be solved, men are assholes to be avoided and promises are only binding on fools who want to believe in them. So, unlike the other girls on campus, boys are not a priority for her. Worse, she sees them as an obstacle to her success!

But during a student party, she meets Jude. Freshly transferred from Harvard to play on Brown's soccer team, Jude is the new star on campus. Handsome and inaccessible, he is the type not to get attached: the perfect candidate for a one-night stand.

But the chemistry is too strong. And though Rocky is determined to run away from him, he is determined to conquer her heart.

About the Author

Rather discreet, Oly TL likes to give free rein to her pen. She passionately ventures into dark, tortured, sensual, and deep universes to communicate the emotions of her characters as accurately as possible. Between intensity, diversity, suspense, drama, and a touch of humor, this French author explores different themes, pains and social issues that are close to her heart.

www.ingramcontent.com/pod-product-compliance
Lightning Source LLC
Chambersburg PA
CBHW031640200726
48289CB00004BA/1019